This Week's *Stories of Mystery and Suspense*

This Week's

Stories of

Mystery and

Suspense

Edited, with a Preface, Notes and an Essay,
"How to Write the Mystery and Suspense Story,"
by

STEWART BEACH

Introduction by
ALFRED HITCHCOCK

RANDOM HOUSE, NEW YORK

Contents

STEWART BEACH

Preface

THE THIRTY STORIES that make up this collection have been taken from issues of *This Week* Magazine published during the past ten years. It seems fair to say that they represent some of the best short fiction which has been written in the field of mystery and suspense—much of it by the top practitioners of this special art in the United States and in Great Britain.

Most of the authors represented are primarily novelists, because they are the best of the short-story writers, too—novelists who only occasionally, as some irresistible idea capable of quick distillation catches their imagination, turn instinctively to the short story for expression. Some authors, respected for mystery novels, are not represented here at all, because they never use the short story.

While all these stories have been selected primarily for their quality and entertainment, they have been arranged to show the wide variety which this type of story takes today. There are straight detective stories, a "whodunit" or two, mysteries with unusual situations—often exotic backgrounds, unexpected solutions—and suspense stories in which tension and raw danger walk. For readers in search of brief relaxation, most of them offer pure enjoyment. For serious students who care to indulge in literary analysis, they show how some of the finest writers in this field go after their effects.

It is a challenging task to select fiction for an audience the size of *This Week*'s. The magazine has presently a circulation of nearly 12,000,000, the largest of any publication in the world, and close to double that number of readers. And readers *will* differ in their individual tastes. What one likes enormously another may find on the dull side. But the one kind of story which almost everyone likes is the tale in which there is a puzzle to be solved, a mystery to be exposed.

In editing this book I am grateful for the assistance of Mrs. Howard B. Tingue, who helped with the selection and arrangement of our thirty stories. And I am particularly grateful, too, to

Mr. Alfred Hitchcock, the master of suspense in motion pictures and in television, for contributing a wise and characteristically light-hearted introduction.

Now here is Mr. Hitchcock, and here are the stories. You are on your own. Read them straight through, or dip in where fancy strikes. Good hunting!

New York City
1957

ALFRED HITCHCOCK

INTRODUCTION

Through the mystery and suspense stories he has brought to the films and television screens, Alfred Hitchcock of England has emerged as the Master of Suspense. Who better to set the stage for these thirty tales? Ladies and gentlemen, Mr. Hitchcock!

THE other day a fascinating statistic was brought to my notice. I was asked to believe that during this year of 1957 some 40,000,-000 prescriptions will be written for tranquilizers to relieve the tensions of the world Americans live in. Now I have no quarrel with any sort of medication. But I believe I have a more pleasant prescription: Take a suspense story . . . Shake well . . . and keep shaking!

From the days when legends of bold deeds and sudden death were sung by minstrels, the suspense story has always enraptured audiences, made them forget for a little while the sorry problems of their own lives. To hold a man spellbound for an hour is to return him refreshed to face tomorrow with a bolder heart.

Wherein lies the magic of the mystery story? I suppose it is the breath of danger, safely encountered in the darkness of a theatre, or blowing up from the printed page in the security of a quiet living room. Presidents and ministers of state have long found relaxation from their own tensions by losing themselves in a story of suspense. So you see the tales of violence which I contrive for the motion pictures and for television have a deeper purpose behind them. And also the stories in this book.

Yes, it is a world of make-believe. You know the criminal will be caught—but how? And would you have it otherwise? These are entertainments, designed to take you out of yourself, to make you believe—while you read or look at a screen—in the reality of what is there. The capture of the criminal rounds out the play, as it confirms the security of the reader when he returns to reality.

So now I commend you to the pleasures of the thirty stories which follow this little homily. I hope I may have prepared you for them properly by the sobering thoughts I have expressed. If stories of tension indeed relieve you of some of your own tensions —as I earnestly believe—then these are just what the doctor ordered.

Hollywood
1957

This Week's *Stories of Mystery and Suspense*

1

PAT FRANK

The Christmas Bogey

THE AIR FORCE holds a particular fascination for
Pat Frank, and the theme of his most recent novel,
Forbidden Area, was a determined Communist plot to
put our strategic bombers out of business. The same
documentary spirit he brought to that story turns "The
Christmas Bogey" into a tale with all the reality of a
newspaper report. In addition to writing novels and short
stories, Mr. Frank has served as a foreign correspondent
both in World War II and in Korea.

WHEN THE AIR FORCE privately evaluated the affair later, delay
in reporting the original sighting received much of the blame.
This delay was the fault of Airman 2/c Warren Pitts, but the
cause of Pitts' lapse never was committed to paper, for it would
sound so emotional and unmilitary. The truth is that Warren
Pitts was only eighteen, and he was homesick, and weeping at
his post.

Pitts was the youngest of five technicians assigned, that morning, to 48-hour duty in the Early Warning Radar shack atop a
wind-scoured hill overlooking the sprawling Thule base in northern Greenland.

It was Tail End Charley duty. Down on the base everybody
was celebrating. There was a USO troupe, including dancers
from Hollywood, at the theater. Pitts had not seen a woman in
three months. There was a Christmas tree, flown from Maine in
a B-36 bomb bay, in the gymnasium. It was the only tree in a
thousand miles. There were parties in the clubs and day rooms,
and turkey dinners in the mess halls, and a mountain of still
undistributed mail and packages. Pitts hadn't received the
Christmas box his folks had promised.

Even in the radar shack there was a celebration of a sort. In
the other room the older men had concocted an eggnog from

evaporated milk, powdered eggs, vanilla extract, and medicinal alcohol. Since Pitts didn't drink, he had drawn the six to midnight watch.

The other room was bright, and warm, and they were listening to Christmas music on the radio, and Sergeant Hake was telling almost believable stories about girls he had known Stateside.

There was no light in the viewing room, so that vision would be sharper. Pitts sat lonely in darkness and watched a thin white sliver revolve in hypnotic circles on the screen.

He wasn't thinking of himself as the guardian of a continent. He was thinking of Tucson's hot sun. He hadn't seen the sun in weeks, and wouldn't see it for weeks more. He said, aloud, "Oh, God, I want to go home."

When at last he looked up there was a fat, green blip winking evilly at him from the upper right-hand quadrant of the screen. How long it had been there he could not guess. It could have come across the Pole, or it might have entered from the east. The radar had a range of perhaps 300 miles. When he first saw the blip, it was closing on the 150-mile circle.

Had Pitts instantly reported this sighting, successful interception would have been possible at Thule, but he didn't. He told the blip to go away. He begged it to go away. On occasion, Russian weather planes crossed the Pole, but always they turned around and went back and he wished this blip would do the same, so he would not have to explain to Sergeant Hake. The blip kept on coming, skirting the edge of the 150-mile circle, as if making a careful detour.

Pitts rose from his canvas chair and shouted, "I've got a bogey!"

Except for Sinatra singing "White Christmas," there was silence in the other room, and then suddenly they were all in with him. Hake watched the blip for three revolutions, and said: "How long you been asleep, kid?"

"I haven't been asleep. Honest I haven't."

The sergeant noted the boy's reddened eyes and the tear channels down his pinched white face. He turned back to the scope.

"What do you think it is?" Pitts asked, fearfully.

"It could be a large flying saucer," said Hake, "or it could be Santa Claus and eight tiny reindeer, or it could be an enemy jet bomber." He reached for the telephone and called Central Radar Control.

That night Lieutenant Preble, a serious young man, had the duty. Ranged along the wall inside Control were many types of radar, including a repeater set from the early warning installation on the hill. Lieutenant Preble switched on this set. As it heated, the blip appeared. He estimated the bogey at 140 miles from Thule, bearing 80 degrees, speed 400 knots, and headed due south.

It could be a Scandinavian airliner bound for Canada and Chicago. And, it could be a jet tanker, on a training flight from Prestwick, Scotland, which had failed to report its position in the last hour.

Or it could be an enemy jet bomber sneaking around Thule.

Whatever it was, Radar Control had a standing order to scramble fighters and alert the batteries if a bogey could not be identified within 60 seconds. That would certainly have been done, except for several human factors.

Lieutenant Preble often played chess with a Captain Canova, an F-94 fighter pilot, and at this moment Captain Canova and his radar observer were in the ready room. In an alert, they would be scrambled—the first ones to face that icy air.

On a base like Thule you will find many poker, bridge, and gin rummy players, but few devoted to chess. So Lieutenant Preble and Captain Canova were firm friends, and Preble knew that this was probably Canova's last duty at Thule.

In the morning, Canova would pack up and board the air tanker coming in from Scotland. Canova's wife was ill and Canova had been given compassionate leave. The tanker's base was Westover Field, Massachusetts, and Canova lived in Boston. He should be with his wife Christmas night—barring accident.

Outside, the temperature was 42 below, and the wind an erratic Phase Three—above 50 knots. If the bogey continued its course and speed, it would be an extreme long-range interception, outside the protective cloak of his radar. So there could very well be an accident.

Preble turned to his communicator and said, "Let's try to raise this bogey. Call the tanker again."

The tanker didn't respond. Preble wasn't worried about the tanker. There had been no distress calls, and near the magnetic pole on top of the world radio frequently went haywire.

They tried the commercial channels. No answer.

Preble took a good hold on the edge of his desk. The blip had closed to 120 miles, but it was now due east of Thule, and moving fast to the south. Each second, now, was taking it away. Unless he scrambled Canova immediately, there would be no chance for an intercept.

He looked at the clock. The big second hand was sweeping down like a guillotine.

Even if Canova shot down the bogey, it might turn out to be a transport loaded with people racing home for Christmas.

But whatever the bogey was, an alarm would stop the USO show in the theatre, and empty the clubs, and send some thousands of troops and gunners and airmen to their posts in the frightful cold, and wreck Christmas. If Canova shot down a friendly plane, there would be no more room for Lieutenant Preble at Thule, or perhaps anywhere.

Preble slammed his hand on the red alarm button, and spoke into the microphone: "Scramble, Lightning Blue! Ready, Lightning Red!"

He looked at the clock, and marked the hour, minute, and second. Canova would be airborne in under three minutes, requesting instructions. But the chase would be long, and would carry beyond the fringe area and guidance of his radar. In his heart, he knew he was too late. Outside, he heard the sirens screaming.

At 6:24 p.m., EST, Christmas Eve, the priority mesage from Thule reached the enormous plotting room of the Eastern Defense Command, Newburgh, New York. A bogey had slipped past Thule. Interception had been unsuccessful, and the pilot had returned to base. The bogey was headed for Labrador or Newfoundland at better than 400 miles an hour, estimated altitude 30,000 feet.

Upon the shoulders of Major Hayden, an ace in two wars but the youngest and least experienced officer on the senior staff, rested the awful responsibility for the safety and security of the vital third of the United States, from Chicago east to the Atlantic. This was normal, on Christmas Eve, for alone among the Master Controllers Major Hayden was a bachelor.

Major Hayden was not alarmed at this first report. The day's intelligence forecasts showed that the world, this season, was comparatively peaceful. Also, it was only one plane, and Major

Hayden did not believe an attack would be launched by one plane, or even so small a number as one hundred.

Besides, the bogey could be reasonably explained. One of his plotting boards showed every aircraft, military and commercial, aloft on the approaches to the Eastern states. The bogey could be a British Comet which had announced it was going far north to seek the jet stream. It could be a Scandinavian airliner looking for Goose Bay. It could be most anything.

Major Hayden ordered a miniature plane set upon the plotting board at the spot this bogey ought to be, according to its projected course and speed. A red flag, showing it was unidentified, topped this plane. He would keep his eyes on it.

He didn't want to bother the General, although the General had visited the plotting room, at six, to look things over. The General always seemed anxious. This may have been because on December 7, 1941, when Major Hayden was a sophomore in college, The General was a major commanding a bomber squadron at Hickam Field, Hawaii, and all his planes had been bombed and shot up on the ground. The last thing the General had said was, "I'm going over to my daughter's, at the Point, for dinner. You know the number. If anything happens call me."

Major Hayden didn't believe that anything, really, had happened yet. Besides, he knew that every Christmas Eve the General trimmed the tree for his grandchildren. He didn't want to break that up.

Major Hayden did call the Royal Canadian Air Force liaison officer, and he did alert the outlying bases, and the border radar sites. Then he waited.

An hour later, reports began to come in. The jet tanker from Prestwick turned up at Thule, its radio out. The Comet landed at Gander after a record crossing. It had not been near Thule. The Scandinavian, it developed, was grounded in Iceland.

Major Hayden fretted. Every fifteen minutes, one of his girls inched the red-flagged bogey closer to his air space. The bogey became the only thing he could see on the board. He alerted all fighter bases north of Washington, and the anti-aircraft people, and the Ground Observer Corps. The GOC was apologetic. It doubted that many of its posts were manned. The GOC would do what it could, but he would have to remember that they were volunteers, and this was Christmas Eve.

When the second sighting came, there could be no doubt of the menace. The Limestone, Maine, radar picked up an unidentified blip moving at 600 knots and at 40,000 feet. It came out of an unguarded Canadian sector. Instead of moving down the coast toward the heavily populated areas, it had headed out to sea, dived steeply, and vanished. It had appeared so swiftly, and left the radar screen so suddenly, that interception had not been possible. Limestone's best night-fighter pilots were older men, and away on Christmas leave.

Major Hayden knew what had happened, and what to expect. The intruder had shrewdly avoided the picket ships, and airfields, near the shore. Then it had crossed the danger zone at tremendous speed.

Once at sea, it had dropped below 4,000 feet—safe from the eyes of radar. Now it would come in at its target, very low, and achieve tactical surprise. Major Hayden called the General.

When the phone rang in the Smith home at West Point, the General, a spare man with iron-gray hair, was balanced atop a ladder, putting the angel on top of the tree, while his grandchildren shrilled their advice and admonitions. Tracy Smith, his daughter, answered the phone, and said, "It's for you, Dad."

The General said, "Tell 'em I'm busy. Tell 'em to wait a minute."

It took the General three minutes to place the angel exactly as he wanted, and exactly straight and upright. "Well," he said, climbing down, "there's the angel that stands guard over this house." At that moment, three minutes may have been the critical factor.

The General picked up the phone. He listened without speaking, and then said, "All right, red alert. Order SCAT. SCAT's all that will save us now. I'm coming."

When he put down the phone the General looked ten years older. His daughter said, "What's up?"

"An unidentified plane," he said, putting on his coat, "off the coast. I believe an enemy."

"Just one?" said Tracy Smith.

"One plane, one bomb, one city," said the General. "Maybe New York."

And he was gone.

Major Hayden flashed the SCAT order to every airfield in his zone. SCAT meant Security Control of Air Traffic. Under SCAT, every plane, military and commercial—except fighters on tactical missions—was to land at the nearest field immediately. In thirty minutes the air must be cleared of everything except the enemy, and our fighters, to give the anti-aircraft batteries and the Nike rocket battalions a chance to work in congested areas.

Very shortly, Major Hayden discovered that on this particular night—of all nights—SCAT couldn't operate properly. In all the big cities, holiday travel was setting records. Planes were stacked in layers up to 20,000 feet over Idlewild, La Guardia, and Newark. Boston, Philadelphia-Camden, and Washington National were the same. And the airways between cities were jammed. He didn't know how long it would be before the Nike rockets could be used. A Nike is a smart rocket, but it cannot tell a transport loaded with 80 people from a jet bomber.

The General came into the plotting room just as the report came in from a lonely spotter at East Moriches, Long Island. A huge jet had come in from the sea at a speed he refused to estimate. It had swept wings, and its four engines were housed in these wings, close to the fuselage. It was bigger than a B-47. It had come in at 2,000 feet, and he swore it was marked with a red star.

The General knew, then, that it was too late, unless he ordered everything shot out of the air. This he could not do—not at Christmas.

A few minutes later a strange plane joined the traffic pattern circling Idlewild, easing itself between two Constellations. It was a jet. One of the Constellations came in for a landing, and then the jet turned on its wing lights and landed. It taxied up to the Administration Building, as if it owned the place, and the blue and red flames of its engines were snuffed out, one by one. Three men got out. They wore strange uniforms.

The Air Force liaison officer at Idlewild called in the news to the General. "Two of them are Poles," he said, "and the other a Czech.

"The plane is this new type Russian 428 that they showed last May Day over Moscow, only this one is fitted out as a weather ship. These three guys said they had been planning this for almost a year. One of them used to live in Hamtramck, and another has an uncle in Pittsburgh, and they all speak English."

"It's wonderful!" the General said. "But it's a miracle they got here. By rights, they should long ago have been shot down."

"Well," said the liaison officer, "they said they had it all figured out. They said nothing means so much to Americans as Christmas."

"Yes," said the General. "They're three smart men. Real wise."

2

MARGERY ALLINGHAM

Bluebeard's Bathtub

WHILE SHE WAS STILL a schoolgirl, Miss Allingham made the exhilarating discovery that she had a flair for writing mystery stories. What is more surprising, staid publishers and critics agreed, so that at an early age she was accepted as one of the most accomplished of the English writers. Of her more than twenty novels, *Flowers for the Judge* is considered a true classic. She is married to Desmond Carter, editor of *The Tatler,* and lives near London.

AT FIVE O'CLOCK on a September afternoon Ronald Fredrick Torbay was making preparations for his third murder. He was being wary because he was well aware of the dangers of carelessness.

He knew, way back before his first marriage, that a career of homicide got more chancy as one went on. Also, he realized, success was liable to go to a man's head.

For an instant he paused and regarded himself thoughtfully in the shaving glass of the bathroom in the new cottage he had hired so recently.

The face which looked back at him was thin, middle-aged and pallid. Sparse dark hair receded from its high narrow forehead and the eyes were blue and prominent. Only the mouth was really unusual. That narrow slit, quite straight, was almost lipless and, unconsciously, he persuaded it to relax into a half smile. Even Ronald Torbay did not like his own mouth.

A sound in the kitchen below disturbed him and he straightened up hastily. It might by Edyth coming up to take her long discussed bubble bath before he had prepared it for her, and that would never do.

He waited, holding his breath, but it was all right; she was going out of the back door. He looked out the window to see her disappearing round the side of the house into the small square

11

yard which was so exactly like all the other square yards in the long suburban street. He knew she was going to hang some linen on the line to air, and although the maneuver gave him the time he needed, still it irritated him.

Of the three homely, middle-aged women whom he had persuaded to marry him and then to will him their modest possessions, Edyth was proving easily the most annoying. In their six weeks of marriage he had told her a dozen times not to spend so much time in the yard. He hated her being out of doors alone. She was shy and reserved, but now that new people had moved in next door there was always the danger of some overfriendly woman starting up an acquaintance with her, and that was the last thing to be tolerated at this juncture.

Each of his former wives had been shy. He had been very careful to choose the right type and felt he owed much of his success to it. Mary, the first of them, had met her fatal "accident" almost unnoticed in the bungalow of a housing development very like the present one he had chosen, but in the north instead of the south of England.

At the time it had been a growing place, the coroner had been hurried, the police sympathetic but busy and the neighbors scarcely curious, except that one of them, a junior reporter on a local paper whose story was picked up by the wire services, had written a flowery paragraph about the nearness of tragedy in the midst of joy, published a wedding-day snapshot and had entitled the article with typical northern understatement, "Honeymoon Mishap."

Dorothy's brief excursion into his life and abrupt exit from it had given him a little more bother. She had deceived him when she told him she was quite alone in the world. An interfering brother had turned up after the funeral to ask awkward questions about her small fortune. He might have been a nuisance if Ronald had not been very firm with him. There had been a brief court case duly recorded in a small item in newsprint. However, Ronald had won his case handsomely, and the insurance company had paid up without a murmur.

All that was four years ago. Now, with a new name and a newly invented background, he felt remarkably safe.

From the moment he had first seen Edyth, sitting alone at a little table under the window in a seaside hotel dining room, he had known that she was to be his next subject. He always thought of his wives as "subjects."

Edyth had sat there looking stiff and neat and a trifle severe, but there had been a secret timidity in her face, an unsatisfied, half-frightened expression in her nearsighted eyes. She was also wearing a genuine diamond brooch.

He had spoken to her that evening, had weathered the initial snub and, finally, got her to talk. After that the acquaintance had progressed just as he had expected. His methods were old-fashioned and heavily romantic, and within a week she was hopelessly infatuated.

From Ronald's point of view her history was ideal. She had taught in a girls' boarding school during her twenties before being summoned home to look after a demanding father, whose long illness had monopolized her life; now at forty-three she was alone, comparatively well off and as much at sea as a ship without a rudder.

Ronald was careful not to let her toes touch the ground. He devoted his entire attention to her, and in exactly five weeks he married her at the registry office of the town where they were both strangers. The same afternoon they each made wills in the other's favor and moved into the villa which he had been able to hire cheaply because the holiday season was at an end.

Two things signed her death warrant earlier than had been Ronald's original intention. One was her obstinate reticence over her monetary affairs and the other was her embarrassing interest in his job.

Ronald had told her that he was a junior partner in a firm of cosmetic manufacturers who were giving him a very generous leave of absence. Edyth accepted the statement without question, but almost at once she had begun to plan a visit to the office and the factory and said she must buy some new clothes so as not to "disgrace" him. At the same time she kept all her business papers locked in an old writing case and steadfastly refused to discuss them, however cautiously he raised the subject. Ronald had given up feeling angry with her and had decided to act.

He turned from the window and began to run the bath. His heart was pounding, he noticed. He wished it would not. He needed to keep very calm.

The bathroom was the one room they had repainted. Ronald had done it himself and had put up the little shelf over the bath to hold a small electric heater of the old-fashioned type. He switched it on now and stood looking at it until the two bars of glowing warmth appeared. Then he went out onto the landing, leaving it alight.

The fuse box which controlled all the electricity in the house was concealed in the bottom of the linen cupboard at the head of the stairs. Ronald opened the door carefully and, using his handkerchief so that his fingerprints should leave no trace, pulled up the main switch.

Back in the bathroom the heater's glow died away; the bars were almost black again by the time he returned. He eyed the heater approvingly and then, still using the handkerchief, he lowered it carefully into the water. It lay close to the foot of the tub where it took up practically no room at all. The white cord of the heater ran up over the porcelain side of the bath, along the baseboard, under the door and into a wall socket just outside on the landing.

When he had first installed the heater, Edyth had demurred at this somewhat slipshod arrangement. But he had explained that the local Council was stupid and fussy about fitting wall sockets in bathrooms since water was said to be a conductor, and she had agreed to let him run the cord under the linoleum.

At the moment the heater was perfectly visible in the bath. It certainly looked as if it had fallen into its odd position accidentally, but no one in his senses could have stepped into the water without seeing it. Ronald paused, his ugly mouth narrower than ever. The beautiful simplicity of the main plan, so swiftly fatal and, above all, so safe as far as he was concerned, gave him a thrill of pleasure as it always did.

He turned off the bath and waited, listening. Edyth was coming back. He could hear her moving something on the concrete outside the back door below and he took a paper sachet from his jacket pocket.

He was reading the directions on the back of it when a slight sound made him turn his head, and he saw, to his horror, the woman herself not five feet away. Her neat head had appeared suddenly just above the flat roof of the scullery, outside the bathroom window. She was clearing the dead leaves from the gutters and must, he guessed, be standing on a stepladder.

It was typical of the man that he did not panic. Still holding the sachet lightly he stepped between her and the bath and spoke mildly.

"What on earth are you doing there, darling?"

Edyth started so violently that she almost fell off the steps. "Oh, how you startled me! I thought I'd just do this little job before I came up to change. If it rains, the gutter floods all over the back step."

"Very thoughtful of you, my dear." He spoke with that slightly acid amusement with which he had found he could best destroy her slender vein of self-assurance. "But not terribly clever when you knew I'd come up to prepare your beauty bath for you. Or was it?"

The slight intonation on the word "beauty" was not lost on her. He saw her swallow.

"Perhaps it wasn't," she said without looking at him. "It's very good of you to take all this trouble, Ronald."

"Not at all," he said with just the right amount of masculine, offhand insensitivity. "I'm taking you out tonight and I want you to look as nice as . . . er . . . possible. Hurry up, there's a good girl. The foam doesn't last indefinitely, and like all very high-class beauty treatments, it's expensive. Undress in the bedroom, put on your gown and come straight along."

"Very well, dear." She began to descend while he turned and shook the contents of the sachet into the water. The crystals, smelling strongly of roses, floated on the tide and then when he turned the water on hard began to dissolve into thousands of iridescent bubbles. The bubbles grew into a fragrant feathery mass which obscured the bottom of the bath and overflowed the porcelain sides of the tub. It was perfect.

He opened the door to call to her and just then she appeared. She came shrinking in, her blue dressing gown strained round her thin body, her hair thrust into an unbecoming bathing cap.

"Oh, Ronald!" she said staring at the display. "Won't it make an awful mess? Goodness! All over the floor!"

Her hesitation infuriated him.

"That won't matter," he said savagely. "You get in while the foam is still there. Hurry. Meanwhile I'll go and change, myself. Get in, and lie down. It'll take some of the sallowness out of that skin of yours."

He went out and paused, listening. She locked the door as he

had known she would. The habit of a lifetime does not change
with marriage. He heard the bolt slide home and forced himself
to walk slowly. He gave her sixty seconds. Thirty to take off her
things and thirty to hesitate on the brink of the rosy mass.

"How is it?" he shouted from the linen cupboard.

She did not answer at once and the sweat broke out on his
forehead. Then he heard her.

"I don't know yet. I'm only just in. It smells lovely."

He did not wait for the final word, his hand wrapped in his
handkerchief had found the main switch again.

"One, two . . . three," he said with horrible prosaicness and
pulled it down.

From the wall socket behind him there was a single splutter-
ing flare as the fuse went, and then silence.

All round Ronald it was so quiet that he could hear the pulses
in his own body, and he could hear no sound at all from the
bathroom.

After a while he crept back along the passage and tapped at
the door.

"Edyth? Are you still there? Edyth? Edyth?"

No. There was no response, no sound, nothing at all.

"Edyth?" he said again.

The silence was complete, and after a long minute he straightened his back and let out a deep sighing breath of relief.

Almost at once he was keyed up again in preparation for the
second phase. As he well knew, this next was the tricky period.
The discovery of the body must be made but not too soon. He
had made that mistake after Dorothy's "accident" and had actually been asked by the local inspector why he had become
alarmed so soon, but he had kept his head and the dangerous
moment had flickered past.

This time he had made up his mind to make it half an hour
before he began to hammer loudly at the door, then to shout for
a neighbor and finally to force the lock. He had planned to stroll
out to buy an evening paper in the interim, shouting his intention
to do so to Edyth from the front step for any passer-by to hear,
but as he walked back along the landing he knew there was
something else he was going to do first.

Edyth's leather writing case in which she kept all her private
papers was in the bottom of her canvas hatbox. She had really

believed he had not known of its existence, he reflected bitterly.

He went softly into the bedroom and opened the wardrobe door. The case was exactly where he had last seen it, plump and promising, and his hands closed over it gratefully. There were bundles of savings certificates, one or two thick envelopes whose red seals suggested the offices of lawyers, and on top, ready for the taking, one of those familiar gray books which the Post Office issues to its savings-bank clients.

He opened it with shaking fingers and fluttered through the pages. The sum made him whistle. Seven thousand two hundred and fifty pounds. Then a drop as she had drawn out fifty pounds for her trousseau. Seven thousand two hundred. He thought that was the final entry but on turning the page saw that there was yet one other recorded transaction. It was less than a week old. He remembered the book coming back through the mail and how clever she had thought she had been in smuggling the envelope out of sight. He glanced at the written words and figures idly at first but then, as his heart jolted in sudden panic, stared at them, his eyes prominent and glazed. She had taken almost all of it out. There it was in black and white: *September 4th; Withdrawal seven thousand one hundred and ninety-eight pounds.*

His first thought was that the money must still be there, in hundred-pound notes perhaps, in one of the envelopes. He tore through them hastily, forgetting all caution in his anxiety. Papers, letters, certificates fell on the floor in confusion.

The envelope, addressed to himself, pulled him up short. It was new and freshly blotted, the name inscribed in Edyth's own unexpectedly firm hand. "Ronald Torbay, Esquire."

He wrenched it open and stared at the single sheet of bond paper within. The date, he noted in horrified amazement, was only two days old.

Dear Ronald:

If you ever get this I am afraid it will prove a dreadful shock to you. For a long time I have been hoping that it might not be necessary to write it, but now your behavior has forced me to face some very unpleasant possibilities.

I am afraid, Ronald, that in some ways you are very old-fashioned. Has it not occurred to you that any homely, middle-aged woman who has been swept into a hasty marriage to a stranger must, unless she is a perfect idiot, be just a little suspicious and touchy on the subject of *baths?*

You must know that I am a dedicated newspaper reader, and after reading about two women who had met with fatal accidents in bubble baths soon after their marriages, I rather began to wonder.

Frankly, I did not want to suspect you because for a long time I thought I was in love with you; but when you persuaded me to make my will on our wedding day, I could not help wondering. And then as soon as you started fussing about the bathroom in this house, I thought I had better do something about it rather quickly. I am old-fashioned, too, Ronald, so I went to the police.

Have you noticed that the people who have moved into the house next door have never tried to speak to you? We thought it best that I should merely talk to the woman over the garden wall, and it is she who looked up the newspaper items I told her about. She even went a little further and found some cuttings from local provincial newspapers, each of which contained a press snapshot of the husband taken at the funeral.

They are not very clear, but even so, as soon as I saw them I realized it was my duty to agree to the course suggested to me by the Inspector. He told me that he had been looking for a man answering that description for over three years, ever since the two photographs were brought to his notice by your poor second wife's brother.

What I am trying to say is this: if you should ever lose me, Ronald, out of the bathroom, I mean, you will find that I have gone out over the roof and am sitting in my dressing gown in the kitchen next door. I was a fool to marry you, but not quite such a fool as you assumed. Women may be silly but they are not so stupid as they used to be. We are picking up the idea, Ronald.

Yours, Edyth.

P.S. On reading this I see that in my nervousness I have forgotten to say that the new people next door are not a married couple but Inspector Batsford of the C.I.D. and his assistant, Policewoman Richards. They assure me that there cannot be sufficient evidence to convict if you are not permitted to attempt the crime again. That is why I am forcing myself to be brave and play my part, for I am very sorry for those other poor wives of yours, Ronald. They must have found you as fascinating as I did.

With his slit mouth twisted into an abominable O, Ronald Torbay raised haggard eyes from the letter.

The house was still quiet, and even the whine of the mower next door had ceased. In the hush he heard a sudden clatter as the back door burst open and heavy footsteps raced through the hall, up the stairs toward him.

3

H. VERNOR DIXON

Trapped!

NOW HERE IS what we'd call an almost perfect suspense story. You know the horror of the situation almost from the start, and share the hopelessness of the principal character. We won't hint at how it comes out, except to call your attention to the fact that the ending is neatly motivated. Mr. Dixon, an old hand at suspense stories, lives in San Francisco.

JOHN WAS READY to leave his office when he noticed a memo on his desk reading: "Silverware. Crane's Warehouse." It was his wife's handwriting. Ellen must have come in while he was out and left the cryptic message. John had to smile. Ellen's assumption that he would know what she meant was so typical.

The silverware had been left to him by an elderly aunt, recently deceased. Some of it was extremely valuable, but Ellen had said it was in odd pieces and unmatched units so that it could not be used at home and they might just as well sell it.

He wondered if "Crane's Warehouse" meant that Ellen had been to the storage vaults to look it over, have it transported home, or appraised, or if she wanted him to do something about it. He wondered just what she meant.

Then he had too many other important matters on his mind. Only that day the city commissioners had informed him that he had been awarded the contracts for the new sewage and outfall systems and the three-million-dollar disposal plant. Every architect and contractor in the state had been after those contracts, and John had won out. Now he had an opportunity to live up to the reputation of the business he had inherited from Ellen's father. The old contractor had been a big man in the state. When he died suddenly and John took over, he'd expected the business to go on as usual. But it had not worked out that way. John had to prove himself. Well, he'd done it now. These contracts meant he was accepted at the top. Ellen would be delighted when she heard the news.

It was dusk when he walked out to the street and headed for the parking lot. At thirty-nine he was a tall, rather broad-shouldered man whom life and the years had treated kindly. His dark brown hair was beginning to turn gray at the temples, but his eyes were clear. A twice-weekly workout at the Athletic Club helped to keep him fit. He believed firmly that a man should keep in shape. But, on the other hand, it had never crossed his mind that his life would one day depend on it.

When he reached his car he started automatically for home. At the first red light, however, he changed his mind. Jimmy was having football practice at high school, which would mean a late dinner. He could drive to Crane's where the silver was stored, and learn if Ellen had made any arrangements.

Crane's was the largest single structure in town. The huge warehouse of brick, cement and old wood occupied an entire square block and spilled over into offices along a side street. The barred windows were all dark. John turned around the corner of the warehouse to the offices, but they were also dark.

He was about to drive away when he saw a man shuffle across the street and unlock a door of the warehouse. John quickly parked the car and hurried to intercept the man, who turned out to be Sam Moran, the night watchman. John had used him on contracting jobs and though he had had to fire him for drinking on the job he still liked the old man.

John explained what he was after, and Moran thought he could at least find out if the silver had been moved. As customers sometimes telephoned after hours, receipts were always left in the watchman's office for goods moved that day.

John followed him into the gloomy warehouse and along a dark corridor that bisected the building. They passed through a heavy door into a tiny room cluttered with baled papers, magazines, some broken chairs, a roll-top desk and a blanket-covered Army cot. The room was overly warm and smelled from the fumes of a smoking kerosene stove.

Moran hung his heavy mackinaw on a hook beside the stove. John thought it was dangerously close to the stove, but his attention was diverted by Moran snapping open the desk and going through a pile of papers. He nodded after a moment, held a piece of paper and said, "Yep, she's been here. Didn't move the stuff, though. Just had it appraised and insured for forty thousand."

A smile tugged at the corners of John's lips. Then the memo on the desk had been simply to let him know that everything was taken care of. That was so like Ellen. The two had such a close affinity that she expected him to guess everything from a few words. A feeling of warmth stole through John that had nothing to do with the atmosphere of the room.

Moran squinted at John. "Y'know," he said, "I'm willin' to let bygones be bygones if you are."

"How do you mean?"

"Don't you remember givin' me the bounce for takin' a drink now and then?"

"Oh," John laughed. "I've never held that against you. You can always come back with me if you ever want to."

"That's mighty nice of you. What say we have a drink on it? I got a nice bottle stashed away down below. How about it, Mr. Mead?"

"I don't know—"

"Now, look, lad, a little one never hurt anybody. Make it a toast to old times."

John didn't want to appear stuffy. "Well," he laughed, "since you're twisting my arm—"

He followed Moran down a long flight of stairs. At the bottom there was a damp concrete wall, with a small steel door about the size and shape of bulkhead doors in submarines. Moran swung it open and stepped into black darkness. John followed him through as soon as a light was turned on. Moran closed the steel door behind them.

John looked curiously about the small room in which he found himself. It was built of solid concrete—walls, floor and ceiling— about eight feet high and twenty feet square. There were some boxes in one corner of the room, some steel filing cabinets and, in the center of the floor, an old kitchen table and two chairs. Embedded in two of the walls were disconnected pipes, broken gauges, rusted dials and valve handles. There was no other entrance to the room except the one they had used. The single source of light was from a battery-type lantern hanging from a valve in the ceiling.

The watchman swung one of the broken pipes around to extract two glasses and a bottle of bourbon. As he placed them on the table he noticed John's eyes traveling about the room. He explained, "This place has been all kinds of things; a control room for furnaces, a bank vault and even a water reservoir. It ain't used for nothin' now."

He poured two husky slugs of whisky into the glasses and shoved one of them across the table to John. The watchman sighed with satisfaction as the whisky warmed his throat, and began talking about old times in the contracting game.

John was anxious to leave. The room gave him a ghostly feeling of unease. But he wanted to be polite, so he sat down and listened to Moran's tales. In spite of his anxiety, he became interested in Moran's reminiscences and injected some stories of his own. They had another drink, talked a few minutes longer, and then John got up to leave.

Moran placed the bottle and glasses back in the pipe and slapped John's shoulder as he passed him to move toward the closed door. As he placed his hand on the steel handle a puzzled expression crept into his eyes. He stared at the door for a moment. Then slowly he raised his hand and placed it flat against the steel. His bushy eyebrows came together in a worried frown.

John stepped forward and placed his own hand on the door. "The steel seems to be warm."

"Yeah."

They looked into each other's eyes for a split second and hastily away. John felt suddenly weak and limp, but he pushed the watchman aside, grasped the steel handle and shoved the door open. The silence of the vault was instantly shattered by an enormous, ear-splitting roar, as if a thousand explosions were taking place simultaneously. Vicious heat battered at them.

The stairway at the end of the corridor had disappeared in a burst of flame, and the corridor itself was a river of fire, sparks, embers and burning beams falling from the floor above. John stepped back, slammed the door closed and was again in the silence of a tomb.

For a moment, John felt that he was going to faint. He leaned weakly against the concrete wall and looked at Moran, who was staring vacantly at the door. John whispered, "That heater started it."

Moran nodded, then turned his head to blink at John. "Man, the whole warehouse is on fire! We're *trapped*."

John closed his eyes and considered the central location of the watchman's dingy office. The fire would spread from there in all directions, racing across the ground floor and then leaping upward to the other floors. The block-square building was eight stories high, each floor jammed with furniture, perishable goods and tons of combustible items.

There was some concrete and steel in the structure, but the building was old and consisted principally of wood. The fire was probably out of control at the moment it started. Fire trucks must be screaming into the adjoining streets, but John knew with terrible certainty that a fire in that building could never be put out until it had collapsed and burnt itself out.

Collapsed over our heads, he thought.

He felt the concrete getting warm against his shoulder and moved away. He placed his hand on the steel door and quickly withdrew it. The door was now actually hot. He looked frantically about the room, searching wildly for a means of escape. There was no other exit. He glanced at the light, which had been left on, and noticed it swaying slightly on the valve. Timbers were probably already crashing against the concrete ceiling. He wondered about its thickness and if it would hold.

The watchman followed the direction of his eyes and gasped, "It's solid. All concrete and steel. Maybe four feet thick. I don't think it will break."

"How about the walls?"

"Same thickness."

A wave of nausea swept through John, and then his weakness drained away. He walked slowly about the four walls of the room, examining the broken pipes. None of them seemed to pierce the walls. They were probably filled with concrete. At least, fire and smoke would not be able to get through. But where, he wondered, was air coming from? There was not a single vent in the walls or ceiling.

He searched the room and under the table found a large manhole in the floor. He got down to his knees and sniffed at the holes in the iron cover. Cool, musty air was in his nostrils. Evidently the manhole went down to a disposal pipe of some kind that was open to outside air. Otherwise he would detect heat. Thank God for that, he thought, as he got back to his feet.

Moran put his bottle and glasses back on the table and helped himself to the whisky. Then he cleared his throat and said huskily, "Ain't there nothin' we can do?"

"I can't think of anything. There's only the one exit, and we can't use that." He saw the fear growing in Moran's eyes and said quickly, "They'll probably be able to dig us out in a day or two."

"If anybody looks."

"Yes."

Moran screamed, "Man, there must be something!"

John did not reply. He looked down at his hands on the table and saw that they were shaking. He tightened his hands into fists. He had to keep control of himself . . .

Don't let me go to pieces. Don't let it happen. I can hold on. I know I can hold on. Just let me hold on till it is over with and someone gets us out . . .

The air in the room was getting very warm. Beads of perspiration appeared on the faces of the two men and the backs of their hands. Moran shifted uncomfortably in the heat, offering the bottle. John shook his head and watched Moran finish the whisky. The watchman's head bobbed drunkenly on his shoulders.

The heat deepened in the room. John took off his coat and vest. In another few minutes he had taken off his tie and shirt. Perspiration was streaming from him. He was afraid to think of what was happening over him, but his brain was intent on visualizing the holocaust, the flames and smoke shooting hundreds of feet in the air, the night made hideous with the roaring of the fire, the crashing of timbers, sections of the building giving way, whole floors crashing through and the pitiful efforts of midget-men directing tiny streams of water.

He thought of the great burning pile settling directly onto the vault in which he was imprisoned, and his brain came up with the parallel image of food being barbecued under clay and hot rocks. For the first time he realized that he and the watchman were actually trapped in a giant oven. They would slowly but inevitably be roasted to death even if the concrete held, which, he then knew, was not possible. Under such terrible heat the concrete would crack and explode and the vault would collapse. But long before that happened he and Moran would be roasted.

John jumped to his feet and rushed around the walls like a trapped animal. He could no longer touch the concrete. Even the metal strap of his wristwatch was becoming too hot for his skin. He took it off and dropped it on the floor. He sank back into the chair at the grimy table and blinked at the watchman, whose head was slowly sinking lower. Moran's skin was becoming a mottled red from the heat. John realized sickly that his own skin probably looked the same.

He looked at death, then, and faced it. Panic left him and the beat of his raging heart became calmer. It was human to hope, but here there was no hope. Even a man in a trapped submarine at the bottom of the ocean could hope that somehow there was a way out. But there was no hope in the vault.

There was but one single, inescapable fact—he would be roasted. A man being strapped in an electric chair had a better chance to live. No one could send a reprieve to the vault. Death filled the room.

John accepted it and turned away from it and thought of his family. Ellen and Jimmy would be secure, at least. There was the business to sell, there was ample insurance and there was the trust fund put aside for Jimmy's education. Ironically, too, the silver in the warehouse would now bring in an additional forty thousand dollars from the insurance policy. There was no worry about their future.

He considered the past, racing through it in his mind to savor its every moment. It had been good. He and Ellen had been in love when they married, and that love had increased and intensified through sixteen years.

They had always been very close. He thought of a favorite remark of Ellen's, "We were truly fated for each other, darling. I think Fate will always play a large part in our marriage." Then she would ask, "Don't you believe that, too?" and he would admit that he did. There had been nothing ordinary about their marriage. Perhaps he could have pushed harder for material success, but now he was just as glad that he had not. It would have taken time from Ellen.

That closeness, that feeling of oneness, was now something to be cherished beyond anything material. That was the real past and all of the pure gold of the past. Even facing death he was content with the way it had been. Life had been good to him . . .

When he heard a telephone ringing he thought his senses were playing tricks on him. He raised his head and, with the action, came out of the fog of heat enveloping his brain. The bell was still ringing. The sound seemed to emanate from the filing cabinets. It was true. There was a telephone working in the room.

He did not wonder why. He got groggily to his feet and shook Moran. The watchman sagged back in the chair, fell sideways and crashed to the floor. His swollen mouth was open and his eyeballs were staring at nothingness. *Was it really that bad already?*

He staggered around the table, bumped against a filing cabinet and burned the flesh of his arm. He shoved the cabinet aside and behind it on a wall bracket, was the phone. John stared at it with fascination. When he lifted the phone from the cradle it burned his hand, but he hung onto it. It took him almost a full minute to wet his lips and clear his throat sufficiently to speak. "Hello?"

A voice crashed in his ear, "My God, is there really someone there?"

John repeated dully, "Hello?"

The voice became hysterical with excitement. "Hey, wait a minute. This can't be. I was just trying the lines to see how many had been burned out. Wait." There was silence for a second, then the voice said, "This can't be a trick. I know where this goes. I'm connected to the vault under the warehouse."

John swallowed hard and said, "That's right. That's where I am."

"You're down there under that fire?"

"Yes. Trapped. The watchman—I— Who is this?"

"Devlin, manager of Crane's. I'm in the main office. This line we're talking on goes down under the vault and across the street. That's why it's working. But I never really thought— Say, who are you?"

"John Mead."

"Not the contractor!"

"Yes. We're trapped. Roasting. We're roasting. D'you hear me?"

"Oh, God, yes. Hold on." There was another short silence, and then Devlin again. His voice was flat, toneless. "Anyone you care to talk to, Mead? I can cut this line in on the city switchboard."

That was it, John thought. He knows too. He said, "Yes, get me Empire 2931."

"Of course. Just hang on."

John closed his eyes and waited, fighting wildly for control. After seconds that seemed years, struggling for the right casual tone, he said, "Hello, Jimmy."

"Oh, Dad. Say, where are you? Mom's been a little worried."

"Yes. I—I'm downtown, Jimmy. Do you hear me all right?"

"Sure. Why not?"

"Where is your mother?"

"She's down the street. Mrs. Overbright's. You know that book league thing they're in together. They gotta talk over—"

John interrupted quickly, "I know." There was no time to call Ellen. There was no time to get Jimmy to go after her. But talking to Jimmy was almost the same as talking with Ellen. He wet his thickening lips and said, "I only have a moment, Jimmy."

"Something you want, Dad? Say, what do you think of that fire? Isn't that a beauty?"

John asked dully, "Crane's?"

"Sure. Even way out here the whole sky is all lit up. Boy, oh boy, what a sight. I wanted to go down and watch it, but Mom—"

John cried, "No, Jimmy, no. You stay home. Do you hear me?"

"Well, sure—but, gee—gee—"

"Look, Jimmy, I just called to say—well—tell your mother—" He paused. What was there to say?

"Yes, Dad?"

"Nothing, Jimmy."

"Say, you sound kind of funny."

He had to hang up. He could not go on. "Good-by, Jimmy. I—I'll be seeing you."

"Sure. Good-by, Dad."

He dropped the phone back in the cradle and then thought of the thousands of things he could have said and was just as glad that they remained unsaid.

He staggered away from the filing cabinet and dropped to his knees by Moran's side. The room was now indeed an oven. Every breath was a searing pain in his lungs. He placed a hand on the watchman's chest and felt nothing. He reached for his wrist and felt the pulse. Moran was dead. He started to stretch out at his side. The phone was ringing again. John crawled across the floor, fought his way to his feet and lifted the phone. "Yes?"

"Mead. Devlin here." He sounded breathless, excited. "You hear me, Mead?"

"Yes."

"There may be a chance. There is no way to get at you. We can't do it. I've been talking with the fire chief. It's hopeless. We can hardly stand the heat even here in the offices. But there may be a chance. Isn't there a manhole there in the middle of that vault?"

"Yes."

"Thank God, it hasn't been plugged. Listen closely. That's the top of a twenty-inch pipe that drops down from the vault, goes under the street and comes out in back of our offices. It's part of an old abandoned drainage system built years ago.

"Now then, firemen are already knocking off the top of the pipe over here. If you can get down in there and crawl through we'll let a rope down from this end and pull you out. I don't know if it can be done. The pipe may even be filled up somewhere. But it's worth a try. You and Sam Moran—"

"The watchman is dead."

"Then get going, man. Don't waste time. Try it!"

John dropped the phone and fell again to his knees. He crawled to the center of the room and placed his hands on the manhole cover. The hot iron burnt his flesh. He pried and tore at the heavy cover, but could not budge it.

Strength. Just a little strength. Just enough strength. He pulled a chair over, broke a leg loose and pried it into the cover. It began to give. He levered the cover out of the hole and shoved it aside. He looked down into blackness.

For a moment he hesitated. He would have to go head first and he had no idea how far he would drop. Then, too, even though air did come through, the pipe was probably well filled with silt.

He thought of his words to Jimmy, "I'll be seeing you," and that decided him. Anything was worth trying, even if he went from one trap to another.

He extended his arms down into the pipe, lowered his head and shoulders and slid down until the cold iron was scraping his shoulders. He let his knees go and then was full length in the pipe and falling and his hands hit bottom. The drop had not been more than seven feet. But his arms would have buckled except for the confining diameter of the pipe.

He felt weak and helpless in the black hole and panic swept through him in waves. He wondered, amazed and astounded, how he managed to retain his sanity. He wanted to yell and scream.

When he felt a slight return of strength he shoved his hands forward and felt the curve of the pipe. His body could not bend enough to make the curve. He squirmed and wiggled and rolled to his back and bent up against the curve and then he was sliding through with his head and shoulders into the curve and his body following after. He clawed at the pipe and pulled himself into the flat horizontal part and rolled over again to his stomach.

He lay there in blackness and reeking mud and forgot his lacerated shoulders in the grateful coolness of the iron and the mud. He lay there for a long while, and then his arms went slowly forward into the silt. It was not very deep, about five or six inches. He squirmed into the ooze and inched forward with elbows and knees.

Slowly, inch by painful inch, he traveled forward through the pipe, trying to reckon his progress and the probable length of the pipe. He knew he had to travel at least two hundred yards, and that logically it could not be done.

He discarded logic and thought only of the inches. Another two or three inches; another, another. He went forward.

Time had no meaning. Even pain ceased to exist. There was but one elemental fact left in the world and that was movement, squirming, wiggling, forward movement. It went on for years and ages and space in time, but it went on. And at the end he felt another upcurve of the pipe and dug his way through deeper silt and rolled again to his back so that his stomach would fit around the curve and shoved himself forward and up.

He heard voices far above echoing in the pipe and then he felt the dangling rope and with all that was left he fought to pull the rope down and smeared it with the blood of his hands as he tied it in a firm knot around his chest and felt himself being lifted, *lifted* . . .

He was conscious of being pulled from the pipe and into the open air below a red and black night and of crowds milling around and shouting and talking and the stretcher and then the ambulance. He could hear the siren and felt the movement of the ambulance and the rush of its progress over the streets. But he felt something deeper, closer, tender and embracing, a part of himself, and knew that Ellen was near.

He forced his eyes open. Ellen was kneeling on the floor of the ambulance, an arm about his head, looking down into his eyes. She was pale, and her eyes were wide but not with fear.

She placed a cool cheek against his and whispered, "John."

"Yes."

"I always said—about us—"

"I know. It's true."

"More than either of us realized, my darling. Years ago—when he was contracting—it was my father who built that pipe."

John relaxed. I guess, he thought, I should have known. He smiled and closed his eyes.

4

AGATHA CHRISTIE

Murder at the Vicarage

AGATHA CHRISTIE has for many years been writing some of the most exciting mystery fiction to come out of England. Her Belgian-born detective, Hercule Poirot, has solved as many intricate crimes by his use of "the little gray cells" as Sherlock Holmes. But Miss Jane Marple, the purely amateur sleuth in this story, is also a favorite of the author—and of her enthusiastic readers. Married to Professor Max E. Mallowan, Mrs. Christie often accompanies her archeologist husband on "digs" in Iraq.

THE VICAR'S WIFE came round the corner of the Vicarage with her arms full of chrysanthemums. A good deal of rich garden soil was attached to her strong brogue shoes and a few fragments of earth were adhering to her nose, but of that fact she was perfectly unconscious.

She had a slight struggle in opening the Vicarage gate which hung, rustily, half off its hinges. A puff of wind caught at her battered felt hat, causing it to sit even more rakishly than it had done before. "Bother!" said Bunch.

Christened by her optimistic parents Diana, Mrs. Harmon had become Bunch at an early age for somewhat obvious reasons and the name had stuck to her ever since. Clutching the chrysanthemums, she made her way through the gate to the churchyard, and so to the church door.

The November air was mild and damp. Clouds scudded across the sky with patches of blue here and there. Inside, the church was dark and cold; it was unheated except at service times.

"Brrrrh!" said Bunch expressively. "I'd better get on with this quickly. I don't want to die of cold."

With the quickness born of practice she collected the necessary paraphernalia: vases, water, flower-holders. "I wish we had lilies," thought Bunch to herself. "I get so tired of these scraggy chrysanthemums." Her nimble fingers arranged the blooms in their holders.

There was nothing particularly original or artistic about the decorations, for Bunch Harmon herself was neither original nor artistic, but it was a homely and pleasant arrangement. Carrying the vases carefully, Bunch stepped up the aisle and made her way toward the altar. As she did so the sun came out.

It shone through the East window of somewhat crude colored glass, mostly blue and red—the gift of a wealthy Victorian churchgoer. The effect was almost startling in its sudden opulence. "Like jewels," thought Bunch. Suddenly she stopped, staring ahead of her. On the chancel steps was a huddled dark form.

Putting down the flowers carefully, Bunch went up to it and bent over it. It was a man lying there, huddled over on himself. Bunch knelt down by him and slowly, carefully, she turned him over. Her fingers went to his pulse—a pulse so feeble and fluttering that it told its own story, as did the almost greenish pallor of his face. There was no doubt, Bunch thought, that the man was dying.

He was a man of about forty-five, dressed in a dark, shabby suit. She laid down the limp hand she had picked up and looked at his other hand. This seemed clenched like a fist on his breast. Looking more closely she saw that the fingers were closed over what seemed to be a large wad or handkerchief which he was holding tightly to his chest. All round the clenched hand there were splashes of a dry brown fluid which, Bunch guessed, was dry blood. Bunch sat back on her heels, frowning.

Up till now the man's eyes had been closed but at this point they suddenly opened and fixed themselves on Bunch's face. They were neither dazed nor wandering. They seemed fully alive and intelligent. His lips moved, and Bunch bent forward to catch the words, or rather the word. It was only one word that he said:

"*Sanctuary.*"

There was, she thought, just a very faint smile as he breathed out this word. There was no mistaking it, for after a moment, he said it again, "Sanctuary . . ."

Then, with a faint, long-drawn-out sigh, his eyes closed again.

Once more Bunch's fingers went to his pulse. It was still there, but fainter now and more intermittent. She got up with decision.

"Don't move," she said, "or try to move. I'm going for help."

The man's eyes opened again but he seemed now to be fixing his attention on the colored light that came through the East window. He murmured something that Bunch could not quite catch. She thought, startled, that it might have been her husband's name.

"Julian?" she said. "Did you come here to find Julian?" But there was no answer. The man lay with eyes closed, his breathing coming in slow, shallow fashion.

Bunch turned and left the church rapidly. She glanced at her watch and nodded with some satisfaction. Dr. Griffiths would still be in his surgery. It was a couple of minutes' walk from the church. She went in, without waiting to knock or ring, passing through the waiting room and into the doctor's surgery.

"You must come at once," said Bunch. "There's a man dying in the church."

Some minutes later Dr. Griffiths rose from his knees after a brief examination.

"Can we move him from here into the Vicarage? I can attend to him better there—not that it's any use."

"Of course," said Bunch. "I'll go along and get things ready. I'll get Harper and Jones, shall I? To help you carry him."

"Thanks. I can telephone from the Vicarage for an ambulance, but I'm afraid—by the time it comes . . ." He left the remark unfinished.

Bunch said, "Internal bleeding?"

Dr. Griffiths nodded. He said, "How on earth did he come here?"

"I think he must have been here all night," said Bunch, considering. "Harper unlocks the church in the morning as he goes to work, but he doesn't usually come in."

It was about five minutes later when Dr. Griffiths put down the telephone receiver and came back into the morning room where the injured man was lying on quickly arranged blankets on the sofa. Bunch was moving a basin of water and clearing up after the doctor's examination.

"Well, that's that," said Griffiths. "I've sent for an ambulance and I've notified the police." He stood, frowning, looking down on the patient who lay with closed eyes. His left hand was plucking in a nervous, spasmodic way at his side.

"He was shot," said Griffiths. "Shot at fairly close quarters. He rolled his handkerchief up into a ball and plugged the wound with it so as to stop the bleeding."

"Could he have gone far after that happened?" Bunch asked.

"Oh, yes, it's quite possible. A mortally wounded man has been known to pick himself up and walk along a street as though nothing had happened, and then suddenly collapse five or ten minutes later. So he needn't have been shot in the church. Oh, no. He may have been shot some distance away. Of course, he may have shot himself and then dropped the revolver and staggered blindly toward the church. I don't quite know why he made for the church and not for the Vicarage."

"Oh, I know *that*," said Bunch. "He said it: 'Sanctuary.' "

The doctor stared at her. "Sanctuary?"

"Here's Julian," said Bunch, turning her head as she heard her husband's steps in the hall. "Julian! Come here."

The Reverend Julian Harmon entered the room. His vague, scholarly manner always made him appear much older than he really was. "Dear me!" said Julian Harmon, staring in a mild, puzzled manner at the surgical appliances and the prone figure on the sofa.

Bunch explained with her usual economy of words. "He was in the church, dying. He'd been shot. Do you know him, Julian? I thought he said your name."

The vicar came up to the sofa and looked down at the dying man. "Poor fellow," he said, and shook his head. "No, I don't know him. I'm almost sure I've never seen him before."

At that moment the dying man's eyes opened once more. They went from the doctor to Julian Harmon and from him to his wife. The eyes stayed there, staring into Bunch's face. Griffiths stepped forward.

"If you could tell us," he said urgently.

But with his eyes fixed on Bunch, the man said weakly, "Please —*please*—" And then, with a slight tremor, he died . . .

Sergeant Hayes licked his pencil and turned the page of his notebook.

"So that's all you can tell me, Mrs. Harmon?"

"That's all," said Bunch. "These are the things out of his coat pockets."

On a table at Sergeant Hayes' elbow was a wallet, a rather battered old watch with the initials W.S. and the return half of a ticket to London. Nothing more.

"You've found out who he is?" asked Bunch.

"A Mr. and Mrs. Eccles phoned up the station. He's her brother, it seems. Name of Sandbourne. Been in a low state of health and nerves for some time. He's been getting worse lately. The day before yesterday he walked out and didn't come back. He took a revolver with him."

"And he came out here and shot himself with it?" said Bunch. "Why?"

"Well, you see, he'd been depressed . . ."

Bunch interrupted him. "I don't mean *that*. I mean, why here?"

Since Sergeant Hayes obviously did not know the answer to that one he replied in an oblique fashion, "Come out here, he did, on the 5:10 bus."

"Yes," said Bunch again. "But *why?*"

"I don't know, Mrs. Harmon," said Sergeant Hayes. "There's no accounting. If the balance of the mind is disturbed—"

Bunch finished for him. "They may do it anywhere. But it still seems to me unnecessary to take a bus out to a small country place like this. He didn't know anyone here, did he?"

"Not so far as can be ascertained," said Sergeant Hayes. He coughed in an apologetic manner and said, as he rose to his feet, "It may be as Mr. and Mrs. Eccles will come out and see you, Ma'am—if you don't mind, that is."

"Of course I don't mind," said Bunch. "It's very natural. I only wish I had something to tell them."

"I'll be getting along," said Sergeant Hayes.

"I'm only so thankful," said Bunch, going with him to the front door, "that it wasn't murder."

A car had drawn up at the Vicarage gate. Sergeant Hayes, glancing at it, remarked: "Looks as though that's Mr. and Mrs. Eccles come here now, Ma'am, to talk with you."

Bunch braced herself to endure what, she felt, might be rather a difficult ordeal. "However," she thought, "I can always call Julian in to help me. A clergyman's a great help when people are bereaved."

Exactly what she had expected Mr. and Mrs. Eccles to be like, Bunch could not have said, but she was conscious, as she greeted them, of a feeling of surprise. Mr. Eccles was a stout and florid man whose natural manner would have been cheerful and facetious. Mrs. Eccles had a vaguely flashy look about her. She had a small, mean, pursed-up mouth. Her voice was thin and reedy.

"It's been a terrible shock, Mrs. Harmon, as you can imagine," she said.

"Oh, I know," said Bunch. "It must have been. Do sit down. Can I offer you—well, perhaps it's a little early for tea—"

Mr. Eccles waved a pudgy hand. "No, no, nothing for us," he said. "It's very kind of you, I'm sure. Just wanted to . . . well . . . what poor William said and all that, you know?"

"He's been abroad a long time," said Mrs. Eccles, "and I think he must have had some very nasty experiences. Very quiet and depressed he's been, ever since he came home. Said the world wasn't fit to live in and there was nothing to look forward to. Poor Bill, he was always moody."

Bunch stared at them both for a moment or two without speaking.

"Pinched my husband's revolver, he did," went on Mrs. Eccles. "Without our knowing. Then it seems he come out here by bus. I suppose that was nice feeling on his part. He wouldn't have liked to do it in our house."

"Poor fellow, poor fellow," said Mr. Eccles, with a sigh. "It doesn't do to judge."

There was another short pause, and Mr. Eccles said, "Did he leave a message? Any last words, nothing like that?"

His bright, rather piglike eyes watched Bunch closely. Mrs. Eccles, too, leaned forward as though anxious for the reply.

"No," said Bunch quietly. "He came into the church when he was dying, for sanctuary."

Mrs. Eccles said in a puzzled voice, "Sanctuary? I don't think I quite . . ."

Mr. Eccles interrupted. "Holy place, my dear," he said impatiently. "That's what the vicar's wife means. It's a sin—suicide, you know. I expect he wanted to make amends."

"He tried to say something just before he died," said Bunch. "He began, 'Please,' but that's as far as he got." Mrs. Eccles put her handkerchief to her eyes and sniffed.

"Oh, dear," she said. "It's terribly upsetting, isn't it?"

"There, there, Pam," said her husband. "Don't take on. These things can't be helped. Poor Willie. Still, he's at peace now. Well, thank you very much, Mrs. Harmon. I hope we haven't interrupted you. A vicar's wife is a busy lady, we know that."

They shook hands with her. Then Eccles turned back suddenly to say, "Oh, yes, there's just one other thing. I think you've got his coat here, haven't you?"

"His coat?" Bunch frowned.

Mrs. Eccles said, "We'd like all his things, you know. Sentimental-like."

"He had a watch and a wallet and a railway ticket in the pockets," said Bunch. "I gave them to Sergeant Hayes."

"That's all right, then," said Mr. Eccles. "He'll hand them over to us, I expect. His private papers would be in the wallet."

"There was a pound note in the wallet," said Bunch. "Nothing else."

"No letters? Nothing like that?"

Bunch shook her head.

"Well, thank you again, Mrs. Harmon. The coat he was wearing—perhaps the Sergeant's got that too, has he?"

Bunch frowned in an effort of remembrance.

"No," she said. "I don't think . . . let me see. The doctor and I took his coat off to examine his wound." She looked round the room, vaguely. "I must have taken it upstairs with the towels and basin."

"I wonder now, Mrs. Harmon, if you don't mind . . . We'd like his coat, you know, the last thing he wore. Well, the wife feels rather sentimental about it."

"Of course," said Bunch. "Would you like me to have it cleaned first? I'm afraid it's rather—well, stained."

Bunch frowned. "Now I wonder where . . . excuse me a moment." She went upstairs and it was some few minutes before she returned.

"I'm so sorry," she said breathlessly, "my daily woman must have put it aside with other clothes that were going to the cleaners. It's taken me quite a long time to find it. Here it is. I'll do it up for you in brown paper."

Disclaiming their protests she did so; then once more effu-
sively bidding her farewell the Eccles departed.

Bunch went slowly back across the hall and entered the study.
The Reverend Julian Harmon looked up and his brow cleared.
He was composing a sermon and was fearing that he'd been led
astray by the interest of the political relations between Judaea
and Persia, in the reign of Cyrus.

"Yes, dear?" he said, hopefully.

"Julian," said Bunch. "What's *Sanctuary* exactly?"

Julian Harmon gratefully put aside his sermon paper.

"Well," he said. "Sanctuary in Roman and Greek temples
applied to the *cella* in which stood the statue of a god. The
Latin word for altar 'ara' also means protection." He continued
learnedly: "In 399 A.D. the right of sanctuary in Christian
churches was finally and definitely recognized. The earliest
mention of the right of sanctuary in England is in the Code of
Laws issued by Ethelbert in A.D. 600 . . ."

He continued for some time with his exposition but was, as
often, disconcerted by his wife's reception of his erudite pronouncement.

"Darling," she said. "You *are* sweet."

Bending over, she kissed him on the tip of his nose. Julian
felt rather like a dog who has been congratulated on performing
a clever trick.

"The Eccles have been here," said Bunch.

The vicar frowned. "The Eccles? I don't seem to remember . . ."

"You don't know them. They're the sister and her husband
of the man in the church."

"My dear, you ought to have called me."

"There wasn't any need," said Bunch. "They were not in need
of consolation. I wonder now." She frowned. "If I put a casserole
in the oven tomorrow, can you manage, Julian? I think I shall
have to go up to London for the sales."

"The sails?" Her husband looked at her blankly. "Do you
mean a yacht or a boat or something?"

Bunch laughed.

"No, darling. There's a special white sale at Burrows and
Portman's. You know, sheets, tablecloths and towels and glass-
cloths. I don't know what we do with our glass-cloths, the way

they wear through. Besides," she added thoughtfully, "I think I ought to go and see Aunt Jane." . . .

That sweet old lady, Miss Jane Marple, was enjoying the delights of the metropolis for a fortnight, comfortably installed in her nephew's studio flat.

"So kind of dear Raymond," she murmured. "He and Joan have gone to America for a fortnight and they insisted I should come up here and enjoy myself. And now, dear Bunch, do tell me what it is that's worrying you."

Bunch was Miss Marple's favorite godchild, and the old lady looked at her with great affection as Bunch, thrusting her best felt hat further on the back of her head, started on her story.

Bunch's recital was concise and clear. Miss Marple nodded her head as Bunch finished. "I see," she said. "Yes, I see."

"That's why I felt I had to see you," said Bunch. "You see, not being clever—"

"But you *are* clever, my dear."

"No, I'm not. Not clever like Julian."

"Julian, of course, has a very solid intellect," said Miss Marple.

"That's it," said Bunch. "Julian's got the intellect, but on the other hand, I've got the *sense*."

"You have a lot of common sense, Bunch, and you're very intelligent."

"You see, I don't really know what I ought to do. I can't ask Julian because—well, I mean, Julian's so full of rectitude . . ."

This statement appeared to be perfectly understood by Miss Marple, who said, "I know what you mean, dear. We women—well, it's different." She went on, "You told me what happened, Bunch, but I'd like to know first exactly what you think."

"It's all wrong," said Bunch. "The man who was there in the church, dying, knew all about Sanctuary. He said it just the way Julian would have said it. I mean he was a well-read, educated man. And if he'd shot himself, he wouldn't drag himself into a church afterward and say 'sanctuary.' Sanctuary means that you're pursued, and when you get into a church you're safe. Your pursuers can't touch you. At one time even the law couldn't get at you."

She looked questioningly at Miss Marple. The latter nodded. Bunch went on, "Those people, the Eccles, were quite different.

Ignorant and coarse. And there's another thing. That watch—
the dead man's watch. It had the initials W.S. on the back of
it. But inside—I opened it—in very small lettering there was
"To Walter from his father" and a date. *Walter*. But the Eccles
kept talking of him as William or Bill."

Miss Marple seemed about to speak but Bunch rushed on,
"Oh, I know you're not always called the name you're baptized
by. I mean, I can understand that you might be christened
William and called 'Porky' or 'Carrots' or something. But your
sister wouldn't call you William or Bill if your name was Walter."

"You mean that she wasn't his sister?"

"I'm quite sure she wasn't his sister. They were horrid—both
of them. They came to the Vicarage to get his things and to
find out if he'd said anything before he died. When I said he
hadn't I saw it in their faces—relief. I think, myself," finished
Bunch, "it was Eccles who shot him."

"Murder?" said Miss Marple.

"Yes," said Bunch. "Murder. That's why I came to you,
darling."

Bunch's remark might have seemed incongruous to an ignorant
listener, but in certain spheres Miss Marple had a reputation for
dealing with murder.

"He said 'please' to me before he died," said Bunch. "He
wanted me to do something for him. The awful thing is I've no
idea what."

Miss Marple considered for a moment or two, and then
pounced on the point that had already occurred to Bunch. "But
why was he there at all?" she asked.

"You mean," said Bunch, "if you wanted sanctuary you might
pop into a church anywhere. There's no need to take a bus that
only goes four times a day and come out to a lonely spot like
ours for it."

"He must have come there for a purpose," Miss Marple
thought. "He must have come to see someone. Chipping Cleghorn's not a big place, Bunch. Surely you must have some idea
of who it was he came to see?"

Bunch reviewed the inhabitants of her village in her mind
before rather doubtfully shaking her head. "In a way," she said,
"it could be anybody."

"He never mentioned a name?"

"He said Julian, or I thought he said Julian. It might have been Julia, I suppose. As far as I know, there isn't any Julia living in Chipping Cleghorn."

She screwed up her eyes as she thought back to the scene. The man lying there on the chancel steps, the light coming through the window with its jewels of red and blue light.

"Jewels," said Bunch suddenly. "Perhaps that's what he said. The light coming through the East window looked like jewels."

"Jewels," said Miss Marple, thoughtfully.

"I'm coming now," said Bunch, "to the most important thing of all. The reason why I've really come here today. You see, the Eccles made a great fuss about having his coat. We took it off when the doctor was seeing to him. It was an old, shabby sort of coat—there was no reason they should have wanted it. They pretended it was sentimental, but that was nonsense.

"Anyway, I went up to find it, and as I was going up the stairs I remembered how he'd made a kind of picking gesture with his hand, as though he was fumbling with the coat. So when I got hold of the coat I looked at it very carefully and I saw that in one place the lining had been sewn up again with a different thread. So I unpicked it and I found a little piece of paper inside. I took it out and I sewed it up again properly with thread that matched. I was careful and I don't really think that the Eccles would know I've done it. I don't *think* so, but I can't be sure. And I took the coat down to them and made some excuse for the delay."

"The piece of paper?" asked Miss Marple.

Bunch opened her handbag. "I didn't show it to Julian," she said, "because he would have said that I ought to have given it to the Eccles. But I thought I'd rather bring it to you instead."

"A cloakroom ticket," said Miss Marple, looking at it. "Paddington Station."

"He had a return ticket to Paddington in his pocket," said Bunch.

The eyes of the two women met.

"This calls for action," said Miss Marple briskly. "But it would be advisable, I think, to be careful. Would you have noticed at all, Bunch dear, whether you were followed when you came to London today?"

"Followed!" exclaimed Bunch. "You don't think—"

"Well, I think it's *possible*," said Miss Marple. "When anything is possible, I think we ought to take precautions." She rose with a brisk movement. "You came up here ostensibly, my dear, to go to the sales. I think the right thing to do, therefore, would be for us to *go* to the sales. But before we set out, we might put one or two little arrangements in hand. I don't suppose," Miss Marple added obscurely, "that I shall need the old speckled tweed with the beaver collar just at present."

It was about an hour and a half later that the two ladies, rather the worse for wear and battered in appearance, and both clasping parcels of hard-won household linen, sat down at a small and sequestered hostelry called the Apple Bough to restore their forces with steak and kidney pudding followed by apple tart and custard.

"Really a prewar-quality face towel," gasped Miss Marple, slightly out of breath. "With a J on it, too. So fortunate that Raymond's wife's name is Joan. I shall put them aside until I really need them and then they will do for her if I pass on sooner than I expect."

"I really did need the glass-cloths," said Bunch. "And they were very cheap, though not as cheap as the ones that woman with the ginger hair managed to snatch from me."

A smart young woman with a lavish application of rouge and lipstick entered the Apple Bough at that moment. After looking round vaguely for a moment or two, she hurried to their table. She laid down an envelope by Miss Marple's elbow.

"There you are, Miss," she said briskly.

"Oh, thank you, Gladys," said Miss Marple. "Thank you very much. So kind of you."

"Always pleased to oblige, I'm sure," said Gladys. "Ernie always says to me, 'Everything what's good you learned from that Miss Marple of yours that you were in service with,' and I'm sure I'm always glad to oblige you, Miss."

"Such a dear girl," said Miss Marple as Gladys departed again. "Always so willing and so kind."

She looked inside the envelope and then passed it on to Bunch. "Now be very careful, dear," she said. "By the way, is there still that nice young Inspector at Melchester that I remember?"

"I don't know," said Bunch. "I expect so."

"Well, if not," said Miss Marple, thoughtfully, "I can always ring up the Chief Constable. I *think* he would remember me."

"Of course he'd remember you," said Bunch. "Everybody would remember *you*. You're quite unique." She rose.

Arrived at Paddington, Bunch went to the Luggage Office and produced the cloakroom ticket. A moment or two later a rather shabby old suitcase was passed across to her, and carrying this she made her way to the platform.

The journey home was uneventful. Bunch rose as the train approached Chipping Cleghorn and picked up the old suitcase. She had just left her carriage when a man, sprinting along the platform, suddenly seized the suitcase from her hand and rushed off with it.

"Stop!" Bunch yelled. "Stop him, stop him. He's taken my suitcase."

The ticket collector who, at this rural station, was a man of somewhat slow processes had just begun to say, "Now, look here, you can't do that—" when a smart blow in the chest pushed him aside, and the man with the suitcase rushed out from the station. He made his way toward a waiting car. Tossing the suitcase in, he was about to climb after it but before he could move a hand fell on his shoulder, and the voice of Police Constable Abel said, "Now then, what's all this?"

Bunch arrived, panting, from the station. "He snatched my suitcase," she said.

"Nonsense," said the man. "I don't know what this lady means. It's my suitcase. I just got out of the train with it."

"Now, let's get this clear," said Police Constable Abel.

He looked at Bunch with a bovine and impartial stare. Nobody would have guessed that Police Constable Abel and Mrs. Harmon spent long half hours in Police Constable Abel's off time discussing the respective merits of manure and bone meal for rose bushes.

"You say, Madam, that this is your suitcase?" said Police Constable Abel.

"Yes," said Bunch. "Definitely."

"And you, sir?"

"I say this suitcase is mine."

The man was tall, dark and well dressed, with a drawling voice and a superior manner. A feminine voice from inside the car, said, "Of course it's your suitcase, Edwin. I don't know what this woman means."

"We'll have to get this clear," said Police Constable Abel. "If it's your suitcase, Madam, what do you say is inside it?"

"Clothes," said Bunch. "A long speckeldy coat with a beaver collar, two wool jumpers and a pair of shoes."

"Well, that's clear enough," said Police Constable Abel. He turned to the other.

"I am a theatrical costumer," said the dark man importantly. "This suitcase contains theatrical properties which I brought down here for an amateur performance."

"Right, sir," said Police Constable Abel. "Well, we'll just look inside, shall we, and see? We can go along to the police station, or if you're in a hurry we'll take the suitcase back to the station and open it there."

"It'll suit me," said the dark man. "My name is Moss, by the way. Edwin Moss."

The Police Constable, holding the suitcase, went back into the station. "Just taking this into the Parcels Office, George," he said to the ticket collector.

Police Constable Abel laid the suitcase on the counter of the Parcels Office and pushed back the clasp. The case was not locked. Bunch and Mr. Edwin Moss stood on either side of him, their eyes regarding each other vengefully.

"Ah!" said Police Constable Abel, as he pushed up the lid.

Inside, neatly folded, was a long rather shabby tweed coat with a beaver fur collar. There were also two wool jumpers and a pair of country shoes.

"Exactly as you say, Madam," said Police Constable Abel, turning to Bunch.

Nobody could have said that Mr. Edwin Moss under-did things. His dismay and compunction were magnificent.

"I do apologize," he said. "I really *do* apologize. Please believe me, dear lady, when I tell you how very, very sorry I am. Unpardonable—quite unpardonable—my behavior has been." He looked at his watch. "I must rush now. Probably my suitcase has gone on the train." Raising his hat once more, he said meltingly to Bunch, "Do, *do* forgive me," and rushed hurriedly out of the Parcels Office.

"Are you going to let him get away?" asked Bunch in a conspiratorial whisper of Police Constable Abel.

The latter slowly closed a bovine eye in a wink.

"He won't get too far, Ma'am," he said. "That's to say, he won't get far unobserved, if you take my meaning."

"Oh," said Bunch, relieved.

"That old lady's been on the phone," said Police Constable Abel, "the one as was down here a few years ago. Bright she is, isn't she? But there's been a lot cooking up all today. Shouldn't wonder if the Inspector or Sergeant was out to see you about it tomorrow morning."

It was the Inspector who came, the Inspector Craddock whom Miss Marple remembered. He greeted Bunch with a smile as an old friend.

"Crime in Chipping Cleghorn again," he said cheerfully. "You don't lack for sensation here, do you, Mrs. Harmon?"

"I could do with rather less," said Bunch. "Have you come to ask me questions or are you going to tell me things for a change?"

"I'll tell you some things first," said the Inspector. "To begin with, Mr. and Mrs. Eccles have been having an eye kept on them for some time. There's reason to believe they've been connected with several robberies in this part of the world. For another thing, although Mrs. Eccles *has* a brother called Sandbourne who has recently come back from abroad, the man you found dying in the church yesterday was definitely not Sandbourne."

"I knew that he wasn't," said Bunch. "His name was Walter, to begin with, not William."

The Inspector nodded. "His name was Walter St. John, and he escaped forty-eight hours ago from Charrington Prison."

"Of course," said Bunch softly to herself, "he was being hunted down by the law, and he took sanctuary." Then she asked, "What had he done?"

"I'll have to go back rather a long way. It's a complicated story. Several years ago there was a certain dancer doing turns at the music halls. I don't expect you'll have ever heard of her, but she specialized in an Arabian Night turn, 'Aladdin in the Cave of Jewels' it was called. She wore bits of rhinestone and not much else.

"She wasn't much of a dancer, I believe, but she was—well—attractive. Anyway, a certain Asiatic royalty fell for her in a big way. Amongst other things he gave her a very magnificent emerald necklace."

"The historic jewels of a Rajah?" murmured Bunch ecstatically.

Inspector Craddock coughed. "Well, a rather more modern version, Mrs. Harmon. The affair didn't last very long, broke up when our potentate's attention was captured by a certain film star whose demands were not quite so modest.

"Zobeida, to give the dancer her stage name, hung on to the necklace, and in due course it was stolen. It disappeared from her dressing room at the theater, and there was a lingering suspicion in the minds of the authorities that she herself might have engineered its disappearance. Such things have been known as a publicity stunt, or indeed from more dishonest motives.

"The necklace was never recovered, but during the course of the investigation the attention of the police was drawn to this man, Walter St. John. He was a man of education and breeding who had come down in the world, and who was employed as a working jeweler with a rather obscure firm which was suspected as acting as a fence for jewel robberies.

"There was evidence that this necklace had passed through his hands. It was, however, in connection with the theft of some other jewelry that he was finally brought to trial and convicted and sent to prison. He had not very much longer to serve, so his escape was rather a surprise."

"But why did he come here?" asked Bunch.

"We'd like to know that very much, Mrs. Harmon. Following up his trail, it seems that he went first to London. He didn't visit any of his old associates but he visited an elderly woman, a Mrs. Jacobs who had formerly been a theatrical dresser. She won't say a word of what he came for, but according to other lodgers in the house he left carrying a suitcase."

"I see," said Bunch. "He left it in the cloakroom at Paddington and then he came down here."

"By that time," said Inspector Craddock, "Eccles and the man who calls himself Edwin Moss were on his trail. They wanted that suitcase. They saw him get on the bus. They must have driven out in a car ahead of him and been waiting for him when he left the bus."

"And he was murdered?" said Bunch.

"Yes," said Craddock. "He was shot. It was Eccles' revolver, but I rather fancy it was Moss who did the shooting. Now, Mrs. Harmon, what we want to know is, where is the suitcase that

Walter St. John actually deposited at Paddington Station?"

Bunch grinned. "I expect Aunt Jane's got it by now," she said. "Miss Marple, I mean. That was her plan. She sent a former maid of hers with a suitcase packed with her things to the cloakroom at Paddington and we exchanged tickets. I collected her suitcase and brought it down by train. She seemed to expect that an attempt would be made to get it from me."

It was Inspector Craddock's turn to grin. "So she said when she rang up. I'm driving up to London to see her. Do you want to come, too, Mrs. Harmon?"

"Wel-l," said Bunch, considering. "Wel-l, as a matter of fact, it's very fortunate. I had a toothache last night so I really ought to go to London to see the dentist, oughn't I?"

"Definitely," said Inspector Craddock . . .

Miss Marple looked from Inspector Craddock's face to the eager face of Bunch Harmon. The suitcase lay on the table. "Of course, I haven't opened it," the old lady said. "I wouldn't dream of doing such a thing till somebody official arrived. Besides," she added, with a demurely mischievous Victorian smile, "it's locked."

"Like to make a guess at what's inside, Miss Marple?" asked the Inspector.

"I should imagine, you know," said Miss Marple, "that it would be Zobeida's theatrical costumes. Would you like a chisel, Inspector?"

The chisel soon did its work. Both women gave a slight gasp as the lid flew up. The sunlight coming through the window lit up what seemed like an inexhaustible treasure of sparkling jewels, red, blue, green, orange.

"Aladdin's Cave," said Miss Marple. "The flashing jewels the girl wore to dance."

"Ah," said Inspector Craddock. "Now, what's so precious about it, do you think, that a man was murdered to get hold of it?"

"She was a shrewd girl, I expect," said Miss Marple thoughtfully. "She's dead, isn't she, Inspector?"

"Yes, died three years ago."

"She had this valuable emerald necklace," said Miss Marple, musingly. "Had the stones taken out of their setting and fastened here and there on her theatrical costume, where everyone would take them for merely colored rhinestones. Then she had a replica

made of the real necklace, and that, of course, was what was
stolen. No wonder it never came on the market. The thief soon
discovered the stones were false."

"Here is an envelope," said Bunch, pulling aside some of the
glittering stones.

Inspector Craddock took it from her and extracted two official-
looking papers from it. He read aloud, " 'Marriage certificate
between Walter Edmund St. John and Mary Moss.' That was
Zobeida's real name."

"So they were married," said Miss Marple. "I see."

"What's the other?" asked Bunch.

"A birth certificate of a daughter, Jewel."

"Jewel?" cried Bunch. "Why, of course. Jewel! *Jill!* That's it.
I see now why he came to Chipping Cleghorn. *That's* what he
was trying to say to me. Jewel. The Mundys, you know, Labur-
nam Cottage. They look after a little girl for someone. They're
devoted to her. She's been like their own granddaughter. Yes,
I remember now, her name *was* Jewel, only, of course, they call
her Jill.

"Mrs. Mundy had a stroke about a week ago, and the old man's
been very ill with pneumonia. They were both going to go into
the Infirmary. I've been trying hard to find a good home for Jill
somewhere. I didn't want her taken away to an institution.

"I suppose her father heard about it in prison and he managed
to break away and get hold of this suitcase from the old dresser
he or his wife left it with. I suppose if the jewels really belonged
to her mother, they can be used for the child now."

"I should imagine so, Mrs. Harmon. *If* they're here."

"Oh, they'll be here all right," said Miss Marple cheerfully . . .

"Thank goodness you're back, dear," said the Reverend Julian
Harmon, greeting his wife with affection and a sigh of content.
"Mrs. Burt always tries to do her best when you're away, but
she really gave me some *very* peculiar fishcakes for lunch. I
didn't want to hurt her feelings so I gave them to Tiglash Pileser,
but even *he* wouldn't eat them so I had to throw them out of
the window."

"Tiglash Pileser," said Bunch, stroking the Vicarage cat, who
was purring against her knee, "is *very* particular about what fish
he eats. I often tell him he's got a proud stomach!"

"And your tooth, dear? Did you have it seen to?"

"Yes," said Bunch. "It didn't hurt much, and I went to see Aunt Jane again, too . . ."

"Dear old thing," said Julian. "I hope she's not failing at all."

"Not in the least," said Bunch with a grin.

The following morning Bunch took a fresh supply of chrysanthemums to the church. The sun was once more pouring through the East window, and Bunch stood in the jeweled light on the chancel steps. She said very softly under her breath, "Your little girl will be all right. I'll see that she is. I promise."

Then she tidied up the church, slipped into a pew and knelt for a few moments to say her prayers before returning to the Vicarage to attack the piled up chores of two neglected days.

5

The Spell

ARTHUR GORDON, who is one of the most versatile practitioners of the short-short form, occasionally dips into the black arts for a theme. Here is such a story, as unusual and as chilling as any we have ever read. Mr. Gordon claims Savannah, Georgia, as his birthplace but he now lives with his family near New York. Most of his short-shorts have appeared in the pages of *This Week*.

EXCUSE ME, SIR, I see that you are smoking—could you possibly spare a cigarette? We are not allowed to have them here. A wise rule, no doubt, in the majority of cases. Lunatics should never be trusted with fire.

But believe me, sir, I don't belong in this place with all these crazy people. Really, I don't! I'm as sane as anyone, as sane as you are. But there you sit in your parked car, free to come and go as you please. And here am I behind these bars . . .

Oh, please don't go away! Don't drive off just because I am talking to you. I won't cause you any embarrassment. Not the slightest. I won't even ask you again for a cigarette.

I suppose you're waiting for someone. Your wife? A friend, perhaps? One of the doctors who work here in the asylum? It doesn't matter. If I see anyone coming, I'll stop talking. I'll go away from the window. But until then, please stay. You don't know what it means to be able to talk like this to somebody on the outside. Somebody who will listen, somebody who might even believe . . .

No, that's too much to expect, of course. But tell me, sir, do I *sound* like a madman? Is there anything irrational in the way I talk? My mind is as good as it ever was; truly, it is. I can solve a problem in trigonometry for you, or recite one of Shakespeare's sonnets. But when I try to tell the truth, they won't believe me.

Sir, you're a gentleman, that's obvious. You have the sympathy and the tolerance, the willingness to hear a man out. I can recognize those qualities for a very good reason. I'm a gentleman, myself.

Oh, you wouldn't think so from looking at me, I know. And you wouldn't think so if you read my medical file. It says that I am David Greenlea, merchant seaman, a hopeless paranoiac suffering from insane delusions. But, sir, I swear to you I'm not David Greenlea, and I'm not insane!

Let me tell you, sir, just how it happened. And let me beg of you not to judge me by the way I look. This broken nose, these gnarled hands—they're not mine, I tell you, they're not mine! They belong to David Greenlea, that's true. But I'm not David Greenlea, I'm not. I'm not. I'm Edgar Greenlea, vice president of the Overseas Shipping Company, with a house on Edgewater Drive and a wife and two fine children . . . oh, you must believe me!

But wait. I'm going too fast. I can see the disbelief in your eyes. And the pity. Yes, the pity. I don't blame you, sir, really I don't. But hear me out, I beg of you. It will only take a minute or two. And it will cost you nothing. Just a cigarette, perhaps, if you're so inclined.

It happened a year ago, almost to the day. I was in my office, as usual. I was in my own body, too, not this tattooed monstrosity that you're looking at. Oh, I know that does sound insane, but let me explain, *please!*

One of our ships, the *Eastern Star*, had docked only that morning. About noon they brought me word that David Greenlea had come ashore, was drinking himself blind in a water-front tavern. David Greenlea, my first cousin, a wretched ne'er-do-well, always drunk or fighting, always in trouble. I had got him his berth on the *Eastern Star*. Without my influence, he would have lost it a dozen times. But there was no gratitude on his part, sir. None at all. Indeed, he hated me, hated me because I was successful, respected, everything he wanted to be—and was not.

Malevolent as he was, I felt responsible for him as a member of the family. And so I went down to that tavern. I found him, drunk and disgusting. I took him into a back room and ordered coffee. We were alone there . . .

Sir, could you *possibly* let me have a cigarette? Just one? Look, I'll stretch my arm through the bars as far as it will go. If you could just put one in my fingers, I'd be so grateful. Really, you don't know how agonizing it is to watch another man smoke when you . . . Oh, thank you, sir, you are most kind!

So I made David drink the coffee. I got him fairly sober, but he kept reviling me. He accused me of secretly loathing him, despising him. I said that I didn't despise him, I only pitied him. When I said that, he gave me a strange look, half drunken and half cunning. Then he smiled. I tell you, sir, I have seen that smile a thousand times since, in my dreams.

"Let me show you a trick, Cousin Edgar," he said, "a trick I learned from a sing-song girl in Hong Kong. A little magic, black or white depending on where you sit."

He took something out of his pocket and put it on the table, and I saw that it was a cone of cheap incense. "First there must be pity," he said, smiling that evil smile, "if the spell is to work. Then there must be a burnt offering, and finally there must be the words."

I thought he was raving, but I decided to humor him. So I . . . Pardon me, sir, could I trouble you for a light? You needn't give me a match, just hold the flame where I can reach it with the tip of the cigarette. That's right. Thank you, sir. Ah, but that's good . . .

So I said to my cousin David, "What words?"

He had the incense lighted, now, and the smoke was rising up between us. He looked at me through it, just as I am looking at you. Then he said the words. Come closer. I'll whisper them to you. Just a little closer. There!

It works! It works! By the ancient and terrible gods, the spell still works! I thought it would, I hoped it would! Oh, I *am* sorry, sir, to leave you in there. But I had to get out, I had to! And this was the only way. I had to change places with you, don't you see? I had to exchange bodies with you, just the way David did with me!

Oh, *please* don't scream like that, and shake the bars. The attendants will come and put you in a straitjacket. Because to them you'll just be David Greenlea, merchant seaman, hopeless paranoiac. And no matter what you say, they won't believe you. You'll have to bide your time, just as I did. You'll have to wait until someone pities you, and then there must be a burnt offering, remember, and then the words. Don't forget the words.

Now I must be going, for I have much to do. Ah, yes, much to do. My cousin David will not be expecting me, not looking like this. What a surprise for David, what a surprise!

I'll take your car, sir, because you won't be needing it any more. Thank you for everything, especially the burnt offering— I mean, the cigarette. Good-by, sir. Good-by.

6

DAVID CHANDLER

12 Flights Up

THE ACTION of this story takes place in 1947, an important point to remember, since it rises out of some of the tense—and often tragic—black-market operations which happened in Europe after the close of World War II. Mr. Chandler has one novel to his credit—*A Little More Time*, published a year ago. Otherwise, his writing is chiefly taken up by short stories and assignments for the movies and TV in Hollywood, where he lives.

IT WAS A NIGHT of intermittent, eccentric rain, bursting into angry little squalls, dwindling to mistlike drizzle, seeming to die only to start again. The agent of the Army Department's Criminal Investigation Division wondered whether she would come out in the rain; he took a table near the window of the coffee shop where he could watch the door.

As soon as she entered the restaurant, though he could not see her face, Stanton knew she was the girl. A gray porkpie of the same wool as her coat shaded her eyes. She was not as tall as the first impression she created yesterday, but that was because she held herself proudly as if she prized what she had. She waited for the hostess to lead her to a table. Her eyes were fixed without focus ahead of her and she pulled at the fingers of the white string gloves that sheathed her hands.

Stanton left a couple of bills on his check beside a small blue teapot, pushed his chair back and walked toward her table. He was a well-built man in his middle thirties, dressed in a loose-fitting double-breasted suit of soft blue flannel. He had graying black hair which he brushed back smoothly from a part on the right side of his head. Over his arm he carried a service trench coat. He did not attempt a smile as he approached her.

"Did you drop this, Miss Linton?" he asked. He placed his credentials, enclosed in a small leather folder, on an empty serv-

ice plate before her. Her eyes, when they looked up at him, gave
no sign of what she was thinking.

"Major Stanton," she said, letting a smile cross her face and
holding the leather folder up to him. "You're an unexpected type
anyway. Do sit down."

He took the chair across from her. She appeared even younger
than her age, but her face, her eyes, her speech betrayed someone who had chosen to draw strength only from herself, and
this gave her a quality he did not often observe in the young.
Her glamour-girl pictures he'd studied in Washington hadn't
done her justice; but most of all, they hadn't even begun to show
her strength of character and the firmness of her manner.

"I don't mind waiting," Stanton told her. "Please have your
dinner."

"You mean to say a smart Army C.I.D. man of your discern-
ment doesn't know I always take dinner in my apartment? This
is just a chance to see some faces before I turn in."

The smile on his face was almost an apology. "I can't say I
know all your habits. I've only been tagging you for two days."

"Hasn't it been dull? No coded messages, no corpses, not even
a phone call?"

A grin creased Stanton's face. "They don't usually come like
you either, Miss Linton. Generally they're wrapped to the ear-
lobes in mink, trimmed in gold accessories and glistening with
diamonds."

She looked swiftly around the crowded restaurant. "Look," she
said, "why don't we go to my place? I'll let you search the whole
flat while the coffee is perking."

Stanton rose with her but was late for her chair. "I'll take you
up on that. But don't ask me to make a search. In the Criminal
Investigation Division I'm known as the heavy-fingered guy who
destroys evidence by the caseful every time he opens a
door."

Her apartment was in one of the apartment-hotels near West-
lake Park.

The elevator boy knew that she belonged on the twelfth floor.
She threw open the door to her apartment, took off her coat and
bag, tossing them easily to a chair, and went to the far end of
the living room where there was a lamp, then turned and sailed
the porkpie expertly to the chair on which she had left the coat
and bag.

"Practice," she explained with mock pride. She held her hand out toward a bookcase. "Pick up a volume of 'The Messages and Speeches of the Presidents' and amuse yourself till I get the coffee on."

She returned to the room, walked to a music box in a corner, inspected a batch of records, returned them to the spindle, and started the turntable. "The lessor likes gypsy music," she told Stanton. "This is Hungarian. We've also got Rumanian—any flavor you like."

"I can't tell one from the other. But I would like to know, Miss Linton, how you can leave home without a word to family or anyone, leave a pretty big job writing high-style copy for 'Modes' and—"

"The interrogation begins?" she asked, her eyes narrowing, amused.

He sprang suddenly from his seat, moodily walked to the window. Far below the rain-swept city was pin-pointed in a million lights. "I'd hoped you were going to be serious," he said bitterly.

"You don't think this becomes me?"

Stanton returned to his seat. "No," he said crisply. "I've seen too much of it. A girl teams with a man, they begin playing both ends against the law and she winds up broken on the pavements from twelve flights up or a washed-out type in cotton drab in the penitentiary."

Her face went grave. She looked at him for a long time. "Sorry," she said, smiling. "I'll see if the coffee's ready."

"I forgot to tell you," he remarked. "I hate coffee."

"How do you feel about *zigeunermusik?*"

"Got any Mildred Bailey?"

She walked to the music box and put an end to the music. Then she went to the kitchen and snapped an electric switch. "Bailey's the best there is, Mister Army Department. You've got an ear for music."

"And people."

She looked away from him quickly, so that all he saw of her was the long clean line of her hair across the shoulders. Her voice, when she spoke, was firm, but she did not look at him. "You want to know what about John English, don't you? We're supposed to be engaged. Well, go ahead, ask me. I haven't seen him in over a year. I haven't got a letter in almost as long—not a message—nothing. The last I heard he still belonged to you people in the Pentagon Building and was in Germany."

"We know all that," Stanton said. "We've been reading every piece of mail he's got or has sent out. We know he hasn't even asked about you in over a year. And we know you haven't written him."

She turned to him slowly, her lips tensing a little, her eyes filmed with tears. "Then what do you want me for?"

"He needs your help," he said through unmoving lips. He let that sink in, then became matter-of-fact. "It was too pat. A girl like you is engaged to an officer with a brilliant record. She's true-blue all the time he's in training, loyal—you see, when I got this hunch I started out by finding out everything about you —loyal while he's in North Africa and Sicily. Patton asks to have him along when he changes commands.

"That's a fair kind of guy, Miss Linton. He gets the Silver Star, a DSC, the stuff you get in the line, and as if that isn't enough, a couple of Purple Hearts. He's with armored spearheads all the way through Germany. He checks in sick after the peace, the first time in his record when he goes to a hospital without being forcibly sick-tagged by a medical officer.

"The doctors find nothing wrong. The old wounds doing okay. But he's tired, shaking. You might say he was cracking up. But you don't Section-Eight a man like Captain Johnny English. He gets a courier job to Naples, a chance to rest-camp in Capri, any duty he wants. No matter what you think about us, we're proud of men like Captain English and we'd do anything we could for him. When everyone else begs to go home, he then asks to be assigned back to Germany."

"He wrote me there was a job still to do."

"But when he came back on leave there was no marriage. No talk about bringing you over with him."

"Something tortured him. He told me, 'I'm in trouble, darling. I'm in more trouble than I ever thought there was in the whole world. No matter what, keep on believing and waiting.' I knew then I'd never leave him. If you're in love with a man you're with him to the very end of the road."

"Then he was changed when he returned from Germany after the war?"

"I hardly knew him. I'd been his girl all through basic training, through OCS, through his first and last experiences with combat but each time I'd seen him he was always the same wonderful, hearty hell-guy who was afraid of nobody. I don't know if he had any fear in him at all."

Stanton's gaze was level on Elinor Linton. "He had fear, but he was stoppering it. Maybe that's what exploded in Germany after the war—in a black-market operation that would stagger you if I told you the full details."

She brought her hand to her throat as if to ease the tight feeling that made it hard to breathe. She went to the window and looked out for a long time. "You've known all along?"

"He had a head start and got involved with quite an organization, but we've known. We couldn't always tell you the score, but we knew he was in the ball game."

"I'd never seen the way he was when he returned. Combat hadn't touched him like that. He wouldn't talk about himself. He chain-smoked endless cigarettes. He spoke through tight, unrelaxed lips, in hard little whispers. He looked behind him as he talked, around him as we sat in a bar, as if everyone was listening to his conversation. He didn't even look like the same man. He was thinner, his eyes troubled; he covered his nice upper lip with a mustache."

"He said if you loved him this is what you had to do? Come to Los Angeles where you'd first met? Cut yourself off from everyone?"

She turned from the window. "You are clever, Mister C.I.D."

He shook his graying head, smiling almost imperceptibly. "Not clever, Miss Linton. I'm the kind who arrives at the truth by being stupid. Nothing else works, nothing adds up and you reach bottom on the list of possibilities. You know, this was to be the last futile try before I turned in my resignation. My working theory had been that you and he broke off when he returned from Frankfort last year. No letters, no mention of you. I figured it turned out to be just another boy-and-girl romance gone with the war. You quit a job you loved, left the New York you loved, and cut off from everyone because you were the kind to take a dead love affair big. I pegged it as heartbreak."

He took out his handkerchief and brought it across his forehead and at his neck just above the collar. "A good guy goes wrong, you want to help him. Someone like you is in trouble, it isn't a routine assignment any more. I've been a long time in this end of the game, Miss Linton. I've put more Silver Stars and

DSC's up for court-martial than I like to remember. And each time I help drive a nail into the coffin I pray they'll have the guts to stand up before the lid is shut in their face."

He went to the window. It had begun to rain hard again, the dark pavements twelve stories below gleaming like long strips of black patent leather. Traffic appeared to be snarled on the boulevard, and the disembodied tooting of auto horns drifted past the window like thin, last wisps of smoke. Miss Linton had begun the gypsy music once more.

Her voice became calculating and defensive, the way it had been when they started to speak. He heard her say: "Mood stuff. 'Hearts and Flowers.'"

Stanton turned his head to her, then resumed studying the city from the window. She was trying to be cold again, and smart. Her kind of smart, he thought. The way they get when they start being loyal to a man. "You're going to string along with his game?"

"I love him."

He turned sharply from the window. "Okay! That's your privilege. A noble woman sacrificing all for love is the best accomplice a man can get. Remember that. I've told you what changed him, I've told you how we feel, but it makes no difference?"

"That's between you and him."

He shook his head angrily. "No. Never mind us. This is between you and him."

"Thanks for the pearls of wisdom. Now if you want to search my place, you may."

"I like your kind of woman," he said, shaking his head at her offer. "Miss Linton, when I first met you I thought you were in this black-market operation with John English. It didn't take me long to see you're not. And I knew what makes you tick: Your man's in trouble, and you're standing by him; nothing makes any difference. I like you, even if you're not going to be on my side." He jutted a finger toward the window. "Even if it means the long jump, or the cotton-drab.

"But I'll tell you this, Miss Linton. I want Johnny English. And I don't want to take him. I want you to give him to me. I want him to come to us by himself." His hand pointed full-length at the window. "There's a jump a lot longer than twelve flights up, Miss Linton. The pain doesn't end quickly, but it's the only way you can ever have Johnny and the love you've kept for so long."

He moved toward the door, his trench coat over his arm. Now he said casually, "Think it over when you see John English later tonight."

Her gaze froze on him. He turned toward the door and took the doorknob in his hand. "He's back?" she pleaded. "You know he's back in this country?"

His eyes closed slowly. Anxious fingers seized the sleeve of his coat. "He's somewhere, all right."

Her hands were prayerful before him. "How do you know?" she cried. "How do you know?"

"We lost track of him in Germany ten days ago, lost him for five full days. Then we discovered he pulled out on us in civvies, and got to Paris. I'd say he's been back a day or so." He started toward the door.

"Don't go," she begged. "What are you going to do now?"

"Nothing," he said smoothly. "I don't even know where he might be except that I'm sure he's not far from you. I'm not going to tail you. When you and John English want me, I'll be at the Ambassador."

She closed the door behind him; stared at its blankness for a long time. After a while she picked up her pouch bag, her coat and hat and went out by the kitchen door, leaving the building by the service elevator.

All the way, in the car, with the windshield wipers thirstily snapping back and forth, back and forth, through the glaze of traffic in the thinning rain, she kept thinking of their cottage, where he had to be. When he was a green recruit in basic training and she was still going to school, they had met on Rocky Point before the cottage. It became theirs, too, in the morning before the sun came up, in the night with the moonlight dancing on the surf. One day, sitting alone on Rocky Point, after he'd gone overseas, she saw a man nailing up on the cottage a sign that read: FOR SALE.

Elinor Linton pulled up to a curb. Traffic near the beach had thinned out, but she kept her eye in the rear-view mirror to make sure she was not being followed. The rain had stopped, the way it does that tells you that it has stopped for good. The cars behind her passed without taking notice. She started again, first circling a block before she headed toward the beach. Her foot on the accelerator was nervous, impatient.

It was absurd what they asked for the house then. "I've bought it for us," she wrote him. "I had just enough for it."

And in New York the last time, he'd said: "Go out there and wait. Don't write if you don't hear from me. Just keep on believing in me. No matter what happens, wait. One day I'll be there."

His face was lean, calculating, deeply troubled; his eyes probed every corner of the bar they sat in. "I'm in trouble, darling. I'm in more trouble than I ever thought there was in the world." Then, suddenly, he had stopped writing and she knew it was part of his telling her to come here to wait and she knew, whatever it was, he had known precisely what he was telling her to do.

When he left the last time, driving in the cab to LaGuardia, "You'll do it, won't you?" he demanded angrily, strangely.

"Yes, darling," she whispered, "yes, yes, yes. But I want to help you."

"I don't want your help! I just want to know you'll be out there, believing in me, loving me, talking to no one, waiting." For a moment she thought his secret would break through. He held her in his arms. "Elinor," he said, "I need you so much."

But it was too painful living alone in the cottage. She had found the flat in town. First she had come out every day, then every week, then, as time, space and new worlds came between them, her visits grew rarer. Yet she knew here, one day, he would come back to her.

The man Stanton had said he was back. Was it a trap? She drew up to the curb again, her eyes on the mirror seeing that no car was behind her. Did Stanton know where they planned to meet? Her foot quivered when she depressed the clutch.

She headed down the incline to the shore road, headlights drilling into the dark; the air grew clear and fresh and smelled clean of the ocean. Now she thrust the car forward with all the power under its hood. She kept her eye in the rear-view mirror too. She was not being followed.

Her heart sank when she saw the house, dark, cold, alone, just as she had seen it so many times. She flung open the door and flicked the light switch. He was not there. "John," she called. "John!" She ran into the kitchen. "*John!*" He was not in the bedroom. His name died in her throat. She ran her hand against her forehead, knocking her hat to the floor; she stared at it as though uncertain that it belonged to her. There was no sign of him. She sat on the edge of a bed and covered her face with her hands. She uttered his name.

At length she went into the living room again. The room was almost ugly in the hard yellow light, yet, as she walked around it wondering what next to do, she began to feel his presence. The feeling would not be denied. *He's here,* she said to herself, eagerly now, *he's here!*

She went out of the house, running to the beach, the sand wet and firm beneath her hurrying feet. The night was black and the surf pounded endlessly. She ran toward Rocky Point calling his name. She reached the first of the rocks when she heard her name. He took her in his arms and whispered her name like a precious, loved, long-awaited thing.

"Darling," she whispered, "you've come back, you've come back."

He kissed her. Her fingers searched the contours of his head hungrily, through his hair, as though she had to make sure this way she was not dreaming. "Elinor," he said, "it's all over. Nothing will ever be between us again."

She put her mouth on his. "Sh-sh," she said, tenderly, "sh-sh."

They walked to the house. He could see the light glowing. "You've left the light on!" he exclaimed, his voice tensing.

She looked at him. "No one will care, darling." She took his arm. "The neighbors know I come here evenings now and then and they also know I'm not very sociable."

The light hurt their eyes for a moment. He kissed her again. "Let me look at you, darling," she said. His hair had grown long and his face seemed thinner, all vertical lines, the bony structure plain beneath the eyes and under the chin. "You've shaved off that mustache," she commented.

"I knew you'd be glad for that."

He seemed distracted now. He kept looking at the light, at the windows. Then he remembered something. "Your car's outside?" And when she nodded her head, "I've got a rented one there, too. They'll think there's a convention on. We've got to go, darling, now, right now."

"But we're all right," she insisted.

"No. We've got to get out of this place."

"But this is where you wanted me."

"Only to wait for me." His speech was so urgent he could scarcely let her talk. He moved away from her, going to the

window to peer out in the darkness. "We *can't* stay here. We're
going. Not later. Now."

"Where, Johnny?"

His eyes on her were strange, frenzied. "I'll tell you where.
Out of the country, that's where. Haven't you figured out what
I've been doing? Haven't you doped why I let them think you
and I were through? Remember how I told you I was in trouble?" He smiled sardonically, a twisted smile. "It was like being
in the lines for a year, a whole year. But now I've beaten them.
We're here; we're almost in the clear." He sat down beside her
and took her hands in his moist, tensed fingers. "We're going to
Tampico, darling," he whispered. "This bunch I was with has
got a ship coming in and the payoff'll be big enough to keep us
in beach cottages the rest of our lives." She turned her head
from him so he would not be able to see the tears that fought
for release from her eyes. "You want to, don't you?"

"But this is our house."

He moved away from her angrily, again to the window, to
probe the iron dark. "All hell is waiting to break loose out there.
We've got to get out of the country. *Fast.*"

Now she knew she would not cry. She did not speak until he
turned from the window to her; then: "Why did you do it,
Johnny; why?"

"Are you crazy?" He moved toward her almost as if to shake
her. The look in his eyes was frantic, harried. "What kind of
thing is that to ask? Because it made me feel good. When the
war was over I felt rotten, I tell you, rotten. How do you think
it was to realize you lived and a lot of guys better than you
were dead? I used to wake up in bed, sweating, burning. I used
to cry. You wouldn't believe it, would you? Captain John English used to cry. I prayed I'd wake up to find the war wasn't over
so I'd have another chance to catch it the way men I'd sent to
die had caught it."

John English made a furious fist with his right hand and
brought it to his temple, as if the pressing eased his head. "I felt
guilty. I felt ashamed. I don't know why, I just did. I wanted to
rest. I wanted to sleep." He laughed bitterly. "I went to the
medics and they sent me to a hospital."

She reached for him, but he moved away from her. "You were
sick."

"I *wasn't* sick! I knew I wasn't. They kept jabbing me and

testing me, but all I wanted was to sleep, to forget. They couldn't understand. Nothing was wrong with me. I just needed sleep." He clenched his teeth. He looked around him, defiantly. "Then I got the deal in Germany. And it was like the war again. You had to be sharp. You *couldn't* sleep—see what I mean? You had to be on your toes. It was dirty, but I was used to dirt; it was rotten but I was used to that. That's why I didn't want you there, why I didn't want you involved—"

The words had been spilling out of him, impatiently, imperfectly articulated and she broke in: "I knew every minute."

He studied her for a moment. "Yet you waited?"

"I love you," she said. "I'll always wait."

The sardonic smile cut into his face again. "Well, the waiting's over." He got up. "We've got a fortune coming to meet us in Tampico. Let's get going."

She shook her head slightly. "You're sick, Johnny, don't you see? You've been sick for a year."

He turned on her, furiously. "What are you talking about?" he shouted. "I never felt better in my life! Come on, we've got to move now."

She did not stir from where she sat. She looked up at him. Softly: "A man from the C.I.D. wants you. He found me—"

His fingers dug into her shoulder. "You let on?"

"No," she whispered, not showing the pain, understanding. "He was very clever."

"He's here—in town?"

"Yes. He's waiting for you. At the Ambassador. His name is Stanton."

John English went back to the window, but before he could draw the shade from the window to look out into the black night, Elinor Linton said: "No, he's not here. He wants you to come in by yourself, Johnny. They want you to know they're looking for you and for you to come to them. It won't go easy with you but it'll be better than a life that ends suddenly from twelve flights up. They'll understand you've been sick, they'll—"

She came up to him, pleading, but he pushed her away angrily. "What are you talking about? If I stand before a court-martial they'll throw the War College library at me. You'd be ninety years old before I got out of Fort Leavenworth."

She shook her head. "Not when they understand you've been sick. Not if you go to the Ambassador on your own."

His angry hands seized her forearms. He shook her violently. "Stop saying I'm sick! I'm in this to the eyes and there's no going back. It's like combat. Don't you see? You're not going to fail me."

"I'm standing by you, darling." Her voice choked thin in her throat. "I'll always be with you. But you need help, and if I went with you I'd lose you forever. I wouldn't be helping you. This thing would be like a cancer; it'd kill everything we ever meant to each other. Trust me, darling; believe me. I'll wait, I'll wait forever, but go to them." He stood over her, shaking her again and then, suddenly, he released her. It was like falling, falling, falling from an endless height.

He was at the door. His mouth was drawn tight. "Are you coming?" he asked.

"No," she scarcely whispered.

The muscles in his face went hard. His eyes flickered and for a moment he looked at her. He slammed the door behind him. She heard a car start and the wheels dig into the road. Then it was quiet and she could hear the rhythmic stroking of her heart.

She had trouble with the lock, but finally the key went in and she opened the door. She dropped her bag and her coat and went in the dark room to the window. The wind blew in cool and steady. Horns were still sounding on the boulevard, the roar of traffic through the open windows coming in like an endless roar. Below, the streets glistened dully; when she looked straight down there was no end to it.

She shivered. She rubbed her shoulders with her hands. At the phone she waited for the operator, then said: "Will you get me a Mister Stanton at the Ambassador?" She felt she could not stand any more. She cradled the phone and went back to the window. But looking down on it was as though she was not standing any more, as though she had not been standing for a long time, in all the years she had waited, as though she had simply relaxed her grip and found that all the time she had been drifting down but now like a falling body she was falling in each second twice with the speed of the last.

The phone rang. She went to it. Her voice was small. "Mr. Stanton? This is Elinor Linton." She took the instrument from before her mouth and covered it with a hand. After a moment she began again: "Elinor Linton. I'm afraid I wasn't very success-ful. I want to thank you for believing in me."

He noticed the tension in her voice. "Where are you, Miss Linton?" he asked coolly.

"Twelve flights up. The easy one."

"Miss Linton," he broke in, "I want you to come here."

"No," she said.

"Miss Linton," he shouted. "Are you there? Miss Linton! I want you to come here. Do you hear me? John English is here and he wants to talk to you. He needs you very much, Miss Linton! Can you hear me?"

She held the instrument in her hand and put her head on the table and she thought she was going to cry, but she did not. She did not cry.

7

VICTOR CANNING

The Mystery of Kela Ouai

DEVON-BORN VICTOR CANNING now lives in the rolling English hills of Kent, where his windows command the immediate prospect of a tennis court, a croquet lawn and lush gardens. His novels of mystery and suspense, intricately plotted, often have unusual foreign settings and quite frequently find themselves later in the motion pictures. While his principal production is novels, Mr. Canning likes to take time out for an occasional short story . . . like this one.

DON'T THINK THAT this is a story of murder. It's true that Harvey Paynton was poisoned. But the story is a love story, and a warning that love can possess a mind as strongly as ever evil can.

It happened five years ago in Africa at a place called Kela Ouai. I don't blame you for never having heard of Kela Ouai, though it's quite important—gold, hardwoods and probably one of the finest tropical disease research stations in the world.

It was a tennis party at the house of Mark Paynton, Harvey's brother. Mark had just served us with long iced drinks, and I was sitting in the shade with Harvey, not talking much, and watching the tennis players.

There were three men and one girl on the court—Mark Paynton, his manager Ralph Hope, Tony Burroughs, who was working for some Colonial survey, and the girl, Margot Lance. I don't play tennis, but I like watching it, particularly when there's a girl as attractive as Margot on the court.

Harvey was lounging in his chair, nursing the tall metal tumbler in his hands, and I could see that he was watching Margot, too. That didn't surprise me at all. In fact it was the trouble, the last bit of trouble, for Harvey was always in trouble over something.

If I couldn't say I liked him, at least I was sorry for him. He was a big, rather handsome man and, at first, gave an impression of being frank, good-natured and generous. But he wasn't. He was a bad hat. And there was nothing he could do about it. He'd tried, I know—but there was something inside him which could never be altered. That was why I was sorry for him and why at times I almost liked him.

He said to me out of the blue, and in a tone which meant clearly that he wanted to talk, "I've been here too long. I've got to get out."

"Where are you going?" I asked.

"Damned if I know." Then, after a pause, he went on, "Some place where money and women don't exist would fit the bill."

He was talking about Margot. She was Tony Burroughs' fiancée and had been out on a visit for two months, and we had all realized what was happening.

We'd also seen it before when Ralph Hope's wife had come. It was just that there was something in Harvey which drew them.

"There's no place like that in this life," I said.

"Not in this life—don't I know it!" He looked at me, and there was an excitement at the back of his blue eyes that disturbed me. I knew his love of the dramatic, and the extravagance of his nature—but even so I wondered momentarily whether the excitement might not be desperation.

"I can't stay here," he went on. "I'm in trouble with Mark, too. You know what an upright stickler he is."

"Money?"

"Yes. Fellow I met in Capetown last year put me on to a good thing—only it wasn't. The money I put in was Mark's. Or rather, from the firm. I know I was a fool, but there you are. That's me."

"Does he know?"

"He hasn't said anything yet. Everything I touch goes to hell. And then nice people like Margot lose their heads over me and won't listen when I try to tell them I'm no good. What's the use of talking about it? I'm going—for good."

"How?" He really had got me worried.

"You'll see." They were the last words I ever heard him speak.

The set finished, and the four players came out of the sunlight back to the table where we were sitting.

They picked up their tumblers from the table, and Margot

lifted the heavy silver jug of orange juice and went round top-
ping the drinks for them.

She served Harvey last, just looking at him and smiling in the
way a woman only smiles when there is love in her thoughts.
He gave her a little nod and held up his tumbler. As she stood
there by his side I saw the three men watching them, and there
was a curious little pause in the talk and laughter.

There was a hardness in Ralph Hope's face, a hint of teeth
biting at a lower lip which made me think of Harvey and Mrs.
Hope. A husband never forgives or forgets a threat to his happiness. The look on Tony Burroughs' face was frankly jealous, so
open that I thought he would say something. Already, I knew,
there had been trouble between them. I was sorry for him, too.
It's no pleasure to lose your girl to another man.

As for Mark, standing a little apart from the others, he had
the air of a man acutely aware of the tensions that existed around
Harvey. He loved his brother, but it was the kind of love that
only gets anxiety and trouble in return.

Margot must have felt the attention she was attracting, for she
put the jug down and then, moving toward Tony, raised her
drink and with a rather exaggerated cheerfulness said, "Well,
here's to all of us."

We all drank, and I saw Harvey put his empty tumbler back
on the table and drop into his chair. Within five minutes he was
dead. There's no need to describe how it happened. Medicine is
my subject, and, although for the past year I'd devoted myself
exclusively to antivenom serums at the research institute, it didn't
take me long to discover that Harvey was dead of a dose of
cyanide of potassium. Those five minutes are unpleasant to remember.

We carried him into the house. A doctor's authority runs as
high as a policeman's at such times, so I took charge. I made
them leave everything on the table as it was, tumblers, jug,
everything. I got Mark to telephone the Commissioner's office
and, knowing he would be a couple of hours getting there, I
insisted that they should all stay in the house. I didn't want anyone wandering about near the tennis court.

Tony and Ralph had trouble with Margot. Mark and I tried
to talk for a while, but nothing made much sense to me. In the
end I went and sat by myself at the window.

Before we had carried Harvey in I had smelt, but not touched, his tumbler. There wasn't any doubt about the smell. The dregs, I guessed, still held enough to kill two or three healthy men. But there was no smell from any of the other tumblers or from the jug of orange juice.

The obvious solution seemed to be that Harvey had put the poison into his own drink and committed suicide. For a while, I almost believed this. Then it just wouldn't make sense. I knew him well. He was used to being in jams. He could be moody and maybe desperate, but there could never be any question of suicide with him. He still liked life too much. Then how and by whom had he been killed, and why?

We had all arrived at the same time at the house. The drinks and tumblers had been carried into the garden, and our tumblers had been filled and we had all drunk before the first game of tennis. The game over, Margot had replenished every tumbler and we had all drunk again—and this time Harvey's drink had been poisoned.

I went back over all our movements so far as the tumblers and the drinks were concerned. I remembered the scene when the drinks were being prepared. Mark's servant was out and we had the kitchen to ourselves. Margot had made the orange juice with Ralph Hope. I remembered he had taken the ice from Mark's refrigerator for the drinks. And I had fetched the tumblers—Mark had a set of tall metal ones in different colors. They, too, had been in the refrigerator because Mark had a theory that it was no good putting iced drink into lukewarm glasses. I'd loaded them onto a tray and the whole lot had been carried by Harvey into the garden, and Margot had poured the drinks while Tony and Mark had handed them around.

I kept at it, but the answer wouldn't come. We'd all drunk from the same jug. The first round of drinks had been harmless —but Harvey's second drink had been poisoned. At first I thought it was something to do with the ice cubes Ralph Hope had put into the drink. One of the cubes could have been bored and filled with the poison and when the ice melted . . . No, the whole jug would have been contaminated.

I thought of the motives people might have for killing him; Tony, jealousy—you never know how strong it is; Ralph—his pride hurt over his wife's still smoldering affection for Harvey, Margot—that was harder, but who knows what goes on in a woman's mind? And then Mark—he might know about the money, might be tired of pulling Harvey out of jams, fearful that one day he'd so something which even he could not fix or live down . . .

When the Commissioner arrived I was no nearer any solution. A verdict of suicide was brought in some days later—largely on my evidence of Harvey's last conversation with me. For me, however, the puzzling thing about the inquest was the behavior of the two women. Margot had got over her shock and she and Tony seemed closer together than they had ever been. But Mrs. Hope who was there was white and stricken and obviously holding herself back from hysterical collapse.

A week later I went to England on a six months' leave. Mrs. Hope traveled back on the same boat and she was still haggard and unsettled. As for myself, the problem of Harvey's death went with me. I couldn't get it out of my mind. Then one freezing December day, walking around the garden at home, it came to me. I knew how and why—just from looking at the goldfish in the garden pool.

When I got back to Kela Ouai, I went at once to see Mark. There was a change in him I had never expected. He had lost weight and seemed to have to make an effort to talk to people, as though his mind was far away in some other world. I went to see him at half-past six in the evening. He was alone in the house except for his servant. He was changing for his bath and he called me up to talk to him. I sat on his bed with the door to the bathroom open while he tubbed and we talked. I was quite frank and he made no evasions at all.

"Mark," I said, "you know that if Harvey had lived he was going away?"

"Yes."

"He was going off with Ralph Hope's wife."

"Yes. How did you know?"

"I traveled home with her. Sea voyages make people talk. Harvey was in money trouble, too—with you."

"He always had been in trouble with me, but I didn't mind. About other people I did mind."

"Ralph Hope is your best friend—maybe your only friend."

"He is." There was no doubt of the sincerity there.

"You murdered Harvey, didn't you?"

"Yes, I murdered my brother. How did you know?"

His voice was flat, unemotional.

"You put a minute solution of cyanide of potassium and water into the bottom of a tumbler and you froze it some time during the morning in your freezer. When it was frozen you added another eighth of an inch of water and froze that. This meant that there was a layer in all of about a quarter of an inch at the bottom of the tumbler, both unnoticeable and harmless until the top layer melted.

"Before we went into the kitchen to prepare the drinks, you slipped out and removed this prepared tumbler from the freezing compartment and put it with the others on the refrigerator shelf. The tumblers stayed there about twenty minutes and then they were brought out and drinks were poured into them.

"You helped hand the drinks around. I expect the one intended for Harvey had some mark, a small chip. You saw he got it. We all drank safely, even Harvey the first time because there was a thin layer of pure ice over the poisoned layer. But ice melts and a little later . . ."

I heard him step out of his bath and begin to towel himself.

"What put you on to this?"

"My talk with Mrs. Hope and some goldfish at home. They were frozen into the ice of our pool. Why did you do it, Mark?"

"Because I loved him." He said it slowly. "Loved him too much to want him constantly wrecking other people's lives. He was bad. He knew it and could do nothing about it. I had to do it for him. I thought I could be judge, jury . . . even executioner. He wanted peace desperately—and I gave it to him."

"And now?"

He came to the door and his face was still, beautifully tranquil.

"Nothing," he said. "I don't think there will be anything for you to do. Since he went I've discovered that no man has the right I thought I had—not even love gives that to one."

He never did finish dressing. I heard the shot as I went down the drive, but I didn't go back.

8

ELLERY QUEEN

"*My Queer Dean*"

ELLERY QUEEN first startled mystery readers back
in the late twenties, when he was created by two enthusiastic young New Yorkers, Frederic Dannay and
Manfred B. Lee. For a long time they made a mystery
of their dual authorship, too, but finally permitted themselves to be unmasked. In addition to their full-length
mysteries, they know the trick of producing a fully
rounded story in short space—with a solution that provides spice and entertainment for the reader.

THE QUEERNESS of Matthew Arnold Hope, beloved teacher of
Ellery's Harvard youth and lately Dean of Liberal Arts in a New
York university, is legendary.

The story is told, for instance, of baffled students taking Dr.
Hope's Shakespeare course for the first time. "History advises us
that Richard II died peacefully at Pontefract, probably of pneumonia," Dr. Hope scolds. "But what does Shakespeare say, Act
V Scene V? That Exton struck him down," and here the famous
authority on Elizabethan literature will pause for emphasis, "with
a blushing crow!"

Imaginative sophomores have been known to suffer nightmares
as a result of this remark. Older heads nod intelligently, of
course, knowing that Dr. Hope meant merely to say—in fact,
thought he was saying—"a crushing blow." The good dean's
unconscious spoonerisms, like the sayings of Miss Parker and Mr.
Goldwyn, are reverently preserved by collectors among whom
Ellery counts himself a charter member. It is Ellery who has
saved for posterity that deathless pronouncement of Dr. Hope's
to a freshman class in English composition: "All those who per-
sist in befouling their theme papers with cant and other low
expressions not in good usage are warned for the last time:
Refine your style or be exiled from this course with the rest of
the vanished Bulgarians!"

But perhaps Dean Hope's greatest exploit began recently in the faculty lunch room. Ellery arrived, at the dean's invitation, to find him waiting impatiently at one of the big round tables with three members of the English department.

"Dr. Agnes Lovell, Professor Oswald Gorman, Mr. Morgan Naseby," the Dean said rapidly. "Sit down, Ellery. Mr. Queen will have the cute frocktail and the horned beef cash—only safe edibles on the menu today, my boy. Well, go fetch, young man! Are you dreaming that you're back in class?" The waiter, a harried-looking freshman, fled. Then Dr. Hope said solemnly, "My friends, prepare for a surprise."

Dr. Lovell, a very large woman in a tight suit, said roguishly: "Wait, Matthew! Let me guess. Romance?"

"And who'd marry—in Macaulay's imperishable phrase—a living concordance?" said Professor Gorman in a voice like an abandoned winch. He was a tall, freckled man with strawberry eyebrows and a quarrelsome jaw. "A real surprise, Dr. Hope, would be a departmental salary raise."

"A consummation devoutly et cetera," said Mr. Naseby, immediately blushing. He was a stout young man with an eager manner, evidently a junior in the department.

"May I have your attention?" Dean Hope looked about cautiously. "Suppose I tell you," he said in a trembling voice, "that by tonight I may have it within my power to deliver the death blow—I repeat, the death blow—to the cockypop that Francis Bacon wrote Shakespeare's plays?"

There were two gasps, a snort, and one inquiring hum.

"Matthew!" squealed Dr. Lovell. "You'd be famous!"

"Immortal, Dean Hope," said Mr. Naseby.

"Deluded," said Professor Gorman, the snorter. "The Baconian benightedness, like the Marlowe mania, has no known specific."

"Ah, but even a fanatic," cried the Dean, "would have to yield before the nature of *this* evidence."

"Sounds exciting, Doc," murmured Ellery. "What is it?"

"A man called at my office this morning, Ellery. He produced credentials identifying him as a London rare-book dealer, Alfred Mimms. He has in his possession, he said, a copy of the 1612 edition of *The Essaies of Sr. Francis Bacon Knight, the Kings Solliciter Generall,* an item usually bringing four or five hundred dollars. He claims that this copy, however, is unique, *being in-*

scribed on the title page in Bacon's own hand to Will Shake-speare."

Amid the cries, Ellery asked: "Inscribed how?"

"In an encomium," quavered Dean Hope, "an encomium to Shakespeare expressing Bacon's admiration and praise for—and I quote—*'the most excellent plaies of your sweet wit and hand!'* "

"Take that!" whispered Mr. Naseby to an invisible Baconian.

"That does it," breathed Dr. Lovell.

"That would do it," said Professor Gorman. "If."

"Did you actually see the book, Doc?" asked Ellery.

"He showed me a photostat of the title page. He'll have the original for my inspection tonight, in my office."

"And Mimms' asking price is—?"

"Ten thousand dollars."

"Proof positive that it's a forgery," said Professor Gorman rustily. "It's far too little."

"Oswald," hissed Dr. Lovell, "you creak. Do you know that?"

"No, Gorman is right," said Dr. Hope. "An absurd price if the inscription is genuine, as I pointed out to Mimms. However, he had an explanation. He is acting, he said, at the instructions of the book's owner, a tax-poor British nobleman whose identity he will reveal tonight if I consent to purchase the book.

"The owner, who has just found it in a castle room boarded up and forgotten for two centuries, prefers an American buyer in a confidential sale—for tax reasons, Mimms hinted. But, as a cultivated man, the owner wishes a scholar to have it rather than some ignorant Croesus. Hence the relatively low price."

"Lovely," glowed Mr. Naseby. "And so typically British."

"Isn't it?" said Professor Gorman. "Terms cash, no doubt? On the line? Tonight?"

"Well, yes." The old Dean took a bulging envelope from his breast pocket and eyed it ruefully. Then, with a sigh, he tucked it back. "Very nearly my life's savings . . . But I'm not alto-gether senile," Dr. Hope grinned. "I'm asking you to be present, Ellery—with Inspector Queen. I shall be working at my desk on administrative things into the evening. Mimms is due at eight o'clock."

"We'll be here at seven-thirty," promised Ellery. "By the way, Doc, that's a lot of money to be carrying around in your pocket. Have you confided this business to anyone else?"

"No, no, of course not," Dean Hope replied.

"Don't. And may I suggest that you wait behind a locked door? Don't admit Mimms—or anyone else you don't trust—until we get here. I'm afraid, Doc, I share the professor's skepticism."

"Oh, so do I," murmured the Dean. "The odds on this being a swindle are, I should think, several thousand to one. But one can't help saying to oneself, suppose it's not?"

It was nearly half-past seven when the Queens entered the Arts building. Some windows on the upper floors were lit up where a few evening classes were in session, and the Dean's office was bright. Otherwise the building was dark.

The first thing Ellery saw as they stepped out of the self-service elevator onto the dark third floor was the door of Dean Hope's anteroom . . . wide open.

They found the old scholar crumpled on the floor just inside the doorway. His white hairs dripped red.

"Crook came early," howled Inspector Queen. "Look at the dean's wristwatch, Ellery—smashed in his fall at 7:13."

"I warned him not to unlock his door," wailed Ellery. Then he bellowed. "He's breathing! Call an ambulance!"

He had carried the Dean's frail body to a couch in the inner office and was gently wetting the blue old lips from a paper cup when the Inspector turned from the telephone.

The eyes fluttered open. "Ellery . . ."

"Doc, what happened?"

"Book . . . taken . . ." The voice trailed off . . .

"Book taken?" repeated the Inspector incredulously. "That means Mimms not only came early, but Dr. Hope found the book was genuine! Is the money on him, son?"

Ellery searched the Dean's pockets, the office, the anteroom. "It's gone."

"Then he did buy it. Then somebody came along, cracked him on the skull, and lifted the book."

"Doc!" Ellery bent over the old man again. "Doc, who struck you? Did you see?"

"Yes . . . Gorman . . ." Then the battered head rolled to one side, and Dr. Hope lost consciousness.

"Gorman? Who's Gorman, Ellery?"

"Professor Oswald Gorman," Ellery said through his teeth, "one of the English faculty at the lunch today. *Get him.*"

When Inspector Queen returned to the Dean's office guiding

the agitated elbow of Professor Gorman, he found Ellery waiting behind the Dean's flower vase as if it were a bough from Birnam Wood.

The couch was empty.

"What did the ambulance doctor say, Ellery?"

"Concussion. How bad they don't know yet." Ellery rose, fixing Professor Gorman with a Macduffian glance. "Where did you find him, Dad?"

"Upstairs on the seventh floor, teaching a Bible class."

"The title of my course, Inspector Queen," said the professor furiously, "is 'The Influence of the Bible on English Literature.'"

"Trying to establish an alibi, eh?"

"Well, son," said his father in a troubled voice, "the professor's more than just tried. He's done it."

"Established an alibi?" Ellery cried.

"It's a two-hour seminar, from six to eight. He's alibied for every second from 6 p.m. on by the dozen people taking the course—including a minister, a priest, and a rabbi. What's more," mused the Inspector, "even assuming the 7:13 on the Dean's broken watch was a plant, Professor Gorman can account for every minute of his day since your lunch broke up, Ellery."

"I beg your pardon," said a British voice from the anteroom. "I was to meet Dr. Hope here at eight o'clock."

Ellery whirled. Then he swooped down upon the owner of the voice, a pale man in a bowler hat carrying a package under one arm.

"Don't tell me you're Alfred Mimms and you're just bringing the Bacon!"

"Yes, but I'll—I'll come back," stammered the visitor, trying to hold on to his package. But it was Ellery who won the tug of war, and as he tore the wrappings away the pale man turned to run.

And there was Inspector Queen in the doorway with his pistol showing. "Alfred Mimms, is it?" said the Inspector genially. "Last time, if memory serves, it was Lord Chalmerston. Remember, Dink, when you were sent up for selling a phony First Folio to that Oyster Bay millionaire?

"Ellery, this is Dink Chalmers of Flatbush, one of the cleverest confidence men in the rare-book game." Then the Inspector's geniality faded. "But, son, this leaves us in more of a mess than before."

"No, dad," said Ellery. "This clears the mess up.

"Because what did Doc Hope reply when I asked him what happened?" Ellery said. "He replied, 'Book taken.' Well, obviously, the book wasn't taken. Professor, you're a communicant of the Matthew Arnold Hope Cult of Spoonerisms: What must the Dean have meant to say?"

" 'Took . . . Bacon'!" said Professor Gorman.

"Which makes no sense, either, unless we recall, Dad, that his voice trailed off. As if he meant to add a word, but failed. Which word? The word 'money'—'took Bacon *money*.'

"And who took the Bacon money? The one who knocked on the Dean's door just after seven o'clock and asked to be let in. The one who, when Dr. Hope unlocked the door—indicating the knocker was someone he knew and trusted—promptly conked the old man and made off with his life's savings."

"But when you asked who hit him," protested the Inspector, "he answered 'Gorman.' "

"Which he couldn't have meant, either, since the professor has an alibi of granite—"

"Another spoonerism!" exclaimed Professor Gorman.

"I'm afraid so. And since the only spoonerism possible from the name 'Gorman' is 'Morgan,' hunt up Mr. Morgan Naseby of the underpaid English department, Dad, and you'll have Doc's assailant and his ten grand back, too . . ."

Later, at Bellevue Hospital, an indestructible Elizabethan scholar squeezed the younger Queen's hand feebly. Conversation was forbidden, but the good professor managed to whisper, "My queer Dean . . ."

9

MIGNON G. EBERHART

The Wagstaff Pearls

FOR SEVERAL YEARS, Mrs. Eberhart has been
delighting *This Week* readers with the adventures of
Mr. James T. Wickwire, a senior bank vice president
with a positive proneness for being mixed up with murder. This is one of the best. In addition to short stories,
Mrs. Eberhart has more than thirty mystery novels to
her credit, many of them laid in Chicago, where she
lived before moving closer to the scene of Mr. Wickwire's
operations—New York.

AT MIDNIGHT the telephone rang and a woman's voice said, "Mr.
Wickwire?"

I had been asleep. I was only half awake. I said, "Yes? Who
—who is . . . ?"

She cried, in an agitated, incoherent way, "This is Frances
Dune. I'm sorry to call you now but—I can't wait. I've got to
tell you. My conscience—" She took a long rasping breath. "It's
the Wagstaff pearls—"

There was a thud and clatter as if the telephone dropped, a
kind of dull crash, and then a scream. It was a terrible scream,
which gradually, as if from an increasing distance, died away.
Then there was nothing.

I pressed the telephone against my ear. Frances Dune was my
secretary, and the Wagstaff pearls were in my care. I knew that
something was very wrong and I didn't like that scream. Suddenly I heard rapid breathing, and somebody began to dial.

I cried, "Miss Dune! What is it? Miss Dune!"

The dialing stopped. "Oh, Mr. Wickwire, I didn't know you
were still on the phone. Miss Dune—I tried to stop her—I
couldn't—"

She sounded hysterical. I snapped, "Who is this?"

"I'm—I'm Muriel Evans. I work in the bank. Mr. Wickwire,
she killed herself—"

80

The scream echoed horribly in my ear, put an edge to my voice. "Where are you?"

"Her apartment," she said unsteadily. "In her apartment—"

"Give me the address."

She gave it to me in a voice that was still shaking.

"Call the police. I'll be right there. Don't let anybody else come into the place. Call them—wait a minute. How did she kill herself? Are you sure she's dead?"

Miss Evans seemed to swallow hard. "She jumped out the window. It's the ninth floor."

With another cold wave of horror I realized that there wouldn't be much use in calling a doctor.

Fifteen minutes later I was dressed and in a taxi. My house is in the upper sixties; we hurtled down Park Avenue. I was all too certain that I knew what had happened. Rarely but sometimes, things like that do happen in a bank. The trusted teller walks away with cash; the reliable cashier disappears with negotiable bonds. This time my perfect secretary had stolen the Wagstaff pearls.

My name is James Wickwire. I am a banker, a bachelor. I am indeed elderly enough to be one of the senior vice presidents. The Wagstaff pearls had been in my care for some twelve years, since Mrs. Wagstaff had died. Her estate was left to minors; its administration was in the care of trustees. I was one of them and I had a power of attorney for the estate.

I was under the authority of the other trustees, but I could open the Wagstaff Estate safe-deposit boxes. In one of those boxes, enclosed in a flat box of blue velvet, the Wagstaff pearls lay and wasted their beauty.

They were rather a nuisance because, twice a year, they had to be taken out of the vault and worn for one entire day.

Banks do many odd chores for old and valued clients and this was one of those chores. Twice a year one of the girls in the bank was sent down to the vault, the pearls were clasped around her neck (next to her skin, one of Mrs. Wagstaff's requirements), and there she sat, reading a book for the entire day.

At closing time, the pearls were returned to their blue box and to the vault for another six months. I could never see that their lustre was in any way improved thereby, but that had been Mrs. Wagstaff's idea. She had charged me directly with the pearls.

It was a cold, raw night with the traffic lights reflected in eerie streaks on the wet pavements, yet I could see Mrs. Wagstaff against the night as clearly, almost, as I had seen her during what proved to be my last talk with her. I could see her bedroom, luxurious with feminine fripperies. I could see her sitting up against the pillow, with her white hair neatly arranged and her veined, small hands caressing the pearls. "They must be worn, you understand," she told me. "Otherwise they lose their lustre. They must be worn by a woman and, Jim—" She was one of the few women who have ever called me Jim—"one of the girls in the bank will have to do it. I'm glad you have such pretty girls working in the bank."

Prettiness is not exactly a qualification for any bank employee. Perhaps my face showed perplexity for she smiled.

"Pearls are meant for beautiful women. I was—they said I was beautiful once," she smiled, and a luminous quality of beauty flashed out and touched something in my heart. "My husband used to say that only beautiful women really love pearls. Beauty calls for beauty." She laughed but rather sadly. "Of course he didn't mean it, but he said that is why, sometimes, a beautiful woman will do anything for jewels—for pearls like these." She sighed. A nurse rustled forward. I kissed her small hand before I went away; I don't know why.

It was my last talk with Mrs. Wagstaff. But I had seen to it that her wishes about the pearls were observed. That is, they were worn regularly. I did not subscribe to her notion about beauty and pearls. I put that down to sentiment. Certainly I could not hold, in effect, beauty contests in the bank. Frances Dune had worn the pearls that day.

That, too, was my own direct responsibility. I had had occasion to be out of the office from noon till after the bank closed. I had returned to my own house about eleven. Miss Dune, looking at my calendar that morning, had reminded me of the pearls, and I had sent her to wear them because I should not require her services. Miss Dune had been my secretary for nearly ten years. She was a tall, extremely plain woman of about forty, very neat, rather meagre somehow, fussy and over-conscientious in a way, but efficient. I had trusted her.

Yet as soon as she spoke to me in that frenzied way over the telephone I knew what had happened. I had left it to her to check in the pearls with Mr. Wazey, manager of the vaults; I had overstepped my power of attorney to the extent of giving him my key, without which he could not have opened the safe-deposit box. Obviously, Mr. Wazey had taken the velvet box, without looking inside it, returned it to the safe deposit box, and gone home. Miss Dune had taken the pearls.

Then, overcome by remorse, she had telephoned to confess it and had jumped out of the window rather than face the consequences. It was tragic and it was pathetic—this plain, hard-working woman conquered by the beauty of a strand of pearls.

And they were beautiful; no question of that. But times have changed. When Mrs. Wagstaff—young then—had been given the pearls, her husband had paid nearly a quarter of a million for them; I knew that. I also knew that their value was nothing like that now. The old-time high market for pearls is no more. The popularity of cultured pearls, flawless, too, but plentiful, has done that.

We arrived at an apartment house not far from the river. Already the street was lighted up. Police cars and an ambulance were there, and there were lights from windows all around and heads craning out of them.

A lieutenant of police, a big, burly fellow, who looked rather strained and white, asked me to identify the body, and I did. The night seemed very cold; my gray topcoat was insufficient to keep out a chill that seemed to clutch my very bones. Then the ambulance moved closer. I went with the lieutenant to Miss Dune's apartment on the ninth floor.

It was a small apartment, a bedroom-sitting room with a tiny kitchenette. It was painstakingly neat and rather sparse and meagre. Like Miss Dune.

A girl sat in a stiff chair; she rose as we came in. I recognized her only vaguely; she worked in the bookkeeping department of the bank, and I rarely saw her.

"I'm Muriel Evans, Mr. Wickwire," she said in a low voice. She was slender, dressed simply in red. She wore lipstick and matching nail polish, a custom I rather oppose in the bank, but certainly if the girls chose to wear nose rings outside the bank it was none of my business. However, she was quiet and well-behaved in a very trying and indeed a terrible situation.

I nodded. "This is the young lady who reported it," I told the lieutenant. I still felt cold and rather sick.

He removed his cap. "I'll have to ask you for a statement,

Miss," he said. "I realize it's been a shock but—" He was sorry for her; I could see that.

She began to talk, and I glanced around the room. She had replaced the telephone upon its cradle. A chair lay on its side on the floor. It accounted for the dull crash I had heard. The window, a long window, too near the floor, was still open. "Miss Dune telephoned to me about eleven," Miss Evans was saying. "I live near here, two streets north. She said she couldn't sleep; she was nervous and she asked me to come. I didn't know her well, but she was rather important, you see, at the bank, being Mr. Wickwire's secretary. Of course I came—and she told me she'd taken the Wagstaff pearls. They were in the vault and—"

"I'll explain that," I told the lieutenant and did so briefly.

The lieutenant said, "Take it easy now, Miss Evans. Was she hysterical?"

"Yes! Oh, yes! I didn't believe her. She said she had to talk —it seemed to come out in spite of herself. She was crying and —well, I didn't believe her. I couldn't. I thought she was ill, nervous, something wrong. Anyway, I went into the kitchen. I intended to make some coffee. I didn't know what to do.

"While I was there I heard her at the telephone. She telephoned to Mr. Wickwire—I could hear her—and started to tell him what she'd done. But then she dropped the phone as if she couldn't go on. I ran from the kitchen and—and she was pulling up the window. I caught at the window and her and—I don't know what I did. But I couldn't stop her—" She put her hands over her face.

The lieutenant put a large hand kindly on her shoulder. "It's been tough—take it easy."

I said, "Where are the pearls?"

The girl, Muriel Evans, looked up with a start. She had light brown hair, parted in the middle and drawn up on her head. It was the kind of hair, fine and soft, that seems to make a nimbus around a girl's face. She had blue eyes, set in finely arched hollows. It struck me that in spite of her shock she was rather attractive. "I don't know," she said. "She wouldn't show them to me. That's why I didn't believe her."

"We'll find them," the lieutenant said. "The pearls or a pawn ticket."

I went to the telephone. "Is it all right for me to use this?"

He hesitated. "Well, the fact is, Mr. Wickwire, it's suicide, but

I have to go through some forms. Fingerprints and all that. Do
you mind using another telephone?"

Miss Evans' blue eyes leaped to sudden darkness. "But it was
suicide! I saw her—"

"I understand," the lieutenant said quickly. "Don't get scared,
Miss. It's not a question of murder. Besides if you'd murdered
her—"

"Oh—" Miss Evans gave a kind of gasp.

He patted her shoulder. "If you'd murdered her you'd have
got the hell—that is, you'd have got out of here. Nobody knew
you were here, did they?"

She moved her head slowly, saying, no, in a whisper.

"Well, there, you see! You'd have got out. You wouldn't have
called the police."

A sergeant and another policeman came in from the hall as I
went out. I took the elevator down and used the telephone at the
switchboard in the foyer, to rout out Mr. Wazey. The boy on
duty watched me, popeyed.

"It's terrible," he said. "Miss Dune was sure upset when she
phoned for the lady in the red coat. But I never thought of—"

I asked him to get me a taxi.

Banks are supposed to operate through masses of red tape and
in a sense they do; they have to. At the same time, in emergency, there are ways to cut some of that red tape. Mr. Wazey
met me at the bank and went into the vaults and got out the flat
velvet box. When we opened it there were pearls lying on the
yellow satin lining. But the sight of those pearls shook me in
a way that even Miss Dune's tragic confession had not done, for
they were not the Wagstaff pearls. They were not pearls at all,
but dull and waxy fakes; they proved that the theft had been
planned. And a moment of passionate impulse, and a carefully
planned theft are two different things.

"I looked at them," Mr. Wazey panted, his round face very
pale. "When I replaced the box I glanced inside it. But I didn't
notice. I'm no connoisseur of pearls. Besides, it was Miss Dune."

She had never been delegated to wear the pearls before that
day. I was fairly sure of that but we checked the records Mr.
Wazey had kept. I could not remember when I had actually
looked at the pearls myself so, for accuracy, I ran down the
entire list of names.

Some of the girls whose names appeared there had married

or drifted to other jobs; and many of the girls had worn the pearls twice or even three times, but practically every girl in the bank had worn the pearls at some time. Miss Busch had worn them three times; Miss Smith, twice; Miss Evans (Muriel Evans, the girl in the apartment), twice; Miss Wilkins, three times—Miss Dune, only once.

But she'd have known all about them from my Wagstaff file, so she had prepared herself for an opportunity. And she had reminded me of the date and made the opportunity. My heart was heavy as I watched Mr. Wazey lock up the vaults. Then I went back through the dismal, rainy night to Miss Dune's apartment.

I had been gone scarcely an hour, but the search of the apartment had been so thorough that it looked as if a hurricane had struck it. Muriel Evans still sat in the armchair. She was pale, and something in the texture of her face made me think (although absently) of a magnolia. The lieutenant had unbuttoned his blue coat and was wiping his forehead. "They're not here, Mr. Wickwire," he said rather desperately. "No pawn ticket Nothing."

I have never been one to shirk my duty, even if unpleasant. I had to report not only to the insurance company but to the trustees of the estate and the officers of the bank, exactly how I had permitted this thing to happen. I made my way past the debris of cushions, books, untidy heaps of clothing to the window and looked down, so far down to the street that I felt queerly dizzy and sick again. Poor tragic Miss Dune who had paid with her life for the pearls, entrusted to me! Again I could almost see the still beautiful woman who had put her delicate old hands in mine and given the pearls into my keeping. I could almost see her smile, and hear her voice.

I stood at the window, it seemed to me, for a long time; in fact I suppose it was only a few seconds while I made up my mind to undertake the only course of action that I could determine. I turned back to the lieutenant. "Is it all right for me to go now?"

The lieutenant nodded. "I'll report to you. We'll get started with the pawn shops and jewelers. We'll get the pearls back."

I thanked him. I said to Miss Evans, "Do you mind coming to my house with me? I have to dictate a full report of this."

The light fell fully on her magnolia face. She nodded, and

picked up her coat. While she preceded me to the elevator I
lingered, to speak to the lieutenant. I gave a concise word or two
of directions and joined Miss Evans as the elevator came.

We found a taxi at once. Neither of us spoke, all the way
up town. When we got to my house I got out my latch key.
"My manservant is on his vacation," I said, and let her into the
hall. "I'm going to have a whisky and soda. In the circumstances,
will you join me?"

She refused but thanked me with a lift of her shadowed,
lovely blue eyes. Then I said, "You might know. Did Miss Dune
have a—well, I suppose one would say a boy friend? Some
man—"

She gave me a quiet but intelligent look. "That occurred to
me, too. You mean, someone might have planned this and might
have influenced her to take the pearls. Yes, I think so. Once or
twice I've seen her with a man. I'm not sure that I could identify him. I might be able to. But I feel sure that she wouldn't
have done that unless she was urged to do it. Some man, someone younger perhaps— But it seems cruel to say or think it."

My study is at the right of the hall, and I took her there and
told her to sit down. A tray with decanter and glasses stood on
my desk. I mixed myself a rather strong whisky and soda, then
I opened a drawer of the desk and took out my revolver.

"What—" Miss Evans began sitting upright.

I took out the box of shells and loaded the gun. "I don't like
the idea of a man. By now he knows what has happened. He
might be dangerous." I put the loaded gun down on the table
and went into the hall to the street door. I opened it. The street
was deserted. I went back to the study and closed the door. The
house was extraordinarily quiet.

I picked up my glass and went to the window. The curtains
had not been closed; the room behind me was reflected in the
glittering, black window panes. I took rather a long drink. Then
I said, "Where are the pearls?"

The figure in the cherry-red dress stiffened.

I said, "You've worn the pearls, twice; once six months ago,
once a year and a half ago. One of those times you changed
them for false pearls. No one saw the difference until today.
Miss Dune saw that they were not the Wagstaff pearls; probably she looked up the record herself. She sent for you tonight
to tell you to give them up and you—"

Her head lifted. "I reported the suicide. I wouldn't have done that if—"

"You had to report it. The boy at the switchboard knew that you were there."

The red dress flashed. I am not a brave man but I had to go on. "You killed her."

I heard then a kind of metallic click behind me. I turned. She was standing beside the table, facing me. Her beauty leaped out like a flame. But she had my gun in her hand, and it was pointed at me.

I am not a brave man and I decided rather swiftly that I wasn't very smart either. "You can't do that!"

"I have to," she said. Her voice was low and melodious, her face as lovely as the stars and as fateful. "The pearls are in my apartment. I intended to hide them, but I'll not have time for that. You'd tell the police. But the pearls were your responsibility and everyone knows how you feel about the bank and—they'll say this is suicide, too." She put her finger on the trigger.

I hadn't heard anyone enter the hall through the street door which I had been at some pains to open. But the study door smashed open and the room was flooded with policemen and the gun went off but the bullet went straight through the ceiling.

"Of course she'd snatch at the idea of some man who might have the pearls. And you had to have an excuse for the gun. That was pretty fast work, sir," the lieutenant said, some time later.

I said wearily, "I had no facts, nothing I could tell you. I could not make so serious a charge without facts. But I thought that if she were guilty, if I accused her and I gave her a chance to get hold of the gun, she'd try to get rid of me. Thanks for getting here as I asked you to do, Lieutenant."

He eyed me over his glass with, I will say, a certain respect. "You are a real detective."

"No, the detective in this case was—well, never mind." He wouldn't have understood. The detective was a lady who had smiled at me and said, "Beauty calls for beauty—that is why, sometimes, a beautiful woman will do anything for jewels."

Yet perhaps he would have understood, for he said, a trifle wistfully, "That girl really stacked up. A beauty, wouldn't you say? You didn't exactly see it at first. But gradually—yes, sir, I guess that Helen of Troy dame might have looked something like that."

He seemed to fumble deep down in his consciousness, for an idea. "I guess that's why she wanted the pearls—" he said, gave me an abashed glance, murmured, "So long as I'm off duty," and lifted his glass toward me.

I lifted my glass, too; but I toasted another, and a **very** beautiful woman.

10

MacKINLAY KANTOR

Night of Panic

MacKINLAY KANTOR has found the martial events
of 1861-65 a fascinating field of research which, as long
ago as 1934, produced *Long Remember,* a novel of Get-
tysburg which won great critical acclaim. His best-selling
novel, *Andersonville,* won him the Pulitzer Prize for
1956. Although "Night of Panic" is strictly a rear-echelon
story of the war, solidly based on fact, Mr. Kantor brings
vividly alive the sudden terror that spread through Washington.

A SCANT TWO HOURS before the fire broke out, Major Willis
Lorrence walked northwest from the President's Park, toward
his father's house near Pennsylvania Avenue.

The Major's horse had a swollen hock, so he had left the
animal in camp and had ridden into Washington across the Long
Bridge in an army wagon. He was free to visit his wife and
other relatives until reveille on the second morning following.

Carriages came dear in Washington; the demand was far
greater than the supply. Each street became a chill morass.
Where there was no provost guard to prevent, the soldiers were
apt to ride on narrow sidewalks heretofore sacred to pedes-
trians; as one looked in any direction under the bare buckeye
trees, he could see mounted figures picking their way among
the strollers.

Such a rider splashed rapidly past the Major now, scattering
a spray of muddy water over the young officer's trousers. Lorrence took out a badly abused handkerchief, and repaired as
much of the damage as he could. Then he walked on to his
father's home. It was only a few rods distant: an old house of
red brick, with a narrow front porch and limestone steps.

Lorrence's wife, Agnes, had received his letter and was watching for him. He put one boot on the bottom step; the door flew
open; she stood there without saying a word.

In the gloom of the front hall, with the door closed and the early dusk of a damp day settling around the house, it seemed momentarily that he and Agnes were locked in their embrace at the bottom of some secret well from which neither time nor war could blast them.

She gave a sharp sob. "I've prayed, but—Willy, I must talk to you."

"Not until I've seen the folks," he said hastily, knowing what was coming. "Is the Senator at home?"

"No. He's taking his constitutional with Dandy. Mother's in the kitchen with Sheila."

They went through the second parlor into the dining room, and Sheila, hearing their approach, lumbered away to find the Major's mother. The elder Mrs. Lorrence came from the kitchen cellar—a plump, ruddy woman. She offered her son the eternal kiss of a warm-hearted mother who accepts the ugliest dictates of national error with unreasoning courage.

"Hector will be here for tea," she began, speaking of the Major's younger brother, Captain Hector Lorrence. "Isn't it fortunate he's still in charge of the mules?"

"And horses, praise be!" cried old Sheila. She kissed the Major's hand as he reached out to stroke her shoulder.

Lorrence knew that, relaxed in the brave heart of his family for a scant twenty-four hours, he could look with calmness on the mutilation or death which a battle might bring—if only Agnes would—

"Sheila's had the kettle on the stove all afternoon," Mrs. Lorrence said, "and she'll prepare tea at once. It won't take a minute."

"I'll need to wash first, and I'll need to borrow Hec's razor. My own was stolen."

He kissed his mother once more, told Sheila to delay with the tea and, drawn by the dull entreaty of his wife's eyes, he followed her to the front staircase. There was a window on the landing. As they went up he saw, through the window, his father approaching slowly from Twenty-second Street.

His father was a figure proud and statuesque in the thickening dusk; he walked slowly, feeling his way with a cane. His narrow-brimmed beaver hat was drawn back as if it should not shade eyes which were inexorably shielded by other means. From Senator Lorrence's left wrist, the little dog's leash drew forward like a tight rein. And Dandy, a ridiculous creature with whiskers and cropped ears and thin tail, wore his harness proudly, and seemed to recognize the trust reposed in him.

"You folks oughtn't to let him go out all the time with just Dandy to guide him."

Agnes said, "He insists on going. He drives to State and to committee meetings and to the White House, but he insists upon taking his exercise with Dandy sole alone."

The Major shook his head. "A blind man for all that, my dear."

"He says he can think better when he's alone, walking that way. When there's a session, he takes a walk in the morning and one before tea, and one after."

"Do we dine early or late?"

"We have late dinner. Your brother won't come from the corrals, most days, until seven o'clock."

"Wait a minute. I must speak to Father before I wash." He ran down the stairs, and met his father as Senator Micah Lorrence hesitated before the dooryard.

Willis took the cane out of his father's right hand and put his own there instead. "I am back again, sir."

"So I observe." The gray-haired Senator was smiling: he groped forward, with the leash dangling from his wrist, to pat his son's shoulder. "We heard about Dranesville, my boy. We need victories, even little ones."

Willis led his father up to the door. Behind them, a stranger halloed: "Sure, and we're all fond of ye, Blind Mike, and many's the time I've seen ye walking the streets of Doverton." He left off his crowing to tell the soldiers and children who were passing, "There goes Senator Mike Lorrence! That's his house, but ye ought to see the house he's got in Doverton, too."

"That's just it," the Major told his father as he guided him through the gloom of the parlor, and fumbled with matches and a lamp. "Doverton! You can walk the streets of Doverton, Pa., and be perfectly safe. But this isn't the Washington it was two years ago."

Dandy had scampered to the kitchen, and the Senator settled himself in a rocker. Willis took his cape and hat from him.

"I feel no fear, my son. If you and young Hector can offer yourselves to face the risks of war, surely I need let no qualms rob me of the satisfaction I gain from my excursions."

In his old room, which was now his wife's, Willy found some candles lighted. Water and shaving things were laid out.

Agnes sat on the edge of the bed with her hands clasped on the black walnut post; Willis could feel her eyes on him. He dreaded setting the mirror in place for shaving, because he knew that he should see Agnes's face—dim and evanescent among the candle flares—and yet living in mortal terror over his shoulder.

He laid the razor aside and poured water into the bowl. He took an unnecessarily long time handling soap and towels. At last, as he plunged his face into the soap foam, the very silence of the woman had driven him to desperation. . . . He must force this issue.

"I told him it wasn't safe," he mumbled through dripping suds, "and it isn't."

Agnes whispered, "Nothing's safe, Will."

He laughed, and got some soap in his mouth. "Well," he said, "in peace times, of course, everybody's safe. That is, from anything but acts of God. Father's infirmity—it's been on him almost since I can remember. His spirit is proportionately strong."

His wife whispered, "What have I got to keep me strong?" and he wished that she would sob, because her voice would not be so terrible to hear.

The Major made a great show of drying his face and neck and arms with a large linen towel. "Aggie, you'll just have to be patient. Look at Mother—"

"I don't want to look at Mother. I come near hating her each time I see how little it affects her! Oh, I know it isn't because she has no love for her sons. Maybe I'll never have as much love for mine—that is, if you live to give me any—"

He laughed, but with a set face.

"Willy. You weren't a soldier when I married you."

"Would you have married me, if I had been?"

"I don't know."

The Major hung the towel on its rack. "You knew that I was from the Point—that I had served in the Indian country—and that I should be subject to call in an emergency."

"Are you trying to point out, sir," she asked, "that I should be thankful because of that?"

Willis choked his exclamation into a half-whisper. "Don't 'sir' me, Aggie!"

He began to shave and for a time there was no sound in the room except the keen scrape of blade against flesh. Hearing no word or sign from Agnes, he turned and saw that she was lying motionless, face down across the bed. His resentment at her attitude now diminished, he stood admiring the contour of her shoulders and the round hips clearly revealed in the frock she wore. "Aggie," he whispered, and then downstairs he heard the doorbell ring.

His brother's voice shocked up through the hall, and Willis stood smiling at the thought of Hector's swift transformation from college student to captain in a remount depot.

Then Lorrence went over and stood beside his wife. "Agnes, dear."

"What?" she mumbled, her face buried in the counterpane.

"You must be sensible."

"I can't!"

"Then you must be brave, if you can't be sensible."

Her murmur reached his ears. "I can't be brave, either. I've tried and tried, but—I'm going crazy with all this."

She lifted herself, her hands spread stiff and deep in the bed. The yellow candlelight made a beautiful woman even more beautiful, but could not quicken her face or drive away its pallor.

"Oh, Willy, don't you understand? I have no courage—not an ounce, not a grain of it! I don't want you to be shot, but every waking hour I do see you shot. I see you lying dead! I—I have nightmares at night, too. Every night. I'll have nightmares until I die!"

He reached out as if to clutch her waist, but Agnes moved beyond the reach of his hands. "Go down to tea, Willis; for pity's sake, finish your shaving and go down to tea! I'm not going. I'd be out of place with all your brave people. It's all right for them, but—" Her voice seemed mounting to a scream, although in fact, she was not screaming—"I can't forget what's going to happen—what might happen. *I can't be brave.*"

In the front parlor, young Hector Lorrence had already done away with three cups of tea. Despite the imminence of dinner, he had cajoled Sheila into making him a sandwich. He got up to salute and embrace his brother.

Hec was skinny and fiercely intent about this business of being a captain; he was trying to raise severe mustaches beneath his snub nose. His detachment had nearly five thousand horses and mules in charge now, although the mules were being sent away to Virginia in droves each day, and were being replaced by horses, as mules were hard to secure.

They had all kinds, Hec said: westerners and Morgans and old fat cobs and dray horses from New York, and a good half of them were in misery. Hec wished to the devil that the army would learn more about the care of horses.

Willis grinned, "Sonny, if you don't object, I should like to hear the Senator's opinion regarding General Stone."

"Your father has gone out," said Mrs. Lorrence, "for a further constitutional."

Willis cried, "Mamma, I wish—"

"Now, now, my boy," she began, "there's no arguing with your father."

Major Lorrence growled, "Dandy couldn't drag him out of the way of a cavalry squad, if some puddle-hopping backwoodsmen met him on a pavement!" His tone was surly and accusing. But even as he spoke, he realized that his ire was directed not so much at his blood relatives as against the woman who lay upstairs. She it was who drained his calm and courage.

Tortured by this realization, the soldier went to the front door and flung it wide, hoping to see his father pacing along the sidewalk.

Old Sheila came past and descended to the lower step, peering into the foggy blackness of early evening, searching not for Senator Lorrence, but for a milkman who should have put in his appearance. "Sure," Sheila intoned, "and the moon is rising behind the clouds."

Willis Lorrence followed her gaze. He was looking south toward the flats below Observatory Hill. "That's not the moon, Sheila. It's too rosy."

"And what could it be but the moon?"

"A fire."

Hec heard him. Hec came to the door, with bread-and-butter still clasped in his hand. "Willy, it *is* a fire. A big one! Look— it's coming up; you can almost see flames!"

Unseasonably discerned and touched with distant orange, the straggling trees along the farther reaches of Twenty-second

Street seemed strangely close. . . . The nervous scraping of windows sounded up and down I Street. A flame shriveled beneath the horizon trees. The whole southwest sky was pink. . . . At last someone remembered to ring a fire bell.

Hec yelled, "Willy, that's square in the direction of the corrals!" He ran out to the side pavement, still carrying his bread-and-butter; without a cap and overcoat and sidearms, he resembled no officer in the world. Willis ran to join his brother under the trees, and he could not see Senator Lorrence anywhere, nor hear the blind man's footsteps prowling the darkness.

And yet—surely feet were hurrying through the mud . . . four feet which galloped. Closer and more violently, the hoofs approached. Against the flare they saw the rider turning the corner.

Hec leaped out into the roadway. "Captain," the stranger yelled, "the stables are on fire!"

Willis ran close, but Hec was mounted behind the messenger before his brother could reach the horse. "Come along, Willy, for God's sake!" the younger brother cried. "Take the first carriage you see!" But the horse had racked only a few paces before it reared and halted. A dark shape slid into the mud. This was not Hector; it was the soldier who had come to summon him. Hector rode up across the opposite pavement and bent low to avoid the tree limbs. Then he galloped away.

The private came limping back to the house. He was breathing heavily. "The Captain told me to dismount," he gasped. "He said that horse couldn't carry double and make speed—"

Major Lorrence cried, "Come on, man!" and fled toward the corner with the soldier gasping in pursuit. Over in Twenty-second Street, wheels were lurching; a buggy with side curtains bounced toward the intersection. The Major snatched at the horse's bridle.

"Commandeered!" he yelled. "This is urgent. Climb out, please!"

"Climb out, hell!" roared a voice from the black heart of the buggy. "I'm Second Assistant Fire Marshal for the District of Columbia."

Willis released his clutch and ran back to grasp the buggy itself. He put one foot on the hub even while it was turning again, and swung himself into the soggy vehicle.

"Who the devil are you?"

"Major Lorrence. My brother's in charge of the corrals."

A big blot in the darkness, a blot that smelled of whisky. "Blind Mike's son?"

"Go on!"

They went bounding across solid ruts and through pools which were not yet frozen. Above the lacquer of the horizon-line, a million sparks and charred wisps were floating high, silver and gold above the ferocious glare.

Hec's messenger, obeying the order to follow at all hazards, had sprung up behind the buggy as Willis climbed into it, and he clung with hands around the wooden bows. The vehicle rocked dangerously from hummock to hummock, and crashed now and then against the bottom of some icy little pond along the way.

Four streets more: there were citizens trying to keep pace on either side: men in shirt sleeves and men in flapping overcoats, soldiers who roared with horrid delight, saluting the catastrophe toward which they ran. The eternal vagabond army of small boys had sprung open-mouthed from every yard of Washington.

They rumbled across a bridge; a solid block of houses and walls whistled past; at the next street corner those in the buggy had their first direct view of the fire.

They looked across unfenced, vacant squares, peopled with sprinting black figures, and they saw the entire plain below Observatory Hill baking in crimson. There were five horse barns built close together all too treacherously. Two of these were a mass of flames. On every side the skeleton corrals were painted stark, each post and rail a separate and tiny sharpness in the golden heat.

Rescuers or would-be rescuers were long since at work. They brandished knives and axes; they vanished periodically from view, and the grumble of their chopping and slashing, the stubborn murmur of the expletives they breathed, seemed as roots to the shrill, unearthly structure of animal lamentation.

Piece by piece, the fences had been torn down, and new apertures gaped on every hand; among these gateways the terrified herds were milling—brown, white, black, roan, sorrel.

As the watchers felt their own eyeballs grow hot at this proximity, the herds approached. They pounded undisciplined out of a life which had brought them nothing but evil; they were ready to visit that evil abroad, as fast as their legs could carry them.

Lorrence found himself standing beside the buggy; the lone soldier had leaped down from the rear springs and was heading toward the hot post of danger where he belonged. He was a hundred yards distant when he met a roaring covey of terror.

These fugitives whinnied and bawled like impossible creatures loping flame-footed out of the Book of Revelations; it appeared for a moment that those fleeing on the outskirts tried to rear and avoid the lone figure in their path; he was knocked down in an instant. But surely none of those murdering feet had found him; for when the vanguard had roared away, Willis could see the stubborn little figure arise once more and go forward through the mud, to dodge and circle each fresh menace that sprang in his direction.

At the last house behind, a mother shrieked her alarm: *"Boys, boys, come into the house!"* The crowd scattered. People scrambled behind fences and tree clumps.

Soon these animal swarms would jam the wooden bridges, they would occupy every street in that quarter of Washington. Somewhere, not many squares back, a blind man was meditating through the night, led by a tiny dog . . .

A horse went down with a groan not ten feet away; another, racing behind it, stamped the shuddering flesh and fell whinnying . . . The refugees circled and sallied; they did not come as a single drove. Already a hundred rival squads cavorted at cross purposes, joined forces, and separated again on secret errands.

The Senator! Blind Mike, fumbling alone . . .

Major Lorrence was running on foot. He dodged two or three deaths in the first hundred yards; back in the painted area behind him he heard the yell of his erstwhile driver, and the splintering of the upset buggy. He collided with a fat woman who stood waving a shawl and hissing at the menace as if it were only a flock of chickens who had come into her yard.

Somehow Lorrence got her up on a porch, but her picket fence was mashed to the ground before he had torn the woman's hands from their clutch on him, and then was running again.

He gulped for air. He could hear horses caroling in the south and east and north; already their advance guard was ahead

of him, carrying outrage into side streets and gardens. Lorrence
was behind a row of houses, and for a while he traveled like
an obstacle racer, scrambling across palings and wooden cistern
curbs, but always hearing the torrent of hoofs that exceeded his
pace.

He was caught in a *cul-de-sac* of hedges and board fences, and
got himself out of it by demolishing a wooden gate that refused
to turn on its hinges. His own home was now only three blocks
away, but those three blocks were infested with destructive
companies. He heard their hooting, like an invisible barricade
thrown up between him and Pennsylvania Avenue.

Muddled feet came scourging behind him like a buffalo herd;
he side-stepped into a narrow lane by a carriage house, barely
in time. The victims fumed by: this detachment was led by a
gray mule which might have been possessed of the veriest
rabies; his foam slapped into Lorrence's face as he brayed.

The Major dashed across H Street: he was only one square
away from his house. He did not know just what he should do,
when at last he had gained the doorstep. No one would be able
to tell him which way his father had gone. He prayed that at
the first confusion which was preliminary to this invasion, the
blind Senator might have directed his steps toward home.

The Sanderson house stood on the corner; Lorrence brushed
the Sanderson shrubbery and plunged across the last open area
between himself and his goal. The landscape seemed strangely
dark, and he wondered why the lights of his house were hidden
from view.

The next moment, a brick wall rose solidly in front; he broke
the shock of his collision with outstretched hands. This wall had
been erected the previous autumn; he had seen it twice, but in
his alarm he had forgotten its existence. The wall was ten feet
high.

There was a gate—there must be a gate . . . he remembered
. . . he came face to face with iron bars, and saw like a caged
prisoner the turbulence which ruled I Street. Windows were
alight, and some doors were open. The lamps and candles
flaming, encouraged by the holocaust—and overhead, the poi-
sonous pink of the sky—these made Twenty-second and I Streets
vivid in unhealthy dawn—a dawn which came at seven o'clock
in the evening.

An outlandish tribe staggered and fought at the end of the street. Another squad of horses poured recklessly from the west, leveling the barberry hedges.

Major Lorrence spoke a word; he drove his body against the gate bars. His father was coming down the street. Somehow the blind man had found his way around the corner, before that racking barrier of flesh and bone blocked it. He was fumbling uncertainly with his cane; his hat had fallen off; but Dandy led him still, straining in his harness.

No arms could wrench this gate from its sockets. There were a half-inch chain and a flat padlock binding it tight. Willis began to climb. He shouted his father's name, and then clapped his jaws shut, fearing lest his cry should increase the Senator's bewilderment.

Willis had his hands on the top round of the gate. Now he got his feet up; but over the gate was an enormous fan-arch of wrought iron, with spikes that drove into the air like fingers of a spread hand. The Major sobbed, and strove to reach the topmost arc. He was spread-eagled above the turmoil. Something had his foot and was holding it tight.

He blinked loose the tears; now he saw Blind Mike, and the man was not alone. A woman had come to his side. It was Agnes. She wore the robe of Chinese silk which Willis had ordered for her Christmas present. He had never seen her wearing it before . . . he thought, "If I'd known that she'd have to run in it, I wouldn't have ordered it so full . . ."

Destruction charged upon them from the buckeye trees; in a contemptuous kind of trance she dragged the Senator aside, and stood for a second looking after the beast which had trod so close.

"Get to the trees," Lorrence heard his voice gasping. "Over by the trees, Aggie!" He felt the bones of his foot bending and yielding as he tried to twist his foot from between metal claws.

Agnes had Dandy under her arm. She held the Senator's elbow. Together they were moving through the mire; and then the herd broke away from baffling angles of the street corner. The first rush of horses took the two figures out of Lorrence's sight; they were prone when the hoofs had passed them by . . . "Do I have to hang here," the Major thought, "and see them crushed?" . . . He got his boot loose, and clambered to the breadth of wall beside the fan-arch. A plunging gray galloped beneath him, and there were others following.

Now came the rear guard, rank on rank, shifting through their course like centaurs in a miraculous game, bawling their way along a path that not even Apocalyptic steeds could tread. Lorrence's feet struck the ground.

He crossed the slough; he lifted Agnes first, because she was on top. She was lying with one arm across his father's body. She opened her eyes and spoke the Major's name. She still squeezed Dandy against her side and would not let him loose, no matter how he wriggled.

"Hurry," Lorrence told his father. "There are hundreds more about!" The Senator was greasy with mud when his son had dragged him up . . . But no sharp hoof had touched them.

She told her husband, later, that when she reached the old man's side, she could remember only what Willis had told her when he taught her to ride: that she should lie as quietly as possible—that her horse would not step upon her if she did so.

And so this miracle of I Street came to pass; and after the Senator had been scrubbed clean by his wife, and after he had drunk several fingers of brandy, he quoted the seventh verse of the Ninety-first Psalm with an emotion seldom heard outside the Senate.

When Agnes had bathed, the Major went up to her room. He found her in bed, with candles close, and he sent old Sheila away, as soon as she had brought the hairbrush which her young mistress requested.

"Hec just stopped in for a moment," said the Major. "The fire's burning low. Horses are running, still, all over this end of town; but the cavalry are rounding them up."

And then he could say no more. He marveled at the beauty of his wife's hands as she plied the brush with steady strokes against her yellow hair. Not yet did he dare to look into her eyes and see the glint of high courage which by her own command she had printed in them, and which he knew they would carry when he was gone from her sight again.

11

BRUCE MARSHALL

The Brigadier Smells a Rat

HERE'S A STORY on the lighter side, but it has
plenty of suspense for the principals. The setting is Vienna just after World War II, when currency regulations
—and outwitting them—were normal facts of life, and
the Cold War had just begun. Mr. Marshall, a Scotsman
who has long been a successful novelist, observed that
somewhat scrambled scene as a lieutenant colonel of
Intelligence in the British Army. We take it that he didn't
always regard its events with too serious an eye.

WHEN I was in the Displaced Persons Division in Vienna last
year a good many people envied me my blonde secretary,
Crystal. I didn't envy myself. Crystal wasn't a very good secretary. However, I couldn't do anything about that, because of
democracy. Perhaps I was a little in love with her, but her loveliness made me shy.

Barbizon-Jones was a red-haired civilian in the Treasury
Branch with only two ideas in his head: foreign exchange and
Crystal. This morning, however, Crystal didn't give him much
chance. As soon as he entered she swayed alluringly out of the
room, to find out how many "t's" there were in "committee."

"The Botticelli girl!" B.J. sighed when she had gone.

"I'm busy," I said. "Would you mind stating the object of
your visit?"

"I came to tell you that the Treasury ruling is that all Polish
currency is unexportable from Austria."

"I've known that for the last two years," I said angrily.

"I thought you'd like to know again. So long, old boy."

Crystal came back almost at once, followed by an elegant
dark young woman.

"Signore, I am in trouble," my visitor said. "I am both an
Italian and a Czech displaced person. My parents were Italian,
but I was born in Prague."

102

"Displaced Czechs in Vienna must apply to the Russians for repatriation," I said. "But if you are still an Italian subject I can help you."

The young woman glanced significantly at Crystal.

"Miss Benton-Hirst, perhaps now you wouldn't mind going and finding out how many 'm's' there are in 'committee,'" I said.

"You may understand better when I tell you that I am La Valdi," my visitor said when Crystal had willowed out sulkily.

"The singer?" I said and made a little bow. Even I had heard of La Valdi.

"Signore, for five years I have not sung. Now I wish to go back to Italy and sing."

"Why haven't you applied for repatriation before?"

"You force me to speak of delicate matters," she said, lowering her long eyelashes. "I was in love with an Austrian pianist. But now the passions are finished. So also are the Austrian schillings. Fortunately I still have here in Vienna Italian lire."

"It is illegal for foreigners in Austria to hold in their possession any currency or currencies other than Austrian." I had learned this rote from B.J. himself when he came in to moon at Crystal.

"Nice things are generally illegal, Signor Maggiore." She fluttered her long lashes tantalizingly. "Ten million lire may be illegal, but you will not deny that they are very pleasant."

"I'm sorry, Signora," I said, determined not to weaken. "You must surrender your lire before leaving Austria. We shall give you a receipt which you will present to the Banco d'Italia. They will reimburse you six months later."

"And how am I going to live until I find an engagement?" My visitor was quite beautiful in her anger. "In that case I shall be a Czech. I shall sing in Prague instead of in Rome. You are foolish, *Maggiore*. A Russian officer who is very fond of me has asked me to the opera tonight. I think that I shall be able to persuade him to exchange my Italian lire for Czechoslovakian kroner. Yes, I'm sure of it."

"But that would not be democratic," I said.

"I begin to think that I do not believe any more in democracy," La Valdi said, and walked out.

Crystal came back again, and I soon forgot my visitor when I started dictating. I was spelling out "Croats" in case Crystal should type it as "goats" when Sanderson came in. Sanderson was an aesthete in the Arts and Crafts Division who wore his medal ribbons in reverse order because he thought they looked prettier that way.

"This time I have not come to ogle Miss Benton-Hirst but to speak about the visit you've just received from La Valdi," he said. "His Majesty's Government is anxious that she be given every opportunity of returning to Italy. You see, because of her dual nationality the Russians are after her as well."

"I fail to understand how it can possibly matter to His Majesty's Government whether a caterwauling soprano is repatriated by ourselves or the Russians."

"I'm afraid you don't understand about culture, old boy," Sanderson said pityingly. "A cold war is fought with all sorts of weapons. Music matters as much as munitions. If La Valdi sings in Rome instead of Prague democracy will be the richer."

"In that case His Majesty's Government ought to alter its exchange regulations." I told Sanderson briefly what B.J. had ruled about foreign currency in the possession of displaced persons.

"But it's monstrous!" Sanderson said. "The man must be made to change his mind."

"I'm afraid you don't know B.J.," I said. "And in any case La Valdi has already taken the bit between her teeth. She's going to the opera tonight with a Russian officer who she says will give her Czechoslovakian kroner for her Italian lire."

"I can't tell you how important this is," Sanderson said. "Tell B.J. that the Brigadier will take a very dim view indeed if La Valdi goes to Prague instead of Rome."

"That still leaves La Valdi," I said. "I don't know where to get hold of her."

I admit I was worried but I was used to being asked to do impossible things. When Sanderson had gone I soon persuaded myself that, foreign exchange regulations being what they were, it was not my fault if the eastern nations gained an opera singer and the western nations lost one. I was trying to tell Crystal how to spell "Herzegovinian" when the Brigadier rang up.

"The subject is that Italian hyena," he began. "You've got to get her back to Italy. It is most important. I shall expect a report at 0900 hours the day after tomorrow that the necessary steps have been taken."

I told the Brigadier about the exchange regulations. "Perhaps, sir, if you were to have a word with B.J.," I said.

"You ought to know by now, Jenkins, that I have no authority where the Treasury is concerned. All that's required is a little initiative. Use your loaf, Jenkins. Repatriate that woman to Italy. I don't care how it's done, but it's got to be done. That's an order. Use your loaf, Jenkins."

As the Brigadier hung up angrily B.J. strolled in to take his before-lunch look at Crystal. But even when I had told him about La Valdi and about what Sanderson and the Brigadier had said he was still adamant.

"I'm sorry, old boy. It's a Treasury regulation." There was a silence during which B.J. popped lugubrious eyes at the back of Crystal's shining head.

I suddenly had an idea. I had never left B.J. alone with Crystal and I was sure he was too nervous to have spoken to her outside.

"Excuse me, I've got to see Davis," I said.

When I came back ten minutes later Crystal had left for lunch, but B.J. was still there, wearing a pleased expression.

"Come clean," I said. "Admit you haven't been talking to her about foreign currency."

B.J. blushed.

"I asked her to come to the opera tonight and I'm glad to say she accepted."

"Look here, B.J., how would it be if you and I were to exchange secretaries? There are no Treasury regulations against that, are there?"

"I hope, Jenkins, that you are not attempting to bribe me." B.J. spoke very coldly. "The Treasury Regulations stipulate that Italian lire must be removed from all repatriates before they leave Austria," B.J. said sternly. "Be careful, Jenkins. From now on I'm watching you carefully." B.J. walked primly out of my office.

All that afternoon I racked my brains to discover a means of obeying the Brigadier's seemingly impossible order. I cursed Crystal even when she spelled correctly.

"You're nasty, and I hate you," she said. "And on top of it all you practically force me into a date with that sissy B.J. Do you want me to make eyes at him until he promises to let that floosie out of Austria with her lire?"

"How ever did you guess?" I asked.

"Darling, I'm not so green as I'm cabbage-looking," she said, looking at me sadly out of her lovely face, but I was not convinced.

Crystal reluctantly promised to do her best and went gloomily to keep her appointment with B.J. Doubtful of her success, I tried to think up another plan. B.J. was the incompetent representative of a set of even more incompetent representatives elected by a woolly-headed public ignorant of the difference between a Greek drachma and an Argentinian peso. It was therefore my duty to revolt. The Brigadier had as good as told me so when he had ordered me to use my loaf.

The solution was simple. That very night, I would drive La Valdi down to the Italian frontier and trust that the military police would take her for my secretary and not search her luggage. My gray pass through the Russian Zone was made out for myself and a driver, but from previous experience I knew that it was unlikely the Soviet sentry would examine it closely.

I drove to the Theater an der Wien in high spirits. But I didn't locate La Valdi until the first interval, parading up and down the vestibule on the arm of her Russian escort.

"Major Malinski is my very good friend," La Valdi said as she introduced us. "He has promised to give me Czechoslovakian kroner for 75 per cent of my lire."

"The Union of Soviet Socialist Republics recognizes the value of great artists," Major Malinski said stiffly in German.

At the risk of an international incident I managed to inveigle La Valdi away from Major Malinski. "I can let you have all your Italian lire in Italy," I said and explained my plan to her. Before she had given her reply, Crystal, looking distressed, came running up.

"I've made all sorts of eyes at B.J., but it's no use," she said. "He says that a Treasury ruling is a Treasury ruling and must be obeyed. He means it, too. This very moment he's telephoning the military police about an Austrian countess caught smuggling Portuguese escudos out of the country."

"I think I shall be trying your very attractive plan," La Valdi interrupted. "If you will be waiting for me a moment I shall be making my excuses to Major Malinski."

She had no sooner left us when the Brigadier approached. He

had his usual smile of unhappy admiration for Crystal, but at me he glared sternly.

"Look here, Jenkins," he said, "I'm warning everybody. I'm having another drive against Commission personnel swanning around with foreign girl friends in army transport. I'm really on the ball about it this time, so use your loaf." He smiled again at Crystal and loped off.

"I don't know what you're up to, but if I were you I wouldn't do it," Crystal said when he had gone. "B.J. smells a rat. And if you ask me, the Brigadier does, too."

"Then back to B.J. and let him smell your golden hair instead," I said. She gave me a beseeching, almost tearful look as she walked away. La Valdi returned and I left the theater with her, feeling in my back the stabbing glances of Major Malinski.

I suppose I ought to have postponed our departure from Vienna until next morning, but I was anxious to get the adventure over and done with, especially after what the Brigadier had said about the new drive against using War Department transport for foreign girl friends. I knew that the Brigadier would not excuse disobedience on one count even if it helped me to obey him on another. So, when La Valdi had packed and concealed the ten million lire under stockings and petticoats, we set out through the deserted streets.

"The signore does not talk much," La Valdi said as we drove on through the frail glory of the moon.

"I'm concentrating," I said, trying to resist the fragrance which came from her. "I don't want to make any mistakes at the exit from the Russian Zone."

But, as I had anticipated, there was no trouble with the Russian sentry. We rolled on. Once again I was conscious of the beauty of the woman beside me.

"The British at the Italian frontier post won't be so easy," I said. "Remember to leave the talking to me."

My fears increased as we left Villach, in the blue and gold beginnings of a new day. If the military police found the lire in La Valdi's luggage, not even the Brigadier's order to perform the impossible could save me from a court-martial.

I cursed the driver of a powerful car which flashed past, almost crowding me into the ditch. I cursed again when the same thing happened ten minutes later. And I cursed more vehemently still when, a few hundred yards further on, I found the second car drawn up across the road with the driver standing in front of it, waving at me to stop. And I went all out when I saw that the driver was Crystal.

"It's B.J.," she said. "After the second act last night he accused me of acting as a decoy while you smuggled La Valdi and her lire into Italy. I suppose he must have guessed the same way as I did. Anyway he was so angry that he even told me that he was coming down to the frontier to watch out for you himself. Indeed, as the car I got hold of is not nearly as fast as B.J., I'm pretty certain he's there already."

"That must have been his car which overtook me before you did," I said. "Well, the only thing to do is to turn back."

"On the contrary," Crystal said, "the only thing to do is to go on. B.J. will have guessed it was you he overtook and will be waiting for you. As far as I can make out we're only about five hundred yards from the frontier post. If you don't turn up he'll come and look for you. Don't forget that his right of search extends all over Austria. It'll be easy enough for him to exercise it as his car is faster than yours."

"But if we go on he'll be even more certain to search us," I protested.

"Not if you do as I suggest," Crystal said crisply. "You'll come with me in my car and the signora will wait here. Ten minutes from now she will drive forward to the post. She will pretend that she is attached to the interpreters' pool. Like that her accent won't be noticed and she probably won't be asked to show her pass. B.J.'s never laid eyes on her so he won't recognize her. Understand?"

There was no time for argument, because at so short a distance from the post B.J. might spot our stationary cars and suspect intrigue. I took the wheel of Crystal's car and drove forward with her, and La Valdi remained behind in mine.

"I thought it a good idea to bring some luggage for B.J. to search." As Crystal said this we rounded a bend and came in sight of the frontier post. And there, sure enough, was B.J. himself, standing beside two military policemen. "It might be as well if you were to pretend to be in love with me," Crystal whispered as I stopped the car. I liked her lips so much that she was still in my arms when B.J. opened the door.

"So this is the form, is it?" B.J. asked acidly. "And I was fool enough to think you'd try it on with the lady herself. I hadn't realized that there was more than duty between you. Corporal, the subject is ten million lire. We're going to search this luggage and see if we can't find them."

Of course they didn't find ten million lire although they almost dismantled the car.

"All the same, I could have sworn," B.J. said as he gave up in disgust. "Anyway, what's the reason of this flight from Vienna?"

"Ever hear of romance?" Crystal asked. But the anger on B.J.'s face changed quickly to alarm. The car I had just got out of was wobbling toward the frontier. Clearly La Valdi drove automobiles less excellently than she sang.

"The things they let loose at steering wheels these days," B.J. said as he ran forward and ordered La Valdi to stop.

I didn't wait to see what happened. I drove on with Crystal into Italy, but I drove very slowly so that even La Valdi could overtake us if she were still free. I very much doubted that she could be.

A quarter of an hour later La Valdi did overtake us, but it was B.J. who was at the wheel. I was so sure he had discovered who she was and was taking her back to G.H.Q. to put her under arrest that I stopped by the side of the road, expecting that Crystal and I would be asked to accompany her. B.J. confirmed my suspicions by drawing up beside me.

"Never try to help ladies in distress," B.J. said through the window. "Brigadier came tearing up to the frontier post just as I'd sat down at the wheel. Threatened to put me under arrest for riding with a foreign girl friend in Army transport. He was so angry about his silly regulation that I knew he wouldn't believe the truth. So I said I was on way down to Venice to buy wine for the mess and had taken a girl from the interpreters' pool to help me with the powwowing. And of course that's what she turned out to be. Might have realized she couldn't be anything else if I hadn't been in such a flap."

"I hope you searched her for ten million lire," Crystal said gravely.

"Not on your life I didn't. The Treasury always knows when a lady's ticketyboo and when she isn't. Well, perhaps I need a little feminine kindness," B.J. said as he let his car into gear. "Tutta La Gondola in tutta la moonlight!"

I didn't drive on at once. I sat looking at Crystal in gratitude and admiration.

"Funny the Brigadier popping up so conveniently," I said. "Did you—"

Crystal smiled and laid her golden head on my shoulder.

"Use your loaf, Jenkins," she said.

I used my lips as well as my loaf and of course I married her, after explaining that there was only one "l" in jealous.

12

MARY ROBERTS RINEHART

Case Is Closed!

FROM THE TIME her first mystery novel, *The Circular Staircase*, was published in 1908, Mrs. Rinehart's lively imagination, careful observation of character and skill at plotting have earned her a fabulous success. Novels, magazine serials, short stories and Broadway plays have kept her in the forefront of American mystery writers. Although "Case Is Closed" was written as a short story, the author liked its plot so well that she later expanded the plot elements into a novel—*The Swimming Pool.*

EVE HAD BEEN going to a psychiatrist for about three months when she came into my room at Oak Hill one morning and announced she was going to marry the man. I sat bolt upright in bed and stared at her. My sister is a pretty woman, ten years older than I am, which makes her almost forty. And as our brother Paul says, she has most of the looks of the family.

"Marry him!" I gasped. "When did all this happen?"

"Why shouldn't it happen?" she said tartly. "We're in love. Does that surprise you?"

"But I thought he had a wife."

"There's such a thing as divorce, Bobbie." I looked at her. It had always been hard to tell about Eve. I suppose every now and then some family has somebody like her; someone who has gone slightly off the rails psychopathically—if that's the word. Both Paul and I thought she had a persecution complex, for she had come back to us from Reno after her divorce, and she pretended to be afraid of her ex-husband, Norris Clarke, as inoffensive an individual as ever lived.

She would not go out of the house during the day if she could help it, although she ranged the grounds at night. And she hated taxicabs—even Joe Smith, who had driven his ancient Ford for thirty years. When we went shopping in New York it was busses or the good old legs and feet, so I would come home limping. And she had put double locks on her bedroom door, and even on her bathroom.

"What the hell's wrong with her?" Paul inquired, after she'd been back a month. "If you ask me, Clarke was damned glad to get rid of her."

We never knew why she had left Norris Clarke. He seemed puzzled as well as relieved about it. She had never been easy to live with. But the first thing we knew was that she was off to Reno. Norris had been what Paul calls a gent, agreed to pay her a decent alimony, and the next thing we knew she landed on us, bag and baggage.

We knew from the beginning that trouble was her middle name, but there was nothing we could do. A part of Oak Hill was hers, and there was plenty of room. There should be a law against families who lived in the luxurious years before two world wars building vast country places and then leaving them to their descendants. So Paul and I—and later Eve—found ourselves with forty acres near White Plains and a twenty-four-room house. And as old Hilda, the family cook for many years, never put a foot beyond the kitchen we had to have a general housework girl as well. Her name was Carrie, and after Eve came believe me she did.

I don't want to sound bitter, in view of Eve's tragedy, but she had been the spoiled beauty of the family until she married almost twenty years before, and after that she had an apartment and a couple of maids to look after her. And she did play the piano beautifully, although this was not an unmixed blessing. For Paul had only his salary as an accountant; and I tried to help out by writing short stories and an occasional thriller. But it is hard to concentrate on my sort of work with a piano played *fortissimo*, which is the way she played. Or with someone wandering in to talk because she is bored with being alone.

It was Doctor Lyons who gave me the first real relief I had in months. The idea was Paul's and it was an inspiration.

"There's something wrong with her," he said. "Either she's really afraid of something or she's crazy as a March hare. See if you can get her to a psychiatrist, Bobbie. It will give her something to do, for one thing, and get her out of your hair. Give her a chance to talk about herself, too. She'll probably love it."

As it turned out, it was not as easy as all that, for Eve was
suspicious. She gave me a long look out of her wide blue eyes
when I suggested it.

"Just why?" she asked. "If you think I'm going to spill my guts
to one of those peeping Toms you can think again."

But I daresay she had been bored stiff, with me shut away as
much as I could manage, and only the big empty house to echo
around her. At least she finally agreed, so it gave me three days
a week to work, for she lunched in town after the sessions and
had a shampoo or a manicure. It was the country she was really
afraid of, not the city. Except for taxicabs.

It wasn't long, either, before we realized that she was, to say
the least, attracted to Lyons. She talked about him constantly,
wore her best clothes when she was going to see him, and came
home fairly radiant. This statement of hers however was more
than I could take that morning. I followed her into her room,
and sat down on her chaise longue.

"Better tell me about it, Eve," I said.

She was filing a broken fingernail at her toilet table, and she
looked at me in the mirror.

"I have told you," she said flatly.

"But what about his wife? Will she let him get a divorce?"

"Of course. Why not? He's fed up with her. I've seen her," she
added complacently. "She's not even good looking."

She glanced in the mirror and gave herself a smile. I could
only stare at her. There were times when it was difficult to tell
whether she was telling the truth, or merely believed she was.
I had begun to think that the line between fact and fantasy
with her was never clearly drawn. This looked serious, however.

"What's he like, Eve?" I asked.

"Like the answer to any woman's prayer," she said, and
grinned at me.

When Paul came home that night I told him the story, and
for once he looked startled. But when I said I ought to see the
man myself he shook his head.

"I'd go slow," he advised. "She's still a damned attractive
woman. Maybe he *has* fallen for her. Maybe her little idiosyncra-
sies wouldn't bother a man with his job. He must see a lot of
crackpots."

But he hadn't talked to Eve. I had.

I made an excuse of having to see an editor to go into town

the next day, but I hardly needed one. Eve was going over her clothes, evidently with a view to a trousseau, and she barely nodded when I said good-by.

On the train I sat next to Frank Nesbit, the man who had rented our gardener's cottage and a bit of ground from us about the time Eve came back from Reno. He had been something to the New York police force, but he had come into some money and retired. He played a good game of bridge, so now and then we had him up for a game, or went down to the cottage. I rather thought Eve interested him. I'd caught him watching her now and then. So I was not surprised when he asked: "How's your pretty sister?"

Then and there I was tempted to talk to him. I don't know what there is about a beard that so far as I am concerned removes a man from the usual competition and puts him in the patriarchal class. But after all he had been a policeman, and what had Eve to do with the police?

"She's all right," I said. "In fact she claims she's going to be married again."

He looked at me quizzically.

"Only 'claims,'" he said. "Any doubt about it, Miss Roberta?"

"Well, you know Eve," I said evasively. "I never know whether she means what she says or not."

He nodded. He knew Eve, of course; her erratic bridge, her night walks, and her curious phobias. Just then however the train drew into Grand Central and we had no more chance to talk.

I had no appointment with Doctor Lyons, so I made one from a telephone booth in the station for three that afternoon. After that I called up my sister Emily, the eldest of the family, and suggested she give me lunch.

She was in one of her frequent intervals without a maid, however. She said she was already having some tea and bread and butter in the kitchen, so that was that. Oddly enough I was almost sure I saw Frank Nesbit when I left the booth, but if I did he was lost in the crowd at once . . .

It is hard to remember exactly my first impression of Doctor Ronald Lyons. So much has happened since, and he played a considerable part in it. I do know that I found him tall, impressive and cool. It was his coolness which threw me off at first.

"Just why do you want to see me, Miss Lothrop?" he inquired, after I sat down.

"It's about my sister," I said, trying to smile. "I daresay that's all we have in common."

"I see." He had a folder in front of him, and he opened it. "Just what is your own impression about her? You know of course that I can't discuss her with you from my own point of view, but I'd be glad to know what you think."

"I don't know what I really think," I tried to explain. "She's better in some ways. It does her good to come here and talk. But yesterday she said something I don't quite understand."

I saw his interest quicken.

"What was that?"

I am afraid I flushed.

"She said she was going to marry you," I blurted, and was relieved to see him smile. It made him look more human, even agreeable. Up to that moment I had thought he resented me.

"You'd be surprised how often that happens," he said. "Not necessarily to me. To any man in my profession. It's one of the curious jumps the mind can make, over all sorts of obstacles. For instance, I imagine she already knows I am married."

It sounded like a question, so I nodded.

"You are to get a divorce," I said. "It's all quite simple. I left her looking over her clothes."

He was quiet for a moment. Not shocked, merely thoughtful.

"Perhaps I'd better talk to you rather frankly," he said at last. "I can say this. Usually after this lapse of time I can read a patient's mind pretty well. I'm only a listening post, you know. They talk. I ask questions and listen to the answers. With Mrs. Clarke it's different. I can go so far. Then there's a wall, and I can't either break it down or go over it. What about this man she married?"

"I always liked him. He was puzzled when she left him."

"She gave him no reason?"

"Apparently not. He thought he had failed her some way. Not been attentive enough, or something of the sort."

"He's not a hot-tempered man, then?"

"No. Rather too mild, perhaps."

I thought he disliked questioning me. As though perhaps it was not ethical. But he made up his mind to go on.

"I think I can account for her statement that I mean to marry her," he said. "It's obvious that she feels very much alone, so she needs someone to depend on, perhaps someone to protect her. You see, I think she is afraid of something, Miss Lothrop. And I think that something is real, not merely in her imagination." I must have looked incredulous, for he smiled. He gave me a cigarette and took one himself.

"Suppose you tell me what you think?" he suggested. "Why did you send her to me? Or let's say to any psychiatrist. There must have been a reason. Was she a perfectly normal child?"

"I didn't know her very well then," I said. "She was ten years older than I was. But there were four of us, and she was the pretty one. She was spoiled, I guess. But she was never particularly afraid."

I remember telling him the rest that day: her fear of taxis, the double locks on her door, and her dislike of leaving the house except at night. He listened carefully, but he said very little. Only as I was leaving he said hesitantly:

"We have to be careful with these cases," he said. "I wish I could break down the wall, for her own sake. My own feeling is that some time, somewhere, she has had a psychic shock, and that after so many years of normal living something has revived it. She may not remember it, or refuse to remember it, but it is there."

At least that is what my layman's mind grasped of what he told me. He said to be tactful with her, and if anything worried me to call him up. Then he smiled and said he was quite happily married, so that I could forget that.

I walked to Emily's after I left. I found her dusting the living room, her hair tied up in a bandanna and gloves on her hands. Emily is a handsome woman, but that day she seemed both tired and exasperated. She put me in a chair, pulled off the bandanna, and eyed me carefully.

"Don't tell me how I look," she said. "You look like the devil yourself. Eve wearing you down?"

"We manage," I said drily. "She has a new idea. She's going to marry her psychiatrist, although he seems to have a perfectly good wife already."

Emily shrugged.

"They often get that idea, don't they?" she said vaguely. "Transference or something, they call it. Don't worry about it, Bobbie. She'll get over it."

"You don't have to live with her," I retorted. "Look, Emily, you remember her as a kid, and I don't. Did she ever have a shock of some sort? Anything to scare her?"

"Eve!" she said. "She was too busy taking care of her pretty little self. She was the darnedest little liar I ever knew. She got me into all sorts of trouble."

"Well, she's good and scared now," I said. "Maybe it's all in her mind, but she thinks someone is threatening her. Listen, Emily, I've been thinking on my way here. Do you remember the winter Mother took her away? I was only nine or so, but they were gone for months, weren't they? Wasn't there something wrong?"

I thought Emily looked uncomfortable, but she laughed.

"So you think Eve had a baby! In Tucson, Arizona, where they had dozens of friends! Don't be a fool, Bobbie."

"They *did* go."

"Of course. Eve had a cough she couldn't get rid of. That's all. She came home well, and got married soon after. In 1930, that was." She glanced at the clock on the mantel and got up. "I'm sorry," she said, "but the kids will be home soon and so will George, and all of them ravenous. If Hilda decides she can't take Eve any more send her to me, will you?"

"Eve?"

"No, for heaven's sake! Hilda . . ."

Somehow that trip to Arizona stuck in my mind, and as Eve disappeared after dinner that night I had a chance to talk to Paul. He listened with interest to my account of my talk with Doctor Lyons, but when it came to the fall and winter of '29 he drew a blank.

"I was in college," he said. "Sure, I knew they went to Tucson. Eve's chest, or something. But I wasn't home much those years. I went to Canada in the summers."

I gave up then and went out on the porch. It was clear moonlight. The shadows were very definite, and before long I was sure someone was standing beside a clump of lilacs at the edge of the lawn. Paul had gone up to bed, and of course the maids were a mile off and sound asleep anyhow. But I was not particularly frightened. I stepped to the edge of the porch and called.

"Who's out there?" I said.

The figure emerged, slowly and rather sheepishly, I thought,

and I recognized Frank Nesbit. He came up to the porch before
he spoke.

"Sorry if I scared you," he said. "I saw a rather rough-looking
man turn in the drive and I followed him. But I lost him in the
shrubbery. He's evidently gone. Nice night, isn't it?"

"Are you sure he's gone?" I asked nervously.

"Heard a car start up. Probably just had—let's say personal
reasons."

I sat down on the top step and got a cigarette out of my
pocket. He lit it for me, but I was still nervous. Suspicious, too,
for he had almost certainly followed me to the telephone booth
that morning. Apparently he read my mind, for I had a feeling that just then he was amused at me. "So you saw me!" he
said. "I guess I'm out of practice. Funny, what a few months
will do to a fellow."

"Why on earth should you follow me?" I asked tartly. "I'm
of no possible interest to you."

"I wouldn't go as far as that," he said. "Matter of fact you're
of a great deal of interest to me, Bobbie Lothrop."

I ignored that. I could see that ghastly beard, and I loathed
the very sight of it.

"Why I go into town is my own affair," I said. "I see editors,
I see publishers, I see—"

"Psychiatrists," he said smugly. "And sister Emily. Maybe
I'm better than I thought after all. I'd give quite a bit to know
what Emily told you. Feel like telling me?"

He sat down comfortably on a lower step and got out a pipe.
I hoped he'd set fire to all that hair, but not a chance.

"What was there to tell?" I asked. And when he merely filled
his pipe and lit it without speaking I went on irritably. "I can't
see it's your affair, but she didn't tell me anything."

"No, I don't suppose she would," he said thoughtfully. "And
Paul doesn't know. He was in college at the time."

"What time? What on earth is it all about?" I demanded. "And
why do you follow me, of all things!"

He knocked the ashes out of his pipe and got up. He was a
big man, and he must have been pretty impressive in a uniform
if he'd worn one. But his face in the moonlight looked set and
hard.

"They say once a cop always a cop," he said. "Just now I'm

worried about your sister Eve. She's scared, you know, Bobbie. Or else why the double lock on her door?"

He smiled when I asked how he knew a thing like that.

"This isn't a large community," he said. "And locksmiths are like the rest of us. They have tongues."

Believe it or not, that is all I got from him that night. He waited until I locked the front door before I heard him leaving, but I felt cold and uneasy as I put out the lights and went upstairs.

I locked my door that night, for the first time I could remember. I slept badly too, waking to try to make sense out of what had happened. Doctor Lyons had said she was afraid, and probably had reason to be, although that's as far as he could go. And Frank Nesbit knew the reason but was not talking.

It was useless to go to Emily again. To her I was simply the little sister, who unaccountably had brains enough to write stories and even an occasional book. And Paul was a complete blank, and not even interested. It seemed to me that my only hope was Doctor Lyons, and after I had put Eve on the train the next morning I drove to a drugstore at White Plains and called him up.

His nurse said he was busy, but after I had given my name and said it was important she relented somewhat. It was ten o'clock by that time. She said to call back at eleven, and I had to agree. It was a long hour. I bought cigarettes and chewing gum, on the theory that if I chewed more I would smoke less. Which is a fallacy. I can chew and smoke at the same time. And do.

That was how I noticed the man. He, too, was evidently filling in the time. He ordered a Coke, bought some pipe tobacco and talked to the druggist now and then. But after the druggist called me Miss Lothrop I was sure he was watching me. As I have no illusions about my personal attractions this interested me, especially as there was something vaguely familiar about him.

He was tall and rather shabbily dressed, and although his hair was gray I thought he was probably only forty or a little more. I was tempted to speak to him, but when I looked at him he turned away abruptly.

It never occurred to me that he might have been the rough-

looking man Frank Nesbit had seen in our drive. Or that the
next time I was to see him he was in our local mortuary, with a
bullet through his head.

I thought Doctor Lyons was annoyed when I called him.
His voice sounded sharp, as though he was in a hurry. He
listened, however, when I told him about Frank Nesbit the
night before, and what he had said about Eve. He said he would
like to talk to him, but when I told him about the Tucson
holiday he sounded more interested.

"How long ago was that?" he asked.

"I think it was the winter of '29-'30."

"And you don't know any reason for it?"

"My sister Emily says Eve had a bad chest. All I remember
is that they seemed to go in a hurry, and Mother was upset
about something."

"It wasn't the usual reason? She wasn't pregnant, or anything
like that?"

"Emily says not. They knew plenty of people in Tucson. They
weren't hiding."

"I see. Well, thanks, Miss Lothrop. It may help, although it
sounds normal enough."

But it had not been quite normal, as I remembered it. We
had been in the town house at the time, and as I drove home I
recalled that hasty exodus of theirs. Standing around childlike
to watch the hurried packing of trunks, Mother's face white and
strained, and the nurse grabbing me by the arm and shutting
me in the day nursery. Curiously enough I did not remember
seeing Eve at all. I daresay she was around, coughing as Emily
said, but I did not remember her . . .

She seemed rather quiet that afternoon as I drove her home
from the train. For once she did not mention Doctor Lyons, and
I wondered about her interview with him. How on earth did
he carry on? What did he say, or do? Probably he took the indulgent attitude of a man confronted by a pretty woman who
thinks she is in love with him.

"I wouldn't want to hurt my wife. You can understand that,
Mrs. Clarke."

And Eve looking at him with her lovely blue eyes, and as
off-balance as any human being could be. Only as it happens
I was wrong. As wrong as anyone could be. For she hadn't

looked up at him with lovely blue eyes. As a matter of fact she had got up and walked out on him!

I had an idea that we were being followed on the way home that afternoon. An old Ford kept its distance behind us, but it went on as I turned in at the drive, and I did not mention it. Frank Nesbit was in his garden as we passed. He waved at us, but Eve ignored him.

"I can't understand how you like him," she said. "I'll bet he's still a policeman. 'Once a cop always a cop.' My window was open last night, and I heard him."

"Why is he worried about you, Eve?" I asked.

"I wish he'd mind his own business," she said. "I can worry about myself. And plenty."

But she was very quiet that night at dinner. Possibly because Hilda had gone to bed with an attack of arthritis, and I had to cook it myself. We all went to bed early, but I could not sleep, and far down the drive I could see a light burning in Frank Nesbit's cottage as though he, too, was wakeful. About one o'clock it went out, and I thought I heard a car start up. Down the road a bit it seemed to backfire, but I was drowsy. I went to sleep after that.

I had to get up early the next morning to cook Paul's breakfast, and I was fighting the huge coal range when the boy came with the milk.

He put down the bottles and stood goggle-eyed in the doorway.

"Haven't heard the news, have you?" he inquired.

"What news, Tommy? It would be news if we could afford a new range."

"Man killed last night," he said importantly. "Nobody knows who he is. His car's in the ditch beside the road not far from your gate. I seen it."

"Killed!" I said. "How dreadful. What happened?"

But before he could answer Paul yelled for his breakfast, and when I came back from the dining room Tommy was gone. Paul raised his eyebrows when I placed his food in front of him.

"Oh, no! Not again!" he said.

"You'd better thank God for lady chickens and their eggs," I said indignantly. "And if it interests you the milk boy says a man's been killed down the road."

"There should be a special place in hell for the man who in-

vented wheels," he observed. "And another for the man who
added an engine to them."

Which shows neither of us doubted that it was a car accident.
We had one every now and then.

There was no sign of Joe Smith that morning, so I fed Paul
and took him to the train. There was a small crowd on the road
beside an overturned car about a hundred yards from Nesbit's
cottage, and Joe's taxi was there, among other cars. But it was
almost train time. We could not stop, and when I went back the
place was practically deserted. Only the sheriff, a deputy and a
State Trooper were there, as well as a photographer from White
Plains, busy taking pictures of the car.

Carrie was taking up Eve's breakfast when I got back to the
house. She was fussing about one of the pantry windows having
a broken lock, but I paid no attention, for Frank Nesbit was
coming up the porch steps.

"Any extra coffee floating around?" he inquired. "I haven't had
time for breakfast."

"The accident?" I asked.

"Yes. If you call it that," he said drily. "Fellow was shot, as a
matter of fact."

"Shot? Suicide?"

"No gun. Looks like a murder. Mind if I get the coffee myself? I need whisky, but it's against my principles at this hour."

I nodded and he went into the house. When he came back
he had a cup of coffee and a plate of toast, and I had to wait
until he had finished. He put down his cup and looked at me.

"Maybe you knew him," he said. "His car registration card was
in his pocket. Name seems to be Cummings. David Cummings?
Ring a bell anywhere?"

I shook my head, and then Eve came downstairs, looking fresh
and beautifully groomed as usual. I remember feeling resentful,
after my own hasty toilet, but Nesbit got up and shook the
crumbs off his trousers. She had that effect on men.

"Well," he said pleasantly, "how's the lovely lady this morning?"

She had evidently decided to be agreeable to him, for she sat
down and draped her housecoat around her.

"I'm all right," she said. "What's this Carrie tells me about
someone dead in a car accident?"

So I knew the vegetable man had already been there, and that

Hilda was certainly having a quick recovery from her arthritis. I drew a long breath of relief, but Nesbit shook his head.

"No accident," he said. "Fellow was shot. Ever know anybody named Cummings, Mrs. Clarke? David Cummings?"

Eve frowned in thought.

"Cummings?" she said. "I don't think so. Why?"

"That seems to be his name," Nesbit said and got up. "Don't worry if the sheriff comes around to talk about it. It was pretty close to your gate."

As a matter of fact the sheriff's car was already coming along the drive, and Nesbit prepared to leave.

"Don't want him to think I'm horning in on his business," he said. "If he wants to put a deputy on the place better let him do it. I don't like people being murdered around here."

The rest of the morning was hectic. Both Eve and I had to look at the body in the local mortuary. Eve did not recognize him, but I did. As I have already said, he was the man I had seen in the drugstore in White Plains.

It upset me, the whole thing. He had been interested in me, I knew. I rather thought too that he had followed me home from the station that afternoon. So after I dropped Eve at the house I walked down to Frank Nesbit's cottage.

To my surprise it was empty and locked up. Looking through the windows it appeared as though he had packed hastily, for there were clothes strewn around the room. His car was gone from the shed too, and I was vaguely uneasy.

There was a deputy stationed on the porch when I reached the house. He looked very comfortable in one of our wicker chairs, and I stopped and spoke to him.

"Do you know Mr. Nesbit, in our cottage by the gate?" I asked.

"Don't know him," he said. "Seen him around, that's all. Ex-cop, isn't he?"

"So he says. I don't know whether it's important or not, but he's gone away. It seems queer, just now."

He spat over the porch rail and lit a cigarette. He looked supremely indifferent.

"Maybe he had some business of his own," he said. "Unless you think he killed the fellow down the road. Got any ideas like that?"

"Certainly not," I said, and marched with dignity into the house.

But the sheriff, coming to question us later that day, was more interested.

"Funny thing," he said, "his lighting out like that. Car's gone, and he's gone. Think he knew this Cummings?"

"I haven't an idea."

"Well, one of the people passing here late last night saw an old Ford parked by the cottage. Place was lit up too. You never know about these city cops. Some of them are mighty handy with a gun."

I think he tried to trace Nesbit after he left, but whatever he did the missing man remained missing. The deputy left and another one took his place at dinner time. He was a lugubrious fellow who said he was to stay in the house that night, and advised us all to lock our bedroom doors.

"Got a killer around," he said dolefully. "Maybe a maniac. Never know what he'll do next."

Emily called up that night. She'd seen the story in the evening paper, and she sounded excited.

"Listen," she said, "was his name really David Cummings, Bobbie?"

"So they say. What about him, Emily? Did you know him?"

Her voice sounded odd, and she took a moment before she answered.

"I've heard the name somewhere," she said evasively. "I'm trying to place it. If I do I'll call you."

It was about nine o'clock when Doctor Lyons telephoned me. He said he had seen about the murder in the paper, and as it was near our place he hoped it hadn't disturbed Eve. I said she was all right, and then he asked me if I was alone, or if there was an extension phone in the house. There wasn't, of course. My dream of luxury is to have one beside my bed, but that time is far off.

I told him, and he asked me if I could come in to the office the next day. He had something he would like me to do for him. As I was glad for any excuse to get out of the house I agreed, and I left on the commuter's train a half hour after Paul the next morning.

There was still no news about Nesbit. His cottage looked blank and dreary as I passed it, and the shed remained empty. There was no reason why I should worry about him, I thought. He was nothing to me. But I was sure he was no killer, and I wondered if anything had happened to him. After all he knew something he would not talk about, apparently something that concerned a danger to Eve. And what had he meant about once a cop always a cop?

For the first time I wondered about his renting our cottage about the time Eve came home from Reno. Had he known she was in some sort of danger? Both Paul and I had laid her terror to fantasy, or perhaps her usual attempt to focus attention on herself. It occurred to me then that the danger was not only real. It might still exist.

When I reached the doctor's office he had evidently left word he was expecting me, for the nurse admitted me at once, taking me to a small consulting room I had not seen before, and he came in rather hurriedly, as though he had left a patient.

"Have you time to do a rather troublesome errand for me, Miss Lothrop?" he asked. "It may take most of the day."

"What sort of errand?" I asked.

He did not sit down. He lit a cigarette, as though he needed it, and looked through me rather than at me.

"This trip to Tucson," he said. "I think we may find the trouble there. I worked around to it yesterday, and she not only refused to discuss it. She got up almost immediately and left. She looked very strange, and I admit frankly I don't like it."

He had me go over quickly what I remembered of that episode, which wasn't much. It seemed to satisfy him.

"Your father was pretty well off at that time, I suppose? Well known, too?"

"Well off until the crash," I said drily. "Dad held on for a couple of years, then he died, and Mother, too. Practically all they left us was the house in the country."

"What about your mother, Miss Lothrop? You say she seemed worried about the trip to Arizona."

"I was only a kid, Doctor. I may have imagined it. She'd always had money and—well, position. She didn't take things easily. The crash virtually killed her."

He seemed interested in Mother, although I didn't see why. But he switched soon to our murder. "This Cummings who was shot. Did you ever see him before?"

"Yes. In a drugstore at White Plains, a couple of days ago. He

seemed interested in me, I don't know why. My sister Emily
thought she remembered his name. But Eve saw him at the mortuary, and she didn't know him at all."

"You're quite sure of that?"

"She was perfectly calm. Which is more than I was."

He looked at his watch and then told me what he wanted me
to do. I was to go to Forty-first Street where the Herald Tribune
kept its back files, and look over the winter of 1929-30.

"Look for your family," he said. "Probably on the society page.
It will give you a date or two anyhow. And see if any of you
were involved in any trouble at that time. Outside of the panic,
of course. Just see what you can pick up."

"You're thinking about Eve," I said. "How could she have been
in trouble? She was only eighteen. She didn't even come out
until the next fall."

"It may not involve her directly at all," he said. "It's just a
chance. But I think we have to take it, if she's to get back to
normal. Once she faces it, it may help."

It was a dirty job at the newspaper office. I was covered with
dried scraps of old newsprint before I finished, and except a brief
notice that Mother and Eve had gone to Tucson in February
there was no mention of the family. But purely by chance I
happened on a picture, and I sat staring at it. The caption underneath said: "Indicted for Murder. David Cummings (left)
handcuffed to Lieutenant Frank Nesbit." Nesbit was beardless,
but I knew him at once, and the dead man, too.

When I had recovered I read the brief résumé of the case.
Cummings, a student at Columbia at the time, had been on inti-
mate terms with a girl of indifferent reputation who worked in
one of the five-and-ten-cent stores. She roomed alone in a tene-
ment on the West Side, and one night she was heard quarreling
violently with some man. The next morning her strangled body
was found in her room, and Cummings had been arrested. He
protested his innocence but the evidence was all against him. I
followed through his trial, a couple of months later. Apparently
the jury recognized his youth, for on its recommendation he was
given twenty years on a manslaughter charge.

So he had been free; possibly with time off for good behavior
he had been out for a year or two. Had he traced Frank Nesbit
and tried to kill him? And had Nesbit killed him instead? If so,
where was Eve in all this? It began to look as though, if she had

known him, Mother had simply taken her away to avoid a scandal. Which is precisely what Mother would have done. I took my report, if report it was, to Doctor Lyons that afternoon, after stopping at Schrafft's for a sandwich and a cup of coffee. To my surprise I found Emily coming out of the office as I went in. She looked flurried and angry.

"So it's your turn!" she said nastily. "I hope he gets more out of you than he did out of me. How can I remember all the boys Eve knew twenty years ago? I was married and having babies by that time."

"You thought last night you remembered the murdered man's name."

"Of course I did. The radio says he's been identified as having killed a girl years ago. That's where I must have seen it."

I didn't believe her. Not for a minute. She was like Mother. A breath of scandal choked her. I was sure she had known Cummings, or had known about him. And not from the papers either. And I found the doctor agreed with me. However, my story left him bewildered.

"One thing is sure," he said. "I cannot picture Mrs. Clarke over on the West Side, at the age of eighteen, strangling a cheap little tart. I think possibly she knew the Cummings boy. I think your mother took her away for the reason you give, family pride. But where in God's name does this ex-policeman fit in? If he arrested Cummings the murder might have been the other way. In other words, Nesbit would be dead."

"Maybe he is," I said miserably. "He's disappeared, anyhow."

It was late when I got home. The papers were re-hashing the earlier crime, and Paul was avidly reading the details. There was still no sign of Frank Nesbit, but thank heaven Hilda was in the kitchen, where she was feeding still another deputy a slab of expensive beefsteak. I heard her talking as I went back.

"Girls ain't changed so much," she said. "We had a pretty wild one of our own twenty years ago. Boys, boys, all the time! I got sick and tired of feeding them."

She shut up when I went in and had the grace to explain about the steak. It was too big, she said, so she'd just cut off the tail. But she had given me an idea, and after dinner I went up to the attic. There was a trunk full of faded old snapshots, and I was in a good many of them. Apparently I had a mania for being photographed, although why I wanted to be I couldn't imagine.

I was a gangling kid with pigtails and braces on my teeth. But
Eve was lovely. Almost invariably there was a crowd of boys
around her, and at last I came on a picture, taken at the pool,
and there was no mistaking a young and good-looking Cummings.

He was muscular and handsome in his bathing suit, but not
at all the sort who would strangle a girl to death. And as I sat
there on the floor I remembered him as I had seen him in the
mortuary the day before, and shuddered.

But outside of the fact that Eve had known him the picture
meant nothing. Nevertheless I carried it downstairs with me,
having had my fill by that time of old dusty records, and I
still had it when the doorbell rang.

I opened the door myself, but it was a moment before I recognized Frank Nesbit.

He had shaved off his beard, and he looked years younger. But
he appeared grim as well as tired, and he more or less staggered into the living room and dropped into a chair.

"Suppose I could have a cup of coffee?" he asked. "I forget
when I ate last. Some time yesterday, I think."

Eve had already gone to bed, and Paul was in the back of the
house, locking up as usual. When he came in and saw Nesbit
his jaw dropped.

"For God's sake!" he said. "In disguise, aren't you? Got quite
a chin after all. I always wondered."

But he was pouring straight whisky while he talked, and Nesbit gulped it down. He looked better after that. He even tried
to smile.

"All right," he said. "Now ask me whether I slept with it under
the sheet or on top!" he said. But the smile was forced. While
I fixed him a tray he washed in the downstairs lavatory, and
he wolfed down the food when it came. It helped, but he still
looked unhappy. He stretched out his long legs and surveyed us
soberly.

"I hate like hell to do this," he said. "But I've been on a long
trail. A twenty-year trail, as a matter of fact. It took me all over
the state the last day or two, but I have to tell you first, Bobbie,
that when I said once a cop always a cop I meant it. I'm still a
detective, and I came here under false pretenses. I had reason
to think your sister might be in danger. Mind if I go back a bit?"

Paul was staring at him as if he had lost his mind, and I felt cold chills along my spine. I knew that our mystery, such as it was, was about to be cleared.

"Shall I call Eve?" I asked. "After all, if it concerns her—"

"Not yet," he said. "Maybe later."

And then, in our shabby old living room, he began his story. As I had more or less expected, it went back twenty years, when the girl I'd read about was killed on the West Side. Cummings had been arrested, claimed he had borrowed a car from a fellow student that night and taken another girl for a drive. She wasn't allowed to leave the house, but she slipped out and met him.

"He'd had the car. We knew that, but nobody had taken the mileage, so this other girl was his only alibi. Only as it happened she denied it absolutely. She said she had been in bed that night, that she barely knew him, and certainly she had never driven in a car with him.

"I couldn't break her down," he said. "I felt sure she was lying, but she sat there looking like an offended angel, and denied it in toto. Moreover her mother backed her up. Said the girl had gone to bed with a headache, that she'd looked in on her at one in the morning, and that she was still there. And before the trial the mother got her out of the State.

"What could we do? Here was a prominent family. Against it we had only the boy's statement, so we kept her name out of the papers. But I never forgot the case. I kept after it, and when the time came I rented the cottage here.

"Young Cummings went up on a manslaughter charge for twenty years, but got a couple off for good behavior. He came out in '47. His people were dead by that time, and he'd been a student, so he had nothing to fall back on. He wrote me now and then, but there was nothing I could do to help him—except answer his letters.

"He drifted to Reno, where he drove a taxi, and one day he took the girl—a woman now—to the railroad station.

"He recognized her, and he wrote me that he would kill her if he ever got the chance, and that he was coming East to do it.

"That's when I got busy on the case. But when he came to see me, the night I told you I'd seen someone in the drive, he had thought things over. What he wanted now was only to have his innocence established. He knew I'd never believed he was guilty, and he hoped I could help him.

"I didn't think there was a chance. I told him so. I warned

him to keep away from me, to give me an opportunity to see
what I could do. But he got impatient. He came back, and as he
left the cottage he was killed.

"But I had learned two things from him, you see. So that night,
after the local authorities took over, I had an interview with
your Hilda."

"Hilda!" I gasped. "Why Hilda?"

He did not reply directly.

"Afraid I broke the lock on one of your pantry windows," he
said. "Scared hell out of Hilda, too. But I got her to talk. You
see, Cummings had an idea he'd been seen bringing the girl back
that night. He wasn't sure, and the man he thought had seen
him had disappeared anyhow." He looked at me.

"Happen to remember a butler you had named Simpson?" he
asked.

I nodded. I was afraid to say anything.

"Well, it was queer about Simpson. Seems he left right after
the case broke. Said he'd come into money and was buying a
tobacco shop somewhere. Only Hilda didn't think he'd inherited
anything. Unfortunately she didn't know where the shop was,
but I had to take a chance. It wasn't easy. This is a big state.
But I did locate him, and he said the girl had been out that
night all night. With Cummings, too. Simpson saw him bring
her back. And, with apologies to your family, they bought him
off."

"Oh, no!" I gasped. "Not Mother. Never Mother!"

"Let's say she believed the girl," he said gently. "Let's say they
all thought Simpson was mistaken, but he could make things
pretty complicated. So they got rid of him. Only it seems he
wasn't mistaken."

Paul spoke, for the first time:

"If the girl was Eve," he said heavily, "she wasn't responsible,
Nesbit. She never has been."

"Responsible or not," he said, his voice once more hard, "she
sent Cummings up for twenty years. And then she killed him."

When neither of us spoke he went on:

"It was a warm night," he said. "My windows were open, and
I suppose she was listening outside. She must have heard him
mention Simpson, and Simpson was the pay-off."

"I don't believe it," Paul said. "It's ridiculous. She doesn't even
own a gun."

"I think she does." Nesbit got up and started for the door, but he moved rather slowly. He seemed to be waiting for something, and as he stood there he heard it.

A gun went off in Eve's room upstairs, and I did not need to be told what she had done. Perhaps he knew it would happen. Perhaps he even knew she had been listening on the stairs as he told the story. But that is one thing I have never asked him. I don't want to know.

You see, I am married to him now, and he's back on the police work he had never left. And one thing a policeman's wife soon learns is that once a cop always a cop. And that a case is never closed until it is over.

13

JOHN DAVIES

The Ghost Wore a Monocle

JOHN DAVIES is fiction editor of *John Bull,* one of the most important of the big British weekly magazines, but he likes to show his authors now and then that he can turn out a story, too. During World War II he served as a lieutenant in the Royal Navy. When he isn't working at his desk in London, or writing in his Essex home, he spends his time sailing off England's east coast.

MRS. WHYMPER COULD BE excused for feeling disturbed when she saw her husband on the other side of the Hotel Metropole restaurant, because by then George Whymper had been dead six weeks.

Mrs. Whymper's soup spoon trembled slightly in her hand as she stared at the quietly dressed little man just sitting down at the table by the window. Then she told herself not to be silly. George was dead, and that was that. This was merely someone that looked like him. She would never have noticed the man at all if it hadn't been for the red rose in his buttonhole. George had always worn a red rose—but, of course, plenty of other men did, too.

What nonsense for her to start seeing things at this stage, after all she had been through!

Nonetheless, Mrs. Whymper couldn't take her eyes off the little man; and, when she saw a waiter lay a menu in front of him, she had a terrible feeling of foreboding. She waited, panic fluttering deep inside her. She saw the little man scanning the menu, and his hand going automatically to his waistcoat pocket.

When he brought out a monocle, Mrs. Whymper fainted . . .

Mrs. Whymper was an important guest, and her "turn" caused quite a stir in the hotel. It also provided a welcome new topic of conversation at the reception desk.

"Poor soul," said Miss Fethering, the cashier. "But it's not surprising, seeing what she's been through."

"What's she been through?" asked the new switchboard girl, from inside her cubbyhole.

"You mean to say you don't *know?*" Miss Fethering's tone expressed the utmost contempt for such ignorance. "Why—that's *the* Mrs. Whymper, the one that was in all the papers when her husband died." Miss Fethering lowered her voice. "Suicide, it turned out to be—he shot himself. A millionaire he was, too."

"A millionaire?" the switchboard girl said. "*She* probably shot him, then, to get the money." The switchboard girl went to the pictures three times a week.

Mrs. Whymper soon got over her scare. She wasn't a woman who was easily shaken, and she felt quite all right again as soon as she had taken herself to task for being so silly as to be upset by the sight of a stranger who happened to look a bit like George. But she decided to cut short her stay at the Metropole. After all, George and she had stayed there together so often that there were bound to be associations.

She decided that the best thing to do would be to get out of London. She would go to the sea—to Torquay.

She went the next day, and was soon congratulating herself on the move. The hotel she had chosen to stay at was very comfortable, and Torquay was somewhere she had never been with George. That was comforting because, although she had tried to put the incident at the Metropole out of her mind, she hadn't quite succeeded. In any event, she enjoyed the first few days of her stay.

Then she saw George again.

She was having tea in the lounge when, happening to glance out of the window, she saw a little man in a dark suit. She would probably never have noticed him in London, but here the soberness of his dress was conspicuous among the gaily attired holiday-makers. And George had always worn a dark business suit and a correct collar and tie, even on holiday.

George's only concession to the holiday spirit had been a Panama hat. This man wasn't wearing a hat, but, as the crowd around him eddied, Mrs. Whymper saw that he was carrying one in his hand—and that it was a Panama.

Mrs. Whymper's face went gray. She made a choking sound in her throat, recovered herself enough to mumble some sort of excuse to her companions at the tea table, and went up to her room. There, shaking with fright, she sat at her window watching for the little man to come back. She dreaded seeing him again, but she was even more afraid she wouldn't, because then she would never know for sure whether it had been George or not.

She sat there until the front of the hotel was dark and deserted. After a hideous night, she was back at the window at dawn. She watched the light grow and she saw the first strollers appear.

She had just assured an anxious maid that she was all right when she saw George again. He was moving toward the beach. He must have passed while she was talking to the maid.

Mrs. Whymper scrambled up from her chair and hurried out of the hotel. She felt she must find out whether the man was George or not. But she lost him. By the time she got outside of the hotel there was no sign of him anywhere. She walked half a mile or so in the direction he had been walking, but in vain.

She saw him again though, when, trembling with reaction, she got back to the hotel. He was sitting in a basket chair on the porch. He was neatly dressed in his sober, dark suit. His Panama lay on the floor by his side, and he was reading "The Financial Times."

George had always read "The Financial Times," even on holiday.

Mrs. Whymper stopped dead in her tracks. She felt the cold sweat of panic break out all over her. Nothing could have made her pass that motionless, terrifying little figure on the porch, and she turned and stumbled away.

The day wore on, and Mrs. Whymper didn't return to the hotel. By evening the management, alarmed by reports from the staff of her odd behavior, had alerted the police.

Meanwhile Mrs. Whymper had returned to London. She had caught the first train she could out of Torquay.

She spent the journey in a state of terror, scarcely daring to look at a fellow passenger in case one of them was George.

She didn't want to chance going back to the Metropole. Instead she went to an obscure little hotel in Paddington. There, behind the locked door of a shabby bedroom, she desperately tried to make up her mind what to do next.

At last she decided to go abroad. To Paris. George had always looked upon Paris as a sink of iniquity. He had always refused to go there, and she hoped and prayed that he wouldn't follow her there now.

She telephoned and reserved a seat on the Paris plane that evening. After that she had just time to go to her bank for money and her passport which, luckily, was in order.

George wasn't driving her taxi, nor was he behind the counter at the bank, and Mrs. Whymper began to feel that she had beaten him after all. By the time she arrived at the airport, she was almost sure of it.

When the flight was called, she made haste to take her seat on the plane. She was reassured to find that there was no one among the passengers that looked even remotely like George. And it could only be a matter of minutes now before she was on her way. The plane's engines were already warming up.

But then, as time passed and nothing further happened, she realized that the flight was being held up for something.

Or someone . . .

Mrs. Whymper suddenly realized, too, that the seat beside her was empty—the only empty seat on the plane.

That was why they were waiting. The seat beside her was waiting for George.

Through a daze of terror, Mrs. Whymper heard the air hostess's polite, well-modulated voice. "Hurry, please," the hostess was saying. "We are late on take-off. Please hurry and take your seat, Mr. Whymper."

Mrs. Whymper saw George come aboard and walk forward to take the seat beside her. She started up in terror and stumbled out into the aisle, putting out her hands to fend him off. But he still came on. His face swam up in front of her and he was smiling dreadfully.

Mrs. Whymper clawed at him, and her voice came out in a thin, awful scream.

"No—no! You're dead . . . dead, I tell you! You're dead, because I killed you! You're dead . . . dead . . . DEAD!"

Then the shrieking babble strangled in her throat and she slumped unconscious to the floor . . .

In his Scotland Yard office, Inspector Bradbury was talking to a Mr. Fortescue, a close friend of the late George Whymper who had been a great help to the police in their inquiries into Mr. Whymper's death.

"It was a tough one," Bradbury said ruminatively. "She did it very cleverly, so cleverly that there wasn't a bit of material evidence worth a damn—but all the same I felt certain she'd killed him." He paused and then said abruptly: "You'd like to see the man?"

"I most certainly would," Fortescue said.

Bradbury depressed a switch. He said: "Ask Detective-Sergeant Hollis to come in."

Mr. Fortescue murmured, half to himself: "It was brilliant—brilliant!"

Bradbury said deprecatingly: "Oh, I don't know—it was more a stroke of luck than anything else, our happening to have the right man."

There was a knock at the door and a dark, unassuming little man came in. Bradbury said: "Mr. Fortescue—meet Detective-Sergeant Hollis. Alias George Whymper."

Mr. Fortescue shook hands with Hollis warmly. He said: "Let me congratulate you on a remarkable bit of work." But then he turned to Bradbury, puzzled. "I don't understand, though, why it worked so well. There is certainly a resemblance between Detective-Sergeant Hollis and poor George, but it isn't very marked. I can't understand how a clever, level-headed woman like Edna Whymper could have been taken in by it."

Inspector Bradbury smiled grimly. He said: "It was the props that did it—the rose, the monocle, the Panama, 'The Financial Times' and so on . . . all the details you were so good as to give us. She never looked beyond them at the man himself. Because she had never, as you also so helpfully told us, been interested in poor George Whymper as a man."

Bradbury frowned. Then he shrugged and shook his head, because this had been a very unpleasant business. He said: "That's what did the trick. With a little help from the greatest detective there has ever been, or ever will be . . ."

He paused. The other two men looked at him inquiringly.

"I mean," Bradbury said, "the criminal's guilty conscience."

14

JOHN D. MacDONALD

There Hangs Death!

MR. MacDONALD is one of those versatile young writers equally at home in short stories and in novels, capable of turning out ingenious mysteries or more tender stories of family life. His books, many of them paperback originals, have sold literally millions of copies. A famous classic legend provides the stuff of this thoroughly modern mystery, indicating that a writer can find story material in the most unlikely places.

THE DEAD MAN was face down on the dark hardwood floor. He was frail and old, and the house was sturdy and old, redolent of Victorian dignity. It was the house where he had been born.

The wide stairs climbed for two tall stories, with two landings for each floor. He lay in the center of the stair well, twenty-five feet below a dusty skylight. The gray daylight came down through the skylight and glinted on the heavy ornate hilt and pommel of the broadsword that pinned the man to the dark floor.

The hilt was of gold and silver, and there was a large red stone set into the pommel. The gold—and the red of stone and red of blood on the white shirt—were the only touches of color.

Riggs saw that when they brought him in. They let him look for a few moments. He knew he would not forget it, ever. The bright momentary light of a police flash bulb filled the hallway, and they turned him away, a hand pushing his shoulder.

There were many people in the book-lined study. He saw Angela at once, her face too white, her eyes shocked and enormous, sitting on a straight chair. He started toward her but they caught his arm; and the wide, bald, tired-eyed stranger who sat behind the old desk said, "Take the girl across the hall and put Riggs in that chair."

Angela gave him a frail smile and he tried to respond. They took her out. He sat where she had been.

The bald man looked at him for a long moment. "You'll answer questions willingly?"

"Of course." A doughy young man in the opposite corner took notes with a fountain pen.

"Name and occupation?"

"Howard Riggs. Research assistant at the University, Department of Psychology."

"How long have you known the deceased?"

"I've known Dr. Hilber for three years. I met him through his niece, Angela Manley, when I was in the Graduate School. I believe he'd retired two or three years before I met him. He was head of the Archeology—"

"We know his history. How much have you been told about this?"

"Not very much. Just that he was dead and I was wanted here. I didn't know he'd been . . ."

"What is your relationship to his niece?"

"We're to be married in June when the spring semester ends."

"Were you in this house today?"

"Yes, sir. I went to church with Angela. I picked her up here and brought her back here. We walked. We had some coffee here and then I went back to the lab. I'm running an experiment using laboratory animals. I have to . . ."

"What time did you leave this house?"

"I'd say it was eleven-thirty this morning. I've been in the lab ever since, until those men came and . . ."

"Were you alone at the lab?"

"Yes, sir."

"Did you see Dr. Hilber when you were here?"

"No, sir."

"Did Miss Manley inform you that she was going to stay here? Did she say anything about going out?"

"She wanted me to go for a walk. I couldn't. I had to get back. We sometimes walk up in the hills back of here."

"Did you know that Miss Manley is the sole heir?"

"I guess I did. I mean I remember him saying once that she was his only living relative. So I would assume . . ."

"Did you know he had substantial paid-up insurance policies?"

"No, sir."

"He opposed this marriage, did he not?"

"No, sir. He was in favor of it. He opposed it at first. He didn't

want to be left alone. But after I agreed to move in here after
we're married . . . you see, he wasn't well."

"You had many arguments with him, did you not?"

Riggs frowned. "Not like you mean. They were intellectual
arguments. He thought my specialty is a sort of . . . pseudo-
science. He was a stubborn man, sir."

"You became angry at him."

Riggs shrugged. "Many times. But not . . . importantly angry."

The study door opened and two men came in. The man in
uniform who had come in said to the bald man, "Can't raise a
print off that sword, Captain. It wouldn't have to be wiped.
It's just a bad surface."

The bald captain nodded impatiently. He looked at the second
man who had come in. "Doctor?" he said.

"Steve, it's pretty weird," the doctor said. He sat down and
crossed long legs. "That sword is like a razor. It was sunk right
into the wood."

"If it was shoved through him and he fell on his face, of
course it would be stuck in the wood."

"Not like that, Steve. It's a two-edged sword. If he fell after
it was through him it would be knocked back. Some of the shirt
fibers were carried into the wound. No, Steve, the sword went
into him after he was stretched out on his face."

"Knocked out?"

"No sign of it."

"Check stomach contents and so forth to see if he was doped."

"That'll be done. But does it make sense?"

"How do you mean?"

"If you're going to kill a man, do you dope him, stretch him
out on the floor and chunk a knife down through him? Now
here's something else. After we got him out of the way we
found another hole in the floor. A fresh hole, about four inches
from where the sword dug in. It's a deeper hole, but it looks to
me as if it was made the same way, by the same sword. And
there was only one hole in the professor."

The captain got up quickly and went out. Most of the men
followed him. Howard Riggs got up and went out, too. He was
not stopped. He saw Angela in the small room across the hall.
He walked by the man outside her door and went to her. She
stood up quickly as he approached. Her face was pale, her eyes

enormous. He took her cold hands in his. "Darling," she said, "they act so . . ."

"I know. I know. Don't let it hurt. Please."

"But he's dead, and the way they look at me. As if . . ." She began to cry and he held the trembling slenderness of her in his arms, murmuring reassurances, trying to conceal from her how inept and confused he felt in the face of the obvious hostility of the police.

The hard voice behind him said, "You're not supposed to be in here." A hand rested heavily on his shoulder.

Riggs turned out from under the hand and released Angela. He looked back at her as he left the room. She stood and managed a smile. It was a frail, wan smile, but it was good to see. He hoped he had strengthened her.

Out in the hall the captain was on his knees examining the gouges in the dark wood. He craned his neck back and looked straight up. The men around him did the same. It was a curious tableau.

The captain gave an order and the sword was brought to him. The blade had been cleaned. He hefted it in his hand, took a half cut at the air.

"Heavy damn thing," he said. He glanced at Riggs. "Ever see it before?"

"It's from Dr. Hilber's collection of antique edged weapons. It dates from the twelfth century. He said he believed it was taken on one of the early crusades. The second, I think."

"You men move back down the hall," the captain said. He plodded up the stairs, the incongruous sword gleaming in his hairy fist. Soon he was out of sight, and they could hear him climbing the second flight. There was silence—and then a silvery shimmer in the gray light of the stair well. The sword flashed down, chunked deeply into the floor and stood there, vibrationless.

The captain came back down. He grasped the hilt with both hands, planted his feet, grunted as he wrenched it out of the floor. He smiled at Riggs. "I look at her and I say she could just about lift a sword like this. She couldn't stick it through the old man, but she could drop it through him."

"You're out of your mind!"

"The other hole is where she made a test run when he was out, to see if it would fall right. She says she came back from her walk and found him. But I find clumsy attempts to make it look like a prowler did it. The jade collection in his bedroom is all messed up. We got to check it against his inventory. Dirt tracked into that room where the weapons are. Silver dumped on the floor in the dining room. If Doc wasn't on the ball, that stage setting might have sold me. *Might* have. But now we know it was dropped through him, and it was no theft murder, even if she tried to make it look that way."

They took Angela in on suspicion of murder. They did not let Riggs speak to her. They told him not to leave town. He did not understand why they didn't arrest him also. He sensed that he was being carefully watched.

Though he was emotionally exhausted that night, it took him a long time to get to sleep. A nightmare awakened him before dawn. In his dream a shining sword had been suspended high over him, in utter blackness. He did not know when it would drop. He recognized the similarity to the legend of Damocles. He lay sweating in the predawn silences until his frightened heart slowed its beat. It seemed then that it was the first time he had been able to think logically of the death of Hilber. He thought carefully and for a long time, and when he knew what he would do, he went quickly to sleep.

He walked into the captain's office at two o'clock on Monday. It was raining heavily outside. The captain was in shirt sleeves. "Sit down," the captain said. "You asked to see me, but I'll tell you some things first. The girl is sticking to her story. I half believe her. Besides, that corpse was in the center of the room with the sword sticking straight up. I can't see anybody throwing it and making it land that way, so we're trying to uncover other angles."

"Hilber had a good academic mind, but not what you'd call a practical mind."

"Keep talking."

"If he wanted to kill himself and make it look like murder, he would try to clear Angela by such clumsy business as the dirt tracked in, the silver on the floor, the disorder in the jade case. He'd never stop to think of the next logical step, that the police would accuse Angela of doing all that to mislead them."

"You try to read a dead man's mind and he can't tell you if you're wrong. You've got more than that, haven't you?"

"This morning I talked to his lawyer and his doctor, Captain, and I went to the house and they wouldn't let me in."

"I know that."

"He had very little money. His illness used up most of it. He had forty-five thousand in insurance, in two policies, one of ten and one for thirty-five thousand. There is a suicide clause in the larger policy."

"So he heaved a sword up in the air and it came down and hit him in the back."

"He was operated on two years ago. The operation was not completely successful. The malignancy returned and this time it was widespread. He had six months to two years, and in either case it would not have been pleasant."

"So?"

"Did you ever hear of the Sword of Damocles?"

The captain frowned. "They hung it on a thread over some joker's head when he wanted to be king, didn't they? It would take a special kind of nerve. Some timing device. Candle maybe. Let's go take a look, Riggs."

They looked. The captain brought the sword along. They experimented. It would have had to drop from the top floor. The railing encircled three sides of the stairwell. Nothing was tied to the railing. Nothing had been fastened to the skylight. They searched for a long time. The captain thought of the possible use of rubber bands, so they would snap back into one of the bedrooms. They could find nothing. The captain rubbed his bald head. "No good, Riggs. The sword had to be dead in the middle. Nothing could have held it. The girl didn't come upstairs. The house was searched after we got here. And who could have held the sword out that far—in the center of the room?"

"Let me look around some more, please."

"Go ahead."

Riggs finally wandered to the study. Dr. Hilber had spent most of his time there. He sat moodily in Hilber's chair and went back over every aspect of the previous day to see if he could remember anything that would help.

They had come back from church. Angela had opened the front door with her key, mildly surprised to find it locked. They had walked back through to the kitchen. He remembered that Angela had wondered if her uncle would put in his usual appearance for Sunday morning coffee, then thought that he was probably immersed in reading one of the many scholarly books that were so much a part of his life. She had decided not to disturb him.

The memory of the morning gave him no clue. The Sword of Damocles had hung over the stairwell. And it had fallen. And the means of suspension was utterly gone, as though it had never been. As though it had vanished. He sat very still for a long moment and then got up quickly.

Angela was released at six. Riggs was asked to perform the experiment again for the city District Attorney and two members of his staff. He and the captain had found the proper material after experimenting with various kinds of thread, and had purchased a sufficient supply of rayon tire cord yarn. Riggs took the sword to the top floor, knotted one end of the yarn around the metal railing, and cut off a piece long enough to reach to the opposite railing. To the middle of that piece he tied a length sufficient to reach to the floor far below. He then tied the sword to the middle of the strand, took the free end around and tied it to the opposite railing. The sword danced and shimmered in the air and grew still.

They all went back down to the main floor. Riggs lighted a match and touched it to the strand of yarn hanging down. It caught at once and a knot of flame raced up the piece of yarn with stunning speed. Soon the heavy sword fell and imbedded its point deeply into the hardwood of the hallway.

By the time they reached the top railing, all traces of the suspension method had disappeared. The heat generated had not been sufficient to leave any mark on the metal railings.

The District Attorney sighed. "It's half crazy, but I guess I've got to buy it."

The captain shook his head and said, "It's the only thing possible. Nobody could have thrown that sword and made it land at that angle—or rather without an angle. And that stuff he used doesn't leave a trace. Without Riggs figuring it out, though, I don't know where we'd be."

The District Attorney stared curiously at Riggs. "How did you figure it out?"

"He was a classical scholar and with this setup—" Riggs indicated the open space above them and the railings. "It almost had to be based on the legend of the Sword of Damocles. That and the second hole in the floor. Those were the clues. He tested the method while we were out. That's why there were two holes in the floor. The Sword of Damocles gave him his idea. Modern technology gave him the method."

And then he was free to go to Angela.

15

MARK DERBY

The Next to Last Bullet

MARK DERBY'S suspense novels have won him wide
acclaim as a master of chilling, fast-moving action. His
most recent is *Echo of a Bomb*. He travels a great deal,
has lived extensively in Singapore, the scene of this story,
and in Sarawak, where he has been accepted by the
natives as one of them. During the early part of the Communist terror in Malaya, he led a group of the legendary
Dyak jungle trackers against the rebels.

THERE WAS a short silence while the smart Malay constable
went out and closed the door and the police lieutenant directed
a glance of inquiry across his desk. Then Martha said, "I believe I'm going to be murdered."

With her great eyes wide and a strand of her hair drawn up
into the slipstream of the big ceiling fan she didn't look alto-
gether real. She was afraid that to the young police officer she
maybe didn't look, or sound, altogether sane.

He said, a little stiff and aloof in his smart tropical uniform,
"Sit down, and tell me what it is we can do for you."

Martha's slim body was stiff in the rattan chair for a moment;
then she relaxed. But consciously. She relaxed with an effort,
and the effort was more obvious than the relaxation. "Over and
over again I've told myself that I must be imagining things,
that I'm new to Singapore, new to the East and . . . and lonely
this past month."

"You don't know anybody here?"

"Only Davy's friends. And now they . . ."

She sighed and started again. "Davy Hunter is my fiancé. I
came out five weeks ago to marry him, but he had to go off and
fix some trouble on one of his company's estates in Sumatra. He
comes back tomorrow, and we were going to be married the day
after."

"But not now?" He blinked uncertainly.

"No," she said quietly. "I'm afraid I'll be dead before then."

He blinked again and threw a glance back at the racket and white shoes in the corner behind his desk and another out through the window at the black monsoon cloud that had been piling up for an hour.

Martha realized that her entrance just before he was due to leave his office might have lost him his game that evening. She made an effort to be brief.

"You asked about my friends here. Well, you'll know about them already, I expect."

He said, "I don't know anything. I only came back off leave yesterday."

"But you saw that." She was pointing to a headline on the front page of the "Straits Times" on his desk: POLICE SEARCH FOR MISSING OFFICER.

He frowned at the news story for a moment and then said, "You have some information for us about Commander Milne—is that it?"

"I only know he's dead," she said. "Murdered. I don't know where you'll find his body. Perhaps you won't."

With a glance of resignation toward his racket and white shoes the lieutenant said, "Try putting me in the picture, will you?"

"The only friends I had in Singapore," she began again, "took me to a party three weeks ago. Andrew Carson and Rob and Rosemary Milne. It was somewhat beyond Johore Bahru at a planter's bungalow, a sort of farewell party to Andrew Carson, who was sailing for home next day. We drove back across the Causeway not long past midnight and turned up the road to the Milnes' bungalow. And half-way along the road it happened."

A sentry marched past the window, his proud Malay profile dark against the glare of the sinking sun.

"A girl dashed across the road under our wheels. Just as if she'd never heard the car or seen the lights. Andrew swerved, and we all fell sideways, and then he stopped and he went back with Rob. They could see nobody and we drove on. Next day in the papers we saw that an Indian girl named Lakshami had been injured when a car ran her down along that road soon after midnight and had died before morning. The police were asking the driver to come forward."

His eyes made no response to the tension in hers.

"But that evening Andrew asked us all to his hotel and told

us he'd decided not to go to the police unless we insisted. Why? Well, he'd just finished three years of dodging terrorist ambushes and fighting communist bandits on a rubber estate in Selangor. His boat was sailing next day, and if he missed it while the police completed their inquiries and the inquest was held he wouldn't get another booking for weeks.

"He was a sick man, and the doctors who'd ordered him home wouldn't let him fly. So we agreed to keep quiet. As Andrew said, how would coming forward have helped anybody?

"And it was the girl's own fault, definitely. She didn't give him a chance; she ran out of the trees in front of us like a mad thing."

Martha closed her eyes. "I can see her now, like a shot from a color movie. A beautiful face, with hair blacker than darkness and a gold skin and gold sari and the most amazing eyes. I only saw her for a split second, but I'll remember her as long as I live."

Her hands went suddenly rigid. As long as I live. The echo of her own words had scared her. Then she made the deliberate effort again, and her hands relaxed.

"So Andrew embarked on the *Chusan* next morning. But that was as far as he got. He was taken ill suddenly while we saw him off and died in the ambulance that came to take him to the hospital. Some sort of food poisoning."

He only nodded to her to go on.

"Death by misadventure, they said. And they said it again the week after, when Rosemary Milne was drowned in her own swimming pool. Perfect health, no sign of struggle, but drowned in five feet of water, while her husband wrote letters twenty yards away.

"There was a gardenia hedge between him and the pool, so Rob didn't see the murderer creeping up while Rosemary drowsed on the water, the way she always did, and seizing her ankles and pulling her silently under."

Her eyes challenged the unbelief in his.

"So that's how I know Bob Milne is dead. He's been murdered. By the man who murdered Andrew and Rosemary. The man who's going to murder me."

"You mean, the husband of the Indian girl who was killed?"

"Yes." She added, "He'd only been married to her two days. His name is Daya Ram. He was a clerk at the East India Bank."

But he didn't even write down the name of the man who was

going to murder her. Instead he found a formula that would get her off his hands. He gave her the name and address of a senior officer. "He's the man you want to see. He'll know all about your case."

Just as she'd told herself a hundred times, the police wouldn't believe her. By the time she was outside, down on the hot pavement again, she had forgotten the senior officer's name . . .

Her flat was unbearable, the flat that was to have been home for Davy and her. One glance around the living room was enough to assure her that she could not spend that night there. She moved straight from the door to the telephone, called the Raffles Hotel and asked for a single room. For one night.

But the Raffles was fully booked. So were the only other hotels she knew of. Panic strode near, but inspiration came suddenly. She called the Tanjong Ru Nursing Home and asked for Jean Sanderson.

They put her through at once, and Martha pictured Jean, at ease in her bed, surrounded by flowers and books and the white phone and piles of letters from friends, not really ill but loving the ease of the fashionable nursing home after a month of nonstop parties celebrating her return from England. Martha had met her on the boat.

After Jean had replied at length to her opening inquiry, Martha asked, "Jean, I want to stay there, too. Can I come tonight?"

"*Dar*ling, I thought you sounded rather *diminuendo*," Jean exclaimed. "But there's not a hope. This place is always booked up weeks ahead. I only got in because four patients died in a row." She added, "But no chance of anybody dying tonight, I'm afraid."

Martha closed her eyes and shivered, despite the choking heat of the gathering storm. It hadn't broken yet and the piled-up suspense of the swollen clouds hanging in the darkness above the island was grimly oppressive.

The next moment she suddenly started telling Jean everything. Loneliness and fading courage had sprung the impulse on her, but the long silence as she came to a breathless finish told her she was going to regret it.

"But, *dar*ling!" Jean cried out at last. "Oh, of course it was terrible for you, losing two friends in tragic accidents one after the other, but if you let it prey on your mind like this you'll end

up by taking these gruesome nightmares seriously. Really you
mustn't!"

Martha didn't protest. Somehow she had half known that Jean
wouldn't be convinced, any more than the police officer had
been. "But I can't stay here, Jean," she declared unsteadily. "The
hotels are all full, and now I've no friends left. Only you."

Hesitantly Jean said, "There's my flat, darling, in Snowden
Court. You're welcome to go there, if it helps at all."

"Oh, yes!" Martha snatched at the offer. "May I tonight?
Now?"

"It'll be horribly cheerless," Jean warned.

"It'll be wonderful!" Martha cut in. "Number ten, Snowden
House, isn't it, and I take a taxi to Mowbray Road."

"Get the key from the caretaker," Jean said, "and if you find
your avenging bridegroom lying in wait behind the kitchen door
be sure to call up and tell me good-by before he gets down to
the strangling!"

With a breathless feeling of relief Martha rang off, ordered a
taxi, collected a few night things and Davy's photo from her
bedroom and fled.

For the next half-hour she methodically covered up her trail,
using four taxis, sidetracking and backtracking like a hunted fox.
When finally she let herself into Jean's fourth-floor flat she
slammed the door and leaned against it in the darkness, her
heart racing, her limbs trembling in the relief of escape.

For the night she was safe. Nobody could possibly have
tracked her through the web she had spun. And even if her
enemy were a yard behind her the lock and bolt on the stout
door would save her. The sheer drop below the windows would
defeat anything without wings.

For tonight she was safe and tomorrow Davy would be back.
Like a prisoner reprieved on the scaffold she whispered a small
prayer of thankfulness and then her hand found the light switch
and flicked it down.

Nothing happened.

She tensed again in the dark room, but realized almost at once
that the electricity would have been turned off at the main
switch when Jean left for the nursing home. That didn't entirely
relax her tension, though. Groping for the master switch in the
back quarters of the unfamiliar flat was something her body
refused to attempt until she had gathered all her resolution. And

then, just as she took a step forward, the storm at last opened
its preliminary bombardment.

There was a blinding flash, followed almost immediately by a
clap of thunder like a planet exploding. But it was neither the
flash nor the thunderclap that sent her reeling back against the
door again. It was the shadow she had glimpsed in the dark cave
beyond the open kitchen door!

She felt safety snatched from her, like a fur coat snatched from
naked shoulders in a blizzard. She didn't know if what she had
seen was real or imaginary; she only knew she hadn't nerve
enough to go into that kitchen.

There was a second lightning flash and it showed her the dark
space beyond the kitchen door empty. So it had been imagination. But her sigh of relief was interrupted by something that
hurled her back into terror again.

The big white electric lamp over her head flashed on.

In the same moment the storm burst like a gigantic hose
turned on the building. She stood blinking in the sudden light,
realizing that somebody must have thrown the master switch in
the kitchen, and then he appeared in the doorway.

The picture of him she had built up in her mind had been un-
cannily true. Those fine eyes, shadowed with suffering and
lighted with crazy hatred, were not the eyes of a stranger. The
handsome face, brown under the rich black hair, was one she
had glimpsed in a hundred waking nightmares. Even his voice,
raised above the roar of the deluge, was like a remembered
voice.

"We will go into that room, Miss Langley."

The revolver in his right hand gestured toward the sitting-
room door. She obeyed like a woman walking in her sleep. In
the long sitting room she took a chair he indicated and faced
him across a small table on which stood a vase of dead spider
lilies and the skeleton key he must have used to get in.

He looked at her, like a man face to face with Destiny, and
said nothing.

"Daya Ram?"

It was no question, really, and needed no answer. He only
said, "You understand, then."

She nodded slowly. She did understand. The grief, the loneliness, the fury, and then the madness. She understood it all.

He said, "I spent this afternoon in your flat, Miss Langley. I intended to have our little talk there, but when I heard you arranging with a friend to spend the night here I decided to come over and wait for you. Here we can be sure of not being disturbed."

"Disturbed?"

"If we are disturbed I shall have to cut our interview short." Breaking the revolver, he showed her two of the six chambers loaded. He looked down at the brass bases of the two bullets as if they were jewels and murmured dreamily, "One for you and then the other for me." After he'd closed the weapon again he said, "But first I want to talk to you."

"And I want to talk to *you*," Martha managed to say clearly. "You have murdered three friends of mine and now you want to murder me. What do you get out of it all?"

"Leave to die," he answered quietly, the liquid accent in his dreamy voice making the words sound like a line from a poem. "Leave to die."

The roaring madness of the storm outside almost drowned the quiet madness of his words. She found herself shaking her head and sighing, "None of them believed me."

"The police?" His full lips were contemptuous. "The police never helped me to find my wife's murderers and today, when you went to them, you found they would not help you. I'll tell you why. They thought you were mad. They thought I was mad, too."

She shivered, but nerved herself to say, "Why do you call me and my friends murderers? You know that isn't true."

He said in his faraway voice, "I know my Lakshami is in her grave and I know who was responsible."

"She was responsible herself," Martha protested. "She ran out right under our wheels. She must have been crazy."

He nodded. "Perhaps. Crazy with fear. An animal had attacked her in the darkness, a vile beast who had long desired her and hated her for her marriage to me. She escaped from him onto that road."

"Then isn't *he* your enemy? Isn't *he* responsible? If you must have revenge, why not on him?"

A naked light flashed in the fine eyes as he answered her. "He was the first—"

"Mr. Carson was driving carefully. He tried to avoid her, but there wasn't time. How can you blame us?"

"I only know," the soft voice lifted a little above a growl of thunder, "I only know that I was the happiest man in the world and that now I am the unhappiest, and you and your friends are why."

She was silent. He was so far beyond any reasoning she could advance. He had made a vow to wipe out those he judged responsible for the death of his bride and then he would kill himself. Already there was a sort of exaltation about him; the longed-for moment of release from life was so close. Within ten minutes now she would be dead and he, released from his vow, would have leave to die at last.

When the telephone bell cut suddenly through the uproar of the storm Martha started violently and for some seconds they stared at each other while the bell rang on.

"You may answer it," he said then.

She rose and crossed to the small table where the telephone stood and picked up the receiver.

It was Jean.

"Well, darling," came the bright, teasing voice, "was he lurking with murder in his eyes like I said?"

"Yes, Jean," she replied, "exactly like you said."

"Darling, you sound so odd." Jean's tone had changed. "Honestly, I don't like the idea of your glooming alone in that flat, so listen. Matron says I can break rules and have you along for a drink. Now."

Martha took a deep breath and said, "Afraid I can't come, Jean dear. Maybe they'll let you have my glass, too, and you could drink it for me. And when you see Davy say hello from me and all my love."

She rang off.

Only for a second had the phone seemed to offer a chance of rescue. Then she had realized that the moment she started calling for help the bullet would smack through her back. Even if help arrived, even if it got as far as the door, there would be only two bodies, still warm, on the Kashmiri carpet when the door opened.

When she sat again at the small table, in obedience to his gesture, there was a photograph lying on it between them. Once again Martha saw the flowerlike beauty of the face that had shot into the headlights of Andrew's car. Daya Ram was gazing at it with such consuming adoration that she could not bear to see it.

She asked, "Where is Commander Milne?"

"At the bottom of the sea," he told her. "I arranged a sailor's death for him."

"Poor Rob!" Her voice trembled. "And poor Rosemary! They had only two months together."

"We had only two days," he said softly.

"And you're not allowing me even that." As his dark brows rose in inquiry she told him, "I was to have been married the day after tomorrow."

His eyes stared deep into hers.

"Then you understand," he said slowly.

"Yes," she said, and that was true. She was learning now what loss meant, loss of all that gave life meaning. She felt strangely close to him, to the broken heart of him if not to the broken mind. She felt no hatred any more and now, suddenly, even her fear lost its sharpest edge. The first inklings of a plan were stirring in the dark coils of her mind.

The storm was moving south. From a distance over the harbor came a few muffled thunderclaps, like the sobs of a small child who has stopped crying. The downpour had lost its violence. To hope for help had been useless from the first. But could she yet help herself?

He looked at his watch.

"Two minutes more and the moon will rise," he said. "Then will be the moment for us to die. I made my vow as the moon rose and that is when I shall keep the last details of it."

Martha had a plan now, but had she nerve enough to stage it? She felt as if she were clinging to a narrow ledge over an abyss while violent winds fought to throw her down.

After closing her eyes and asking for strength she said, looking down at the photo of Lakshami. "I think she must have loved you very much." She stole a glance at him through her eyelashes. He held his left wrist arched and something told her that it was now the second hand of his watch that he was frowning over so closely.

The revolver rose and pointed at her breast.

"I think," she went on, still gazing down at the photo, "she must have been thinking of you in the moment that picture was taken. Don't you think so?"

And yes, she had guessed correctly. His eyes could not resist
the photograph, the face he had loved so tragically. They turned
for a last glance of agonized tenderness at its delicate beauty
and in the second Martha acted.

She sprang forward, and her hand, armed with despairing
strength, seized the gun. Before he could snap out of the trance
into which her words and the face of his lost bride had betrayed
him and summon his reserve of maniacal strength the black gun
had been wrested from his hold. Martha, closing her eyes, aimed
it at the window and fired a single shot.

A single shot. Then, as he came at her with his mad, tragic
face contorted, she turned the gun round and held it out to him.

When he snatched it from her she spun round, closed her eyes
again, clamped her hands over her ears and whispered, "Good-
by, Davy," in case it was goodby.

Suspense then, tearing a great wound in her consciousness for
three terrible seconds, and then she stiffened at the report of the
second shot.

A sob like a small child's burst her lips, and she stumbled to
the door, blind with tears and groping desperately for the
lock . . .

"You took a fearful chance," the gruff police officer protested
when she'd told her story half an hour later. "A fearful chance.
Passing a loaded gun to a homicidal maniac and turning your
back on him! Why didn't you throw it out of the window? Or
hold him up with it till my chaps got there? They'd just pulled
up their patrol car outside when you fired; after Mrs. Sanderson
rang the station I sent them along to see how you were."

Martha said, "I understood him, you see. He had two shots
left, one for me and one for himself—one for revenge and the
other for death. And I 'was sure he wanted death more than
revenge, if he couldn't have both.

"It seems an odd thing to say after what he did to my friends,
but when the time came I wanted to help him. So I fired the shot
he'd intended for me and . . . and gave him back the bullet
he'd saved for himself. Surely he's better off now than waiting
to be condemned to a lifetime in a madhouse."

"He was mad, all right," the officer put in grimly.

"It wasn't his mind I understood," she said quietly, "but his
heart. That was broken, too."

He didn't look sympathetic enough for her to complete her

explanation. It was quite a simple one, in fact. Merely that she loved as Daya Ram had loved.

And that night, when she had taken out again the golden future she had folded away and saw it stretch magically again before her, the future with Davy, she drifted smiling into sleep. But smiling on a tear-stained pillow.

Tears for three friends who wouldn't be at her wedding now. For three friends . . . and one enemy.

16

I. A. R. WYLIE

Crack-up at Curtain Time

IN A LONG CAREER of writing, Miss Wylie has
published some twenty-five novels, together with many
serials and short stories for the top magazines in this
country and in England. An Australian by birth, she
has long made her home here and she lives on a farm
not too far from New York. This story we liked particularly because of the sharp way it focuses on the conflict
of ambition and essential decency in the world of the
theatre.

SHE BLEW into the restaurant like a gust of high wind and
the celebrities, near-celebrities and celebrity-hunters with whom
the place was packed looked up at her. And continued to look.
Not that she was beautiful. No such term could be applied to
the blunt-featured, passionate young face and flaming hair. But
she was so ardently alive. Paul Bedlaw, seated in conspicuous
solitude at his habitual table, smiled an amused recognition. He
waved a long amber cigarette holder in her direction, and her
thunderous eyes, searching the crowd, incredulous of what they
could not find, came over to him, sulkily, like a puppy who has
had a tin can tied to its tail and is still mad.

He did not rise. "Lunching alone, Toughy?"

"The name is Francey Benson," she told him, scowling. "Anyhow, Mr. Bedlaw, you don't know me from a hill of beans."

"Oh, but I do. You've been Young Toughy to me ever since
you blew up on your lines in 'Eggs and Omelettes' and threw
a vase at the prompter. I mentioned it in my column. Sit down
and share my steak with me—unless you've really got a date."

"I had. It's stood me up." You didn't allow yourself to be
asked twice by Paul Bedlaw, not if you knew where you were
going, as she did. She didn't even allow the waiter to pull out
her chair for her. She pulled it out herself.

"Who is the date?" Bedlaw inquired lightly.

156

"Peter Carmichael."

"Ah, yes. He was in the 'Eggs and Omelettes' scramble, too. I remember writing that if Mr. Carmichael could learn to make himself audible he might go far—"

As though he had been conjured up by the sound of his own name a young man blundered his way to their table. He came to an abrupt halt. He was a large young man. He loomed. Paul Bedlaw sat back. He murmured fretfully, "Mr. Carmichael, I presume."

The newcomer took no notice of him. His face was scarlet and he was breathless and perspiring. For a moment at least he and the girl across the table were violently and exclusively aware of each other.

"Francey—I'm so darned sorry, I couldn't help it. Arnot sent for me. He kept me waiting. But he's given me a swell supporting part in 'Sunrise'—almost a lead."

"How nice!" she said venomously.

"Francey—I thought you'd be pleased, too."

"Mr. Carmichael," Paul Bedlaw interrupted, "scenes are for the theater—not for restaurants. Miss Benson, having graciously consented to share my steak with me—"

"Oh, go to hell," the young man interrupted rudely—"and take your steak. Francey, you know how much it means to me—"

"Sure. More than I do."

The boy's generous, impulsive mouth set in hard lines. "O.K. Eat his damned steak. After the show I'll be waiting for you. But I won't wait again. I swear I won't."

"Thanks for warning me."

The furious shadow receded. Bedlaw divided the steak precisely. "A violent young man. Rather unwise. A promising career can be wrecked by treading on critical toes—"

She said quickly, "You're not to lay for him, Mr. Bedlaw."

He considered her from under his heavy eyelids. "Why? Are you going to marry him?"

"He thinks so. I don't—not any more."

"How sensible. Theatrical marriages can be hell. You may make a team—like the Lunts. More likely one of you begins to pull ahead. Then over goes the apple cart. You'll travel faster in single harness, Toughy." He added whimsically, "Of course with a good driver at the reins."

She said sullenly, "I don't like that name."

"It isn't pretty. But then you aren't either. And you are tough, aren't you? You've got the theater in your blood. Nothing is going to stop you, is it?"

"No," she said between her teeth.

He was still appraising her. But now he was dead serious. "No—not beautiful. But you're like a flame-thrower. You'll carry across the lights and set fire to all the stuffed shirts and padded bosoms—even, maybe, a critic—if you get the chance."

"I'll never get the chance. Once an understudy," she said bitterly, "always an understudy."

"The understudy of Grace Manners has a whale of a chance."

"Of what?"

"Let us say—a crack-up."

She looked back smolderingly into the white old-young face. "What does that mean?"

"You know. You get around. She's been 'out' for three years. A nervous breakdown is the polite word for it. They're keeping her under lock and key and their fingers crossed. The merest trifle," he said gently, "would set her on the skids again. And then, my Toughy, it would be up to you."

"There won't be any trifle."

"Suppose there were?" His white, well-shaped hand rested briefly on hers. "You know, I've had my weather eye on you for a long time. It's part of a critic's job to pick winners—before they win."

She said scornfully, "She won't crack. Tonight's her last chance—"

"Suppose I were a magician? Suppose I made it your first big chance?"

"You could have my shirt," she told him passionately.

"That, my Toughy, I shan't ask of you. I have a shirt."

She shared a dressing room with stout old Maudie Roberts who had been famous in vaudeville days and now played only the smallest bit parts. Francey couldn't understand how anyone could accept ultimate defeat with such robust good humor. She'd never accept defeat. When her chance came, as it must come because she wanted it fiercely, she'd seize it with both hands and never let it go. Nothing—no one, would weaken her. Not even Peter. Not even loving him. It was a mistake to love anyone. Paul Bedlaw had said so. And he knew.

Maudie chattered incessantly. Hitherto the warm old voice had beaten unheeded against the girl's closed mind. Now suddenly the words concerned her. She had to listen.

"The skunk broke her heart. She'd made him more than he'd made her, and I guess he couldn't forgive. She began to drink to forget. Theater folk live on their nerves. When my old man died I went to pieces, too. If I didn't take to drink I guess it's my weak stomach I have to thank for it."

Maudie looked at her companion, affectionate and tolerant. Francey Benson was dressed as Grace Manners would be dressed, ready, at a moment's notice, to take her place. Once she'd taken it, she'd hold fast to it. Old Maudie knew her kind —young, hungry and ruthless. "We're all rooting for her, my dear. She's one of us. We all know what it's like to be down and out and to live for a comeback. You will, too—one of these days."

Someone tapped at the door, and it was as though the tension that held the whole theater on this opening night had clamped down upon these two women, too.

"Miss Benson—it's Miss Manners. She wants to see you."

Francey applied more lipstick. But her hand shook. "What does *she* want with me?"

"You'd best find out, my dear," Maudie said . . .

Francey stood defensively with her back to the door, behind the woman seated at the dressing table. They measured each other in the mercilessly lighted mirror. They were dressed alike in white Victorian ball gowns that showed their shoulders— young, radiant shoulders and shoulders heavily powdered, already faintly, ominously hollowed. Francey had never seen the worn gray face without its brilliant make-up that made them almost of an age and so singularly alike. It was as though she were confronted with a ghastly, mocking travesty of herself.

"Sit down, Francey. Please. Don't stand there staring at me. You look like a ghost—my own ghost. Did they choose you, I wonder, to haunt me?" She gave a little laugh. It did not reach the burnt-out eyes. "To keep me sober?"

Francey took the chair by the door, sitting stiffly upright, like a wary, uneasy child. But she could still see that gray and tense reflection. She was suddenly angry. It was almost an indecency to flaunt decay so nakedly.

"I'm frightened," Grace Manners said. "Any actress who is worth her salt is frightened." She was trying to speak casually, calmly, but the fear shook her. "A first night is an ordeal by fire. But some of us can outlive failure. I can't." She stretched out her hand for a cigarette. It was a white hand, already veined and slightly puffy. "I had to talk to someone." Her voice was husky—a whisky voice, Paul Bedlaw had called it cynically— but it still had its heartbreaking warmth. "I had to talk to you—"

"But why?"

"It will be like talking to myself. You *are* myself, you know, waiting on the doorstep for the door to open. One night it opened for me. One night it will open for you. But, please God —just not tonight."

"Miss Manners, I ought to go. You haven't much time—"

"So little—don't take it from me."

"I—I don't understand—"

"But you do—you must. I'm not old—only a few long years older than you are. Do you think I've forgotten what it felt like to be you? I, too, waited in the wings and prayed God to strike another woman down for me. And one night God answered—as He might answer you. I didn't even feel a twinge of pity. I hardened my heart. That was my great mistake. Hard hearts are brittle; they break easily."

"She's crazy," Francey thought scornfully. But she was shaken by an unreasoning panic.

Suddenly the slender, white-clad figure turned on her. "Wish me luck, Francey. Please. Those people out there are waiting for me to fall and break my neck. It will be something for them to talk, laugh and write about. But you—to whom it would mean so much—help me."

"What can *I* do?"

"Don't—don't pray against me. Don't wish me harm. Don't want so much to take my place. You will—quite soon, perhaps. But don't let it be tonight."

She was actually pleading, humbly, with the urgency of anguish. "You're strong. No one yet has hurt and broken you. Have pity. Remember that one day you may be sitting where I am sitting. You will know, perhaps, that there is someone out in front—someone whom you loved and trusted with your life— waiting to laugh and shrug his shoulders and be at last quit of you. That someone young and unhurt is at your back and waiting too. You will long for just one hand to be stretched out in reassurance and good will. You will be so terribly alone."

They hadn't heard the knock or the opening of the door. A stage hand set a great basket of red roses beside the dressing table.

"There's a special message for you, Miss Manners. You were to be sure to read it—now."

The man was gone.

At the heart of the roses was something hard and darkly glittering. As though drawn by an invisible magnet Grace Manners lifted the secret thing from its ambush. To the golden neck of the champagne magnum a red ribbon held an open card. She read aloud from it, her voice sick and broken. "A greeting from an old admirer. A farewell stirrup-cup."

She was on her feet now, shaken by wild laughter. "I didn't know he hated me so much." She held the thing high in both hands. She looked, Francey thought, already drunk and disrupted.

"Well, why not? Only *he* knows how much I need it. Pour one out for me, Francey. They say the Borgias poisoned their enemies with nectar served in gold goblets. We haven't a gold goblet, have we? But there must be something—"

Francey had taken the bottle from her. She had strong, sure hands. The foam poured over them. So this was what Paul Bedlaw had meant. "I'll be out there beating my hands to ribbons for you. My piece will be already written. Tomorrow it will welcome a newly risen star."

She held out the brimming glass. Then suddenly she emptied it on the floor. She emptied the whole bottle so that she stood forlornly yet somehow triumphantly, in the midst of a dark, widening stain.

"I *do* wish you luck. Go in and win."

At eleven-thirty it was over. There was no need for Francey to wait. The cheers followed her into the stage-door alley and Paul Bedlaw waited for her in the midst of a crowd still cheering Grace Manners' success. Bedlaw's dead white face was like a clown's mask under the brilliant lights. "What happened? What went wrong?"

She stood quiet for a moment, considering him. "Nothing.

She sent a message. She thanked you—for your vote of confidence."

"Listen, Toughy—"

"The name," she said gravely, "is Francey. Just Francey Benson." She brushed past him. But now she was smiling to herself —"And I have a date."

17

Q. PATRICK

Murder in the Alps

LIEUTENANT TRANT, the suave young New York detective who is the protagonist of this story, has appeared in a good many short stories and mystery novels. His specialty is murder, and the fact that he is on holiday in Switzerland when this story opens is no handicap to him in quickly reaching the solution of the crime. Q. Patrick, like Ellery Queen, is the pseudonym of a pair of authors who also write under the name of Patrick Quentin.

YOUNG LIEUTENANT TRANT of the New York Homicide Bureau sat in the palm lounge of Switzerland's most elegant winter sports resort, feeling bored. Around him, international skiers, turned night owls, were dancing and laughing as if Europe were still a playground. In the third week of a month's vacation, Trant was tired of mountain climbing, glamour and skis. His one authentic enthusiasm—his passion for murderers—had been starved.

He watched the dancers, hoping rather wistfully that one of them would drop dead under mysterious circumstances.

Jimmie, the British ski instructor, paused at his table, bringing with him a strong smell of liniment. Trant, who had his own aches and pains, asked sympathetically, "Hello, Jimmie. How's the arm?"

"Still somewhat painful, sir."

Jimmie, with his sun-bleached hair and lazy smile, had been imported by an astute management to make the British clientele feel "at home abroad." He was the dream boy of the English guests, particularly the female ones, and knew it. He was also colorfully informed as to the gossip of the Hotel St. Laurent. Trant, who took an unorthodox interest in the backstairs of life, had made the Yorkshire-born ski instructor his particular crony.

"And what of our girl friend and company tonight, Jimmie?"

He nodded across the lounge to a corner table where two young men and two girls, well sun-tanned, were making a stormy but striking quartet.

"Lady Mavis' party, sir?" Although Jimmie's speech and presence would have done credit to a duke, his British training kept him invariably respectful. "I'm afraid trouble may be brewing again, sir."

"Trouble," remarked Lieutenant Trant, "is something which Lady Mavis Marriner carries around like a pocketbook."

Jimmie grinned. "She is a bit of what you might call a magnet, sir."

"A magnet for males."

Trant alerted, for at the other side of the palm lounge the blonde had risen in apparent pique. Turning her back contemptuously on her companions, she skirted the dancers and made her way to Trant's table. She sat down and gave him a blinding smile which she then switched to Jimmie.

"Jimmie, darling, be an angel and rescue my pocketbook from those dreary people." As Jimmie hurried obediently off, Lady Mavis, England's prettiest, wealthiest and probably most irritating bright young thing, moaned to Trant: "Darling, be nice to me. You're the only bearable male in Switzerland."

Lieutenant Trant, whose taste in women was also unorthodox, felt a certain weakness for Lady Mavis although, apart from a torrid physical appeal, she had nothing to recommend her. She was both silly and selfish and, although she worked overtime to fascinate every man in sight, she remained—he was sure—technically as virtuous as a police matron.

"What's the trouble tonight, Mavis?"

She shrugged. "My dear, so stupid. Just because that divine Larry Howard happens to think I have a talent for the films, Carlos smolders. And that revolting Claire Howard. Really, she thinks I'm trying to steal her husband! So vulgar and American of her."

From this rambling statement, the experienced police officer in Trant deduced that Lady Mavis, who was currently engaged to the Mexican playboy, Carlos Villanueva, had been vamping the multimillionaire Hollywood producer, Larry Howard, thus infuriating both Howard's wife and her own fiancé.

"Really," continued Mavis, batting her huge lashes and looking almost unbearably luscious, "jealous people are so dismal. Let's dance."

Lady Mavis' dancing was an expert seduction. Sinuous in Trant's arms and headily perfumed with *Tantalizing*, she murmured: "You really are intriguing. So mysterious. I'm sure you do something fascinating."

Trant, who knew he was being exploited merely to make Carlos Villanueva and the "divine" Larry Howard that much more dismally jealous, grinned at her affectionately.

"I'm only clay in the potter's hands."

They went back to the table. Jimmie had brought Lady Mavis' pocketbook. Mavis dazzled at him.

"Jimmie, you're a duck. Please be a lamb and wax my skis. We're starting early tomorrow and I've got to have them done tonight."

Jimmie, all ducal gallantry, said: "Of course, Lady Mavis."

"They're in the cabin. My maid will let you in. Just bring them back and put them on the porch when they're done."

As Jimmie disappeared, Mavis said to Trant: "There's still nothing like English service, is there? Darling, let's dance again."

Lady Mavis danced long and shamelessly enough with Trant to drive her erstwhile companions, one after the other, from the lounge.

Having achieved her objective, she withdrew in pursuit of other game. Trant got trapped into an emotional chess match with the hotel manager and it was one-fifteen before he escaped to his own elegant front room. As he opened the window, an eccentric mountain squall roared in from the darkness outside, scattering everything off the tables and toppling a lamp. He started to restore order, reflecting that Lady Mavis was like a Swiss wind gust. She too toppled everyone in her path . . .

He awoke next morning at nine to an agitated Swiss voice saying: "*M'sieur . . . M'sieur.*"

It was the assistant manager announcing anxiously that the manager wanted him immediately in Lady Mavis' chalet. When they reached the little lodge, cradled in pine trees, which was the hotel's most expensive accommodation, they found the manager alone in the living room, looking distracted.

"M. Trant. *Mon Dieu,* I need the policeman. Lady Mavis disappear."

He told Trant what he knew. Lady Mavis' Paris-imported maid had come, as usual, from the servants' wing, to make morning tea at seven and had found the chalet empty. She was familiar with all of Mavis' clothes and was sure that none of them were missing except the red velvet dress she had worn the night before.

Ignoring the hovering assistant manager, the manager concluded: "Ah, M. Trant, if I telephone the *préfecture* there is perhaps the unnecessary *scandale*. But you, *Monsieur*—one hears of your so great reputation with the unpleasantnesses of America."

Trant, modestly silent, began to search the room and then moved into the bedroom. The bed was neatly made. The heavy plate glass window was shut. The wrap Lady Mavis had worn the night before was slung over a chair. There was an overpowering—even for Mavis—odor of *Tantalizing*. A glance at the dressing-table showed a bottle of the perfume almost empty. Intrigued, Trant traced the odor to an area by a deep, blue armchair where it seemed at its strongest. He dropped to his knees and observed a faint darkish stain on the flowered carpet. It was still a trifle damp. He discovered a similar smaller stain on a pillow from the sofa in her room.

"*Alors*, is it blood?" asked the manager.

"I don't think so." Trant moved to the window, pushed it up and peered intently at the sill. He gave a little grunt. "Look."

At his side, the manager looked. Caught on a wood splinter was a scrap of red velvet.

Trant gazed soberly down the steep sloping bank to a large snowdrift among the pines. A few minutes later, he, the manager and the assistant manager, with shovels, discovered Lady Mavis in the snowdrift—dead.

Crouched by the body, Trant felt a cosmic pity for Lady Mavis and all other foolish young women who reap what they sow.

"I'm afraid that she's been murdered. Probably smothered by a pillow from the sofa in her room," he added sadly.

But only part of him was sad. The other part was musing on Mavis' murderer as a hungry owl might muse on a mouse . . .

They moved around the side of the chalet to its little front porch which faced away from the hotel's façade toward the glistening Alps. Mavis' skis were balanced precariously against the wall. Since the *"scandale"* was now inevitable, the assistant manager was commissioned to telephone Lausanne.

Trant remarked almost plaintively: "Now the police are coming, you won't need me."

"But yes, *Monsieur.*" The manager was wringing his hands. "All the way from Lausanne they must come. And such questions, such crudities . . . Ah, please."

Trant beamed and called after the assistant manager: "Send Jimmie, and his roommate."

Soon Jimmie arrived with one of the Swiss ski instructors. From their distraught faces, it was plain they had been told the news.

Trant said: "Did you wax Lady Mavis' skis last night, Jimmie?"

"Yes, sir."

"When did you bring them back?"

"At one, sir."

"What did you do?"

"I knocked. Lady Mavis answered she was going to bed—to leave them on the porch."

"Then what?"

"I went to my room, sir."

Trant turned to the Swiss ski instructor. "You check on that?"

"Yes, sir. I wake up when Jimmie comes in. We sit a while to talk."

"What time was it?"

"Just after one, sir." He glanced at the large silver watch on his wrist. "I look at my watch when I wake up."

At that moment the assistant manager returned with a little old man whom Trant recognized as the night bus boy. The assistant manager said:

"*Monsieur,* André has something to say."

"Ah, *Monsieur,*" began André. "*C'est terrible. C'est . . .*"

"Speak English," said the manager severely, "in front of the distinguished detective."

André announced: "Last night at one-thirty sounds the buzz-buzz from the chalet of Lady Mavis. I hurry here. I knock. Answers a man's voice in English: *Is all right. Only Lady Mavis has trouble with the window. Now is fixed.* I say: Okay, I leave."

"One-thirty." Trant watched him. "What was this man's voice like?"

"From a foreign land. Not from England. Not from France. Heavy with foreign accent."

The manager flung up his hands. "Ah, she is engaged to the Mexican gentleman."

Trant made no comment. He stood a moment reflectively. Then he said: "I'm going to need an assistant. Since Lady Mavis' murderer was certainly here at one-thirty, Jimmie is alibied. Can I have him?"

"But of course, *Monsieur*."

Trant patted Jimmie's arm. "Find Mr. and Mrs. Howard and Mr. Villanueva. Tell them the manager wants to see them in his office. And use that well-known tact."

In the manager's chic office, Trant and the manager questioned the three suspects.

Mrs. Claire Howard, a vivid red-headed ex-actress with a knife for a tongue, said:

"I'm prostrated by grief. couldn't be sorrier if the python at the Bronx Zoo kicked the bucket."

Although she made no effort to conceal her resentment of Mavis' behavior with her husband, she was firmly alibied by the testimony of an elderly Italian prima donna who swore she had been telling Mrs. Howard's fortune between one and one-thirty.

Larry Howard was more conventionally distressed than his wife. He fussed with his hand-painted tie, looked more like a movie idol than any of the stars on his payroll and kept repeating: "So tragic . . . such a lovely girl . . . so gifted . . ."

He too had what seemed like a perfect alibi. After leaving the palm lounge the night before, he had run into a big-game-hunting friend and had spent the significant time period in the hunter's suite, discussing the most sportsmanlike way of killing a zebra. The hunter corroborated this.

After these two had apparently cleared themselves, Carlos Villanueva was pitifully without defense. The elegant, mournful-eyed Mexican denied having been in his fiancée's chalet but had absolutely no alibi. All he could say for himself was that, humiliated by Mavis' shameless flirtation with Larry Howard, he had paced the moonlit mountainside for hours in an attempt to console himself.

"But Mavis was my heart," he announced with Latin fervor. "You cannot accuse me of murdering my *corazon*."

After he had gone, Trant no longer looked bored. In fact there was a gleam of pleasurable anticipation in his eyes. The manager said: "So we are left with this Villanueva, yes? No alibi—the foreign accent, not of England, not of France."

"Foreign accents can be assumed," suggested Trant mildly. "And it's too early to talk of alibis."

The manager looked alarmed. "You mean others of my guests could have killed her?"

"They could have killed her," Trant agreed, "but they didn't."

"Monsieur, you do not tell that you know who is this murderer!"

"Oh, yes," murmured Trant with an exasperatingly casual shrug, "I've suspected it for half an hour. Now I'm sure."

The manager stared. "*Zut!*" he said . . .

The manager, now in a state of blind adoration, fell in with Trant's requests. They were simple. He merely wanted to interview the three suspects individually in Lady Mavis' chalet. While the assistant manager went off to arrange this, Trant stationed the night bus boy in Mavis' bathroom with instructions to emerge if he heard the foreign voice he had heard the night before. Once he was at his post, Trant and his assistant moved into Lady Mavis' bedroom. Trant sat down, lit a cigarette and offered one to Jimmie.

"Mr. Howard's coming first, Jimmie. When he arrives, I want you to wait in the living room in case I need help."

"Very well, sir."

Trant's gray eyes were pensive. "Jimmie, you've had plenty of experience with rich women on Swiss vacations. You can help me on a point of psychology. A lot of them throw their bonnets over the Alps, don't they?"

Jimmie grinned. "They're apt to be in a holiday mood, sir."

"Exactly. But Lady Mavis was different. That's the point about her. She vamped like Salome but when the time came to crash through, it's my hunch she went colder than a Pilgrim mother."

"That's how I'd sum her up, sir."

"All right, Jimmie, before Mr. Howard arrives, let's assume for a moment that I'm the murderer." Trant smiled contentedly at this hypothesis. "Lady Mavis certainly hurled her all at me last night. Suppose I'd taken her up on it and come here to the chalet expecting a Big Romantic Moment. What would I have got? The don't-touch-me-you-nasty-man routine.

"Suppose I was vain, used to easy conquests. Suppose I got rough. Suppose she rang for the bus boy. Suppose I was married for example, and realized what an awkward spot I'd be in if the bus boy reported an attempted assault to the manager. Say I put the pillow from the sofa over Mavis' face to keep her from calling out when the bus boy knocked, planning to reason with her later and to calm her down. Okay. The bus boy came.

"I invented some trouble with the window to explain the ring and to get rid of him. Later—after André had gone—I realized to my horror that I had been rougher than I thought. I had smothered Lady Mavis."

Trant looked at his own hands as if they were the hands of a smotherer.

"There was Lady Mavis lying in the chair—dead. I got into a panic. Wouldn't death from smothering look very like death from exposure? If I dropped the body out of the window and closed the window, she might not be found in the snowdrift for some time and, when she was found, they might think she'd died accidentally from exposure. At least it was safer than leaving her there in the armchair. How's that fit, Jimmie?"

Jimmie's blue eyes had widened. "It fits, sir. But what about the foreign accent?"

"Oh, I left out a couple of details. The accent, for example. And the spilled perfume." Trant nodded to the stained area on the carpet. "The perfume's simple. There was that stain on the rug and on the pillow from the sofa. Although the murderer was rattled, he knew he had to remove them. He used the perfume, but I'm afraid he didn't completely succeed. The police analysis will show what the stain is."

"What is it, sir?"

Lieutenant Trant rose. Suddenly he seemed depressed.

"He was rather a vain murderer. As the glamour boy of the Hotel St. Laurent, he was used to conquests. He thought that Lady Mavis, with her 'darlings' and 'angels,' should be as much of a pushover as the others. It must have been humiliating when he came into this chalet last night as a Don Juan to find that Lady Mavis just thought of him as a presumptuous under-

ling. It was frightening, too, to know that she was going to
report him to the manager. That would have meant a quick
end to an excellent job."

Jimmie sprang to his feet.

"But the stain rather gave him away," continued Trant quietly.
"The small one on the pillow probably smeared off your strained
arm. But the one on the rug—I suppose a tube of the stuff
dropped out of your pocket and got stepped on in the struggle.
You had to use that perfume, didn't you, not only to remove the
stain but to kill the smell of liniment."

"But . . ."

"The skis gave you away too, Jimmie. You say you put them
on the porch at one o'clock. The porch faces in the same direction as my room. Last night at one-fifteen there was a wind
squall which scattered my things. Certainly it would have toppled those precariously balanced skis. No, you brought the skis
in here first and took them out onto the porch after you'd killed
Lady Mavis—after the wind squall at one-fifteen.

"And I'm afraid your neat alibi can be broken too. Your
roommate said he woke up when you came in. He woke up because you deliberately awakened him, didn't he? But before
you awakened him, you switched the hands of his watch. It was
easy to stay awake yourself until he fell asleep again and then
to turn the hands forward to the correct time."

The ski instructor's ducal composure had fled and with it his
elegant accent. He was a frightened little mill boy again and,
lapsing into a broad Yorkshire dialect, he cried:

"Yer caan't say thaat a'me, zur. She war craazed fur me. She
assked me ter coom oop. Ah didn't knaw . . . Ah didn't meean
her—"

The bus boy burst out of the bathroom. "That is it!" he announced. "Is the same foreign voice I hear last night."

Jimmie swung to him. "Eh, maan, yer caan't—"

"That's all we needed," interrupted Trant quietly. "People
almost always revert to their natural dialect when they're rattled, Jimmie. No wonder André thought that Yorkshire brogue
of yours was a foreign accent."

He nodded the bus boy out of the chalet. Alone with Jimmie,
he felt a twinge of sadness.

He said: "You didn't mean to kill her. I'm sure of that and

I'll do everything I can when the police come. I'm sorry, Jimmie.
I set a trap for you. I feel like a heel."

Jimmie had managed to turn himself into the model hotel
employee again. He smiled a ghost of his engaging smile.

"That's all right, sir. After all, it's your job, sir."

There were times when Lieutenant Trant took a low view of
his profession.

This was one of them.

18

KEM BENNETT

Death at Attention

DURING WORLD WAR II, Kem Bennett was a
British Army major who worked extensively with the
Resistance because of his flawless knowledge of French-
men's French. He was parachuted into France on occasion or landed by plane at night on secret Maqui airfields. Since the war he has devoted his entire time to
writing, sometimes in England, occasionally for long
stretches on Spain's Costa Brava. He now lives with his
wife and two small children in Sussex.

AS THE FREIGHT TRAIN slowed down, clattering noisily over a
maze of points at the approach to a marshaling yard, a corner
of the tarpaulin covering one of the cars lifted and a head poked
up cautiously to stare into Birmingham's yellowish night.

Presently, satisfied that there were no witnesses, the owner
of the head heaved himself up over the side. He reached in to
pull out a small black Gladstone bag, paused for a calculating
second and jumped. He hit the oil-blackened cinder track along-
side the rails, stumbled and recovered himself expertly.

Then, crouching, he ran swiftly across the tracks until he
reached an eight-foot wall over which he threw his bag. He
leaped, caught the top of the wall and chinned himself before
throwing a leg sideways. In an instant he was on the other side
of the wall in a murky slum street. Acrobatic.

The man dusted off his clothes and bent, searching for the
bag he had thrown over the wall. The beam of a flashlight came
across the narrow street from a doorway on the other side,
pinning him in its glare. A calm voice said, "Looking for something, mate?"

Fanatic's eyes glared with anger and hatred at the light. The
man was red-haired and plain-featured; high cheekbones, colorless eyebrows and lashes, a thin, wicked mouth. Only his eyes

were other than ugly; they were fiercely alive, dominating the face beneath them. "I dropped a bag," he snarled.

"Dropped's the word! Nearly brained me with it, mate." The young policeman moved out from the doorway, flashlight in one hand and the bag in the other. He was big and imperturbable and confident. "What were you doing on railway property?"

"Taking a short cut."

The policeman smiled; a sorrowful smile, bulging with disbelief. "Tell it to the magistrate. I'm running you in for trespassing with suspicion of felony."

Redhead's thin mouth opened to argue, twisting itself into a reluctant smile which was belied by the naked anger in the eyes above it. The policeman shook his head. "Don't tell me I can't do it, mate, because I can. Now, what's your name and ad—"

It was a swift whiplash of a punch which came streaking out of the darkness. It caught Police Constable Baron accurately in the solar plexus. Air rushed from his lungs, and searing pain doubled him up. Redhead swooped to seize his bag but found it gripped irremovably. Winded or not the policeman was a fighter.

Viciously, Redhead yanked at the bag. The strength of the big policeman's clutching hand alarmed him. He hit out again. Once, twice—quick, vicious blows to the face which jerked the policeman's head back with blood flowing from bruised lips.

Abandoning the bag, Redhead turned to run. His footsteps clattered and resounded in the deserted alley. Baron staggered in pursuit, arriving at a road junction some fifty yards away ten seconds after the man had turned. The street was empty.

Baron cursed under his breath. Clean getaway. He was humiliated and angry. He had taken Redhead for a sneak thief, and sneak thieves were generally respectful of policemen . . .

Sergeant Martin looked up as his subordinate entered the police station. He saw the worn Gladstone bag in Baron's hand, and his beefy, butcher's face beamed. But he wiped off the smile and listened sympathetically when Baron told his story. Then he made a telephone call, circulating a description. Prowling police cars in the city began to keep an eye out for redheaded men who presumed to lay violent hands on a copper.

The hunt—a middling sized, routine kind of hunt—was up.

When Martin had finished he put down the telephone. "What you got, Charlie?"

Police Constable Baron had been sticking his nose into the Gladstone bag. He had a matchbox in one hand and a gray-painted iron plate about six inches in diameter in the other. "Tools," he said. "And these." He laid the matchbox open on the desk. Sergeant Martin stared doubtfully at two slim aluminum cylinders lying in a bed of cotton wool.

"Detonators." Baron had been an Airborne sergeant in Hitler's war.

Sergeant Martin frowned, seeing safes in his mind's eye and trying to reconcile Redhead's description with that of one or two known cracksmen. It didn't fit.

Baron read Martin's thoughts. He shook his head. "I don't think so, Sarge. Mechanic's tools these are, not safe-breaker's."

In a dubious silence the two policemen stared at the detonators. Little things. Inoffensive to look at. Not what a respectable mechanic carries in his tool bag, though.

Baron blew his sore nose tenderly and remembered the vicious desperation of the man with red hair. "If you ask me, Sarge," he said suddenly, "we ought to give the railway people a call. Ask 'em what trains they've had through during the last hour or so."

Sergeant Martin was a sound, old-fashioned policeman, content to take a tip from a better brain. He promptly reached for the phone and dialed a number. There was a wait. Presently he asked a question. Papers crackled at the other end of the line . . . *mumble, mumble.* Martin listened, grunting uninterestedly as a list was read out to him.

Suddenly he said: " 'Old it! Say that again." The man said it again. Martin murmured his thanks and replaced the receiver. A worried frown crumpled his big red face.

"Eleven forty-eight through the yards," he said. "Ammunition train consigned to the naval dockyard at Portsmouth: loaded with depth charges. Cor! You don't think the geezer could 'ave been fiddlin' with a trainload of depth charges, do you, Charlie?"

Birmingham Police headquarters heard Sergeant Martin's report and instantly phoned Scotland Yard in London. They talked

to the Special Branch, who occupy themselves with matters
such as sabotage and treason. The Special Branch listened with
flattering intensity. They had heard of Redhead.

It was their considered opinion that the trainload of depth
charges had better be investigated. They would send an expert.
Meanwhile, the Special Branch suggested, it would be a fine
thing if Redhead could be picked up. Would Birmingham
please make every effort in that direction?

Birmingham acted. The railway stations suddenly swarmed
with policemen. Vehicles on the way out of the city found themselves being flagged down so that sternly polite men could peer
and probe at their contents. Certain addresses, furnished by the
Special Branch in a hushed conspiratorial voice, were raided or
watched. It became a wearisome thing to be known to have
certain strong political opinions in Birmingham that night . . .

The village with the picturesque name of Bishop's Itchington
lay about thirty miles to the southeast of Birmingham. At one
o'clock in the morning it was usually quite dark and quite silent: not on this particular morning, however. Fate had parked
destruction upon its threshold, and it was feverishly alive.
Lights shone from all the cottages. There were coaches parked
in lines on three sides of the green. Uniformed police helped
the cottagers to move their smallest and most precious possessions.

When Major Peter Paradine Harcourt arrived just after half-
past one, only a single coach remained. Silence hung over the
village again—the silence of abandonment, oppressive and
charged with apprehension. He told his driver to pull up behind the coach. As he got out of the car, he saw a thin, uniformed police superintendent hurrying the last of the still
bewildered villagers into the coach. Then the driver started the
engine, and the superintendent slammed the door.

"Good evening," Harcourt said.

The superintendent wheeled. "Good evening. I didn't see you
arrive. You're Major Harcourt from the Special Branch?"

"Employed by it—for my sins."

"My name's Benbow. Officer in charge."

They shook hands. Harcourt, a big, burly man in a tweed
suit, enveloped Benbow's slim fingers with a great hand which
was warm and dry and hardened by the handling of tools.
"Where is the wretched thing?" he asked.

"Standing on the line about five hundred yards away. The train should never have been stopped so close to a village, but once the engine driver heard what he was pulling, he stopped it dead and rushed away muttering that he was going to complain to his union. One can't really blame him."

Harcourt's laugh was big, matching his physical immensity. "Sometimes I wish I had a union myself; tonight, for example."

The police officer's smile appeared again. It changed his face, wiping away the austerity which responsibility and conscientiousness had graven in the features. "When will the thing go off?" he asked.

Harcourt shrugged. "I can't tell, but if a man takes the risk of sabotaging a trainload of depth charges it's probable that he'll want to get his money's worth. If I'd done the job I would have set the delay so that the explosion would take place where it would do most damage."

"In the dockyard at Portsmouth?"

"Why not? It would be just as easy to arrange it that way. Anyhow, if the man only intended to destroy the depth charges they would have gone up within half an hour of his leaving the train—and they haven't, so we're safe in assuming that they won't until the time when the train should have arrived at Portsmouth. Between ten and eleven tomorrow morning."

"*Safe* in assuming?" Benbow's right eyebrow was climbing up his forehead. "You and I have different ideas of safety!"

His companion's big shoulders shrugged. "In my business I have to weigh what evidence I have and decide whether it's worth trying to investigate. In this case I've decided that I have ten hours' grace. If I'm wrong I shall know very little about it."

Major Harcourt turned and walked back to his car, which looked as swift and powerful as a fighter aircraft. He took a knapsack, heavy with tools, from the back seat and slung it over one shoulder; then a powerful electric lantern with two reflectors, one to make a beam, the other to spread a diffused light.

Lastly he went round to the luggage compartment and took out a black box like an electrical circuit tester. "Microphonic gadget," he explained, pointing to the box. "If it's a clockwork mechanism I shall hear it with that and be back in no time. On the other hand, if it's some sort of chemical time fuse, it could take me hours . . . Let's pray it'll be a clock."

Benbow nodded, then took off his cap and wearily rubbed

his forehead with a long-fingered hand. He looked like a tired musician forced into uniform by the pressure of some great emergency. Certainly he was not a usual type of policeman. "Are you sure you don't want any help?" he asked.

Harcourt smiled at him. "Don't be offended if I say it's not a job for amateurs. I'm a professional. God knows why, because it would seem to be a profession with little future in it. Force of habit, I suppose. I started to play with unexploded bombs early in the war and I've never stopped."

Harcourt turned toward the car. The driver was sitting alert and silent at the wheel. "Beat it down the road a bit, Bates," Harcourt instructed. "If I make a bloomer your car might get bent, and that'd break your little heart, I know."

Bates grinned. "Sooner stick around, sir, if I may."

"Well, put the car somewhere safe and come back here, but keep away from the train."

"Yessir."

Harcourt picked up his black box and lantern. "What's the best way to the train?"

"Along this road until you come to a bend, then over the fence and across the fields."

Harcourt nodded. "If I'm not back in an hour, make yourself comfortable because you'll have a long wait."

Benbow stood by the driver's window and watched Major Harcourt stride away, huge and confident and competent. The big man's walk was buoyant, and Benbow shook his head admiringly. "Major Harcourt is either a fool, or he believes in God," he said to Bates. "And I'm sure he's not a fool." . . .

Police Constable Baron was sitting at a table in the office of Birmingham's Chief Constable. He was glad of the chance to sit down because his bruised solar plexus ached and it hurt him to breathe. All the same, he did not begrudge the need to work into the small hours of the morning.

Five minutes passed in silence before the Chief Constable's brittle, incisive voice clipped across the room. Baron waited, looking respectfully attentive.

"He's not in any of the hideouts the Special Branch gave us," the Chief Constable said, thinking aloud rather than dispensing information. "He's not in any of the hotels, or pubs, or doss houses or cafés. He's not been seen in the railway stations nor in any vehicle leaving Birmingham. Where do you think he is, Baron?"

Baron frowned. It was not every day that he was asked for an opinion by his Chief Constable, who was quick to commend intelligence but even quicker to wipe the grin off the face of a fool. Baron knew that this was a critical moment in his career. "If he was a Birmingham man, I'd say he'd be at home," he said. "But he wasn't a Birmingham man. His accent was a mile off. That being so, if I'd been him, I'd've taken meself off as quick as I could."

"By rail?"

"I don't see why not, sir. Four trains left during the time between his escape and the alarm being raised."

The Chief Constable leaned back in the big Tudor chair which was his one and only attempt to relieve the stark efficiency of his office. "Special Branch think he'll be bound for Portsmouth. They are sure that he set a mechanism so that it would explode when the train arrived at the dockyard, and they think he'll want to be in the city to observe the damage after the explosion."

"He'll not get there tonight, sir," Baron commented. "Not by rail; no connection."

"Precisely what I was thinking." The Chief Constable's voice had softened. "If he's trying to get to Portsmouth by train, he can go by Oxford, arriving at seven-fifty, or through London, arriving at eight-forty."

Baron thought hard and took a risk. "Had I better go to Portsmouth and wait for those two trains, sir?"

The Chief Constable smiled at him, knowing exactly what he had been thinking. "Yes. We'll lay on a car for you with a good driver. If you make it a pinch at Portsmouth I'll put you up for promotion." . . .

Major Harcourt walked steadily until he reached the bend in the road and then crossed to climb over the fence. On the other side he found himself in a damp mushroom-dotted pasture and he set off in the direction of the stationary train. Hereabouts the track was slightly embanked so that the dark silhouette of the train loomed above him against the night sky. Everything was still. The moon, high in its orbit, was shining silver upon the earth, making even a freight train look beautiful.

Harcourt stopped near the train to grind his cigarette out under his heel; no more cigarettes for an hour or two. The loaded cars waited for him patiently, looking as commonplace as a row of suburban houses—thirteen of them, he counted. Unlucky number. The silence was oppressive, sitting in his ears like cotton wool. He shouted in order to reassure himself. "Which of you, you black beggars?"

The silence mocked him. "Guess," it said.

He went to the car nearest to him and yanked with his great hand at the ties of the tarpaulin. The rotten rope snapped. He stared at his hand. It was shaking. Excitement. At the beginning excitement always stirred him. It was later, when weariness and discouragement had worked in him for an hour or two, that fear sidled into his mind, insidious as a worm in an apple.

It seemed to Harcourt that the mechanism would be unlikely to be in the cars at the extremities of the train. Redhead would have avoided the risk of being seen by the guard or the engine driver and would have boarded a car somewhere near the middle. Or would he? What a little guessing game it was!

He stuck to his first choice and climbed up, heaving the loosened tarpaulin aside bit by bit until the depth charges were revealed. There they were, in rows, inoffensive as tar barrels. The electric lantern clicked on, making a pool of yellow brilliance in the night. Harcourt fished in his knapsack for the metal plate which Baron had discovered in Redhead's tool bag. It matched. It was a cover-plate belonging to a depth charge. With any luck he would find a canister with its plate missing. He prayed for the luck.

The symptoms of excitement were familiar to Peter Harcourt. They were physical and material; adrenalin pumping into the blood, nervous tension expressing itself in cold perspiration in the small of the back.

Not so material was a familiar feeling in the air which he now recognized and cursed bitterly. Feeling? It was more of a presence; something like the mystery that will make a dog's hackles rise without tangible cause; or like the terror that waits outside a child's door at night.

He knew it. It was an old acquaintance. It was death, standing at attention, waiting for a mechanism to operate; waiting for an impudent fellow called Peter Harcourt who persisted in walking in its shadow.

None of the depth charges in the first car was short of its cover-plate, nor was there any sign of their having been tampered with. Harcourt used the black box, careful as a doctor chasing a tremor in the beating of a human heart. He heard no clockwork ticking. He moved to the next car and tore away the tarpaulin. He worked in a methodical frenzy; looking first, listening, heaving his equipment from one place to another, climbing into car after car after car . . .

The hours passed. Two o'clock, three, four, five o'clock. In Bishop's Itchington, Bates detached himself silently from the side of Superintendent Benbow, who was watching the train from a vantage point in the garden of the public house. Bates tried the back door of the pub. It gave—nothing like the imminence of cataclysm to make even a prudent publican forget to lock his back door. Bates slipped inside and switched on the light. He put a kettle on the fire burning in the range; then took some coats from a peg and draped them over the window. They would stop the light from attracting Benbow's attention; and what the eye didn't see Bates knew that the heart wouldn't grieve about.

When the clock on the wall of the inn-keeper's kitchen said five-fifteen, Bates was bending over the white scrubbed oak table stirring a brew of tea with a tin spoon. He sniffed the brew and noted its color with satisfaction. Strong—proper five-o'clock-in-the-morning tea, it was. Infantry-man's tea. Life-saving tea.

There was a bottle on the dresser at one end of the room. Bates uncorked it and poured a scrupulous measure of rum; then he filled a mug with tea and laced it with the rum. When he had repeated the performance he put the teapot back on the hob to draw and went out through the back door.

"Cuppa tea, sir?" Benbow turned and smiled a grave smile. "Thank you, Bates. What's the sentence for breaking and entering?" Bates coughed and stared at the sky. "Dunno, sir." His superior chuckled. "I was on the point of doing the same thing myself. What's the time?"

"Just after a quarter past five, sir."

Benbow nursed the hot mug of tea with his cold hands. A quarter past five—that meant Harcourt had been at it for three and a quarter hours. It was a long time to work in that special and particular loneliness which went with the danger of extinction. He felt his stomach cringe at the thought. The thought of responsibility nagged at him and a loathing for his inactive part in the business welled in his throat. "Give me the mug," he said. "I'll take them both and drink mine with Major Harcourt. . . ."

Benbow stood looking up at the train. "I've brought you a mug of tea, Harcourt."

Peter Harcourt's head appeared above the side of the car, and his deep voice, burdened with strain and weariness, snarled: "What are you doing here?"

"Bringing you a mug of tea."

The big man stared down at the fine face illuminated in the glare of his lantern. Smug blighter! He was in a rage, hating the criminal mechanism in the train, hating the thought of death, hating himself, hating Benbow, hating everybody. He leaned down, saying "Thanks," in a surly voice.

"No luck?"

"For God's sake! Would I be here otherwise?"

"Of course not." James Benbow's voice was quiet and gentle. "What are you doing now?"

Harcourt laughed; a bitter noise in the darkness. "Taking the cover plates off the detonator pockets one by one. It wasn't a clock after all. Furthermore the swine screwed the plate back on again after planting the mechanism. It's my guess he had a delay and some priming all prepared and screwed to a spare cover plate; that would account for the one we found in his tool bag."

Benbow absorbed the information. It brought a worried frown to his face. "How many have you done so far?"

"About twenty-five, I think . . . which leaves a few hundred to go. What's the time?"

"Five thirty-two."

Harcourt drained his mug, drinking with huge gulps, then leaned over holding it in his hand. "Catch," he said, "and get to hell away from this train. I've got to get a move on."

Benbow put the two empty mugs side by side on the track at his feet. He lifted a foot and put it on the stuffing box protruding from the wheel nearest to him. He heaved himself upwards and over the side of the car. "Give me a screwdriver. With two of us there's a chance. You'll never find it alone."

"It's not worth it, you fool. One man's life, perhaps, not two."

Benbow took off his hat and started to unbutton his greatcoat. "They're for ships fitting out to go to Korea," he said. "Portsmouth told us that." He reached into Harcourt's knapsack and found a screwdriver.

Harcourt glared at him. Then, suddenly, he nodded. "All right. If you insist, but you're a fool." He was counting on his fingers. "Five hours," he said. "*Maybe* five hours . . . what a way to earn a living!

"Listen. Be careful! More careful than you've ever been in your life. When you lift a cover plate, lift it gently. Treat it as if it was made of angel's feathers. Redhead might have had the time and the wit to put an anti-lifting device in with the mechanism. Feel for a thin, thin wire and if you find one beneath a plate, freeze and lower the plate infinitely slowly back into place.

"Then tell me . . . and for God's sake don't shout!"

Police Constable Baron sat on a bench in Portsmouth railway station with a newspaper on his lap which he occasionally pretended to read. He had been there for an hour. The train from Oxford, transfer station for a man traveling from Birmingham to Portsmouth, had arrived forty minutes earlier. Redhead had not been aboard it.

An alternative train remained; from London, due in at eight forty-two.

In his sports coat and gray flannel trousers, Baron contrived to look unlike a policeman. He was alone—or apparently alone. Two uniformed policemen strolled from place to place in the station. Keeping in the background, five or six plain-clothes men watched Baron while Baron watched the crowds flowing about him. The trap was set. Now the question remained: Was the bait sufficiently tempting? Would Redhead take the risk of coming to Portsmouth to see for himself the result of his devilish ingenuity?

The unfamiliar weight and bulk of an automatic pistol reposed in a shoulder holster under Baron's left arm. More than anything else this reminded him of the urgency of his task. He had not carried a weapon since leaving the army—except a truncheon, which he had now, slung down his trouser leg and available through a hole cut in his pocket.

Baron hoped it would not come to shooting—too damned impersonal. His heart's desire was to get his hands on Redhead;

to take him by strength and skill; to wipe out last night's defeat. He thought of smashing his fist into the pale face of the man, and smiled.

Presently the great clock above him said eight thirty-seven. He rose to his feet and moved forward to the barrier which a ticket collector was opening in preparation for the arrival of the London train. The ticket collector stared at him for a moment, caught sight of the slight bulge made by Baron's truncheon and grinned. "After someone?"

Baron looked solemn. "I'm waiting for my aunt," he said slowly. "She's a great big woman with a black beard and a cast in her eye. If you see her, mate, pass the word."

The ticket collector blinked, then grinned and nodded. "I'll scream me ruddy 'ead orf," he said. " 'Ere it comes."

The train steamed short-windedly into the bay, pompous and deliberate as an alderman maneuvering toward the front row in a civic photographer's group. Doors swung open. The stream of passengers started; a trickle of local commuters without baggage, then thrifty men and women carrying their own bags, finally the prosperous citizens strolling along behind loaded porters. Baron's gaze moved deliberately from one face to another, hoping, peering, discarding.

The queue at the barrier swelled and thinned. Baron finished examining the faces near to him and stared toward the end of the platform. His face set in an expression of disappointment; not only was Redhead's face mirrored on the screen of his memory but the man's gait and manner as well, and none of the remaining travelers matched the image.

Charlie Baron sighed, shut his eyes for a second and swore under his breath. A Special Branch man in plain clothes who had walked up behind him as the crowd thinned murmured: "Don't stop lookin', mate. I've often missed 'em half an inch from my nose."

At the far end of the train the guard climbed down and walked just ahead of a group of porters pushing a barrow down the platform. Within a few yards of the barrier the porters overtook the guard, who stood aside to let them pass.

Then the guard reached the barrier and stopped to talk to the ticket inspector. He pushed up his peaked cap. Baron stared at him incredulously.

It was Redhead, by all that was wonderful!

Baron's heart leaped, and he took a deep, joyful breath. Redhead a railwayman! It explained how the man had known the destination of the depth charge train; how he had entered a station in Birmingham without being noticed by a booking clerk. Nothing in a railway station is more inconspicuous than a railwayman.

"Hey," Charlie Baron shouted happily. "You with the red hair—I want you."

Fanatic's eyes stared at him. Baron tensed and for a split second the two men faced each other. Then Redhead turned to run.

Baron cleared the barrier in a great hurdler's leap and was off, going like a deerhound. This time he had breath; enough to play with, enough for his heart to sing inside him. Redhead also knew how to run, but in fifty yards Baron gained ten. As the end of the platform came near, sloping down toward a network of lines and points, he was on the heels of the guard.

There was a smile on his face as he dived into a flying tackle. On concrete a flying tackle is not the sporting amiability it is on soft turf. Charlie Baron could not find it in himself to mind. His shoulder struck and his arms locked themselves above Redhead's knees. The saboteur crumpled and crashed down on the unyielding concrete.

They slid for ten yards before the impetus of their locked bodies was spent; then Baron stood up, a triumphant smile on his face. He had bruised his elbow badly but he was so thoroughly anaesthetized by excitement that pain did not register.

Redhead stayed where he was, knocked out by the impact of his head with the concrete, Baron locked a handcuff around the limp, outstretched wrist . . .

James Benbow stared at his hands with great disgust. Whether they trembled with fear or with plain fatigue hardly seemed to matter, for he had ceased to feel any shame of being afraid. But trembling hands interfered with the job he had to do— unscrew four bolts, ease up a cover plate with a delicate levering twist of a screwdriver, feel beneath it for a trip wire, peer into the firing tube with the aid of the electric lantern, gently probe the hole with a long piece of wood to make quite sure it was empty, then go on to the next canister.

He had lost count of the number of depth charges he and

Harcourt had investigated. He had even lost count of time, but a pale morning sun shining down on his back could only mean that time was running out. His screwdriver slipped and he banged his knuckles for the twentieth time against hard iron. "Damn," he said viciously. "Damn and blast them to hell forevermore!"

Peter Harcourt bellowed with laughter. "Go on, old boy—blast away. It helps."

Benbow smiled ruefully and sucked his bleeding knuckles.

"Have a cigarette," Harcourt offered.

"What? On top of this pile of diabolic machinery?"

"It's not so risky as all that," Harcourt replied. Out came a cigarette case from his hip pocket. "There comes a time when it's more dangerous not to smoke," he said. "Let's smoke. I loathe self-discipline."

At nine-eighteen they finished the canisters in one car, and at nine twenty-two they started on the canisters in the next.

"How many more to go?" Benbow asked presently.

"Six more carloads."

"What's the time?"

"Nine twenty-five."

"So we'll be in the danger period in half an hour?"

"Up to our necks."

At nine-thirty a noise broke the deadly monotony of their labor. They jerked erect, tools in hand, to stare in the direction of the sound. It was Bates, running, crashing through hedges, stumbling over fences. He was bellowing at the top of his voice. "Major Harcourt! Hold it, sir! They got him!" Bates was nearer. "They got him, sir! At Portsmouth."

Harcourt was looking at his watch. Nine-thirty. His voice suddenly boomed across the mushroom-dotted pasture. "Stop! Go back, Bates! Phone Portsmouth. Tell 'em to get the swine here as quickly as possible."

Bates was quite close to them. They saw the triumphant grin spread over his face "I told 'em, sir. He's on his way. The Navy's bringing him."

Harcourt bellowed with joy. "Bless you, Bates! I love you like my brother! Now get away from this train!"

Bates saluted and ran back in the direction he had come from. Harcourt turned back to Benbow, who was smiling. "So the

Navy's bringing him," the policeman said. "In a rowboat, I suppose."

Peter Harcourt laughed. It was catching. They laughed together, with hysteria on the edge of their amusement. Then Harcourt picked up his screwdriver. "Shall we risk it and do the rest of the car while we're waiting?"

Benbow looked at him and nodded. "Yes," he said, and was proud to say it.

Harcourt unscrewed two bolts remaining in the coverplate he had been working on when Bates appeared. The plate gave more easily than most. He stiffened, then lifted the thing gently, gently, until his big fingers could slide underneath. There was no wire, but there *was* something fastened to the underside of the plate—the thing they had been looking for. He lifted it clear of the depth charge. "Let's go!"

They scrambled over the side of the car and ran twenty yards into the field. Dexterously Harcourt tore away the black waterproof cloth covering the mechanism and took the priming, eight ounces of commercial gelignite and a dry gun-cotton primer, away from the detonator at the end of the time fuse. Then, with a quick expert movement, he slipped a nail from his pocket into a hole in the brass barrel which housed the striker. Now it was safe. The feeling in the air about them departed. Death was standing at ease . . .

It was not a rowboat but a Fleet Air Arm helicopter. It arrived at two minutes to ten, landing in a field prudently clear of the railway and close to Bishop's Itchington. Benbow was waiting. He did not waste time. "Thanks," he said to the pilot. "See you later." Then he turned to Police Constable Baron. "Well done, Baron. That was the best pinch you'll ever make. Unlock your end of the cuffs and give them to me."

Baron unlocked the manacle from his own wrist. Benbow took it. "Watch him, sir," Baron said. "He's a tricky beggar."

Benbow nodded, and looked hard at Redhead. The man was sour and silent. Blood had dried on his face. His nose was swollen and puffy. On his forehead there was a great abrasion—concrete. "Come on," Benbow said grimly. "At the double!" He jerked the handcuffs, and Redhead was forced to trot in the direction of the village.

Bates was waiting for them in the big Lagonda with the en-

gine running. "Get in." Redhead got in. The car roared up the
road. They approached the place where Peter Harcourt had
climbed the fence the night before. Bates clamped on the
brakes and the car skidded to a halt. "Out," Benbow said. "Get
the car away from here, Bates."

Harcourt stood up and threw down his screwdriver as Benbow came up with the prisoner.

"When?" he said to Redhead.

"Wouldn't you like to know?"

"Yes." Harcourt jumped down to the track. He took the
handcuff from Benbow and snapped it shut on a link of chain
hanging down from the side of the car beside him. "There you
are and there you stay," he said. "You know when the thing's
timed to blow. You stay here until it does, or until you tell me
where it is so that I can disarm it."

There was no reply. Redhead was wooden-faced and sullen.
Loathing stared out of his eyes—for Harcourt, for Benbow, for
the world, for the whole human race which he so greatly
despised. Harcourt smiled at him. "Leave yourself plenty of
time," he said softly. "I shall want to know the answers to a lot
of questions before I remove the mechanism—why you mined
the train, who employs you, who pays you, who else is in the
racket—"

"I didn't know that policemen were allowed to commit murder!" Redhead was quite calm.

Harcourt shook his head. "Not murder. If you don't spill it,
you'll just be committing suicide, that's all. Make yourself
comfortable. We shall be in the garden of the pub you can see
in the distance. If you want to answer the questions, wave your
hand. We shall be watching you with field glasses."

Redhead opened his mouth and words poured from his lips;
dreary, blasphemous words. Harcourt and Benbow left him to
his blasphemy and hurried away across the pasture in the sun-
shine.

When they reached the village Bates was waiting for them
in the garden of the public house. He had put a table and two
chairs close to the hedge so that they could sit and watch in
comfort. He had cooked breakfast. It was laid ready on the
table; ham and eggs and toast and a monstrous pot of tea.
Baron was propped against the hedge, watching Redhead
through field glasses.

Harcourt sat down thankfully, overwhelming a flimsy garden chair with his big body. "Bless you, Bates," he said. "Has it gone off yet?"

"No, sir. We put it there under the rosebush."

Benbow and Harcourt looked in the direction of the policeman's pointing finger. The mechanism they had taken out of the depth charge, less the priming and detonator, lay, business end upward, on the black soil of the rosebush. The percussion cap was still intact. When the mechanism operated it would explode, making about as much noise as a child's toy pistol.

"So far, so good," Harcourt said. "Now we've got time to think. Do you think he'll bust?"

James Benbow poured two cups of tea with luxurious deliberation, then slowly shook his head. "I doubt it, I'm afraid. He's no amateur. He'll know that the English police would never handcuff a man to a train that might explode and he'll deduce that we've found the thing and removed it."

Harcourt grinned with wicked delight. "He'll deduce until he's blue in the face, but he won't be sure. If I were in his place I should be very, very frightened."

"So should I," Benbow agreed, "but neither you nor I are fanatics. The man looked to me like a born martyr. I think he's the kind that would keep his mouth shut even if he were sure he was going to die."

The loaded minutes ticked by, James Benbow, thinking back to his own emotions during the long night that had passed, imagined what Redhead had to be feeling and wondered. "To be blown to pieces must be about the quickest death that could be devised," he said, lighting a cigarette and pouring himself a third cup of tea. "I wonder why it's so beastly to contemplate."

Harcourt answered authoritatively. He was a specialist in the subject. "I think it's the thought of mutilation. Violence. Being blasted into eternity. Most of us want to die in bed with our boots off; to have time to think about it." He glanced toward the railway where the figure of the saboteur was just distinguishable to the naked eye. "That poor devil must be sweating it out!"

A bleakness came into Benbow's eyes. "Let's not be sorry for him," he said coldly. "It is not his fault that he failed to kill hundreds of sailors and stevedores. He's going to get off too lightly as it is. In wartime we could shoot him, but in this lukewarm contest we are conducting at the moment we cannot. A police state would be less scrupulous and more logical."

Harcourt smiled wryly, then gestured toward the thing under the rosebush. "Like me to go and pop it back?" he asked.

Benbow smiled in return; a tired smile full of self-knowledge. "Don't mistake me," he said. "I wouldn't want to fight them with their own weapons. I'm old-fashioned enough to believe that truth will win in the end and that no end can justify unspeakable means."

It was twenty-five minutes past ten. Baron shouted suddenly: "It looks as if he's waving, sir . . . He *is!* Yes, he's waving."

Harcourt was grinning triumphantly. Without a word he and Benbow set off in the direction of the railway line. Then, before they were five yards on their way, there came the sound of a sharp crack behind them. The striker in the mechanism had driven forward and the percussion cap had exploded. They stopped in their tracks to stare at one another.

"He was trying to take us with him," James Benbow's voice was suddenly weary and disillusioned. He detested the thought that such fanaticism could exist in the world.

Peter Harcourt, with the tiny explosion of the percussion cap still ringing in his ears, nodded and set his jaw. "We'll go and talk to him about it," he said quietly. "I wondered if he'd try that one."

They strode forward again, two tired and determined men with cold anger sitting in their hearts. They had only one thought between them. Redhead had to be cracked—like an egg —and the yolk of vital information he carried had to be dragged out of him.

Five hundred yards is three minutes of fast walking. When they had covered a hundred yards, Redhead started to scream.

Harcourt glanced at Benbow. "He might have been meaning to take us with him," he said, "but I believe he's cracked now. Can you hear him yelling?"

Benbow nodded. They increased their pace.

Harcourt said: "Well, are you going to talk?"

The man mouthed silently for a second. Then, expressed as a torment of words, his fear burst from him. "I'll talk. I will. I will. I promise. But get the bombs out of the charge first. It's time. It's time, I tell you!"

Harcourt's eyes widened. "Them!" he said. "Two? Did you lay two mechanisms?"

The answer was a wail of terror. "Yes. Yes, two of them. One at the bottom, one at the top. Quickly. Quickly!"

"Get away from this train!"

It was a sudden roar of urgency, spoken with all the force of the big man's lungs. Benbow leaped to obey. His hand came forward with the key of the handcuffs. It seemed wrong that Harcourt might die and Redhead live, but he could not leave the man chained as he was. He unlocked the manacles.

Aboard the car where the mined depth charge lay, Harcourt seized a stick and probed the gaping hole of the firing tunnel. He felt a second bomb lying at the bottom of the tunnel and knew that he was as near to being a dead man as any soldier covered by a sniper's rifle. His arm plunged down the tunnel, his fingers groping for the bundle of waterproof cloth and high explosive. He could not reach it.

Forcing himself to move without panic, he reached in his tool kit for a telescopic grab. Extended, it was a long steel arm like the shaft of a golf club with spring-loaded jaws at its end. He thrust it gently down the tunnel until it met resistance, then allowed the jaws to close. He pulled and the bundle shifted slightly before the cloth tore and the weight came off the end of the grab.

Harcourt knew that all that remained between him and death was a copper wire already eaten away to breaking point by the corrosive chemical surrounding it. He knew that all it needed was a slight jar or a few more seconds of corrosion and it would break, allowing the striker to fly forward.

He lowered the grab again and took another grip on the bundle; then he lifted, infinitely gently, holding the steel shaft between his thumb and second finger. The bundle shifted and came up the tunnel, making a little dry noise as it scraped against the sides.

Five seconds later he had it in his hands. There was no longer any time for skill or delicacy. With perspiration soaking into his clothes and with hope in his heart, Peter Harcourt took a firm grip on the thing with his right hand, then leaned backward with it at the end of a stiff arm and hurled it like a grenade, far out into the field beside the railway line.

It sailed gently through the air in a parabola and when it struck the ground it exploded . . . harmlessly, with a spiteful sharp detonation which frightened the birds from their perches in the trees and sent a black column of smoke and earth climbing up to heaven . . .

"The first and cardinal principle of demolition is to duplicate the means of initiation," Peter Harcourt said in Bishop's Itchington pub forty minutes later. "I thought I should never forget that as long as I lived, but I did. I was so stupidly, ridiculously relieved to see the first bomb that I forgot to look for another."

Bates poured whisky into two glasses, while Baron stood smugly in the background. Superintendent Benbow picked up his drink and sniffed it. "Redhead blew," he said. "I worked on him before he had time to get cool. He had a lot to say. Quite useful, I should say. Quite." He smiled and picked up his drink. "Well, here's to us. It's a long time since two men so well deserved a drink. I look toward you, Major Harcourt."

"Thanks, old man," Peter said. Then, after staring for a second at the whisky in his glass, he looked up. "Oh Lord!" he said suddenly. "What a hell of a way to make a living!"

19

SAX ROHMER

The Mystery of the Vanishing Treasure

SOME FORTY YEARS AGO Sax Rohmer created
the character of Dr. Fu Manchu. The villainous doctor
has been the subject of countless novels, several films
and both radio and television series. Mr. Rohmer has
traveled extensively in Egypt and the Far East, where he
has gathered many of the exotic backgrounds for his
fiction and plays. He was a long-time friend of the late
great magician, Houdini, and has a special interest in
magic, which forms the theme of this story.

MAX LOOKED DOWN into the face framed in an upturned fur
collar which nestled against his shoulder. Frosty air had heightened Jan's perfect coloring. "Happy, darling?" he asked.

She glanced up, squeezed more tightly against him as they
walked on. "Frighteningly happy, Max."

"Frighteningly?"

"Just seems too wonderful to last." Their footsteps made a
pleasant crunching sound in the snow. "Here's Steevens. Now
you can deliver your mysterious message."

The chauffeur was grooming a smart convertible outside the
garage. His naturally sad expression changed when he saw
Jan.

"Good morning, Miss Jan. I've stopped that squeak. Nothing
serious. Good morning, sir."

"Good morning, Steevens."

Jan knew that Max rather liked Steevens, who had been with
her father, Colonel Wharton, for two years, although, the first
time Max met Steevens, he had asked her where he came from.
He was haunted by a vague impression that he had seen the man
before.

"Orders from the colonel, Steevens." Max gave that provoca-

tive half-smile which sometimes irritated but had always fasci-
nated Jan. "Sorry, Jan. Secret orders! Let's step inside for a moment, Steevens."

Jan made a childish grimace, as Max and the chauffeur went
into the garage. It was Jan's twenty-first birthday. Drawing her
left hand out of the warmth of her coat she feasted her eyes on
an extravagantly beautiful diamond and sapphire ring which
gleamed on her finger. Her engagement to Max Finlay would
be announced at the big party taking place that night. She kissed
Max's ring and put her hand back in the pocket of her coat
as he came out.

She took his arm; snuggled up to him as they started back to
the house.

"It's mean of Father not to let me into the secret of his vanish-
ing-treasure trick. *You* know, and even Steevens knows!"

"Not really, Jan. Steevens does one little job and I do another.
But neither of us knows how the substitution is worked."

They crunched on through the snow again, and suddenly:
"Greta and her father are coming tonight," Jan said. "Their ship
has been delayed." She tried to keep a wistful note out of her
voice. "I know the subject is taboo, darling, but I can't help
wondering if you're quite sure. You did tell me that at one
time you were in love with Greta. And she's very pretty."

Max pulled up short. "I'm sorry I ever told you, Jan. I wasn't
out of college. Please forget it."

Max watched her in an unhappy way. Then, detecting the
beginning of a smile on her lips, he held her in his arms during
a long kiss. "You almost made me think you meant it."

They walked on in silence. Max was unlike any of the other
men who had made love to Jan. He brushed things aside so
lightly. It wasn't what he said but what he left unsaid which
sometimes annoyed her.

Presently, he paused. He was looking at a motorcycle to which
a sidecar was hitched. It was the property of Steevens on which
he traveled between his lodgings and Colonel Wharton's house.
The sidecar served for light shopping.

"We shall have to go back, Jan. Steevens' motorbike reminds
me. Something I forgot to tell him."

"All right, darling. You go. I'll hurry on up. Mother is working
herself to death over the party, as usual. I must report for
duty."

"Soldier's daughter!"

Max kissed her again, and turned back . . .

Jan found her mother, in gloves and overall, working like a stevedore. Mrs. Wharton, light-footed, alert and nearly as slim as her daughter, possessed a fund of vitality which seemed to be inexhaustible. Jan was so strikingly like her that no one could have mistaken the relationship. Jan changed quickly, and soon the two were doing the work of three housemaids.

"Your father has never grown up." Mrs. Wharton spoke happily. "He loves a party." She changed the position of a side table. "Gives him an audience for his conjuring tricks. I have banned the sleight-of-hand, but of course we're going to have the vanishing treasure!"

"I know," Jan nodded. "Max is assisting him. Father's so proud of it, because Houdini showed him how to do it."

"Well"—Mrs. Wharton sighed—"it's certainly very intriguing, and it seems to amuse everybody."

Half an hour passed before Jan began to wonder what had become of Max. Traitorous doubts threatened to steal back. Going up to her room to make herself presentable for luncheon, she glanced out of the window, and her heartbeat changed to an odd rhythm.

Max was climbing in over a stile, beyond which a footpath led to the crossroads. Dr. Underhill, Greta's father and their nearest neighbor, lived near the crossroads, less than a mile away . . .

Jan came downstairs just as Max shed his wet rubbers on the porch, and began to hang up his topcoat in the lobby.

The phone rang. Mrs. Wharton, who carried a large bowl of flowers, looked out from the lounge.

"Be an angel, Max, and take the call for me."

Jan was too far away to catch the beginning of the conversation, but she heard the end, heard Max say, "I'm terribly sorry, and disappointed. But I still hope to see you."

He hung up, and she said, "Who was that, Max?"

"Greta. Her Aunt Margaret has been taken seriously ill. They're driving up to London and might have to stay the night. Bad luck, isn't it?"

"Very bad luck." Jan's voice sounded unfamiliar. "I'm sorry. You were away quite a long time, Max. Did you take a walk?"

Max gave his provocative half-smile. "Right to the crossroads and back, darling . . ."

When early winter dusk fell, the house became a fairyland of twinkling lights. A great log fire blazed in the library.

Jan, a vision in palest blue, knew that she looked charming— and she knew that Max was proud of her.

When the colonel announced his daughter's engagement, he said, grinning impishly at Jan, that he was sorry she hadn't picked a soldier instead of lawyer. But he added:

"Max Finlay is a rising young barrister with a bright future, and when he's a High Court Judge any one of us may have cause to be glad that he's a friend of ours!"

Max responded modestly. Jan loved the easy resonance of his voice. There followed the usual chorus, cheers, popping of corks, exhibition of gifts, and a threat of tears from Mrs. Wharton.

Dancing was resumed. Jan and Max went out onto the porch. Max stooped and kissed a white shoulder as he helped Jan into her coat.

"Max darling!"

"Tell me you're happy, as I am, Jan. Something seems to be worrying you. What is it?"

Jan found it hard to answer.

Moonlight touched the snow-robed garden with magic. Max's kiss had thrilled her. If only that wretched cloud hadn't come down again when she had seen him climbing over from the field path! But his frank statement of where he had been had banished it. They had often taken the same walk together.

Jan told herself, bitterly, that she was a jealous little cat. But then, following the phone call from Greta, she discovered that Max had retired as her father's assistant, proposing their friend Phil Dwyer as a substitute. This would leave Max free during the time that everybody else watched her father's illusion.

"Nothing is worrying me, Max—really—"

Max put his arm around her, tightly. "Champagne makes some people morbid!"

"Does it?" Jan peeped up at him over the furry collar. "Tell me, Max, why did you let Father down tonight? I mean, why did you change your mind?"

Max laughed and hugged her closer.

"Surely that's not your worry? The colonel agreed that as I assisted at Christmas, and again at New Year's, some of them might suspect collusion. Bad showmanship, Jan. It's a long time since Phil appeared in the act, and I briefed him as soon as he arrived. What's wrong with that?"

"Nothing, darling. Isn't it a divine night?" Soft strains of a Cuban melody stole over the frosty air. "Let's go in and dance."

It was nearly midnight when calls for the colonel's celebrated trick became insistent. He always waited for this moment.

Jan, flushed and happy, came into the library, Max's arm around her. Max placed her comfortably, smiled and moved away as Phil Dwyer moved into an adjoining chair.

"Mustn't monopolize you, darling!" Max whispered.

The log fire had been stoked up by Steevens, who had arranged seats to accommodate all the guests. Colonel Wharton announced that he would try to perform a very difficult magical feat for the secret of which he was indebted to the great magician, Houdini. He would require someone to assist him. And he beckoned to Phil Dwyer—who tried to look surprised.

To Phil he handed a silk hat, instructing him to take up a collection of valuables from the guests. "Don't be modest. Fill it up. And I don't want any cheap stuff . . ."

As Phil took the hat, Jan, looking around, realized that Max had gone. He wasn't in the library!

The cloud swept blackly down. She slipped away, searched the house, looked into the garden. But Max was not there. All her misgivings, all her doubts, crystallized into a maddening conviction. He had crept out to meet Greta.

She ran up to her room. The shades hadn't been drawn, and moonlight poured silver onto the rugs. Aimlessly, her eyes burning, her hands shaking, Jan crossed to the window.

Max, wearing rubbers, and a topcoat over his dress clothes, was hurrying across the field path toward the crossroads, his footsteps shadow-painted in the snow.

In the library, when Jan came back, Colonel Wharton had reclaimed the laden hat. It contained two diamond brooches, a wrist watch, a string of pearls, a wallet containing a roll of notes, and other valuables, nineteen items in all. The colonel was appealing for one more offering "to make it a round figure."

Jan slipped in like a ghost and sat down, unnoticed, on a settee by the window. Then her father saw her, and crossed, hat in hand.

"I don't believe *you* have subscribed, Jan!"

Jan smiled wanly, and drawing the diamond and sapphire ring from her finger, dropped it in the hat.

"Hullo!" the colonel lowered his voice and raised his heavy eyebrows. "Will Max approve?"

"I don't know. He's not here."

Sensing a lovers' quarrel, the colonel said no more, but he reflected, uneasily, that they had started rather early.

The magical operation continued. The treasure was transferred to a linen bag, which was then tied tightly, the knots being sealed with a guest's signet ring. A ballot-box was introduced.

Phil Dwyer distributed little scribbling-blocks and pencils.

Each guest was asked to think of any spot within a reasonable radius of the house and write it down. Entries were folded to fit into the slot of the box. When all had voted, the colonel removed the lid and tipped the voting papers out onto his table.

Three different volunteers divided and subdivided the votes, each time into two parts, one of which they rejected. When, by means of this process, only three papers remained, the youngest guest was called upon to make a final choice, and to read out what was written there. She read:

"Beside the old well in Dr. Underhill's garden."

There was laughter, part ironical and part sympathetic, when those who knew told those who didn't that the spot chosen was nearly a mile away! But the words struck a chill to Jan's heart. "Dr. Underhill's garden." It was to Dr. Underhill's garden that Max had gone!

Colonel Wharton raised his hand. "The challenge is accepted. Nothing is impossible to a magician. Before I disintegrate the contents of this sealed bag and speed the atoms on their way, I want a search party to be ready to leave. Who will drive?"

"I'll drive!" Jan's clear voice rang around the library. "I know the place, and my car's right outside."

"Now choose two other volunteers."

Every man there volunteered, but Jan selected General Vondy, with whom her father had served, and Mr. Attenburg, the family solicitor.

Colonel Wharton picked up the sealed bag.

An attractive young widow who had contributed a diamond bracelet, whispered to her escort (owner of the wallet in the bag), "You haven't seen this before, Ray. You're going to get the fright of your life!"

"I command you," the colonel intoned impressively, "to fly to the old well in Dr. Underhill's garden."

And he tossed the bag into the heart of the blazing fire!

A moment of stupefied silence followed, broken only by the widow's laughter, as fragments of red hot wire, bits of glass and metal glowed in the flames. Threaded pearls were seen apparently to dissolve . . .

Jan drove along snowy roads, over a surface which, in the headlights, seemed to be made of powdered diamonds. Not another car was sighted during the journey. This may have been fortunate, for although she drove with mechanical steadiness, Jan's thoughts were far away.

Max couldn't possibly love her—or he wouldn't have left her, on this night of all other nights, and stolen off to see someone else. He must have fixed a meeting that morning, when she had seen him coming back. Then there had been a change of plan, and Greta had called him to make a later date.

Why, Jan asked herself desperately, had he ever become engaged to her, if it was Greta he really loved? And, whatever had happened between them, why couldn't Greta leave him alone, *now?*

Fate had stepped in. By a freakish coincidence, she had been given the chance to convince herself—to find them together . . .

Jan swung right at the crossroads and drove along a winding lane bordered by jewelled Christmaslike trees. "Here we are!"

She pulled up where a long low house lay back from the lane.

"All in bed, Jan?" Mr. Attenburg asked. "Or are the Underhills away?"

"I think they're away."

Jan's voice was no more than a whisper.

"Where's this old well? I've never seen it."

"It's to the east of the house, and not far from the wall beside the lane." Jan was mystified, but a welcome doubt had crept in. "Did you bring the flashlight, General?"

"All ready, my dear!"

Jan leading, the search party moved up to the dark house, turned left across a border and went through a gap in a hedge.

"Strictly speaking, this is trespass!" the lawyer declared.

Strictly speaking, it wasn't the shortest way, but it had enabled Jan to satisfy herself that the back of Dr. Underhill's house was in darkness, like the front.

Presently, Jan leading with the flash lamp, they came to a low, stone wall bordering the property, and there was the ancient wall, said to be of Roman origin.

"Good God! What's this?" the general said.

A man lay sideways in the snow beside the wall, his arms and legs tied. A haggard face, disfigured by adhesive tape, stared up at them.

Jan checked a scream, stooped, looked still more closely. "It's *Steevens!*" she cried out.

After a moment of consternation, the men went to work to free the chauffeur. His limbs were stiff, and although his teeth chattered, speech burst from him:

"A hold-up, Miss Jan! He was hiding by the well—a man with a handkerchief tied over his face! Just as I put the bag down, I found myself looking right into the barrel of a big automatic! He made me turn around and fixed me as you saw. He grabbed the bag and ran to where I'd left my bike. A minute afterward I heard him start up!"

"Do you mean the bag containing the jewels and money?" Mr. Attenburg asked.

"Yes, sir. It was my job to bring it here. I've done it many times. But nothing like this ever happened."

"I don't understand," General Vondy declared. "We all saw the bag in the colonel's hand three minutes before we left the house, saw him throw it into the fire!"

"No you didn't, General." Jan spoke wearily. "I don't know how Father does it, but a duplicate bag is substituted and the real one passed out to Steevens who's waiting to take it to the selected place. You can't suppose Father would throw his friends' jewelry into the fire!"

"But the selected place is decided by votes!" Mr. Attenburg objected.

"The lottery is faked, sir," Steevens assured him. "Must be. I knew the place this morning. Mr. Finlay told me. The stuff was handed out to me tonight by Mr. Dwyer before any voting started!"

"Some rogue found out what was to happen!" the general shouted. "You were followed!"

"No, sir, I had the road to myself all the way. That I can swear."

The news brought back by Jan and the search party staggered everybody. Colonel Wharton was deeply mortified. He undertook, failing capture of the thief, to replace all missing items which were uninsured. Steevens, chilled to the bone, had been sent out to the kitchen to restore circulation with a hot grog. The colonel was telephoning the local police.

Jan felt dizzy. Amid a babel of excited conversation, she alone remained silent. Before leaving Dr. Underhill's, they had aroused the housekeeper, called the colonel—and had learned that the doctor and Greta were in London.

Where, then, was Max?

Suddenly, every voice became stilled.

Max walked in, carrying the sealed bag, which he dumped on a table!

"I am sorry if you people got alarmed. But nothing to worry about. You'll find everything here."

There followed a forward rush. Max stepped aside, crossed to Jan, who felt as though she had been suddenly hypnotized, and put his arm around her. "Where's your father, darling?"

"On the phone in his study. But, Max—"

"Where's Steevens?"

"In the kitchen."

"Let's join the colonel."

Colonel Wharton had just hung up as they walked in. "I don't know where the devil you've been all night, Max, but have you heard the news?"

"I'm here to report it, Colonel."

Jan recovered consciousness. She tried to hide her ringless left hand. "Max has brought the bag back!" She spoke almost hysterically. "Listen to them out there!" she cried.

Colonel Wharton started for the door.

"One moment, Colonel." Max detained him. "Everybody's property is safe, I assure you. But before you go in, I think you should know the facts."

The colonel sat down again, stared from Max to Jan. "I'm the most bewildered man in all England!"

Max planted Jan in an armchair and sat on one arm of it.

"The facts are these: I had occasion to see Steevens again this morning after I had given him his instructions about the place he had to go to tonight. I found him—that is, I heard his voice

—in the toolshed. He was saying to someone, 'Look the ground over now, Jim. Then be outside here right on from dark. I'll signal you.' "

Colonel Wharton made a choking noise.

"I hid and waited for the other man to come out. Steevens' face has always been vaguely familiar to me, but I had never been able to place him until I saw the other man. He was James Dyker, convicted some years ago of a jewel robbery at Croydon. Seeing him, I remembered Steevens.

"Steevens had been in charge of the jeweler's shop at the time. He was found gagged and locked in a cellar. I happened to be in court on another case at the trial, and as Steevens' story hung together he was discharged. Dyker got five years. He must just have come out."

"But why," the colonel demanded explosively, "did you allow me—"

"I apologize, Colonel, but the robbery had to be attempted before we had a case. I followed Dyker this morning. And when he turned right at the crossroads I knew where he was going. There's a short cut by a footpath, and I was hidden near the old well before he climbed the wall and took a careful look around. The plot was plain. This was the spot—and they were going to follow the same routine!"

"You should have notified me immediately!"

Max smiled his half-smile.

"Maybe it was a gamble, but I couldn't resist playing Sherlock Holmes! Tonight, I was back in the same hiding place well ahead of time. I took the liberty of borrowing your service revolver, Colonel."

He laid it on the desk. Colonel Wharton repeated the inarticulate sound.

"Dyker arrived soon after me and waited behind a hedge. Then Steevens came along. The loot changed hands, but I waited. Steevens allowed Dyker to truss him up and leave him lying there by the well. Dyker ran back to the motor bike and had just got there when I jumped for him! He carried an automatic in an arm holster, but before he had it free, I hit him an almighty crack on the skull with the butt of your gun, and bundled him into the sidecar—"

Suddenly from outside a speeding engine whined and then they heard brakes screaming.

"That will be the police, Colonel. You'll find Dyker tied up and locked in the toolshed. Make sure of Steevens."

Colonel Wharton left the study as if jet-propelled. Then, before Max could detain her, Jan ran out after him!

A barrage of inquiries met the pair, but Jan was back almost as Max reached the door—the diamond and sapphire ring sparkling again on her finger. "Max darling!" He almost crushed her in his arms. "Say you forgive me!"

He paused, stared into anxious blue eyes.

"What for?"

"Never mind what for. Just say you forgive me."

20

DAVID SAVAGE

Killer in the Club Car

HERE'S A STORY that will make you take an extra
look at your fellow passengers next time you ride in the
club car of a train. We liked it because it is an exciting
suspense tale with the excitement growing out of a quite
commonplace setting. David Savage, the author, works
in television and radio and writes fiction in his spare
time. He is married, the father of three children, and
lives not far from New York.

THE NEWSPAPER ACCOUNT of the hold-up read: "Officer Reynolds
is survived by his wife, Anna, 32, and their seven-year-old daughter, Annabel.

"A strange development in the investigation was disclosed this
afternoon when police revealed that out of the scores of eye witnesses questioned, they were able to extract a coherent description of the gunman from only one, a twelve-year-old girl who had
been waiting outside the door of the store for her father. The
girl, whose name the police have withheld, watched the entire
holdup through the glass door and, although too terrified to give
an alarm at the time, she was able later to give the police what
they consider an amazingly accurate description."

George Saxon put his glass back on the small steel table that
was bolted to the floor of the club car and shook his paper open
to the sports page. In the next chair Susan Saxon used the edge
of her comic book to push one of her blonde pigtails back over
her shoulder.

The train lurched slightly and slowed as the brake shoes
scraped against the wheels.

Suzy twisted around to look out the window.

"Why are we stopping?" she asked.

"One Hundred and Twenty-fifth Street," her father said.

"Oh," said Suzy and turned back to her book.

As the train squeaked to a halt, she turned again to look down at the brightly lit cross street. "When do we get to Portland?"

"Six something," George said. "The porter will wake us in time," he added, anticipating her next question.

"Will Mummy meet us?"

"Of course. Now, read your book. You have to go to bed in a few—"

George looked down at his daughter and cut off his words abruptly. Suzy's comic book fell to the floor, and she was staring past her father to the rear of the car, her blue eyes wide with undisguised horror. George snapped a quick glance in the same direction.

A young man, perhaps thirty years old, stood just inside the door, scanning the car for a vacant seat. He wore a neat gray flannel suit, tweed topcoat and a brown snap-brim hat.

George turned back to Suzy. "What's the matter? Are you sick?"

Suzy didn't answer but her eyes had lost none of their look of terror.

The young man spotted an empty chair, a few seats beyond and across the aisle from George and Suzy, and walked slowly between the other passengers, shrugged off his coat and sat down.

Suzy's right hand clutched fiercely at her father's sleeve and she cowered in her chair. George put his hand on her knee and tapped it gently. "Suzy! What's the matter?"

She yanked her head around to look up at her father. "That's him," she said in a whisper.

"That's who?" George turned, looked around him vaguely.

"Him," Suzy insisted. "The man I saw this afternoon."

George immediately relaxed. He smiled down at her. He said. "Couldn't be, darling. He's—"

"It *is*," Suzy said. "I know it is."

"Now, look," George said quietly. "You're upset and I don't blame you, but you can't just—"

Suzy's eyes opened even wider. "Daddy, I'm *not* wrong. It's him. I'm positive." Her voice rose above the whisper. "You've got to—"

"Suzy!" George said sharply, "Now, stop it." He patted the bare knee once again. "You're tired and overwrought. Anyway, it's bed time."

Suzy slumped in her chair, stared sullenly at the floor. George looked up and across at the young man giving his order to the white-coated porter. He studied him carefully for a long moment, then shook his head. It had been a terrible ordeal for his child and now, obviously, her fears were jumping her into what might well be an extremely embarrassing situation.

Suzy had told the police that the gunman was wearing a dark suit, gray hat and a battered trench coat. Also that the man had worn a thin mustache. The most important bit of description she had given had been a small heart-and-arrow tattoo on the gunman's left wrist.

George turned his eyes back to his daughter. She was biting her lip and staring blankly at her hands, folded loosely in her lap.

He glanced back across the aisle just as the young man reached into his left trousers pocket, extracted a bill and stretched his arm out to place it on the porter's tray.

The coat and shirt sleeves slid back, and on his left wrist was a blue and red tattoo—a small heart, pierced with an arrow.

It was only a fraction of a second, but in that instant, the young man glanced at George, looked down at his wrist and then very slowly back to George. It was too late to pretend he'd been looking elsewhere. George stared back and his insides knotted in fear as the man's eyes shifted to Suzy and narrowed perceptibly. There was but one thing to do—get Suzy out of there. As casually as he could, George stood up and reached for Suzy's hand.

The young man across the aisle got slowly to his feet and yawned. George dropped Suzy's hand, and the young man pretended to look for something in his pockets. When he patted the breast pocket of his coat, he did it with one finger, an eloquent indication to George that a gun was hidden beneath.

From the forward end of the car, past the tiny bar, came the huge figure of the porter who had earlier shown George and Suzy their berths. George reached in his pocket as the porter approached and withdrew a dollar bill.

"Would you please see my daughter into her berth?" he asked, proffering the bill. "Second car back—upper two."

The porter's dark face split in a wide grin.

"Sure thing. It'll be a pleasure."

"I don't want to," Suzy said. "Besides—"

"Right now, Suzy," George snapped.

"Come along young lady." The porter offered a hamlike hand which Suzy ignored. She got to her feet and glanced quickly at the young man whose slitted eyes were unwaveringly studying her. She turned to George.

"If you won't believe me, who will?"

George bent down and kissed her. "I'll be along in a few minutes, dear. Stop worrying and get a good night's sleep. We'll be home before you know it." He patted her shoulder as she scuffed off behind the porter, then stepped back and sat down, relieved. At least Suzy wasn't in the same car.

"That was a stupid move," said a voice in his ear.

George turned. The young man was now sitting in the chair vacated by Suzy. He spoke very softly. Over the clattering noise of the train, no one but George could possibly have heard him. The young man smiled, bent down and retrieved the comic book from the floor. George got a momentary glimpse of a black gun butt.

"You sent her to bed without her book," the young man said.

"I'm afraid I don't know what business that is of yours," George replied, stiffly.

"I always mind my own till I see someone else doing it for me," the man said. "That's a smart little girl you have there, Mister."

"She is," George said, "but I don't see what that has to do with you."

"Don't you?"

"No I don't." George reached for his beer, changed his mind and started to rise. "Now, if you'll excuse me, I'll—"

"Sit down and stay there," the man ordered quietly.

"Now, wait a minute," George began.

"You wait a minute. I saw your kid looking at me—looking at me like she'd seen me before. I read the papers and I can add two and two. Maybe it's lousy bad luck we wind up on the same train, and then again, maybe it's not so bad."

"I haven't the foggiest idea what you're talking about," George said, in a last, blind groping for a way out.

"Don't hand me that, Mister," the man snarled. "Let's just say the kid's right and let it go at that—but that don't make either of you any better off."

"You can't start anything here, and you know it," George said, giving up the pretense. "Now—"

"Shut up," the man whispered hoarsely. "I still got the gun. There's one slug in a cop. Do you think I give a damn where the rest of 'em go? In you? In your nosy kid? I don't, Mister. Believe me, I don't." He ran a forefinger across his upper lip as though expecting to find something other than the smooth skin. "One or a dozen," he muttered, "that seat don't get any hotter."

George looked at the grim, cruel face—the cold gray eyes, the thin tight lips. He leaned back in his seat, made a steeple with his hands, rubbed them against his forehead.

"What do you want?" he asked.

"Out," said the gunman. "Out—and you and your kid are it."

"Leave her alone," George said, suddenly. "Leave her alone or so help me, I'll—"

"You won't do anything—anything but what I tell you and I *will* leave her alone."

"What do you want?" George asked again.

"I told you. Now listen—hard." The gunman shifted in his seat. "You thought that was pretty cute—getting your kid out of here. Big hero stuff. You between me and the kid. In case you don't know it, you couldn't have played it better—because I'm going to change all that."

"What—?" George began, but the gunman interrupted.

"Shut up," he ordered. "I'm doing the talking. Right now, you're between me and the kid. In two minutes, it's going to be the other way around. Your kid's in upper two—two cars back. Do you know where I'll be?"

George knew the answer. He waited.

"In *lower* two."

George had a momentary impulse to scramble out of his seat and take his chances against the gun. He tightened.

"Don't try it, Mister," the gunman said. "I got an idea what you're thinking, and you can take this or leave it. The first one I head for is the one who's got the finger on me—your kid. Don't think anybody in this car's going to be a hero and stop me."

George sagged visibly. "You touch her and I give you my word—"

"That's right in your lap, Mister."

"How?"

"Like I said, I'll be in lower two. First stop's Stamford. I look out the window and there's no cops—no fuss—no nothing—the kid and I get off. I get her a nice comfortable hotel room—I don't touch her—and like that comic says, 'Away I go.'"

"But," George began.

"Yeah—comes Stamford—I look out the window and there's cops—I can spot them, Mister, even out of their monkey suits." He paused and the pale eyes narrowed even more. "Remember —I'm in *lower* two, and a forty-five slug makes a big dent in an upper berth."

He rose quickly and stood for a moment looking down at George. "Good night," he said cheerfully. He strode to the rear entrance, yanked it open but was gone. George looked frantically at his fellow passengers.

One or two of them glanced briefly up at the young man as the door opened, and then went back to their drinks, their papers or their conversations.

Two cars back, the gunman parted the curtains of lower two and slid into the berth. He lay back and contemplated the curved metal base of the upper berth, and smiled sardonically.

In the small men's lounge at the rear of the same car, four husky young men in khaki sat playing a weary game of poker.

One, a bit older than the others and with a craggy, lined face, wore the stripes of a master sergeant. The other three were privates. None of them was looking at his cards. They were staring in puzzlement at the figure of a little girl in a night gown who stood in the curtained doorway, tears streaming down her face.

"Look, kid," one of the privates said softly. "You had a nightmare—a bad dream. Now, you please hop back in the sack and leave us alone."

"Please," Suzy sobbed. "Please believe me. I haven't even been to sleep."

The sergeant tossed his hand onto the table, stood up and stepped to the entrance. He squatted and held Suzy gently by the arms.

"Want I should go back to your berth with you?" he asked.

Suzy pulled one arm free from the huge, gentle hand and wiped her sleeve roughly across her eyes.

"No—no—just believe me. He's got a gun—I know—and he killed a policeman—I saw him do it. And now he's in the same car with my daddy."

"Okay-okay," the sergeant said soothingly. "Tell you what." He turned his head and winked at the other three. "We don't want things like this going on, but it'll take a little figuring. You scoot back to your berth and me and my buddies will figure out something. Okay?"

"You do believe me," Suzy said, in a surge of relief.

"Of course," said the sergeant. "We all do."

There was a chorus of "sures" from the other three and Suzy again wiped her eyes on her sleeve, smiled weakly and turned away. The sergeant touched her lightly on the head as she went. Then he stepped back to the game.

"Deal," he said.

"It's all dealt," said a private. "I already bet two bits."

"Next game I play's gonna be in a Turkish bath," said a third soldier, disgustedly.

"What's the matter with you?" the sergeant demanded. "Get in or get out."

"Look behind you," said the private.

The sergeant turned, stared and threw down his hand.

Suzy stood there again, not in tears, now, but in utter panic.

The sergeant started to rise, but Suzy darted past him, slid in a tight little ball onto the leather covered bench, and buried herself from sight under the pile of Army overcoats. The soldiers swapped puzzled looks for a silent moment.

"Any of you boys seen a little girl?"

The young man in the gray flannel suit stood casually in the entrance.

"My daughter," he continued. "She has awful nightmares. I shouldn't have left her."

The three privates looked at the sergeant. It was his play. The sergeant turned his back on the man in the doorway. "What would a little girl be doing in here?" he asked. "Gimme three cards," he added to the dealer.

"I thought she was in her berth," the young man said. "She's not. I thought she might have wandered down here."

"How old is she?" one of the privates asked.

"About—er—twelve."

"Nothing that age around here. If you happen to spot one around twenty-five, though, send her along, huh?" The sergeant chuckled. "I'll raise you four bits," he said to the dealer.

The young man turned to go and glanced briefly at the pile

of coats. "Thanks, fellas. If you see her, I'll be in the club car."

"Yeah. Sure—sure," the sergeant rumbled.

As the green curtains fell together behind the young man, the sergeant reached out and snatched the overcoats from Suzy's trembling form. She sat up, looked wildly about, started to speak and then froze.

The young man stood, again, in the curtained entrance. His right hand was under the left side of his coat.

"What is this?" he demanded. "A game?"

The sergeant stood and shuffled his feet in embarrassment. "That's what she told us, Mister. Isn't it?"

The young man relaxed.

"I only wish it was," he said, sadly. "She's only out of the sani—the hospital a week now." He stepped into the room. "Come along, dear."

Suzy, in stunned terror, got to her feet. She looked with utter disbelief at the sergeant.

"You're a soldier," she said, in a choked voice. "You're supposed to protect people."

"Look, kid," the sergeant growled. "Do what your father says. Run along. You can get people into trouble, acting like this."

Numbly, Suzy walked to the curtains. The young man shook his head sadly and followed.

In the club car, George Saxon looked at his watch and groped in the jumble of his mind for a way out. There was less than ten minutes before the train stopped at Stamford.

The door opened and Suzy entered, followed by the gunman. Suzy was dressed. She sat next to her father. The gunman sat next to her.

"You all right?" George asked, taking one of her hands in his.

Suzy nodded. "What's he going to do? Why did he make me get dressed?"

"Do what he says, honey," George told her. He looked into the unblinking gray eyes of the man. "He won't do anything."

"You're both smart," said the gunman. "I don't want to hurt nobody." He looked down at Suzy. "Not you *or* your father."

The clatter of the wheels became louder as the door opened again, and at the same time, the hiss and scraping of the brakes drowned out conversation. The four soldiers filed in, weaving against the sway of the train. All but the sergeant were carrying their caps in their hands, and two of them carried their overcoats over their arms. The sergeant held his cap slightly in front of him in his right hand. It was obviously wrapped around something. They stopped in a line, the sergeant directly in front of the gunman.

"Hi, there." The sergeant grinned at Suzy. "Still up?"

Suzy stared at the floor.

"We're getting off at Stamford," the gunman said. "Can I buy you boys a drink?"

"No, thanks," said the sergeant, pleasantly. "We had a few beers. Just came in to ask you to settle a bet."

The train lurched and slowed. The soldiers each reached out an arm to brace themselves over the heads of George, Suzy, and the gunman. The two overcoats, hanging from outstretched arms, screened them from the view of the other passengers.

"A bet?" asked the gunman. "Why me?"

"We figured you're the only one on the train who could," the sergeant told him.

"I don't get it."

The sergeant let his cap fall to the floor. In his big right hand, he held the neck of a beer bottle, broken in the middle, its jagged edges pointing at the gunman's face.

"I dropped this back there," he said casually, "and we got to wondering. Then we made a bet. Johnny, here, says 'yes.' I say 'no.'"

The man's face was an unblinking mask as he stared at the sharp points of glass.

"Yes or no to what?" he asked in a choked whisper.

"I say 'no,'" said the sergeant. "I say a guy packing a rod wouldn't have the guts to go for it if a thing like this was a few inches from his face." He moved the wicked points a fraction closer to the upturned face in front of him. "What do you say, Mister? Settle the bet. It's just a question of guts, I guess."

The gunman's lower lip quivered slightly, and his right hand moved slowly upward toward his left armpit. The razor-sharp points of glass moved an inch closer. Tiny beads of sweat suddenly appeared on his forehead and the right hand fell back. The bottle didn't waver.

George put his arm stealthily around his daughter's shoulders and drew her closer.

Slowly, the gunman let both arms relax and hang over the

sides of his chair. His body slumped. His face was the color of putty.

"What say?" asked the sergeant.

The brakes grabbed harder and the train slowed suddenly, but the sergeant's hand didn't move.

The two soldiers on his right then braced themselves and wedged him tightly.

The gunman's eyes traveled from the bottle to the four pairs of unsmiling eyes above him. Then he spoke and his voice was a hoarse muttering. "I—I guess you'd win, Sergeant. He wouldn't have the guts."

Slowly, the sergeant removed his hand from the wall above the gunman's head, and gently, he reached under the gray flannel coat. He handed the heavy, black automatic to the soldier on his left . . .

Half an hour later, after the police had taken their prisoner in handcuffs from the train and it was once again rolling north, George Saxon tucked Suzy into upper two and waited there till she slept.

Back in the club car again, he smiled gratefully at the four soldiers. "What tipped you, Sergeant?" he asked.

The sergeant sipped his beer. "When I'm worried about my kid," he said, "I don't go looking for her with a forty-five. Best tailor in the world can't hide the bulge that one of those things makes."

"That all? Just the gun?"

"No," said the sergeant, quietly. "When Johnny asked him how old she was, he told us 'about twelve.' If she was my kid, I'd know exactly—not 'about.'"

George grinned. "I'll be darned," he said. "And all I can do is buy you boys a beer?"

"No," said the sergeant.

"Huh?" said George.

"Buy us two. We're thirsty."

George looked at the four faces. They were all grinning, now. He signaled the porter, and laughed aloud.

21

CYRIL HARE

Murderer's Luck

CYRIL HARE is the pseudonym of an English judge who likes to dabble in fictional crime in his off-the-bench hours. He has written a number of fascinating novels dealing neatly with the reasons men (and women) may commit murder. The story, he tells us, was suggested by an incident which once came to his attention. The fictitious Progress Club which forms the setting is patterned on a real one. We won't tell you its name, but it *is* in London's Pall Mall.

EVERYBODY who knows London knows the Progress Club. It is one of the most impressive buildings in Pall Mall, and every line of its architecture proclaims that for the best people Progress stopped in 1850 or thereabouts. I am not a member, but my friend Prothero is, and I was his guest there at dinner recently.

Prothero likes to call himself a "criminologist." Murder is his hobby, and I have long since lost count of the famous crimes which he has "written up." I was not surprised, therefore, that among the friends of his who joined us in the smoking-room after dinner was a rather exalted official at Scotland Yard, by the name of Wrestall.

Over our coffee and liqueurs Wrestall happened to ask me whether I had been in the club before.

"Yes," I told him, "but not for several years. I remember that the last time I was here the member who entertained me was Sylvester Kemball."

It was not a very tactful remark, seeing that Kemball had quite recently been hanged for murdering his wife. But my companions took it in good part.

"I have always thought," said Prothero, rather pontifically, "that the Kemball case was one of the most successful examples of modern detective methods. It was a great triumph for our

214

police organization—and for you personally, Wrestall," he added.

"If you say so," said Wrestall modestly. "But as a matter of fact, it was only by the merest stroke of luck that we obtained the evidence to bring it home to him."

"Luck!" said Prothero. "When you come to think of it, it is astonishing how often the most astute and careful criminal is defeated by some quite unforeseen accident—often by an extravagantly unlikely event which he could not possibly have guarded against. Take the Abertillery murder, for example . . ."

But we never took the Abertillery murder. A man in the far corner of our group interrupted him without ceremony. "The unluckiest murderer within my recollection," he said, "was Anthony Edward Fitzpatrick Pugh."

Everybody turned to look at him. He was not much to look at —a small, insignificant fellow with a disagreeably complacent expression. I recollected that his name was Hobson and that, like myself, he was present as the guest of a member.

"Pugh?" Prothero contrived to make the name sound almost insulting. "I think I am tolerably well acquainted with every crime of any significance during the last century and a half, and I have never come across the name before. Wrestall, are you familiar with the case of the homicidal Mr. Pugh?"

Wrestall shook his head.

"You see, Mr. Hobson," Prother went on. "You appear to be the possessor of knowledge quite unknown even to Scotland Yard. I hesitate to make the suggestion, but are you quite sure of your facts?"

"Perfectly. Would you care to hear them?"

"We are all ears." Prothero settled himself in his chair with an indulgent smile.

"It's a very simple story, really," said Hobson, "and I only mention it because whenever the subject of bad luck comes up, it always brings Pugh to my mind. Mind you, he deserved his luck, as people generally do.

"He was a disagreeable type, selfish and greedy as they make them. His bad luck began when he entrusted practically the whole of the fortune he had inherited from his parents to a get-rich-quick schemer in the City. He should have known better, of course, but there it was. He lost the lot. Then he brought an action to recover his money. He secured a judgment quite easily.

Ten thousand pounds and costs. But it's one thing to get a decision from the courts and quite another to make it effective, as Pugh found out.

"His lawyers went through the usual motions, of course, which added quite a tidy figure to the costs Pugh had to pay. It was no good. Their man went gracefully and artistically bankrupt. Pugh could whistle for his money—it simply wasn't there.

"What made things still more aggravating for him, destitution didn't seem to make the slightest difference to the debtor's style of living. He lived on his comfortable estate in Sussex. He continued to travel up to London every day with a reserved seat in a first-class smoker, and the porters touched their caps to him. Poor Pugh lived in the same neighborhood and caught the same train, traveling third-class non-smoker, thinking about his ten thousand pounds every mile of the way.

"The secret of the happy bankrupt's prosperity, of course, was that he, personally, never owned anything. Every stick and stone of the Sussex mansion, the pedigreed Jerseys in the park, the racehorses in the stables, the money that paid the servants' wages and the butcher's bills and the first-class fares to London was the sole, separate property of his wife—who was, incidentally, a very attractive, good-natured woman, and much too good for her scamp of a husband.

"That daily encounter on the railway station platform made Pugh feel positively murderous. One could hardly have blamed him if one fine morning he had slaughtered the man out of hand. But Pugh wasn't that sort. Money was what he cared about—not revenge. Killing his debtor wouldn't have got his ten thousand back. What he wanted was to find some means of putting money into his debtor's pocket, where he could get at it.

"He thought the matter over in his cold-blooded way, and hit upon a very simple, logical solution. The fellow had made his property over to his wife. Pugh proposed to reverse the process. He could be fairly certain that in such a set-up the lady would have made a will leaving everything to her husband. He had only to put her out of the way, and there would be more than enough money in the husband's hands to satisfy his little claim. That was his calculation, and, as it turned out, he was dead right.

"Once having made up his mind to commit the murder, he carried it out with great simplicity and ease. He discovered by observation that his intended victim was in the habit of driving herself into Worthing every day. To get to the main road she had to go through a gate across the drive which was kept shut on account of the cows.

"Pugh concealed himself behind a hedge at that point, waited till she came along, and then shot her through the head at close range as she got out of the car to open the gate. He used an old German pistol he had picked up years before. Then he walked quietly away, leaving the pistol. He saw no reason why anyone should connect him with a woman to whom he had never even spoken in his life. And, indeed, there was none."

"Then how was he convicted?" asked Prothero.

"He wasn't," Hobson replied. "I never said that he was. I merely said that he was the unluckiest murderer within my recollection, and that was strictly true. You see, although he had been absolutely right in his calculations and completely successful in his crime, he never got his ten thousand pounds.

"Pugh had been so careful to avoid being suspected himself that it had never occurred to him to wonder who would be likely to be accused of the crime in his place. But of course when a rich woman with a penniless husband is murdered, there is one obvious person for the police to pick on, if you don't mind my putting it that way, Mr. Wrestall. If Pugh had thought the matter out a little more carefully, he would have seen that this was also the one person he couldn't afford to have convicted.

"When the authorities began to look into the case against the husband, Pugh's bad luck started to operate in earnest. It turned out that the couple had had a flaming row that very morning and that the wife was actually on her way to see her lawyer about making a new will at the moment when she was killed.

"It turned out, further, that the pistol Pugh used was the dead spit of one owned by the accused and—so he said—lost by him only a week or two before. That made quite a sizable case against him, but the crucial piece of evidence arose from the unlikeliest stroke of luck you could imagine.

"A witness was found to prove that the husband was near the scene of the crime within ten minutes or so of the critical moment. He was the prisoner's gardener, and he had no business to be there at all at that hour. His presence was due solely to the fact that his wife had scalded herself by upsetting a kettle and he was on his way to telephone for the doctor. Result: The alibi which the defense tried to set up was blown to bits, and the husband was hanged.

"His conviction, of course, deprived him of all rights in the deceased's estate and he died as penniless as he had lived. You may say, then, that Pugh lost ten thousand pounds just because a gardener's wife was a bit clumsy taking a kettle off the hob. Oh, he was unlucky all right! So, when you come to think of it, was the chap who was convicted."

There was a long pause, and then Hobson's host said, "Where is Pugh now? I've an idea our friend Wrestall might be interested in a little talk with him."

"Oh, he's past all that," Hobson said. "Pugh killed himself six months after the unfortunate ending of the trial. Not from any remorse, you understand. The thought that now he never *could* get his ten thousand pounds drove him to desperation."

"By the way," Prothero said, "what was the husband's name? I don't think you mentioned it."

Hobson didn't seem to have heard the question. He was looking at his watch. "Heavens! I'd no idea it was so·late!" he exclaimed. "I've a train to catch at Victoria. Do you mind if I rush away now, old man?"

His departure broke up the party and as I am not fond of late hours, I took the opportunity to thank Prothero for a pleasant evening and made my way out. As I went, I caught sight of Wrestall, looking, it seemed to me, distinctly thoughtful.

I found Hobson just outside hunting for a taxi. As I may have indicated, I had not taken to the man very much, but I had my car round the corner and Victoria Station was on my way home, so it seemed only decent to offer him a lift.

"I suppose the husband in your story was Sylvester Kemball?" I asked, as we took the corner by Marlborough House.

"Oh, yes," said Hobson complacently.

"And his execution was a complete miscarriage of justice! How horrible!"

"Oh, you needn't waste any pity on *him*. He deserved all he got. His treatment of his wife alone merited hanging."

"You seem to know a lot about him," I observed.

"Well, she was my aunt. The only relation I had in the world."

I said no more until we were passing Buckingham Palace.

"When did you come to learn the truth about your aunt's murder?" I asked him.

"About half way through Kemball's trial," said Hobson calmly. "I knew Pugh fairly well, and I used to discuss the evidence with him. One evening we were dining together, and he got a bit tight. He slipped out something that he hadn't meant to say, and I broke him down. He told me the whole story."

"What on earth did you do?"

"Nothing at all. I looked at it this way: Kemball was every bit as bad as a murderer. I think he would probably have killed my aunt anyway, if Pugh hadn't got in first. And hanging Pugh wouldn't have done her any good. Besides, the fact is that I couldn't afford to see him hanged."

"What do you mean?" Thank heaven, Victoria was just ahead. I could hardly bear the man's presence any longer.

"Well, I was a poor man and I was my aunt's next of kin. If Kemball was acquitted, it meant that her will leaving everything to him was good. If he was convicted, I scooped the pool. I am sure my dear aunt would have preferred to have it that way."

I stopped the car with a quite unnecessary jerk. Hobson got out.

"Thanks for the lift," he said. "Perhaps I shall see you again some day. I'm putting up for election to the Progress, by the way."

I wondered, as I drove home, whether I ought to warn Prothero about this candidate for his club. I decided not to do so. After all, I am not a member.

22

FRANCES AND RICHARD LOCKRIDGE

Death on a Foggy Morning

THE LOCKRIDGES have been entertaining mystery readers for some twenty years with their stories of that genial couple, Mr. and Mrs. North. Besides novels, the Norths have been regulars on both radio and television. Captain Heimrich, the state trooper who is the protagonist of this story, has also appeared in a number of novels. Before turning to fiction, Mr. Lockridge was dramatic critic on the New York *Evening Sun.* Mrs. Lockridge used to be a newspaper woman herself.

IT WAS WALTER BRINKLEY's first contact with the New York State Police, as it had also been his first contact with violent death. He found the police courteous and patient: telling them what had happened somehow lessened the impact of the violence, so that the quivering of his nerves lessened. It was true that they continued to call him "Professor," an appellation which, although accurate enough, he preferred to hear used in a classroom, which this certainly was not.

"The fog had lifted, then?" the uniformed sergeant said, and the other policeman held his pencil ready. "You appreciate it might make a good deal of difference."

Mr. Brinkley nodded his head. His thick white hair glinted in the sunlight which, at that hour of an April morning, poured into his living room.

"Just," he said. "Very suddenly. Ten minutes before I went down I could hardly see the road. Then I could see the mail box, and that Mr. Beale had been by and put down the flag." He paused. "I call it the flag," he said, a little anxiously. "The arm, you know? The—indicator? That shows when there is mail to be picked up?" He was anxious to be clear. At the same time, he felt he was too anxious. A fussy old man, they would think him. In short, a professor. No wonder . . .

"Yes, professor," the sergeant said. "And you went down and —found Mr. Gray?"

He had. It was all clear in his mind—too clear. He had walked down his driveway, which ran straight up from Hayride Lane for three hundred feet, to his comfortable white house. He had walked in the warming sun of an April morning, and had walked with spring in his steps. He had taken the mail out of his box and looked up and down the road, as one does. And there, not a hundred yards away to the north, just by the big lilac clump at the corner of the Farmers' land, a man lay in the shallow roadside drainage ditch. Walter Brinkley ran, then.

The man was Martin Gray, who lived up the lane half a mile or so, who walked down the lane a mile each decent morning and walked back up the mile, for his health's sake, and who was dying when Brinkley knelt beside him, though he still managed to speak. Now the sergeant wanted to get his last words down very carefully, and Walter Brinkley repeated them as carefully as he could.

"He said," Brinkley told the policeman, " 'Wrong side. Wrong side.' He spoke more loudly than—than one would have expected. Then he said, 'No! No!' I suppose as—as a kind of protest?"

"Probably," the sergeant said. "When he saw the car coming at him. Then?"

"Then—'No!' again and then, 'No con—' And then—then he died." It was all clear—dreadfully clear. "I was trying to lift him up," Walter Brinkley, professor emeritus of English, said in a fixed voice, and looked at the sergeant through fixed eyes.

"Nothing you could have done," the sergeant promised him.

And the trooper who was taking notes said, "C-o-n? That was what it sounded like?"

"Well," Brinkley said, and knew he was being fussy again. "Yes. Or k-u-n, perhaps. As if . . ." He felt that they were being very patient with a white-haired, elderly man—an absurdly meticulous man. "That was what it sounded like," he said, firmly, and then, by way of showing he was not unaware of idiom and knew a little about the world, "A hit-and-run case?"

"Looks like it," the sergeant said. "Didn't see him in the fog. Thought he was dead or—didn't care, long as he could get away. Probably no other car in sight. Well—thanks, professor. Nothing you could have done you didn't do. Probably want your evidence when we catch up with him."

They seemed very sure they would catch up with the motorist who had killed Martin Gray, Professor Brinkley thought, watching the police car go down the drive. Poor Gray, who had come to North Wellwood only two years ago, retired in his late fifties with, obviously, plenty of money; a strong and active man, considerate of his health. A man with a pretty, much younger wife and a pretty daughter by an earlier marriage. Professor Brinkley, a widower and sometimes lonely, returned to his study and work on "American Regional Accents" (tentative title). It was best to return, as quickly as one might, to life's routine.

The police routine had already begun. When a car hits a man hard enough to crush him, the car is damaged. Right front fender, most probably, in this case—car moving south in Hayride Lane, meeting a man, walking north. The man walked to face traffic (if he knew his way around) and stepped out into the roadway because he had to get past a big lilac clump growing too close to the road's edge. Considering the fog, an accident. Until the driver left the scene, and a man dying. A crime, then.

Since Brewster, New York, is north of North Wellwood, the discovery of a light car in a Brewster garage, undergoing repairs on a dented left front fender, seemed without significance. It seemed that until routine disclosed that the car was registered in the name of Constance Gray, and that Constance Gray was Mrs. Martin Gray. Then the matter seemed one for Captain M. L. Heimrich, New York State Police, whose concern is homicide.

Constance Gray was not at home; she was in New York, and neither the maid nor the pretty, sobbing girl—Mary Gray, a senior at North Wellwood high school, called from class to be told of her father's death—knew where Constance could be reached. She was expected back in the late afternoon, expected on the train due in Brewster at five-twelve.

Questions are best based on information, and Heimrich, late into the case, had less of it than he could have wished when, with Sergeant Forniss, he waited for the five-twelve on the station platform. He knew that Constance Gray was twenty years, at least, younger than her husband; that Martin Gray had retired three years before at the age of fifty-five from what appeared to have been a lucrative insurance business; that he had been a widower for some ten years when he remarried and that Mary, who had just passed seventeen, was his only child. Heimrich also knew what Gray, dying, had found strength to say to Professor Brinkley.

Heimrich would have liked more to go on as he watched a pretty blond woman in a powder-blue spring suit come down the steps of a coach of the five-twelve. A policeman must, however, go on what he has.

If the pretty blond woman, with piquant face and wide blue eyes, had driven her car across the road—on the "wrong side"—to kill her husband, there was nothing in her face to show it. Her face was gay. Her hair was immaculately in place. Probably what she had gone to New York for, Heimrich thought, moving toward her. To have her hair done. "Mrs. Gray?" he said, and she stopped. She looked up at two solid men, and her wide eyes widened.

"State Police," Heimrich said, and watched her face, and her face told him. There could be no doubt her face told him, her eyes told him. Constance Gray was afraid. Because they were policemen, she was afraid. It was as easy as that—and, for an instant, Heimrich realized that, watching her, pretty and gay-faced, he had wished it wouldn't be.

"Oh!" she said, as if her breath caught, and then again, "Oh!" And then, which was quite unbelievable, "I knew I should have reported it. I really *did* know that. But it didn't seem to hurt him."

Heimrich is used to remarkable statements, particularly by murderers. He could remember none more remarkable than this. Here was a woman who had guided a car across a road so as to kill her husband with it, and who said now that she should have reported this—should "really" have reported. And—that being killed hadn't seemed to hurt. He looked down at her in disbelief. He felt his face falling open, human astonishment triumphing over professional detachment. He pulled his face together. He said, "What are you talking about, Mrs. Gray?" and his voice sounded hard in his own ears.

She looked bewildered then. He had seen that expression on many faces. All bewildered innocence she was now.

"The deer?" she said. "Isn't it about the deer?"

So that was it. One had to give her credit. But not too much.

"It's not about a deer," Heimrich said, and told her flatly what it was about. She began to tremble, then, and put her hands over her face and did (Heimrich thought without sympathy) such other things as she thought appropriate. They took her home, then, to the big white house on Hayride Lane. There her step-daughter ran into her arms and clung to her, and Constance Gray, her own face set, seemed to try to comfort the girl. A very competent actress, Heimrich thought of Constance Gray.

After she had had time enough, she pushed the girl away, gently, and turned to Heimrich and said, in a quite level voice, "Tell me about it, please." Heimrich told her, but not that her husband had died saying her name—part of her name. There would be time for that, later. She said, "You think I—" and then, "How can you think that?" And this, too, was appropriate enough.

"Now, Mrs. Gray," Heimrich said. "I don't think anything yet, naturally." (Which was not really true.) "You didn't see your husband on the road? Didn't run into him? By accident, natu-rally."

She had not seen Martin Gray—not after they left the house at about the same time, he for his walk, she in the car. He had started north on the left side of the road, and had waved at her. She had driven north to Brewster. There had been a little fog.

"Why do you think—?" she said, and again did not finish, but instead said, "I loved him. We loved each other." And her voice shook at that.

Heimrich waited. Then he said, "You hit a deer? That's how your fender was dented?"

"Yes," she said. "I hit a deer. Only a deer. Is it any use to tell you?"

"Now, Mrs. Gray," Heimrich said. "It's of use, naturally."

She had been two or three miles on the road to Brewster. The fog had lifted. She had not been driving fast. The deer came out of nowhere in one great leap; a big deer, which scrambled and slid on the road surface. "Afterwards," she said, "there was froth on my windshield." She had braked, skidded a little, felt the jar as the car struck him.

"He half fell," she said. "But then he didn't fall. He leaped away—up the bank and away. He didn't seem hurt."

But her voice seemed to die away as she told of the deer. It was, Heimrich thought, as if she lost faith in her story even as she told it. Yet it was not, intrinsically, an improbable story. Few motorists drive long in Northern Westchester without narrowly missing—or not missing—deer charging across roadways. If deer and car survive, there is nothing to report to authority. Then, why the tableau of guilt on the station platform? Explanation of a guilt reaction which could not wholly be concealed. Probably. Of course, the Grays had not lived long in deer country.

A telephone rang in another room. The call was, the maid came to say, for Miss Mary. "That boy—the Beale boy," she said, in a certain tone. The pretty girl, pretty for all the redness of her eyes, ran out of the room.

Constance Gray watched her, and Constance's eyes narrowed a little. She turned back to Heimrich and said, "Her—boy friend. Martin and I are rather—" and stopped with that, and put her hands over her eyes. After a time she took them down and said that she was sorry, and that she was all right now.

"Why do you think it wasn't merely a—a dreadful accident?" she asked him, and her voice was steady.

It was time to tell her, then, and Heimrich told her what her husband had said, dying. Her blue eyes seemed to darken as she listened. And, Heimrich thought, fear grew in them.

"He said, 'No, Con,'" she repeated, when she had heard. "That was it? As if—as if it were, 'Don't, Con!' That's what you think?"

There was no need to answer.

"And," she said, "'Wrong side.' And I would have been on the wrong side to hit him. That's it, too?"

"Now, Mrs. Gray," Heimrich said.

"Because he was older?" she said. "That's what you think? Or—just for the money. The insurance? Double indemnity for accidental death. You'll find that out." She had begun to speak very rapidly. "A hundred thousand dollars," she said. "To kill Martin for. To—"

Suddenly, she began to say, "No. No. No . . ." over and over, as if she would never stop.

Mary Gray ran back into the room, then, and looked at Heimrich with anger. "Go away!" the girl said, in the voice of youth's angry rebellion. "Go away. Leave her alone!"

Heimrich nodded to Forniss with that, and the two tall, solid men did as the girl said, since hysteria is inarticulate, and since Heimrich needed to know more before he could ask more. He did not say that they would be back, since there is no point in saying what is obvious.

Heimrich did know more the next morning, had more to go on, as he drove toward the Gray house—Constance Gray's house now—at a little after eight. He knew that the insurance money went to Constance Gray, along with a good deal more money.

He knew that Martin Gray had been popular enough, certainly had had no "enemies." If one did not count young Rodney Beale, high school senior, who had done some muttering about people who thought they were better than other people because they had a lot of money. (The point apparently being that Martin Gray had considered Rodney, eighteen and a part-time grocery clerk, an unsuitable husband for his daughter.) But boys of eighteen often mutter against fusty parents who have themselves forgotten love.

He was abruptly distracted from his sorting of information. A car came briskly toward him, and the car had no driver. *No driver at all!* It had a passenger, sitting at the right of the driver's seat. There was nobody behind the wheel. Heimrich's car winced toward the side of the road. But then the approaching car swerved abruptly to the right and stopped beside a rural mail box. Heimrich laughed, soundlessly, at himself.

A good many rural route men drove in that fashion, needing only a car with automatic transmission—sat on the wrong side, but the side nearest boxes, drove with left hand and foot, and so avoided much sliding across seats to take mail out of boxes and to poke it in. All the same, it was somewhat alarming to see when a car so driven came head on. And all the same, it was rather risky. In an emergency, a man on the wrong side of the driver's seat wouldn't have much control. Not much con—

Wrong side. No con— Wrong side of the *car,* not of the *road!*

Heimrich drove on, but not to the big white house he had been headed for. He drove to another house like it, but half a mile north on Hayride Lane. He said to the gray-haired man there, "When Mr. Gray said 'con' and stopped, did it sound like an emphasized first syllable? As if he might have been going to say '*Con*stance?' Or—"

"I've been worrying about that," Professor Brinkley said, in a worried voice. "I was afraid they would think I was just being —fussy. Unemphasized, I'm quite sure. The indeterminate sound of the vowel, you know. And—"

"Yes," Heimrich said, "as if he really meant to say control."

Heimrich drove into North Wellwood, then, and to the small

cottage where Thomas Beale, driver of rural route No. 2, lived
with his wife. Not that Beale would be there; he would be on
the route. But—

Beale was there. His wife said so. In bed with one of his
migraines. And had been the day before. And—

"Tom's nephew is taking the route for him," Mrs. Beale said,
and was anxious, and twisted her apron in her hands. "Rod, that
is. There's nothing wrong, is there?"

"I hope not," Heimrich said, going as far as he could go. He
drove two blocks to another cottage, where the Whitney Beales
lived with their son, Rodney, but he did not go to the door. He
waited in his car for an hour or more before Rodney Beale, driving as his uncle drove—as what boy of eighteen would not,
given an excuse?—turned into the driveway.

He was a big boy. All the same, his instinct was to run. Heimrich could see that in his tense body, his working, frightened
face.

"Well, son?" Heimrich said.

"*I didn't mean to,*" the boy said. "He just sort of stumbled out
in front of me and—I— *He was dead.* I couldn't *do* anything.
Wasn't he dead?"

"No," Heimrich said. "I don't say it would have made any
difference if you'd got help. But—he wasn't dead."

"Nobody would have believed me," the boy said. "After—I've
been saying things about him. And—"

"We might have," Heimrich said. "We might still. But—you'll
have to come with me now, son."

A boy can panic, Heimrich thought, driving away from the
Brewster substation of the New York State Police, the spring
afternoon warm about him. Anybody can panic. Probably the
boy hadn't meant to kill. Not consciously meant to kill. So probably it wasn't actually murder, which is Heimrich's special concern.

Heimrich turned his car into Hayride Lane once more, toward
Constance Gray's big white house. There he would have what
amounted to an apology to make.

23

MICHAEL GILBERT

Scream in a Soundproof Room

HIS MYSTERY NOVELS are earning Michael Gilbert increasing prestige in this country as they have for a number of years in Great Britain. Mr. Gilbert, during professional hours, is a London solicitor, but during World War II he was a British Army major ending up in Intelligence. He has that English knack for sensing an unusual situation and dealing with it sensitively, which is at its best in this story from behind the Iron Curtain . . . and from a soundproof room.

IT WAS second nature in Orloff to watch people without appearing to do so.

So, as Ladislas Petrov walked slowly up and down the handsome, paneled room that was partly his old drawing room and partly his new library, Orloff took out a lighter, lit a cigarette, and put away his lighter, and polished his nails and examined the toes of his own boots. Though his eyes rested rarely on his host his attention was on him the whole time.

The precaution was unconscious, the fruits of the life that Orloff had lived: nearly forty years of it since, as a boy of ten, he had started by carrying messages for the anarchist underground.

How old had he been when he had first been flogged? Fourteen was it? Or fifteen? How old when first condemned to death, and saved by some quirk of the absolute monarchy? Saved to see that monarchy go down in blood and dust and bitter humiliation; saved to see himself, as Party Secretary, the effective ruler of the country that had once hung him to a steel ring and beaten him.

It was purely unconscious, because Orloff had no reason now to distrust or to fear Ladislas Petrov. Petrov was that rarity, a Communist leader who had succeeded in reaching retirement. Rich, no longer ambitious, politically secure, dangerous to no one, he lived on in his handsome villa at Provst, a living exception to the rule that no revolutionary man dies in his bed.

"It is the joinery which is so clever," he said. "You see? Each edge dovetailed to the other, but the dovetails hide each other successively, so that in the end, no joint appears."

He stroked with his finger the clean poplar wood which, fashioned into book shelves and pediment, ran the length of the wall.

The man who had fashioned it was in the room with them. He had completed his work on the bookcases and the presses and was finishing now the woodwork of the new door. Orloff had noticed the door as he came in. It was solid and very heavy, but so beautifully balanced and hung that it moved to a finger's touch. You would imagine almost that a breath would open or shut it. When it closed, it slid into the jamb with that soft kiss that meant fitting to a hundredth of an inch on every side.

"We have fine carpenters still in our country," he agreed.

"You must not say 'carpenter.' I made that mistake myself at first. A carpenter is a man who builds houses. He has a big saw, to cut beams, and a heavy hammer, to drive nails." Petrov made a pantomime of sawing and hammering and laughed at his own clowning. "This man is a cabinet maker. He is a craftsman, a precision worker."

Although the workman was within hearing and took in every word they said, both men spoke about him as if he were not there, or had no proper understanding.

Orloff turned his searchlight attention on him for a moment. He was a big, brown-faced, white-haired man with a smile. An unusually good advertisement for the regime.

"You pay him?"

"Nothing, but for each day's work I give him a month's privilege ticket. If he works here twelve days he will be able to live well for a year—is that right?"

Finding himself addressed, the man smiled and bobbed his head. A privilege ticket enabled him to buy, at low cost, the extra fats and meat and milk that, in the normal way, only senior party members could enjoy.

"It is good work. It makes a handsome room."

His eye was still on the man. On his face, his hands, his canvas sack of tools. Orloff's intelligence picked up one fact—two facts—but failed, for the moment, to translate them.

"I gave some thought to it," agreed Petrov complacently. "First, we designed the shutters." The shutters flanked the long, single window which looked straight across Lake Plerny. They were cleverly designed but did not entirely conceal the fact that the windows themselves were barred, like the windows of a cell, by steel bars. Even in retirement a revolutionary leader could not neglect certain safeguards.

It would be a difficult room to attack, thought Orloff. One narrow, barred window. One heavy door. He had no doubt that under the fine paneling was steel plate. The walls were so thick that they were almost soundproof. An easy room to defend. But why think of that now? There was no fighting nowadays. No opposition. They were getting fat. Fat and soft.

Petrov suddenly laughed. "We are all three cabinet makers," he said. "You realize that? All three in this room."

It was true, thought Orloff. Difficult to realize now, as you looked at old Papa Petrov. Difficult to see in him the fighter, the man who had held the post office for nearly a week in the first May rising, held it with a handful of men and boys, little ammunition and no food.

Even more difficult to see the ruthless prosecutor of the purges. The man who had placed his own brother on trial for treason and countersigned the order for his execution without emotion. The man who, when everyone else had cried, "Halt," had gone one step further—and then another.

Who had shot, with the guilty Rabotkin, the innocent Kometsy. Who had said, as Kometsy was prosecuted and handed to the Security Police, "He is innocent now, perhaps. But he has the look of a man who may be guilty some day."

Orloff found himself thinking of things he had not remembered for many years, things he had thought buried under the heap of the intervening time. Those had been days when every man carried his head loose on his shoulders.

Why did his mind come back to Kometsy? Perhaps because he had been the greatest, and the last, of the victims. And as an oak, when felled in a thicket, brings down a host of lesser trees, so had tumbled all Kometsy's friends.

His secretaries. His family. His department. His friends. His wife had taken poison. There was a brother, Andreas. Something about Andreas? He had escaped. By great good fortune Andreas had been in Washington at the time of the trials, and by better fortune had had his family with him.

So rapidly had these thoughts passed through Orloff's mind that he found Petrov was still laughing at his own stupid joke.

"I have made and unmade many cabinets in my time," he repeated.

But Orloff was still looking at the workman, who had just finished his work on the door jamb with a few strokes of a spokeshave. A first-class workman, indeed, thought Orloff, who knew something of most things. Not one to massacre his material and then hide the scars behind sandpapering and putty. His finished product was clean wood, cleanly worked.

"Was your father a carpenter?" he asked suddenly.

"Indeed, greatness," said the man, speaking for the first time, "and his father before him."

"I thought it might be so," said Orloff. "You do not often see tools like this now."

It was a gauger plane that had caught his eye. A lovely instrument of bright steel and brass. He picked it up and twirled the gauge screw which regulated with micrometer precision the depth and set of the blade.

"It would take you—what—a year—to buy such a tool?"

"More, greatness," said the man. "I work little for money. Many of these my father left me. Others came to me before— before the Liberation."

Orloff nearly smiled. He guessed that if the man had been alone he would have said something very different.

He was packing away his tools now, with careful hands, as a surgeon might lay aside his instruments. Each chisel with its edge hidden in a wad of oakum, the graded drills, the curious gouges, the small, thin, heavy, brass-backed saw.

When he had done he bobbed to the two men asking leave to withdraw himself from their presence.

Petrov smiled, and made a gesture of dismissal with his hand. The man opened the door and ambled through, then he turned, smiled again, and closed the door behind him.

The little sigh which it made hung on the air.

Petrov moved again to the window. Below the terrace wall the waters winked in the setting sun.

"When I die," he said, "I will leave instructions in my will for my coffin to be taken out and sunk in the middle of the lake. They say it is bottomless—an old volcano—"

"I think," said Orloff, in his hard, incisive voice, "that you should check up on that man. The sooner the better."

"That man?"

"The man who's just left. Who does he call himself?"

"I never asked him his name," said Petrov. "The local co-operative sent him."

"Even local co-operatives have been known to make mistakes," said Orloff, drily.

"Are you sure you're not—"

"—letting my suspicious mind run away with me? No. I'm not sure. But my suspicious mind has just told me two things which my eyes saw five minutes ago. Do you remember the gauger plane? It would cost you—in this country today—oh, thirty dollars. Would a man like that earn thirty dollars in a year? In three years?"

"But he told you," said Petrov. "It came down to him from his father."

"That sort of plane did not exist five years ago."

"I see," said Petrov. He walked across to the fireplace and touched the bell. "Are you sure?"

"I know about these things," said Orloff. "It is a precision instrument, first invented for the aircraft industry, in America. But it was not only the plane. Did you not see his hands?"

"I saw them," said Petrov. "But they said nothing to me. What did they show to you?"

"Fresh blisters. Blisters from this job he has been doing here in the past twelve days. In the palm, from the butt of his chisel. On the side of the index finger from the handle of his saw."

"Why not?" said Petrov. "He has used both chisel and saw. I have seen myself."

"A carpenter," said Orloff, contemptuously. "And the son of a carpenter. A man who had handled tools since he was in knee breeches. Those parts of his hands would be like leather. And a third thing—"

His voice was so sharp that Petrov stopped pacing and stood still, looking at him.

"*Why has no one answered your bell?*"

"It is that old fool, Sebastian," said Petrov. "He is getting deaf. If he is not in his pantry he does not hear the bell—"

"Perhaps," said Orloff.

He walked across the room, his feet noiseless on the heavy carpet, and turned the handle of the new door. It turned quite freely. But the door remained shut.

He threw his weight back, once, twice. So little impression did he make that he might have been pulling against a tree.

"He has locked us in?"

"From the feel of it," said Orloff, "I should surmise that the door has been screwed to the jamb with half a dozen very long screws. You'd best try the telephone, though I should guess it is little use."

Petrov seized the instrument, listened a moment, jiggling it, and then put it back. "Dead," he said.

"Does your window open?" Orloff asked.

"The bars—"

"I had no intention of getting out of it. I wished to shout for help."

He had crossed the room as he spoke. Petrov came with him. Something seemed to have happened to the window. The catch could be opened, but their combined strength could not move the sash by a fraction up or down.

Quite suddenly the air in the room seemed stifling. Orloff ran to the mantelpiece, picked up a heavy iron candlestick, ran back, and swung it hard at the glass.

The next moment the candlestick had clattered to the floor. The glass was scarcely scratched.

"Bullet proof," said Petrov. For some reason he had dropped his voice to a whisper. "That man—could he have been Andreas?"

"It might have been," said Orloff. "It cannot be coincidence that his name was in my mind, too. I hardly knew him, but there was something in the look. Sit down, man, and stop sweating."

"What—how—what does he hope to do?"

Good God, thought Orloff, with a spasm of disgust, I was right. The old man's gone soft. There's no fight left in him.

"Sit down," he said again. "If he aims to suffocate us, the less air we use the better. It's a big room. Someone will come soon."

"Not before morning," said Petrov. "Not unless we can attract attention."

"A lot can happen in twelve hours," said Orloff. "If I am not back by nightfall, my own office will start to panic." For the first time that afternoon a very faint smile appeared round his lips. "They'll probably think I've crossed the Curtain."

"Stop talking," said Petrov. His voice was high. Like a woman about to plunge into the emotional depths of a tantrum.

Orloff looked sharply at him. Then he heard it, too.

Somewhere behind the bookshelves, behind the beautiful paneling, and the clever joinery: a deep, purposeful, purring, clicking, pendulum note.

"Maybe we haven't got twelve hours after all," said Orloff, resignedly. "Maybe not even one."

It was not too bad until Petrov started to scream.

24

ERLE STANLEY GARDNER

Flight into Disaster

IT SEEMS A LONG TIME AGO that Erle Stanley
Gardner created Perry Mason, the lawyer and private
detective who has probably appeared in more mystery
novels than any other private eye in fiction. A lawyer
himself by training, Mr. Gardner has long since made
fiction his business. His novels have sold millions of
copies—so many that he rarely finds the time to devote
himself to short stories. This one he wrote specially for
This Week—a spy story with a Wyoming setting.

ONLY ONCE BEFORE had the woman in the club car ever known
panic—not merely fear but the real panic which paralyzes the
senses.

That had been in the mountains when she had tried to take
a short cut to camp. When she realized she was lost there was
a sudden overpowering desire to run. What was left of her
sanity warned her, but panic made her feel that only by flight
could she escape the menace of the unknown. The silent mountains, the somber woods, had suddenly become enemies, leering
in hostility. Only by running did she feel she could escape—
by running—the very worst thing she could have done.

Now, surrounded by the luxury of a crack transcontinental
train, she again experienced that same panic. Once more there
was that overpowering desire to run.

Someone had searched her compartment while she had been
at dinner. She knew it was a man. He had tried to leave things
just as he had found them, but there were little things that a
woman would have noticed that the man didn't even see. Her
plaid coat, which had been hung in the little steel closet so
that the back was to the door, had been turned so the buttons
were toward the door. A little thing, but a significant thing which
had been the first to catch her attention, leaving her, for the
moment, cold and numb. Now, seated in the club car, she strove

to maintain an attitude of outward calm by critically inspecting her hands. Actually she was taking stock of the men who were in the car.

Her problem was complicated by the fact that she was a compactly formed young woman, with smooth lines, clear eyes, a complete quota of curves, and under ordinary circumstances, a latent smile always quivering at the corners of her mouth. It was, therefore, only natural that every male animal in the club car sat up and took notice.

The fat man across the aisle who held a magazine in his pudgy hands was not reading. He sat like a Buddha, motionless, his half-closed, lazy-lidded eyes fixed upon some imaginary horizon far beyond the confines of the car—yet she felt those eyes were taking a surreptitious interest in everything she did. There was something sinister about him, from the big diamond on the middle finger of his right hand to the rather ornate twenty-five-dollar cravat which begged for attention above the bulging expanse of his vest.

Then there was the man in the chair on her right. He hadn't spoken to her but she knew that he was going to, waiting only for an opportunity to make his remark sound like the casual comment of a fellow passenger.

He was in his late twenties, bronzed by exposure, steely-blue of eye. His mouth held the firmness of a man who has learned to command first himself and then others. The train lurched. The man's hand reached for the glass on the little stand between them. He glanced apprehensively at her skirt.

"Sorry," he said.

"It didn't spill," she replied almost automatically.

"I'll lower the danger point," he said, raising the glass to his lips. "Going all the way through? I'm getting off at six o'clock in a cold Wyoming morning."

For a moment her panic-numbed brain failed to appreciate the full significance of his remark, then she experienced a sudden surge of relief. Here, then, was one man whom she could trust. She knew that the man who had searched her baggage hadn't found what he wanted because she had it with her, neatly folded, fastened to the bottom of her left foot by strong adhesive tape. Therefore the enemy would stay on the train as long as she was on it, waiting, watching, growing more and more desperate, until at last, perhaps in the dead of night, he would . . . She knew only too well that he would stop at nothing. One murder had already been committed.

But now she had found one person whom she could trust, a man who had no interest in the thing she was hiding, a man who might well be a possible protector.

He seemed mildly surprised at her sudden friendliness.

"I didn't know this train stopped anywhere at that ungodly hour," she ventured, smiling.

"A flag stop," he explained.

Across the aisle the fat man had not moved a muscle, yet she felt absolutely certain that those glittering eyes were concentrating on her and that he was listening as well as watching.

"You live in Wyoming?" she asked.

"I did as a boy. Now I'm going back. I lived and worked on my uncle's cattle ranch. He died and left it to me. At first I thought I'd sell it. It would bring a small fortune. But now I'm tired of the big cities, I'm going back to live on the ranch."

"Won't it be frightfully lonely?"

"At times."

She wanted to cling to him now, dreading the time when she would have to go back to her compartment.

She felt the trainmen must have a master key which could open even a bolted door—in the event of sickness, or if a passenger rang for help. There *must* be a master key which would manipulate even a bolted door. And if trainmen had such a key, the man who had searched her compartment would have one.

Frank Hardwick, before he died, had warned her. "Remember," he had said, "they're everywhere. They're watching you when you don't know you're being watched. When you think you're running away and into safety, you'll simply be rushing into a carefully laid trap."

She hoped there was no trace of the inner tension within her as she smiled at the man on her right. "Do tell me about the cattle business," she said . . .

All night she had crouched in her compartment, watching the door, waiting for that first flicker of telltale motion which would show the doorknob was being turned. Then she would scream, pound on the walls of the compartment, make sufficient commotion to spread an alarm.

Nothing had happened. Probably that was the way "they" had planned it. They'd let her spend one sleepless night, then when fatigue had numbed her senses . . .

The train abruptly slowed. She glanced at her wristwatch, saw that it was 5:55, and knew the train was stopping for the man who had inherited the cattle ranch. Howard Kane was the name he had given her after she had encouraged him to tell her all about himself. Howard Kane, twenty-eight, unmarried, presumably wealthy, his mind scarred by battle experiences, seeking the healing quality of the big, silent places, the one man on the train whom she knew she could trust.

There was a quiet competency about him, one felt he could handle any situation—and now he was getting off the train.

Suddenly a thought gripped her— "They" would hardly be expecting her to take the initiative. "They" always kept the initiative—that was why they always seemed so damnably efficient, so utterly invincible.

They chose the time, the place and the manner—give them that advantage, and . . .

There wasn't time to reason the thing out. She jerked open the door of the little closet, whipped out her plaid coat, turned the fur collar up around her neck, and, as the train eased to a creaking stop, opened the door of her compartment and thrust out a cautious head.

The corridor was deserted.

She could hear the vestibule door being opened at the far end of the Pullman.

She ran to the opposite end of the car, fumbled for a moment with the fastenings of the vestibule door on the side next to the double track, then got it open and raised the platform.

Cold morning air, tanged with high elevation, rushed in to meet her, dispelling the train atmosphere, stealing the warmth from her garments.

The train started to move. She scrambled down the stairs, jumped for the graveled roadbed by the side of the track.

The train gathered speed. Dark, silent cars whizzed past her with continuing acceleration until the noise of the wheels became a mere hum. The steel rails readjusted themselves to the cold morning air, giving cracking sounds of protest. Overhead, stars blazed in steady brilliance. To the east was the first trace of daylight.

She looked for a town. There was none.

She could make out the faint outlines of a loading corral and cattle chute. Somewhere behind her was a road. An automobile was standing on this road, the motor running. Headlights sent twin cones of illumination knifing the darkness, etching into brilliance the stunted sagebrush shivering nervously under the impact of a cold north wind.

Two men were talking. A door slammed. She started running frantically.

"Wait!" she called. "Wait for me!"

Back on the train the fat man, fully dressed and shaved, contemplated the open vestibule door, then padded back to the recently vacated compartment and walked in.

He didn't even bother to search the baggage that had been left behind. Instead he sat down in the chair, held a telegraph blank against a magazine, and wrote out his message:

THE BUNGLING SEARCH TRICK DID THE JOB. SHE'S LEFT THE TRAIN. IT ONLY REMAINS TO CLOSE THE TRAP. I'LL GET OFF AT THE FIRST PLACE WHERE I CAN RENT A PLANE AND CONTACT THE SHERIFF.

Ten minutes later the fat man found the porter. "I find the elevation bothering me," he said. "I'm going to have to leave the train. Get the conductor."

"You won't get no lower by gettin' off," the porter said.

"No, but I'll get bracing fresh air and a doctor who'll give me a heart stimulant. I've been this way before. Get the conductor."

This time the porter saw the twenty-dollar bill in the fat man's fingers.

Seated between the two men in the warm interior of the car, she sought to concoct a convincing story.

Howard Kane said, by way of introduction, "This is Buck Doxey. I'm afraid I didn't catch your name last night."

"Nell Lindsay," she said quickly.

Buck Doxey, granite-faced, kept one hand on the steering wheel while he doffed a five-gallon hat. "Pleased to meet yuh, ma'am."

She sensed his cold hostility, his tight-lipped disapproval.

Howard Kane gently prodded for an explanation.

"It was a simple case of cause and effect," she said, laughing nervously. "It was so stuffy in the car I didn't sleep at all.

"So," she went on quickly, "I decided that I'd get out for a

breath of fresh air. When the train slowed and I looked at my
wristwatch I knew it was your stop and . . . Well, I expected
the train would be there for at least a few minutes. I couldn't
find a porter to get the vestibule open, so I did it myself, and
jumped down to the ground. That was where I made my mistake."

"Go on," he said.

"At a station you step down to a platform that's level with
the tracks. But here I jumped onto a slanting shoulder of gravel,
and sprawled flat. When I got up, the step of the car was so far
above me . . . well, you have to wear skirts to understand what
I mean."

Kane nodded gravely. Buck turned his head and gave Kane
a quartering glance.

She said, "I guess I could have made it at that if I'd had sense
enough to pull my skirt all the way up to the hips, but I couldn't
make it on that first try and there wasn't time for a second one.
The train started to move. Good heavens, they must have just
thrown you off!"

"I'm traveling light," Kane said.

"Well," she told him, "that's the story. Now just what do I do?"

"Why, you accept our hospitality, of course."

"I couldn't . . . couldn't wait here for the next train?"

"Nothing stops here except to discharge passengers coming
from a division point," he said.

"But there's a . . . station there. Isn't there someone on duty?"

"Only when cattle are being shipped," Buck Doxey explained.
"This is a loading point."

"Oh."

She settled back against the seat, and was conscious of a re-
assuring masculine friendship on her right side, a cold detachment on her left side.

"I suppose it's horribly ravenous of me, but do we get to the
ranch for breakfast?"

"I'm afraid not," Kane said. "It's slow going. Only sixty feet
of the road is paved."

"Sixty feet?"

"That's right. We cross the main transcontinental highway
about five miles north of here."

"What *do* we do about breakfast?"

"Well," Kane said, "in the trunk of the car there's a coffee pot and a canteen of water. I'm quite certain Buck brought along a few eggs and some ham . . ."

"You mean you stop right out here in the open and cook?"

"When yuh stop here, you're in the open, ma'am," Buck said and somehow made it seem his words were in answer to some unjustified criticism.

She gave him her best smile. "Would it be impertinent to ask when?"

"In this next coulee . . . right here . . . right now."

The road slanted down to a dry wash that ran east and west. The perpendicular north bank broke the force of the north wind. Buck attested to the lack of traffic on the road by stopping the car squarely in the ruts.

They watched the sun rise over the plateau country, and ate breakfast. She hoped that Buck Doxey's cold disapproval wouldn't communicate itself to Howard Kane.

When Buck produced a battered dishpan, she said, "As the only woman present I claim the right to do the dishes."

"Women," Buck said, "are . . ." and abruptly checked himself.

She laughingly pushed him aside and rolled up her sleeves. "Where's the soap?"

As she was finishing the last dish she heard the motor of the low-flying plane.

All three looked up.

The plane, which had been following the badly rutted road, banked into a sharp turn.

"Sure givin' us the once-over," Buck said, his eyes steady on Kane's face. "One of 'em has binoculars and he's as watchful as a cattle buyer at a loading chute. Don't yuh think it's about time we find out what we've got into, Boss?"

"I suppose it is," Kane said. Before her startled mind could counter his action, Buck Doxey picked up the purse which she had left lying on the running-board of the car.

She flew toward him.

Doxey's bronzed, steel fingers wrapped around her wet wrist. "Take it easy, ma'am," he said. "Take it easy."

He pushed her back, found her driving license. "The real name," he drawled, "seems to be Jane Marlow."

"Anything else?" Kane asked.

"Gobs of money, lipstick, keys and . . . Gosh, what a bank-roll."

She went for him blindly.

Doxey said, "Now, ma'am, I'm goin' to have to spank yuh if yuh keep on like this."

The plane circled, its occupants obviously interested in the scene on the ground below.

"Now—here's something else," Doxey said, taking out a folded newspaper clipping.

She suddenly went limp. There was no use in further pretense.

Doxey read aloud, " 'Following the report of an autopsy surgeon, police, who had never been entirely satisfied that the unexplained death of Frank Hardwick was actually a suicide, are searching for his attractive secretary, Jane Marlow. The young woman reportedly had dinner with Hardwick in a downtown restaurant the night of his death.

" 'Hardwick, after leaving Miss Marlow, according to her story, went directly to the apartment of Eva Ingram, a strikingly beautiful model who has however convinced police that she was dining out. Within a matter of minutes after entering the Ingram apartment, Hardwick either jumped or fell from the eighth story window.

" 'With the finding of a witness who says Frank Hardwick was accompanied at least as far as the apartment door by a young woman whose description answers that of Jane Marlow, and evidence indicating several thousand dollars was removed from a concealed floor safe in Hardwick's office, police are anxious once more to question Miss Marlow. So far their efforts have definitely not been crowned with success.'

"And here's a picture of this young lady," Buck said, "with some more stuff under it.

" 'Jane Marlow, secretary of scientist who jumped from apartment window to his death, is now sought by police after witness claims to have seen her arguing angrily with Frank Hardwick when latter was ringing bell at front door of apartment house from which Hardwick fell or jumped to sidewalk.' "

Overhead, the plane suddenly ceased its circling and took off in a straight line to the north.

As the car proceeded northward, Buck put on speed, deftly avoiding the bad places in the road.

Jane Marlow, who had lapsed into hopeless silence, tried one more last desperate attempt when they crossed the paved road. "Please," she said, "let me out here. I'll catch a ride back to Los Angeles and report to the police."

Kane's eyes asked a silent question of the driver.

"Nope," Buck said decisively. "That plane was the sheriff's scout plane. He'll expect us to hold you. I don't crave to have no more trouble over women."

"All right," Jane said in a last burst of desperation, "I'll tell you the whole story. Then I'll leave it to your patriotism. I was secretary to Frank Hardwick. He was working on something that had to do with cosmic rays."

"I know," Doxey interrupted sarcastically. "And he dictated his secret formula to you."

"Don't be silly," she said, "but he *did* know that he was in danger. He told me that if anything happened to him, to take something, which he gave me, to a certain individual."

"Just keep on talking," Buck said. "Tell us about the money."

Her eyes were desperate. "Mr. Hardwick had a concealed floor safe in the office. He left reserve cash there for emergencies. He gave me the combination, told me that if anything happened to him, I was to go to that safe, take the money and deliver it and a certain paper to a certain scientist in Boston."

Buck's smile of skepticism was certain to influence Kane even more than words.

"Frank Hardwick never jumped out of any window," she went on. "They were waiting for him, and they threw him out."

"Or," Buck said, "a certain young lady became jealous, followed him, got him near an open window and then gave a sudden, unexpected shove. It *has* been done, you know."

"And people *have* told the truth," she blazed. "*I* don't enjoy what I'm doing. I consider it a duty to my country—and I'll probably be murdered, just as Frank Hardwick was."

"Now listen," Kane said. "Nice little girls don't jump off trains before daylight in the morning and tell the kind of stories you're telling. You got off that train because you were running away from someone."

She turned to Kane. "I was hoping that *you* would understand."

"He understands," Buck said, and laughed.

After that she was silent . . .

Overhead, from time to time, the plane came circling back. Once it was gone for nearly forty-five minutes and she dared to hope they had thrown it off the track, but later she realized it had only gone to refuel and then it was back above them once more.

It was nearly nine when Buck turned off the rutted road and headed toward a group of unpainted, squat, log cabins which seemed to be bracing themselves against the cold wind while waiting for the winter snow. Back of the buildings were timbered mountains.

The pilot of the plane had evidently spotted the ranch long ago. Hardly had Buck turned off the road than the plane came circling in for a landing.

Jane Marlow had to lean against the cold wind as she walked from the car to the porch of the cabin. Howard Kane held the door open for her, and she found herself inside a cold room which fairly reeked of masculine tenancy, with a paper-littered desk, guns, deer and elk horns.

Within a matter of seconds she heard the pound of steps on the porch, the door was flung open, and the fat man and a companion stood on the threshold.

"Well, Jane," the fat man said, "you gave us quite a chase, didn't you?" He turned to the others.

"Reckon I'd better introduce myself, boys." He reached in his pocket, then took out a wallet and tossed it carelessly on the desk.

"I'm John Findlay of the FBI," he said.

"That's a lie," she said. "Can't you understand? This man is an enemy. Those credentials are forged."

"Well, ma'am," the other newcomer said, stepping forward, "there ain't nothing wrong with my credentials. I'm the sheriff here, and I'm taking you into custody."

He took her purse, said, "You just might have a gun in here."

He opened the purse. Findlay leaned over to look, said, "It's all there."

"Come on, Miss Marlow," the sheriff said, "You're going back in that plane."

"That plane of yours hold three people?" Findlay asked.

The sheriff looked appraisingly at the fat man. "Not us three."

"I can fly the crate," Findlay said. "I'll take the prisoner in, lock her up and then fly back for you and . . ."

"No, no, no!" Jane Marlow screamed. "Don't you see, can't you realize, this man isn't an officer. I'd never get there. He. . . ."

"Shut up," the sheriff said.

"Sheriff, please! You're being victimized. Call up the FBI and you'll find out that . . ."

"I've already called up the Los Angeles office of the FBI," the sheriff said.

Kane's brows leveled. "Was that because you were suspicious, Sheriff?"

"Findlay himself suggested it."

Jane was incredulous. "You mean they told you that . . . ?"

"They vouched for him in every way," the sheriff said. "They told me he'd been sent after Jane Marlow, and to give him every assistance. Now I've got to lock you up and . . ."

"She's my responsibility, Sheriff," Findlay said.

The sheriff frowned, then said. "Okay, I'll fly back and send a deputy out with a car."

"Very well," Findlay agreed. "I'll see that she stays put."

Jane Marlow said desperately, "I presume that when Mr. Findlay told you to call the FBI office in Los Angeles, he gave you the number so you wouldn't have to waste time getting it through an operator, didn't he?"

"Why not?" the sheriff said, smiling good-humoredly. "He'd be a hell of an FBI man if he didn't know his own telephone number."

The fat man fished a cigar from his pocket. Biting off the end and scraping a match into flame, he winked at the sheriff.

Howard Kane said to Findlay, "Mind if I ask a question?"

"Hell, no. Go right ahead."

"I'd like to know something of the facts in this case. If you've been working on the case you'd know . . ."

"Sure thing," Findlay agreed, getting his cigar burning evenly. "She worked for Hardwick, who was having an affair with a model. We followed him to the model's apartment. They had a quarrel. Hardwick's supposed to have jumped out of the window. She went to his office and took five thousand dollars out of the safe. The money's in her purse."

"So she was jealous?"

"Jealous and greedy. Don't forget she got five grand out of the safe."

"I was following my employer's specific instructions in everything I did," Jane said.

Findlay grinned.

"What's more," she blazed, "Frank Hardwick wasn't having any affair with that model. He was lured to her apartment. It was a trap and he walked right in."

Findlay said, "Yeah. The key we found in his vest pocket fitted the apartment door. He must have found it on the street and was returning it to the owner as an act of gallantry."

The sheriff laughed.

Howard Kane glanced speculatively at the very young woman. "She doesn't look like a criminal."

"Oh, thank you!" she blazed.

Findlay's glance was patronizing. "How many criminals have you seen, buddy?"

Doxey rolled a cigarette. His eyes narrowed against the smoke as he squatted down cowboy fashion on the backs of his high-heeled riding boots. "Ain't no question but what she's the one who jimmied the safe, is there?"

"The money's in her purse," Findlay said.

"Any accomplices?" Buck asked.

"No. It was a combination of jealousy and greed." Findlay glanced inquiringly at the sheriff.

"I'll fly in and send that car out," the sheriff said.

"Mind if I fly in with yuh and ride back with the deputy, Sheriff?" Buck asked eagerly. "I'd like to see this country from the air once. There's a paved road other side of that big mountain where the ranger has his station. I'd like to look down on it. Some day they'll connect us up. Now it's an hour's ride by horse . . ."

"Sure," the sheriff agreed. "Glad to have you."

"Just give me time enough to throw a saddle on a horse," Doxey said. "Kane might want to ride out and look the ranch over. Yuh won't mind, Sheriff?"

"Make it snappy," the sheriff said.

Buck Doxey went to the barn and after a few minutes returned leading a dilapidated-looking range pony saddled and bridled. He casually dropped the reins in front of the ranch "office," and called inside:

"Ready any time you are, Sheriff."

They started for the airplane. Buck stopped at the car to get a map from the glove compartment, then hurried to join the sheriff. The propeller of the plane gave a half-turn, stopped, gave another half-turn, the motor sputtered, then roared into action. A moment later the plane became the focal point of a trailing dust cloud, then raised and swept over the squat log buildings in a climbing turn and headed south.

Jane Marlow and Kane watched it through the window until it became but a speck.

Howard Kane said, "Now, Mr. Findlay, I'd like to ask you a few questions."

"Sure, go right ahead."

"You impressed the sheriff very cleverly," Kane said, "but I'd like to have you explain . . ."

"Now that it's too late," Jane Marlow blazed indignantly. "You've let him . . ."

Kane motioned her to silence. "Don't you see, Miss Marlow, I had to get rid of the sheriff. He represents the law, right or wrong. But if this man is an impostor, I can protect you against him."

Findlay's hand moved with such rapidity that the big diamond made a streak of glittering light.

"Okay, wise guy," he said. "Try protecting her against this."

Kane rushed the gun.

Sheer surprise slowed Findlay's reaction time. Kane's fist flashed out in a swift arc, just before the gun roared.

The fat man moved with amazing speed. He rolled with the punch, spun completely around on his heel and jumped back, the automatic held to his body, his eyes glittering with rage.

"Get 'em up," he said.

The cold animosity of his tone showed that this time there would be no hesitancy.

Slowly Kane's hands came up.

"Turn around," Findlay said. "Move over by that window. Press your face against the wall. Give me your right hand, Kane . . . Now the left hand."

A smooth leather thong, which had been deftly knotted into a slipknot, was jerked tight, then knotted into a quick half hitch.

The girl, taking advantage of Findlay's preoccupation, flung herself on him.

The bulk of Findlay's big shoulders absorbed the onslaught without making him even shift the position of his feet. He jerked the leather thong into a last knot, turned and struck the girl in the pit of the stomach.

She wobbled about for a moment on rubbery legs, then fell to the floor.

"Now, young lady," Findlay said, "you've caused me a hell of a lot of trouble. I'll just take the thing you're carrying in your left shoe. I could tell from the way you were limping there was something . . ."

He jerked off the shoe, looked inside, seemed puzzled, then suddenly grabbed the girl's stockinged foot.

She kicked and tried to scream, but the wind had been knocked out of her.

Findlay reached casual hands up to the top of her stocking, jerked it loose without bothering to unfasten the garters, pulled the adhesive tape off the bottom of the girl's foot, ran out to the car, and jumped in.

"Well, what do you know!" he exclaimed. "The damn yokel took the keys with him . . . So there's a paved road on the other side of the mountains, is there?

"Come on, horse, I guess there's a trail we can find. If we can't they'll never locate us in all that timber."

Moving swiftly, the fat man ran over to where the horse was standing on three legs, drowsing in the sunlight.

Findlay gathered up the reins, thrust one foot in the stirrup, grabbed the saddle, front and rear, and swung himself awkwardly into position.

Jane heard a shrill animal squeal of rage. The sleepy-looking horse, transformed into a bundle of dynamite, heaved himself into the air, ears laid back along his neck.

The fat man, grabbing the horn of the saddle, clung with frenzied desperation.

"Well," Kane asked, "are you going to untie me, or just stand there gawking?"

She ran to him then, frantically tugging at the knot.

The second his hands were freed Kane went into action.

Findlay, half out of the saddle, clung drunkenly to the pitching horse for a moment, then went into the air, turned half over and came down with a jar that shook the earth.

Kane emerged from the cabin holding a rifle.

"All right, Findlay, it's my turn now," Kane said. "Don't make a move for that gun."

The shaken Findlay seemed to have trouble orienting himself. He turned dazedly toward the sound of the voice, clawed for his gun.

Kane, aiming the rifle carefully, shot it out of his hand.

"Now, ma'am," Kane said, "if you want to get that paper out of his pocket . . ."

She ran to Findlay, her feet fairly flying over the ground despite the fact that she was wearing only one shoe and the other foot had neither shoe nor stocking . . .

Shortly before noon Jane Marlow decided to invade the sacred precincts of Buck Doxey's thoroughly masculine kitchen to prepare lunch. Howard Kane showed his respect for Findlay's resourcefulness by keeping him covered despite the man's bound wrists.

"Buck is going to hate me for this," she said. "Not that he doesn't hate me enough already—and I don't know why."

"Buck's soured on women," Kane explained. "I tried to tip you off. He was engaged to a girl in Cheyenne. No one knows exactly what happened, but they split up. I think she's as miserable as he is, but neither one will make the first move. But for heaven's sake don't try to rearrange his kitchen according to ideas of feminine efficiency. Just open a can of something and make coffee."

Findlay said, "I don't suppose there's any use trying to make a deal with you two."

Kane scornfully sighted along the gun by way of answer.

Jane, opening drawers in the kitchen, trying to locate the utensils, inadvertently stumbled on Buck Doxey's private heartache. A drawer containing letters, and the photograph of a girl.

The photograph had been torn into several pieces, and then laboriously pasted together and covered with Cellophane.

The front of the picture was inscribed "To Buck with all my heart, Pearl."

Jane felt a surge of guilt at even having opened the drawer, but feminine curiosity caused her to hesitate long enough before closing it to notice Pearl's return address in the upper left-hand corner of one of the envelopes addressed to Buck Doxey . . .

It was as they were finishing lunch that they heard the roar of the plane.

They went to the door to watch it turn into the teeth of the cold north wind, settle to a landing, then taxi up to the low log buildings.

The sheriff and Buck Doxey started running toward the cabins, and it was solace to Jane Marlow's pride to see the look of almost comic relief on the face of the sheriff as he saw Kane with the rifle and Findlay with bound wrists.

Jane heard the last part of Doxey's hurried explanation to Kane.

"Wouldn't trust a woman that far but her story held together and his didn't. I thought you'd understand what I was doing. I flew in with the sheriff just so I could call the FBI in Los Angeles. What do you know? Findlay is a badly wanted enemy spy. They want him bad as . . . How did *you* make out?"

Kane grinned. "I decided to give Findlay a private third-degree. He answered my questions with a gun. If it hadn't been for that horse . . ."

Buck's face broke into a grin. "He fell for that one?"

"Fell for it, and off it," Kane said.

"If he hadn't been a fool tenderfoot he'd have noticed that I led the horse out from the corral instead of riding him over. Old Fox is a rodeo horse, one of the best bucking broncs in Wyoming. Perfectly gentle until he feels it's time to do his stuff, and then he gives everything he has until he hears the ten-second whistle. I sort of figured Findlay might try something before I could sell the sheriff a bill of goods and get back."

It had been sheer impulse which caused Jane Marlow to leave the train early in the morning.

It was also sheer impulse which caused her to violate the law by forging Pearl's name to a telegram as she went through Cheyenne.

The telegram was addressed to Buck Doxey, care of the Forest Ranger Station and read:

BUCK I AM SO PROUD OF YOU. PEARL.

Having started the message on its way, Jane looked up Pearl and casually told her of the torn picture which had been so laboriously pasted together.

Half an hour later Jane was once more speeding East aboard the sleek streamliner, wondering whether her efforts on behalf of Cupid had earned her the undying enmity of two people, or had perhaps been successful.

When she reached Omaha two telegrams were delivered. One was from Howard Kane and read simply:

YOU WERE SO RIGHT. IT GETS TERRIBLY LONELY AT TIMES. HOLD A DINNER DATE OPEN FOR TONIGHT. YOU NEED A BODYGUARD ON YOUR MISSION AND I AM FLYING TO CHICAGO TO MEET YOU AT TRAIN AND DISCUSS THE WYOMING CLIMATE AS A PERMANENT PLACE OF RESIDENCE. LOVE, HOWARD.

The second telegram was the big surprise. It read:

I GUESS I HAD IT COMING. PEARL AND I BOTH SEND LOVE. I GUESS I JUST NEVER REALIZED WOMEN ARE LIKE THAT. YOURS HUMBLY, BUCK DOXEY.

25

ARTHUR GORDON

The Warning

FLYING SAUCERS have often been the subject of
speculation, but we doubt that you have ever read a story
which will give you more conviction of their existence
than this one. Mr. Gordon used to be a lieutenant colonel in our Air Force and he writes here with a knowledge
of how generals—and colonels—act and talk. The documentary quality of the writing will convince you that
you are standing in an office of the Pentagon—looking
over the shoulders of two men facing the dimensions of
unknown disaster.

THE GENERAL HALTED his restless pacing to stare out of the
window. Dusk was settling stealthily over the Pentagon. Across
the river, above the lights of Washington, the flood-lit dome of
the Capitol stood out boldly against the sky.

The General lit another cigarette. He was a stocky, bull-
shouldered man with a furrowed face and steel-wool hair. On
the wall behind his desk was a photograph showing him standing beside an early model B-17. He had led the first American
heavy-bomber raid against the Germans in 1942. Only a decade
ago. He rubbed his hand wearily across his eyes. That was war.
This was nightmare.

The inter-office phone spoke sharply. "Colonel Courtney's
here, sir!"

The General turned quickly. "Send him in."

The door opened and Courtney appeared, a slender, fair-
haired man wearing a leather flying jacket. His face was lined
with fatigue, but his eyes were alert and his salute was sharp.

The General ignored it. "Never mind the formalities, Court.
My God, I thought you'd never get here!"

"Sorry, sir. Head winds most of the way."

"I know. You must be bushed." The General kicked a chair

252

forward. "Sit down, man. The Secretary's waiting to see us, but I want a word with you first. Cigarette?"

"Thanks." Courtney took one, lit it, inhaled deeply. He looked up at the older man. "Does the Secretary know anything about this yet?"

"Not yet." The General was pacing again. "I just didn't have the guts to tell him until you got here. I kept hoping you'd bring back word that the man was insane."

Courtney's mouth tightened. "I wish I thought so."

"Did you talk to him again?"

"Yes. For as long as the doctors would let me, which wasn't very long."

"Couldn't budge his story?"

"Not an inch."

"What's he like?"

"Oh, typical, I'd say. Tough, unimaginative—fanatically loyal, of course. In pretty bad shape, physically. But not stupid. And not delirious. And not insane."

The General slammed his hand down on the desk. "Dammit, Court, I just won't believe it!"

The younger man shrugged faintly. "The Japs probably didn't believe we had a certain bomb, either, until it fell on Hiroshima."

The General stared at him without speaking for perhaps ten seconds. Then he picked up a folder from the desk. "Come on," he said. "Let's go."

They went through the maze of corridors, past offices empty now and dimly lit. Their heels rang sharply in the silence. "Was it cold up there?" the General asked irrelevantly.

"Not very, sir," the Colonel said. "Damp, though."

They came to the suite of offices with the neat blue-and-white lettering beside the door: *Secretary of the Air Force.* The pretty civilian receptionist smiled at them. "Go right in, gentlemen," she said.

The man behind the desk stood up as they entered. He had a strong face, disciplined, calm. He held out his hand to the General. "Well, Bob, what's on your mind?"

The General turned slightly. "This is Colonel Courtney, sir, one of our better men in A-2. I know you'll excuse his rumpled appearance. He just flew non-stop from Alaska."

"I've heard good reports of Colonel Courtney," said the Secretary pleasantly. "Learned to speak fluent Russian, haven't you, Colonel? Among other interesting things."

"Yes, sir," Courtney said.

The Secretary indicated two chairs. "Sit down, gentlemen." He spoke into a concealed microphone. "No interruptions, please, unless it's something very urgent." He clicked it off.

The General looked down at the folder in his hands. The words *Top Secret* were stamped across it in red. "Damned if I know how to begin."

"Why not at the beginning?" the Secretary suggested mildly.

"All right," the General said. "At the beginning." He stood up and began to pace again, hands jammed into his pockets. "Remember the day last week when three of our F-86's disappeared somewhere in the Aleutians?"

The Secretary looked grave. "I do indeed."

"Well," said the General, "that's apparently when it began. Although of course we didn't know at the time . . ." He frowned and was silent.

"Didn't know what?" the Secretary asked at length.

"What had happened to them. We still don't, really. You had my report. The possibility that they had strayed over Russian territory and got themselves shot down was eliminated because they never broke radio silence. They'd have screamed bloody murder if somebody had started shooting at them. We figured they must have smacked into a mountain in a fog. But we never spotted any wreckage, and we flew all the sorties that lousy weather would permit . . ." His voice trailed off again.

"You're still looking, aren't you?"

"What? Oh, yes, we're still looking, but . . ." The General wheeled into position in front of the desk, lowering his head like a bull. Courtney sat motionless, watching him. Here it comes, he thought.

"Four days ago," the General said, "a report filtered through to the commanding officer at Base 42 up there. The gist of it was that a parachutist had come down on Kodiak Island, had been picked up—injured—by natives, and was being cared for in one of their more inaccessible villages. The C.O. assumed, of course, that it was one of our missing boys and got a helicopter in there right away. The story was true—it was a parachutist, all right. But he didn't belong to us. He was a Russian fighter pilot."

The Secretary's eyes flicked briefly to the great wall map at the end of the room. "Kodiak? Why wasn't he picked up by our radar screen?"

The General ran a harassed hand through his hair. "I think, sir, I had better finish the story. Then, if you . . ."

The Secretary nodded. "Sorry. Go on."

"This Russian was in very bad shape. He had three smashed ribs—evidently the result of a rough landing—and they had perforated his lung. He also had a compound fracture of one ankle and a badly frostbitten face. He was conscious, but he couldn't speak a word of English, and the rescue team didn't know Russian. Nobody did, at Base 42."

The General took a cigarette from a crumpled pack and lit it. "They flew him back to their hospital and notified us. We didn't like the sound of it and sent Courtney up there right away. He got his first interrogation report back to us via a B-36 training flight that was scheduled anyway." The General opened the folder and took out two typewritten sheets. "I have it here in the form of a statement. It's not long. May I read it to you?"

The Secretary leaned back in his chair. "Go ahead."

The General tamped out his cigarette and began to read in a flat, unemotional voice: " 'I, Vladimir Suvurov, Captain in the Air Forces of the U.S.S.R., do solemnly swear that the following statement is true in every particular. On May 5, at approximately 1430 hours, I was leading one half of my fighter squadron, two flights of three planes each, on a routine training run between Khabarovsk and Vladivostok, a distance of some 600 kilometers . . .' "

"MIGs?" asked the Secretary sharply.

"He wouldn't say, sir," Courtney replied. "He's ultra security-minded. But they were probably the new Russian jet job. They have three Groups in the Vladivostok area. None has been seen south of the Yalu river—yet."

Again the Secretary glanced at the map. "How far from Vladivostok to Kodiak?"

"Over three thousand miles, sir," Courtney murmured.

The Secretary whistled almost soundlessly. "They have any sort of carriers out there?"

"Not according to our naval intelligence, sir."

The Secretary said, "Go on, please, Bob."

The General went on reading: " 'We were flying at 6,000 meters when I observed, higher than our line of flight, but directly ahead, an unfamiliar type of aircraft. It had no wings, but was shaped like a thick coin. It seemed at first to be stationary, but as we approached it drew away at a high rate of speed. I judged it to be two or three times the size of our larger bomber.' "

The General glanced up grimly. "Sounds familiar, doesn't it?"

The Secretary was leaning forward. "Go on."

" 'I immediately notified my control tower at Vladivostok and requested permission to pursue the object. This was granted, and I was instructed to force it to land, or if necessary to shoot it down. I asked for confirmation of this last part of the order, but my radio ceased to function and I lost contact with my base.' "

The General wet his lips and turned a page. It made an audible rustle in the silence.

" 'The object withdrew toward the east. I led my two flights in pursuit at maximum speed. We gained slowly. As we drew nearer I could see that the object seemed to consist of two discs, one on top of the other. Both discs were rotating at very high speed. I could not tell whether they were counter-rotating or not. Between the discs was a darker area that seemed to be stationary . . .' "

The Secretary said harshly, "*Rotating* discs?"

The General nodded. "Some sort of gyroscopic principle, evidently." He went on reading: " 'The object remained just out of cannon range. We pursued it eastward until I knew we must be over the Sea of Japan. Our fuel supply was limited, but I was sure my comrades would follow me, even past the point of no return. Since I could not communicate by radio, I glanced at them frequently in my rear-view mirror. I was watching when they began to explode. There was no smoke, no fire. They disintegrated.' "

The General took out a handkerchief and passed it across his forehead. His dry voice continued: " 'I think my wing-man escaped. He went down suddenly in a steep dive, but under control. When I last saw him, he was heading west . . .' "

"Lost his nerve," said Courtney drily. "Can't say I blame him!"

"Well," said the General, "this Suvurov had plenty of guts. Listen to this: 'I was determined to close with the object. I fired my cannon, with no apparent result. We were now at 11,000 meters and climbing. The object suddenly changed course. It flew back and hovered directly over me.

" 'My fighter ceased to answer its controls. I felt a tremendous upward pressure, as if my plane were being dragged into the stratosphere. My ears began to pain me badly, and my oxygen supply seemed inadequate. When my altimeter needle touched 14,000 meters I became unconscious. I remember nothing more until my parachute opened approximately 1,000 meters above the ground.'"

The General looked up again. "He still doesn't know where he is—thinks he came down somewhere in northern Japan." He hesitated. "There's one more short paragraph: 'I thank the military forces of the United States for their kindness and medical treatment and urgently request that I be returned as soon as possible to my command.'"

He tossed the typewritten sheets onto the Secretary's desk and sat down. Nobody spoke. The Secretary picked up a paperweight made to resemble a B-47. He put it down. He said, with exaggerated calm, "I don't blame you for being upset by this story, Bob. But I think I see a few flaws in it. For example, if he was unconscious, how did he pull his rip-cord?"

Courtney coughed. "I think I can explain that, sir. I asked him the same question. He hedged a bit, but I gather they've developed a barometric gadget for high altitude parachute jumps. If the flier blacks out, the 'chute opens automatically at about 3,000 feet." He glanced at the General. "I'll pass that along to Wright Field, of course."

"But if his plane disintegrated," the Secretary demanded, "why didn't he disintegrate, too?"

"He doesn't think his plane disintegrated, sir. He thinks they got it."

"They?"

"Whoever-whatever was in the disc. He thinks they had no use for him, so they just threw him out—not knowing about his 'chute. But they kept his plane." Courtney shifted his feet and stared at the carpet. "If that is true, then, they've probably got one of our F-86's, too."

The Secretary braced his arms against the desk as if he were forcing something away from him. "It must be a hoax! Some kind of fantastic Oriental hoax!"

The General opened the cardboard folder again. "You've already seen these, sir. Here's that photo taken some time ago by one of our photo-recon boys 35,000 feet over Labrador. You can see the dark round object quite clearly. Of course, our photo interpreters decided it was just a Navy weather balloon wandering around in the stratosphere.

"Then here are the reports from those two B-29 crews flying night missions in Korea. You remember the planes were in widely separated areas, and yet three members of each crew reported seeing near midnight a circular object that flew along with them emitting blue flames."

"But, dammit, man, those objects were described as being very small! Their size was estimated at—"

"You can't always judge size at night in the air," the General said. "Anyway, if you concede the existence of small ones, you may as well grant the possibility of a big one!"

"I noticed," said Courtney drily, "that we didn't concede anything in our statements to the press. We said, in effect, that we saw them, but we didn't believe them."

The General glared at him suddenly. "What the hell else could we say?"

"Take it easy, Bob," the Secretary said. He bit his lips. "Tell me, Colonel Courtney, what time of day did this parachutist come down on Kodiak?"

"I asked the rescue crew that question, sir. They didn't know, for sure. Apparently the natives are pretty vague about time. But it was daylight, all right, because a couple of them actually saw him come down."

"In other words, if his story is true, he was carried three thousand miles in about three hours—perhaps less."

Courtney nodded. "Probably much less; otherwise he'd have been suffocated, or frozen, or both."

The Secretary got up, walked to the end of the room, stared at the map for a moment. He turned around slowly. "I think it's important not to get too excited. Excitement doesn't exactly help clear thinking. For the moment let's assume the impossible. Let's assume there is some—some mechanism loose in the sky which can fly at supersonic speeds, which can create its own magnetic field, blanket radio transmission when it wants to, even destroy pursuing fighters by concentrated sound waves or some other method. Who created such a thing? Where did it come from?"

The two officers stared at the floor. They said nothing.

"If Suvurov's story is true," the Secretary said, "we can't

suspect the Russians. It must have been a hell of a jolt for the
C.O. at Vladivostok."

"Must have caused an even worse shock in the Kremlin," the
General said. "Six new jet fighters tangle with a—with a something. One comes back. My God, they must be scared stiff!"

"And since they don't know who's responsible," the Secretary
said softly, "they must blame us."

"Us?" The General sounded startled.

"Who else would be suspected of putting a secret weapon over
Siberia? After all, we hold Japan."

"But they'd have protested!" the General objected. "They'd
have raised merry hell with us in the UN!"

"Not the Russians, General," Courtney said. "They'd figure we
were talking to them in the one language they understand.
Force!"

"But they haven't done a thing! They haven't reacted in any
way!"

"They've hardly had time," the Secretary said grimly. "After
all, they had to fly a badly frightened pilot back to Moscow. Had
to interrogate him, had to evaluate this fantastic thing . . ." A
phone buzzed on his desk. He picked it up. "Yes?" He held it
out toward the General. "For you."

The General took the instrument, listened, put it down slowly.
"Message from Base 42," he said slowly. "Suvurov is dead. Pneumonia, plus complications."

Courtney stood up and moved over to the window, "That's
too bad." He cleared his throat. "I liked him, poor devil. He
was a brave man."

Silence sang in the room. Seconds ticked into a minute, two
minutes. The General kept his eyes fixed on the Secretary. Something in the man's face reminded him of a trapped animal.
Courtney stared out of the window. The phone buzzed again.

The Secretary picked it up. "Yes?" he said again. "What?"
They saw his expression change. "No! Are you sure?" He raised
one clenched fist and shook it in a sudden gesture of elation.
The jumble of excited words continued for a moment, then was
gone. The Secretary put down the phone. He said, hoarsely,
"That was the Defense Secretary, gentlemen. He's just come
from a conference at the White House. The Russian Ambassador
was there, so excited he could hardly talk. It seems he'd just

got a call from Moscow. There's been a complete change of policy in the Kremlin. They're lifting the Iron Curtain, gentlemen. This—this could really be the beginning of peace!"

The three men stared at one another. Nobody spoke. At length Courtney raised his leather-clad arm and pointed through the window. "Look," he said in a whisper.

The others joined him. Red and unwinking, a point of light hung just above the horizon. More than fifty million miles away, the great planet glowed through the icy chasms of space.

The General wet his lips. "That's—that's Mars, isn't it?"

Courtney nodded. "The war-god's planet."

Silence again. Then the Secretary uttered the thought that was in the minds of all of them. "Maybe they sent us a warning —a warning to stop these murderous wars before it's too late.

"Maybe," he said, and his voice shook a little, "maybe they sent us a messenger of peace!"

26

GEOFFREY HOUSEHOLD

Secret Information

WHEN HE WROTE *Rogue Male,* just before the beginning of World War II, Geoffrey Household came into fame as the author of what has been called one of the great suspense stories of all time. Except for the interruption of his service during the war as a British Army officer in the Middle East, attached to Intelligence, he has been at this pleasant business of concocting suspense stories ever since. This is a gentle one—but it will make you hold your breath.

IT WAS the nearest he had ever come to sending an agent to his death. Her death, rather. He admitted that he shouldn't have taken the risk, that a man with his experience of women should have known better; but there he was with the enemy order of battle—all along the southern fringe of the Iron Curtain from Bratislava to the Black Sea.

The list was complete, and accurate up to the previous Saturday; and there wasn't a chance of getting it out to the West. No handy secret wireless. No landing grounds. Not a trustworthy agent who had the remotest hope of being given a passport in time to be of use. Theotaki had found his job much easier when operating under the noses of the Gestapo.

He was a Rumanian of Greek origin, with all a Greek's hungry passion for the ideal freedom which had never in practical politics existed, and never could. He had also the Greek's love of adventurous intrigue for its own sake. One gets used to the trade, he would say. Steeple jacks, for example. They couldn't be thinking all the time about risk. They took, he supposed, meticulous care with all their preparations—blocks and tackle, scaffolding, belts—and then got on with the job.

He admitted, however, that this had been an occasion for desperate measures. The only chance he could see of getting that enemy order of battle into hands that could appreciate it

261

was D-17. D-17 was going the very next day to Stockholm to
be married. She would never have been allowed to leave, but
it was hard, even for communist bureaucrats, to think up a
really valid excuse for preventing a citizen—an entirely useless
citizen whose parents were living on the proceeds of their
jewelry and furniture—from taking herself off to Sweden and
matrimony, when a firm request for her had been passed through
diplomatic channels.

Alexia—D-17—was a very minor agent: somewhat too enthusiastic, said Theotaki, for her sister had been mishandled by
the Russian advance guards when they entered Bucharest and
had died the following week. The unfortunate incident had had
some effect on Theotaki's ideals of freedom, too. But he never
confessed to emotion. To judge by his jowled, dead, decadent
face, you wouldn't have thought him capable of feeling any.

Since he had moved before the war in the social circle of the
parents and their two daughters, he knew Alexia very well. She
had, of course, no idea that he was in any way responsible for
the occasional orders received by D-17. She couldn't have given
away more than the three names of the other members of her
cell—at least she couldn't up to the time when Theotaki was
forced into gambling against his better judgment.

He kept her under observation all the morning. She was shopping for a few clothes and necessary trifles that she could much
better have bought abroad.

She was obviously happy. Well, why wouldn't she be? She was
a tense and lovely woman in her middle twenties escaping to
her lover and doing a bit of buying to please his eyes. When,
however, she sat down, alone, in the huge barren hall of a cheap
café, she was ashamed of herself. Theotaki guessed it from her
bearing, from the uncertainty of her eyes.

To be ashamed of yourself for being happy was, he explained,
one of the most damnable, minor, nagging aches of political
tyranny. Your personal tastes and joys could not be altered by
the common discontent, yet you felt they should be. Love and
the feel of dress to a woman—they don't come to an end because
your country is enslaved and terrorized.

So that was the position—D-17 sitting in a café, thinking of
her beloved with one half of her mind, and with the other her
duty to hate; and Theotaki moving behind her to find a table,
not too far away, where she couldn't see and greet him.

He took one of the café's illustrated papers in its cane frame, and began abstractedly to write a poem across the blank spaces of an advertisement. When he had finished his drink, he paid his bill and sent the waiter to Alexia with the paper. He then vanished from his table and stood talking to a casual acquaintance by the door, whence he could watch in a mirror the effect of his inspiration.

Alexia received the paper as if it were expected. Theotaki approved her presence of mind, and well he might. Any gesture of surprise could have led—if the waiter earned a little extra money by giving information to the police—to prolonged questioning of both of them.

She glanced idly through the coarse rotogravures of factory openings and parades, and found the doodling of some previous reader. There were girls' heads and jottings for a commonplace love poem to sweet seventeen.

Among the half lines, the notes for promising rhymes, was a phrase, *your garden at three in the morning* continually repeated, toyed with and crossed out because no order of the words could be made to scan. Then came a row of Capital D's, as if the lovesick doodler, failing to succeed as a poet, had tried to design the most decorative letter with which to begin his work.

D-17's garden at 3 A.M.—the message would have been instantly clear to Theotaki. But he didn't expect the same alertness from D-17; he only hoped. As a man of imagination he had, he insisted, the keenest sympathy for romance, and therefore thought it more than likely that Alexia would be too absorbed by justifiable dreams to notice his vulgar scribbling. He was very pleased with her indeed when her hand began to fiddle with ash tray, saucer and salt cellar arranging them into a group of three to show, if there were anyone watching her, that she had read and understood . . .

D-17's garden—or rather her parents'—was a reasonably safe spot for a rendezvous. A high but climbable wall separated its overgrown shrubbery from the state-disciplined bushes of a public park. In happier days Alexia and her sister had been very well aware of its advantages.

High-spirited young ladies, said Theotaki. Yes, and they had had their own uproarious methods of discouraging unwelcome suitors. When he dropped over the wall that night, for the second time in his life, he remembered that ten years earlier there had been a cunning arrangement of glass and empty cans to receive him, and a crash that woke the uneasy summer sleepers in four blocks of flats.

This time there were only silence and soft leaf-mold. Theotaki in a whisper reminded the darkness of his last visit. He warned the dark shapes of the bushes that if they were not alone they had better say so, for he was about to speak of the relationship—the 1951 relationship, that is—between himself and Alexia.

Alexia detached herself from her background, and assured him that she was alone. As proof of his authority, he told her the names and numbers of the other members of her cell and described their recent activities.

"Will that do?" he asked. "Or do you want more details, D-17?"

She murmured that she couldn't know . . . that she would never have believed it possible . . . that never in all her life had she respected him—or anyone—so much . . .

Theotaki apologized for being desperate. Caution—caution, he told her, was the only road to success. There was no hurry, no room for either risks or enthusiasm. Still, sometimes—regretfully—one had to improvise. Where was it safe to talk?

She led him away from the wall into a tunnel of green darkness, and begged him to say what he wanted from her. Always that dangerous feminine enthusiasm. Yet it was a little forced. Theotaki could tell by her voice that she was uneasy at the unexpected mixture of her social life—such as it was—with her very secret service.

He apologized again for his inefficiency, for the urgency—which had compelled him to appeal to her directly.

"It isn't fair to any of us," he said.

"Whatever happens to me, I shall not talk," Alexia assured him in a passionate whisper.

Theotaki considered the eager, small-boned body with the pitying eye of a professional. It would be capable of exquisite suffering, but he was inclined to share Alexia's faith in its resistance. Torture had little effect upon a flame. Better technique was to confine it closely and have patience until it went out. He reckoned that about three months would be enough to draw out full confession from an Alexia who by then would be Alexia no longer . . .

"You are in love?" he asked.

"Doesn't it stand to reason?"

Theotaki quickly answered that he hadn't doubted it for a moment. Nor had he. She wasn't the type of woman to marry, just to escape from the country, without love. No, he wanted to know what she would answer—to hear the worst from her own lips.

He remembered the man who taught him his trade. He liked to remember him very carefully, for, since the man was dead, there was no other method of consultation. This teacher of his used to say that a female agent was every bit as good as any male. What she lacked in attack, she made up in human understanding. But never, the dead man had insisted, never choose a woman in love!

Something of this, by way of warning, he repeated to D-17.

"I think your friend did not understand women," she answered.

Theotaki explained that his friend had not implied that such a woman's devotion would be any less because she was in love, nor that she would be likely to sacrifice the cause to her private happiness. No, he had only meant that any woman of outstanding intensity was, when in love, Love Itself. She became possessed by hormones and happiness, and ceased to bother with details.

"And I wouldn't choose any woman but a woman in love," Alexia laughed. "Because until she is, she's only half alive."

Theotaki admitted it was true, at any rate, that her will dominated her environment. Yes, there was something in that. The spirit of a woman in love could burn its way through armor plate.

"But don't forget my friend's experience," he warned her. "He was a man of very wide experience. And so be a little more careful over details than you would be ordinarily. Just to compensate."

He gave her the precious sheet of foolscap, closely typed over with the positions, the strengths, the armor of corps, divisions and independent brigades.

"Learn that by heart," he said, "and then burn it. Burn it and crush the ashes. When you get to Stockholm, make an excuse, as soon as you probably can, to be alone, and go straight to the address you will read at the bottom of the sheet. Say you come from me, and recite your lesson. That's all. Then you can be happy with a good conscience. I, your leader, tell you so."

When she had vanished into the house, Theotaki flowed, inch by careful inch, back over the wall. He walked from the park to his flat through streets deserted by all but the police. Several times during the journey he showed his papers. He was a privileged person, kept rather contemptuously by the Ministry of the Interior for the sake of his general usefulness. Nobody could possibly have suspected Theotaki of any idealism.

D-17—well, what D-17 did when she was alone in her bedroom could only be reconstructed from his knowledge of her and the story that reached him weeks later. She had a quick, reliable memory, and in the gray hour before dawn she learned those dull military numerals as conscientiously as she had learned poetry for school examinations. She would remember, said Theotaki—who had practiced, earlier in his career, the same exacting, desperate memorizing—every fact and figure for the rest of her life.

She must have sat down about sunrise, in the last of her spare time, too excited to sleep, to write to her fiancé. That was like her. She was rich in forethought and expedients. Her departure might still be delayed by some incalculable change in the official mind. If it were, her lover would have a letter to comfort him. If it were not, they would read the two pages together, and laugh for relief from their common fears.

Then, when the letter was in its envelope and stamped, came all the fuss of leaving: the weeping mother, the insistence that she should have enough breakfast, the last-minute closing of her four suitcases, the drive to the station.

At the frontier Theotaki took up direct observation again, for, if D-17 should walk into trouble, he wanted to have first news of it. He was astonished at the ease, the gallantry of her departure. The Rumanian officials searched two of her cases and left the rest unopened. It was the starry-eyedness, her own infectious certainty that no one could stop so innocently blissful a girl which carried her through. That grim frontier post, on both sides of the line, was all bows and smiles.

Theotaki could go no further. That he had been allowed to come so far, and on the flimsiest of excuses, was a severe test of his nuisance value to his Ministry. He hastened back to Bucharest, very relieved but unable to get rid of an aching nervousness.

He assured himself that she could have no further difficulties, but she had still to cross a frontier between Budapest and Prague; and at Prague, before she took the plane to Stockholm, there would be a last, thorough and envious examination of her papers and her baggage.

Theotaki spoke of Alexia's journey as if he had been on the train with her. In thought, hour after hour, so he was. He knew to the minute—though that of course was mere calculation of schedules—when the blinds of the train would be pulled down so that no passenger might see the possible presence and activities of Russian troops: 136th Assault Division, Alexia would say to herself, and inevitably her mind would run over and bare details of its strength and its experimental bridging equipment. She wouldn't be able to help this silent recitation and would try to stop herself forming the mental words lest they might be magically overheard.

All that was true enough. Nevertheless Alexia, as he heard afterwards, had passed most of the journey in a dream of romantic confidence.

She turned the future into the present with an audacity that no mere man could have imitated and which she didn't even recognize as unreal—with the result that when police and customs and their informers on the train gave her a look, they saw only a girl neither immorally rich nor suspiciously poor, and much too happy to have anything upon her conscience.

At Prague, however, the solid and bad-tempered Czechs turned her inside out. They flung the upper layers of her bags aside and angrily rummaged the bottom for anti-social contraband. They interrogated her. They gave her a fresh batch of forms to sign. And when they had punished her so far as they could for wanting to leave the Russian orbit at all, they had to allow her to leave it.

After that it was all plain sailing. She was met by her fiancé on arrival, and Swedish smiles passed her straight into their country and let her loose in a blue and white Stockholm which sparkled like her mood.

It must have been very difficult for D-17 to shake off fiancé and future parents-in-law and the odd score of hospitable friends who were determined to cherish her; but she did it. She had, after all, long experience in concealing her intentions. Somehow she established her right to a moment of privacy and claimed it. She delivered her message, word perfect, and kept the taxi waiting and was back in her bedroom in half an hour.

Then she started, said Theotaki, to unpack. He heard of that unpacking when he met his Stockholm correspondent in the quiet course of their business, and even then they couldn't laugh. He was right; he had never come nearer to sending an agent to certain death.

On the top of the first case Alexia opened was her writing-pad, just where she had hastily thrown it in the unworldly light of dawn after finishing that last, all-absorbing letter to her fi-ancé. The bag was the only one of the four that had never been examined by Rumanians or Hungarians. The Czechs had gone like burrowing dogs for the bottom while scattering out the top.

In the pad, hidden only by its flimsy cover, was the sheet of foolscap, gloriously forgotten, not crushed at all to ashes, not even burned, which Theotaki had given her with such delicate precautions.

27

OCTAVUS ROY COHEN

A Case of Nerves

BACK IN 1925, when *Collier's* developed the short-short, Octavus Roy Cohen was one of four authors the editors asked to produce thirteen of these brief stories a year. Of the four—Rupert Hughes, Zona Gale and Sophie Kerr were the others—it is a matter of record that Mr. Cohen was the only one who met his commitment to the satisfaction of the editors. In fact, during a three-year period, he had fifty-nine short-shorts accepted by *Collier's* without a rejection. Mr. Cohen lives in Los Angeles now, has slowed down a bit on production, but still turns these stories out with professional skill.

REGARDING DALE GRAYSON strictly as an architect (which I was never entirely successful in doing), there were several major flaws: Her figure was too perfect, her complexion too good, her lips too exciting and her clear gray eyes too lovely. We had few clients, but even the most staid forgot much too readily that Miss Grayson was chockful of technical ability. Each of them appeared to become obsessed with the idea that he could best talk business with her in a night club after an evening of theater.

Of course, this was good for the firm of Warren & Grayson in a business way, but at the same time it was infuriating. As the senior member of the firm, I preferred riding to the top on brains. But nature had decreed otherwise. Only I knew how smart the young lady was. Only I preserved the clinically impersonal attitude. Or, at least, I kidded myself that I did.

Just recently my confidence in Miss Grayson had been justified, which was how we happened to find ourselves in the Blue Penguin, quarreling bitterly at five o'clock in the afternoon.

She glared at me and said I couldn't do it, and I informed her for the dozenth time that I'd already done it. "The architectural firm of Warren & Grayson is no more," I told her. "It has been dissolved. You are now strictly on your own, and therefore in no

economic position to tell Philips, Schirmer & Lee to go jump in
the creek."

"I'll tell them anyway."

"That doesn't make sense," I argued. "That's one of the half-
dozen best firms in the country. They saw the plans with which
you won that competition. They picked you on ability, strictly.
I'll bet they were even surprised to discover you were female,
or am I wrong?"

"You're not wrong. That's what comes from having a name
which can be either masculine or feminine."

"But after recovering from their shock, they repeated their
offer, didn't they?"

"Yes. All three of them."

"Accept their offer, Dale. You'll be made—"

"Not by Philips, Schirmer & Lee, I won't. Can't you understand, Steve, that all I want is to continue with you? We started
this firm with nothing but ourselves. We can get to the top,
together. That's the way I want it."

"Your viewpoint," I told her, "is not architectural. I'd say it
was tainted with biology."

"Is that bad? And even if it is, can I help it?"

I took her hand—which was a tactical blunder, because it was
a nice, warm, responsive hand. "You're off base," I told her.
"You've forgotten how much your profession means to you. You
went through Michigan the hard way, reaching for your professional degree. That proves that architecture means more to you
than anything else in the world. Now you've got a chance to
tie up with the best, to be recognized . . ."

"What would you do?"

"I'll get along. Keep the same office, most likely. Fortunately,
I'm not worried, financially, and never have been. I skidded
through M.I.T. because it was there for me."

She said, "You never even took biology as a minor course, did
you?"

"That has nothing to do with what we're discussing. You've
got your big chance, and I'm compelling you to take it. And if
you start looking like that, I'll . . ."

But she wasn't looking at me. She was staring at the young
lady at the table adjoining ours. I heard Dale say, "Pardon me,
but you look ill . . ." and the young lady nodded and said she
was feeling quite badly.

I took time out to inspect our neighbor. She was quite something to look at, once I got the dazzle of Miss Grayson out of my eyes.

She was about thirty years of age, and weighed perhaps one hundred and forty, which—statistically—might give you all the wrong idea. She wore her years gracefully, even proudly, and the avoirdupois was picturesquely distributed. She had red hair and a lovely complexion, and, after taking note of those good points, I observed that she seemed to be having lots of no fun.

A drink sat on the table in front of her, but she hadn't touched it. She sat holding the edge of the table as though to brace herself, as though the room was refusing to hold still for her. I heard Dale saying, "Is there something I can do?"

The redhead gave her a wan, grateful smile. She said, "If you'd help me to a taxi . . ."

Dale motioned to me. I dropped a bill on the table, and grabbed my hat and coat. We ranged on either side of the redhead and started for the door.

I'm a fairly hefty guy, but there were moments when I needed all my strength to keep the girl from falling. She wore a tense, fixed smile; a gallant effort to keep people from knowing that she wasn't well. We escorted her through the front door and motioned to a taxi. I helped her in, and asked whether she was feeling better now and where did she want to be driven? But she didn't answer.

I looked at Dale. "She's fainted," I said. "She's really in bad shape."

She hadn't told us where to send her, she hadn't given us her name. The taxi driver caught on to the situation and suggested a hospital. Dale shook her head. "Poor kid," she said. "We'll take her to my apartment. When she snaps out of it, we'll let her decide what to do."

Dale lived on East Fifty-sixth Street, just around the corner from the Blue Penguin. Her suggestion seemed to make sense and to be humane to boot.

The cab stopped in front of the door. We convoyed our charge through the lobby—refusing assistance from the ancient and portly doorman—and up to Dale's second-floor apartment in the self-service elevator. We took her through the big, comfortable living room—with Dale's drawing board and paraphernalia near the window looking more incongruous than usual—and thence into the bedroom. We placed her on the bed, and then Dale shooed me out of the room.

I was sorry for the redhead, but grateful, too. She had interrupted our quarrel before it had gotten too tense, too involved. I knew what would have happened: Dale would have accused me of being noble and I'd have gotten mad: I'd have said she was stubborn and foolish, and then she'd have gotten twice as mad.

All I knew for sure was that any young architect was entitled to swap his right arm for a chance to go in with a firm like Philips, Schirmer & Lee, and silly sentiment shouldn't be permitted to stand in the way. Just because Dale and I had been partners since we'd both gotten out of the Navy at the end of the war, just because we enjoyed working together, and laughed at the same jokes—well, there's a limit to the sacrifice any man should let a girl make on the altar of loyalty.

Abruptly Dale emerged from the bedroom and stood there staring at me. Her face was white, her gray eyes clouded with fright. She was still a delectable morsel of brunette loveliness, but new recognition of that inescapable fact still didn't keep me from realizing that something was radically wrong.

I went to her. I could see our guest stretched out on the bed. Dale said, "Steve! She's not just ill. She's been shot."

You don't grasp a statement like that instantly. It's too unexpected, too startling. I stood staring like a dope, wondering where Dale had cooked up such an idea, wondering why we happened to get messed up in it, wondering what one usually did with shot young ladies. Dale led me to the bed, and said, "Look!"

She had loosened the girl's clothes. There wasn't much blood, but what little there was gave me a sickish feeling. I bent over to examine the spot where Dale had torn away some filmy material.

It was a bullet wound, all right, kind of small and round and purplish where it wasn't stained crimson. The girl's breathing was dangerously shallow, her eyes were closed.

"Why didn't she tell us?" I asked, not because I expected an answer, but rather to release some of the tension that was crowding in too fast. "She wasn't shot in the restaurant. She must have walked in there. Why didn't she call a cop?"

Dale said quietly, "She was trying to protect whoever shot her."

"That's foolish," I said, "even though it makes sense." I took a grip on myself and tried to become the dominant male. "We'd better call a doctor. And the police."

I reached for the bedside phone, but just before I lifted the receiver from the cradle, it rang sharply. Dale said, "Whoever it is, get rid of 'em."

I said, "Hello!" and a man's voice came harshly to my ears. It said, "Don't cut off. This is important."

I was annoyed. I said, "Listen, fella . . ."

"You listen to me. You've got a girl up there named Maxine Collins. She's been shot. I'm sending a doctor over. He'll be there in five minutes. Don't do anything until you talk to him." The phone clicked at the other end. I told Dale what had happened. She looked as puzzled as I felt.

"The man who phoned must be the one who shot her."

I nodded. "He must have been hanging around the Penguin. Probably followed us here, and got your name from the doorman."

Dale asked, "What should we do, Steve?"

I didn't like the way things were shaping up. I said, "Our boy friend said the doc would be here in five minutes. Maybe we can learn something from him. The two men must know each other."

"Yes . . . And the doctor will have to report a gunshot wound to the police, won't he?"

"That's the way I understand it." I saw that Dale was beginning to go to pieces. I put my arms around her and said, "Steady, kid. I'm sorry we stumbled into this, but we'll be all clear in a little while."

My words didn't do much good, because she turned toward me and started to cry. I held her close and stroked her hair and said soothing things, and the more soothing I got, the more she cried. Finally she said, "At least we know her name is Maxine Collins."

I couldn't figure what that had to do with the price of lettuce so I merely agreed that we knew it. After a while Dale backed away from me and said, "I'm all right now, Steve."

"Sure you are."

"You—you're not a good comforter."

I said I was sorry, that I'd try to do better next time. I also said I hoped the doc would get there pretty soon. The whole deal was something I wished had happened to two other people.

The buzzer sounded. I patted Dale's shoulder and went to answer it.

The man who stood there, holding a little black bag, didn't look impressive. He was somewhere in his early forties, about five-six in height and he couldn't have weighed more than one hundred and thirty, soaking wet. He took off his hat, showing pale, wispy hair. He didn't remove his topcoat. He said, in a high, nervous voice, "Where is she?"

"You're the doctor?" I inquired.

"Of course I'm the doctor."

"Who sent you here?"

"What business is that of yours?"

I was getting sore. I looked down at him and said, "Let's start over, Doc. The young lady in the next room seems to be in a pretty bad way. She needs expert attention. And the police need information. This apartment belongs to Miss Grayson, here. I'm a friend of hers. That's what business it is of mine."

His manner was resentful, almost hostile. He said, "You're delaying my examination. I would suggest you permit me to go in there, and ask your silly questions later."

I glanced at Dale, and she nodded. As I stepped back to give him room, I said, "What is your name?"

"My name doesn't matter."

He strode into the bedroom. There wasn't any door. When Dale had decorated her apartment, she'd had it removed, and heavy draperies hung there instead.

Dale came close to me and whispered, "What do you make of it, Steve?"

"He's an unpleasant little monkey," I answered.

"Why should he act that way?"

I lighted a cigarette and tried to concentrate.

"This *could* be the answer," I said. "Somebody shoots Miss Maxine Collins. The assailant has a medical friend. He wants his victim to receive proper attention fast. But he doesn't want his identity known. So he sends his friend, and the friend doesn't want us to know too much, either, for the simple reason that he doesn't want to get caught in the middle of any such awful mess if he can help it."

"Could be that way," Dale admitted. "But it's still a little sour. His attitude was belligerent. The script wouldn't call for that," she added.

"The poor little guy is as jumpy as seventeen dollars' worth of Mexican beans. If he's doing this for a friend—and if it turns out wrong—he will lose his license."

She shook her head. "It isn't that way, Steve."

"Why are you so sure?" I asked her.

"Intuition." She stood staring thoughtfully at the draperies separating the two rooms. "What do we do now?"

I wasn't too sure. I didn't like the set-up any better than she did. I, too, detected the strong aroma of trouble. I said, tentatively, "We'll hear what he has to say. Then we'll make him phone the police from here and wait until they arrive. It'll be their baby then."

Dale said, as though the words meant something, "She must be terribly in love with him."

"Who must be terribly in love with whom?"

"Maxine Collins with the man who shot her."

"For some reason," I stated, "you've got love on the brain. Who's to say it wasn't a woman?"

"I am. She wouldn't cover up that strong for a woman."

There wasn't any arguing with her. Ever since we'd gotten together at the Blue Penguin she'd been that way. She'd completely discarded her scientific attitude and was letting her emotions take over.

I put my hands on her shoulders and turned her so that we faced each other. "Listen," I advised, "we've gotten ourselves involved in something that's none of our business. We've been charitable and generous . . . and maybe even a trifle foolish. Our job now is to wish Miss Collins all the luck in the world, and to see to it that our puny little doctor doesn't pitch any curves."

She stood motionless, looking thoughtful. I said, "Don't do it!" and she looked at me innocently and asked, "Don't do *what?*"

"Don't start getting ideas."

"Can I help it if—"

"Yes, you can help it if. You and I are going to drift with the current. It's healthier that way."

Dale wasn't paying any attention: She never does when she's got her mind made up. She smiled in my direction, and nodded,

as though she agreed with herself. That made it unanimous—all
except me.

"I ought to be in the bedroom with them," she said.

"Why?"

"You know perfectly well why. Don't doctors have nurses present when they're attending woman patients?"

I shook my head. "You lost me long ago. You're not a
nurse . . ." Then an idea hit. "I know! You're a woman!"

"Said under other circumstances, I might take that as a com-
pliment," she replied. "As it is, I regard it as an insult. You mean
I'm merely curious: Is that it?"

"Yes."

"You're right." She tiptoed across the room, pressed against the
door frame, and pulled back the draperies just far enough to
peep into the bedroom.

She made an exceedingly pretty picture standing there, so
pretty that I momentarily forgot the unhappy situation into
which we had been projected. She looked much more like an
architect's delight than like an architect.

I was busy enjoying myself just looking at her when I happened to glance at her face. It was set and stern, and she was
frowning. She flashed a look in my direction and motioned me
to join her. At the same time, she put her fingers on her lips—
enjoining me to silence.

I crossed the room, quiet as two mice. She gestured toward
the bedroom. I took one look and stood rigidly.

What was happening in there was strictly not the way a doctor
should be acting with a badly wounded patient. Our visitor
wasn't paying the slightest attention to Maxine Collins—nor was
there any evidence that he'd concerned himself with her from
the time he entered the room.

He was standing beside the bed, holding Maxine's shiny,
patent-leather handbag. He was taking things out of it, and
stuffing them into his pocket. He was working swiftly, and with
almost frightening concentration, as though time was pressing
hard. But the thing which riveted my attention was the stuff he
was taking from Maxine's bag.

Jewelry! Bracelets, rings, pendants, necklaces. Diamonds,
rubies, emeralds, sapphires. He was transferring them from the
handbag to his topcoat pocket, and he was doing it with the
swift, furtive motions of the thief. It was astonishing from a

dozen angles, most amazing of which was the fact that Miss Collins should be packing that much wealth around with her.

Dale led me back to the far side of the living room, almost to the foyer. She said, "He's not a doctor."

I agreed.

"He must be the man who telephoned. He had to come up after those things, so he said he was sending a doctor. That was to fool us."

"Right. Did you get a good look at that stuff?"

"Yes," she said.

"Costume, or real?"

"Only a man would ask that. It's genuine."

I didn't argue, but she elaborated, anyway. "In the first place, I can tell. In the second place, that's what he came for. It also constitutes the motive for the shooting."

I said, "I wish I were less of a conscientious citizen."

"What does that crack mean?"

"It looks like I've got to do something."

She grabbed both my arms. She said, "Don't you go getting any noble ideas, Steve Warren. I won't stand for it."

"What do you want me to do?"

"Something sane—for once in your life. The little man came up after the jewelry. He's got it. Let him keep it. After he goes, we'll phone for a real doctor, and for the police. It's only a matter of a few minutes . . ."

I looked down at her with fresh interest. She was worried— about me. That was nice: it was one of the nicest things that had ever happened to me. I had a sudden impulse to tell her that, plus a few other things, but this seemed to be a particularly inappropriate time and place.

I had no intention of arguing. What Dale had said was simple, logical and right. And we'd probably have played it just that way if suddenly, from the bedroom, there hadn't come a gasping, choking sound . . . the sort of noise that makes your muscles twitch.

Dale said, "Maxine!"

I moved fast. I barged into the bedroom with Dale right behind me. Doc was standing by the bed, tense as a hairspring. His pale eyes were narrowed, and there was a light in them I didn't like. His wispy hair was mussed up—not much, but enough to give him a crazy appearance.

I said, "What goes on here?"

His voice had a metallic quality. He said, "I don't need any help."

"I think you do." That was Dale. "Who are you?"

He stared at her, saying nothing.

"You're not a doctor," she stated.

The pale eyes of the little man flickered. You could see that he was jittery, and that he was holding himself in check with great effort.

I glanced at the girl on the bed. What I saw didn't make me happy. She must have been a truly magnificent-looking girl once, but not now. A gray shadow hovered over her.

Then, suddenly, she moved. Her lips opened and a long sigh escaped. Then came two or three rasping breaths, a convulsive movement of her body . . . and a terrible, abrupt relaxation. Her eyes were open, staring at the ceiling—seeing nothing.

A little sob broke from Dale, but I hadn't needed that to tell me that Maxine Collins had reached the end of her journey. I'd seen other people die, but never like this. A hot, unreasonable anger surged over me.

Dale had gone to the bedside. She was holding Maxine's wrist: she put her ear down to the girl's lips, trying to detect the breathing that was no longer there. Her stricken gray eyes flashed me a message.

Now there was no further need for argument or debate, no fancy theories about being—or not being—a good citizen. If we'd sized things up right, the shooting of Maxine Collins was no longer just a shooting. It was murder.

The one telephone in the apartment was on the table beside Dale's bed. I started for it. The voice of the little man crackled across the room, "What are you doing?"

"I'm phoning for the police."

I reached for the instrument. Then I heard a sharp cry of warning from Dale, and I looked at the man we called Doc.

His right hand had come out of its topcoat pocket. It was holding a gun.

"If you touch that telephone," he said steadily, "so help me God, I'll kill you."

You think you know what you'd do in a situation like that, but when the time comes you don't do it. You suddenly realize that it's the real thing, not a motion picture.

If it had been a picture, I'd have known precisely how to act. I'd have ordered Dale to stand out of the line of fire, I'd have transfixed a cowering murderer with a fierce and steady eye, I'd have started slowly across the room, knowing his courage could not stand up against mine.

Maybe he'd shoot: maybe not. It wouldn't matter either way, because if he did shoot—he'd miss. Then I'd wrap up his puny frame in my big arms and hold him until the cops came. I'd be the personification of virtue triumphant and I'd marry the boss's daughter and win seven refrigerators and four electric dishwashers on a quiz program.

But things gave no promise of working out that way. Facing us across the dead body of Maxine Collins was a little man who was cornered and desperate: a man who had committed one murder and who had nothing to lose by committing two more.

The fact that he was obviously terrified wasn't any help, either. A nervous finger can pull a trigger before it means to, a frightened man can do things that a sane, level-headed person would never think of doing.

I don't know what I'd have done if I'd been alone in the room with him. But of this much I was certain: I wasn't going to make any play that would increase the danger to Dale. After all, there was nothing we could do to help Maxine Collins. I realized I had a double job on my hands: first, to keep Dale from making any move; second, to handle the situation as quietly and calmly as possible in the effort to soothe the jittery visitor.

Dale said suddenly, "If you aren't going to phone, Steve—I will."

I said quickly, "Hold it, kid. The guy's serious. You're going to work for Philips, Schirmer & Lee. You'd be playing a dirty trick on them if you got yourself killed."

She looked at me oddly. At first she didn't tumble to what I was trying to do. Then I saw comprehension commence to dawn in her eyes, and she picked up the cue. She said, "I wasn't going to take that job, anyway."

The little man looked at us as though we were crazy. He snapped, "Hey! what kind of double-talk is that? And whatever it means, cut it out."

"Okay, Doc," I said with what I hoped was an air of superb nonchalance. Then: "By the way, you're *not* a doctor, are you?"

"Of course not."

"Who are you?"

"What difference does it make?"

"It's easier to use a name, and it wouldn't be right just to go on calling you 'Doc,' would it?"

He thought it over, and then shrugged. "You won't get a chance to tell anyone, so what have I got to lose? I'm Oliver Slocum."

"How do you do, Mr. Slocum. I'm Steve Warren. Architect. This is Dale Grayson. She's been my partner till I dissolved our firm so she could take a better job."

It was working. I was making it tough on Oliver. He couldn't figure my angle—but he was trying, and that was all to the good, because it gave him something to think about besides the spot he was in.

He said, "No use play-acting, Warren. You'd better start feeling sorry for yourselves."

"That wouldn't get us anywhere, would it?"

"No. I've got a job to finish."

"Us, you mean?"

"Yes."

Dale said, "I wonder whether you could, really."

"Could what?"

"Kill us in cold blood, just like that."

He moistened his lips. "I wouldn't want to. But what else is there to do?"

Dale was really in there pitching. As far as I could see, we were gaining nothing but time. But even that helped. Maybe the doorbell would ring, maybe the maid who serviced the apartment would remember that she had forgotten something and come barging in. There were a thousand maybes, all unlikely, but each having its tiny ray of hope.

Looking at it from Oliver Slocum's angle, there really wasn't much for him to do except knock us both off and walk out of there. It was that simple. Certainly they'd never be able to tie him up with us, so he'd be safe unless they connected him with the girl on the bed. And even if they did that, it'd be the hard way because they'd find her in Dale's apartment with no proof that Oliver also had been an actor in the drama.

I said, "Look, Oliver, why don't we go into the living room and talk this thing over? We didn't ask for this, and we don't like what we've got. There must be some answer other than the one you're thinking."

I could sense that I'd made the only possible approach. The frightened little man had a meticulous mind. He, too, was looking for a way out. Our apparently casual acceptance of a ghastly fact had already had some soothing effect. My idea now was to get him out of sight of Maxine's body. Then he might really listen to reason.

He waved us into the living room. He remained a safe distance from us, so that I couldn't hope to jump him. He motioned us to the couch and suggested that we sit at opposite ends of it. He pulled up a straight chair, and sat facing us. He was still coiled tight . . . and the gun was still steady. I reminded myself that with that very gun Oliver had just committed a murder.

"Get it off your chest, Oliver," I suggested. "Maybe we can work something out."

He said, shrilly, "You're not fooling me. I know what you're doing. You're trying to make me relax so you can get to me. You won't succeed. The first move you make . . ."

"Okay, Oliver. Maybe I *was* thinking of that. But it happens that I believe you. I'm also afraid of you. We've had quite a demonstration of what that gun can do."

Dale said, "Why did you kill her, Oliver?"

He wanted to talk, all right, but he went at it the hard way. He said, "She took the jewelry from me. She said she was going to return it."

"Who?" asked Dale patiently.

"Maxine. And she refused to go away with me. Even after she'd told me . . . anyway, she wouldn't."

"You were in love with Maxine?"

"Of course. Certainly I was. That's why I took the jewelry in the first place: so she and I would have a chance."

Dale's voice was quiet, soothing.

"Look, Oliver," she said, "you've got to remember that we don't know what you're talking about. Why not tell it from the beginning? Who are you? What do you do?"

He blinked at her. He said, almost apologetically, "Of course you don't know. For fifteen years I've been confidential secretary to William G. Huntingdon. You've heard of him, haven't you?"

"Yes," I lied. "Of course."

That seemed to give him a certain satisfaction.

His voice was steadier . . . almost as steady as the gun he held, the gun which never wavered.

"At first I just worked for Mr. Huntingdon. At his home, not his office. Then his wife started calling on me for things. I became a sort of combination errand boy and housecat."

"They pushed you around, didn't they?"

"They didn't know I existed."

The picture was getting clearer now: a little man with an overwhelming inferiority complex.

He seemed surprised to find himself talking. Surprised and pleased. He'd had things bottled up inside for a long time. I suppose he was telling himself that it didn't make any difference how much we knew because—at that moment—he was convinced we'd never live to tell it. The whole thing would have been fantastic—if it had been happening to somebody else.

Dale's eyes rested on mine for a moment, briefly. She was telling me to give Oliver Slocum his head, to keep him talking, to play for time, to give him a chance to work off some of his tension. Oliver drew a deep breath, hesitated for a moment, then looked at us again.

"I was in love with Maxine," he went on. "She said she was in love with me. I always doubted that, though I didn't tell her so. I am so much older. I'm not . . . well, not her type. I never believed her until today . . . and then it was too late."

Murderer or not, I felt sorry for the little man. Dale and I sat quietly, waiting for him to go on.

"For years it's been growing on me: the Huntingdons having so much and me having so little. I couldn't see any future for myself unless . . . well, how was I to accumulate any money? I thought that maybe, with money, I could hold Maxine . . .

"Mrs. Huntingdon has a lot of jewelry. When she's not wearing it, it's kept in the safe in the Huntingdon home. Recently she wore a lot of it. This morning she gave the jewelry to me just as they were starting out for a long week-end trip. She handed it to me casually and told me to put it back in the safe. Maybe what got me was that she trusted me so implicitly: the poor little mouse of a man who wouldn't have any impulse to steal, who wouldn't ever need money, who couldn't possibly have a romance in his life."

His voice was bitter. "They left the house. I didn't put the jewelry in the safe. I went to my own apartment in a shabby little building near where the Huntingdons live. I telephoned Maxine. I told her I'd come into money, and that we were going off together.

"In the middle of my packing, I went downstairs for something. I left the jewelry in my half-packed suitcase. When I got back, Maxine was in the apartment.

"She had found the jewelry. She said I had to return it. I don't know yet whether she was simply afraid, or whether she cared for me and didn't want me to get in trouble. Anyway, I told her I wasn't changing my mind. I was getting out, and she could come or not as she wanted. She said she wasn't going to let me make a fool of myself: If I wouldn't return the jewelry, she would. That was when she told me she already had it in her bag.

"I tried to stop her. I had this gun. I tried to scare her with it. She started to open the door. I shot her. I don't know why. Maybe I meant to: maybe I didn't. But that doesn't matter: it's still murder.

"I knew the bullet had hit her, but I thought it wasn't serious. She walked down the hall. Lots of people were there. I didn't dare follow. Apparently no one had heard the shot.

"I followed her into the street and around the corner to the Blue Penguin. I waited outside. I saw her come out with you two, and then come here. I talked with the doorman, found out that the apartment belonged to Miss Grayson—and got the number. I telephoned about sending a doctor. My idea was to get the jewelry—and to get away. I walked up to this apartment when the doorman was busy. I . . . I'm sorry Maxine is dead, but being sorry won't bring her back. I've got the jewelry and I'm going to keep it. There's always a chance that they won't find me." He looked at us, almost pleadingly. "So I'll do whatever else I have to do," he finished. "You understand, don't you?"

Dale and I looked at each other and nodded. There was something more pathetic than sinister in the little man: he'd almost made us forget that he was talking about killing us.

One thing we got out of his explanation: he wasn't fooling.

He said he'd do whatever else he had to do, and he meant it. It was up to us to convince him that he didn't have to kill us. I had the feeling that time was running out.

It was Dale who made the opening gambit. She said, "What's done is done. Just walk out of here, and we'll give you whatever time you need to make a good start."

"And then . . ."

"We'll notify the police." She motioned toward the next room. "We'd have to."

"And you'd identify me. . . . Oh! don't deny it. Even if I trusted you, it wouldn't work. The cops would get the truth out of you. They'd pick me up in a hurry."

"Won't they, anyway?"

"No," he stated reasonably. "Not if you're dead. They won't think of me at all. They'll spend an awful lot of time trying to find out where Maxine fitted into your lives. Since she didn't belong anywhere, they won't get far on that line of investigation . . . but all the time they're trying, I'll be getting farther away. Eventually, they'll bring me into it, but not until after they've wasted most of their effort on you two."

One thing I'll say for Oliver Slocum: his reasoning was unassailable.

"Finding two dead women and a dead man in the apartment," he continued, "they'll immediately suspect some sort of a triangle. I'll leave the gun here. It isn't registered to me." He smiled cheerfully. "You see how it is, don't you?"

Yes, we saw how it was. His only chance for safety was to make sure we couldn't tell anyone, ever. We were dealing with a desperate, frightened little man who had gambled his last chip. He had nothing more to lose. He had much to gain.

We tried new arguments, we made promises. We could have saved ourselves the trouble. He was polite and even apologetic. The whole thing was silly: me, a big, husky guy; Oliver Slocum, a scared shrimp.

The more I considered it, the more apparent it became that the next play had been checked up to me. Things couldn't continue this way indefinitely. I was willing to do nothing—but the cards hadn't been dealt that way.

No chance of surprising him. There was still the width of the room between us. I watched Slocum's face, and didn't like what I saw. He was nerving himself for the payoff. He got up sud-

denly and went to the radio. In seconds the room was filled with
music. Plenty loud. He pressed his back against the radio and
stared at us.

If you've ever boxed and have waited for the gong announcing
the beginning of a bout; if you've ever played football and tensed
yourself for the opening kickoff . . . then perhaps you'll know
what I felt. Getting ready to do something because it had to
be done—because I was there and no other choice was possible.
I tried not to think about what might happen to Dale or me.

I'd been toying with an ash tray which was perched on the
end table next to me. I threw it suddenly, straight at Slocum's
head. Before it got halfway across the room, I started after it.

I didn't even hear the gun. All I knew was that something hit
me in the left shoulder and spun me around. Then I got a
glimpse of Dale dashing past me. Even through a sudden haze of
dizziness and nausea, I saw her grappling with Slocum.

I heard the little man swearing in a low, tense, frightened
voice. I saw him rip open the door of the hall closet. He shoved
Dale inside. I was leaning against the wall of the foyer, near that
same closet. Something hit me on the jaw. It was the barrel of
the gun. I suppose Oliver was afraid to fire again. We were very
close to the front door then and the sound would most certainly
have carried, even above the blaring of the radio.

He pushed me into the closet and I fell flat on my face. The
door slammed shut. I heard the key turn. I lay there, feeling
weak and sick and helpless. Dale apparently had forgotten all
about Oliver Slocum and Maxine Collins . . . and even about
Philips, Schirmer & Lee.

She was holding my head in her lap and saying things which
were sweet and soothing and silly. Then she got up and the
closet was bathed in light as she snapped the wall switch. Inside
the closet were a few of her coats, and above them a shelf holding boxes of various sorts. It was a sort of storage closet as well
as a place to hang coats. I saw her try the door. She rattled it
and banged on it. All she got by way of response was a derisive
hoot from a hot trumpet on the radio.

This was strictly something that shouldn't be. Everything had
gone wrong, and was getting wronger by the second. All except
one thing: Dale's solicitude about me. That, I could take with
enjoyment in spite of how awful I felt.

My position was definitely inglorious. My shoulder felt as

though it had been paralyzed. My jaw was one throbbing ache. I tried to sit up, and flopped back again. Dale seemed to have the idea that I was dying. I assured her that I wasn't: I felt much too terrible for that. For a runt of a man, Slocum had sure done a good job.

I said, "Why didn't he . . ."

"He didn't have a chance. I grabbed his wrist. After he hit you, he seemed to go to pieces. All he was thinking about then was getting away. It was awful . . . and oh, darling! You're not badly hurt?"

"No," I said, "I'm not too . . . hey! what did you call me?"

"You heard me." She stood up and rattled the door again. She stamped on the floor. "Times when I don't want to," she snapped, "I hear every sound from every other apartment—and they complain about noises from here. Now, when it's important . . ."

By holding onto the wall with my good hand, I managed to drag myself upright. I glanced at the shelf, hoping to find some sort of instrument which would help me pry the lock. I tried forcing the door with my uninjured shoulder, but the pain spread all through my body, and I gave it up as a bad job. I felt shaky and all-gone: that absurd feeling you get when you're about to faint.

But I had seen something. I pointed to a box on the shelf.

"Those," I said, "what are they?"

"Light bulbs."

"Give me. Quick!"

She handed me the box. Eleven beautiful, lovely, new one-hundred-watt bulbs. I said, "Hand 'em to me one at a time, but fast. Keep your back to this wall."

She did what I told her. And as fast as she put 'em in my hand, I slammed each bulb against the floor.

Unless you've ever dropped a light bulb, you've no idea what it sounds like. To me, each explosion made more noise than Oliver Slocum's revolver.

Eleven explosions: as close together as she could hand me the bulbs and I could let fly. The neighbors hadn't paid any attention to Slocum's shot, but if they heard these at all, they'd have to pay attention. It sounded like the Battle of the Bulge. The little closet was filled with broken glass . . . and I fell right in the middle of it.

What I remembered of the next half hour was largely confusion, made bearable by Dale's concern over my welfare. She did a lot and talked a lot, but it all came to me through a fog.

I remember someone ripping open the door in response to Dale's insistent banging. The building superintendent was there, plus a couple of goggle-eyed tenants and three uniformed policemen. Another policeman was on the phone talking to someone at Homicide, and I heard him saying, "Yeh, Lieutenant—one dame dead as a mackerel and this here guy and his babe locked in a closet . . . Uh-huh! Glass all over everywhere . . . Talk? . . . Well, *he's* kinda punch drunk, but the babe, she's talkin' our ears off."

Somebody put me on the couch. A couple of detectives came in and started getting the story from Dale. A doctor had showed up—a real one—and Dale wasn't giving the police all the co-operation they thought they were entitled to. She wasn't self-possessed any longer. She was hysterical, and what she was most interested in was whether I'd live. She said I had to because she worked with me.

"Listen, lady"— That was a detective talking— "We don't care who you work for. What we want to know is who killed the redhead in the other room, who socked you and this lad in the closet, who busted all that glass, who had a machine gun up here, and what did he look like?"

Dale gave him the story. Before she was halfway through, they'd taken down some notes and one of the detectives was on the phone telling somebody to put out a wail for a guy named Oliver Slocum for murder, attempted murder, kidnaping, burglary and other assorted felonies. He came back from the phone rubbing his hands and promising us that they'd get Mr. Slocum in no time.

They took me to the hospital, trundled me to an operating room, and it was hours before I knew anything at all . . . and even then Dale had to tell me.

"You'll live," she said, "to become the country's greatest architect and the father of at least half a dozen small architects."

"How about Oliver?"

"He won't be the father of any. They picked him up quite promptly. He confessed, and also apologized to me quite sweetly when they brought him up here for identification."

"Do I look as terrible as I feel?"

She regarded me critically. "Worse. Much worse. You need a permanent caretaker."

"Has that got anything to do with your recent remark about becoming the father of a lot of little architects?"

"Naturally."

"But you understand that that's strictly personal."

"It's bound to be. And since we've decided that, it seems I'd better notify Philips, Schirmer & Lee Monday morning."

I agreed that it was just as well. After all, a dignified and important firm like Philips, Schirmer & Lee would never stand for having the offspring of a rival architect cluttering up their office. It might have been my delicate condition, but that argument seemed more valid than any Dale had advanced.

She was sitting very close to the bed when the nurse came in and told her time was up. She asked for just three more minutes alone with me. The nurse went out, and Dale bent over me. Her lips were smiling, but she was crying, too. "Y-you haven't said anything, Steve . . . Not one single important thing."

I pulled her face down to mine and managed to kiss her adequately despite the lopsided condition of my jaw.

"You've always known I love you," I said. "And we'll keep the firm of Warren & Grayson alive. But after office hours . . ."

"Yes, I know." She was still crying. "While you were still under the anesthetic I sketched a sign for the door of our apartment . . ." She held up a piece of paper for my inspection. It read:

WARREN & WARREN

Do Not Disturb

28

KEN W. PURDY

The Haunted Hour

ONE OF THE COUNTRY'S leading experts on automobiles—from ancient museum pieces to modern sports
cars—Mr. Purdy has often written about his enthusiasm
in articles and in books. For most of his professional life
he has been a magazine editor, but now and then he
turns his hand to fiction, warmly, sympathetically, with
such stout characters as you find here in Helen Winton,
jet pilot's wife—and not quite sure she can take it. This
is one of those quiet suspense stories lived out in the
heroism of a wife's emotions in her own living room,
haunted by the fear of a husband's sudden death.

HELEN WINTON LET the phone slide out of her hands into its
cradle and sat staring at it in numb horror. Of all the accouter-
ments of a machine-mad age, she hated telephones most—more
than airplanes, even. The hours she had spent waiting for that
black voice to speak had so embittered her that even when it
brought good tidings she felt little lessening of hatred; and it had
brought no good tidings this time.

"This is Johnny Douglas at the field, Helen."

"How are you, Lieutenant?"

"Good. Look, Helen, uh, we just got a call from Mac. He was
over the Bonetown range and his fire went out. He . . ."

Helen Winton saw her eyes blur and the awful sickness of
fear welled up in her.

"Johnny, is he down?" she whispered. "Did he get down?"

"Don't know yet, Helen," the voice said. "He just called once,
said it had quit on him. He wouldn't talk while he was trying
to start it again, you know—too busy. I'm sure he's okay, Helen,
and I wouldn't bother you with it at all except that he's on that
gunnery show—lots of brass out there, radio and newspaper guys
—and I was afraid you'd hear some exaggerated cock-and-bull
story on the air!"

"I see," Helen said. She didn't see, at all.

"You be stout, now," Douglas went on, "and I'll phone you again the minute we hear. Don't worry, Mac's a good boy, he'll be all right. You be stout. Good-by, Helen."

"Good-by," Helen said. "Thank you."

She moved away from the telephone and tried to think. Her heart was thumping and she sat down hard. She wanted to remember what Mac had said that morning about the gunnery test. Had he mentioned ground targets, or had it been sleeves, towed high up? She couldn't remember, and it mattered terribly. To lose an engine at 10,000 feet was bad, but it wasn't necessarily deadly. To lose it on a run for ground targets, with nowhere to go, no chance to jump, maybe not even time enough to get the gear down . . .

She stood up abruptly and walked over to stare out the window. The flat ground around the house seemed to dance in the desert sun. There hadn't been a cloud in the sky for weeks.

When they had first come out to the desert, after a gray, wet winter at Mitchel Field, the unfailing hot sun had been a delight; but the Wintons were Vermont people, and after a few months Helen had begun to pray for rain. Or gale or flood or thunderstorm—anything to break the monotony of a brassy sun hanging endlessly in a cloudless sky.

Of course it wasn't alone the monotony of the weather that had begun to turn Helen against this bright land. There was another reason for her disquietude, and she knew well enough what it was—the jets. At Mitchel Mac had flown P-51's, the last propeller-driven operational fighters the Air Force had. A P-51 seemed as safe as a baby carriage to Helen now.

It was the jets that scared her witless. The jets didn't seem like airplanes to Helen. The noise they made, an obscene, unearthly bellowing, was not an airplane's noise; these planes were built to kill, and it seemed to Helen that they killed impersonally and indifferently. They would even kill you on the ground; suck you in at one end, roast you to death in a twinkling at the other.

Most of all, they moved at speeds that affronted intelligence: 600, 700, 800 miles an hour and more. And if the engine quit, there was little glide in them, they came down like rocks . . .

The phone rang again and Helen spun around to get it. It was Janie Marshall.

"Wondered if you were home," Janie said. "I thought I'd drop over."

"All right," Helen said. "Sure. Come on over."

"Right," Janie answered crisply. "Can I bring anything? Pick up the kids or anything?"

"No, thanks, the baby's asleep and Mac Junior's over at the Barretts'," Helen said.

"I'll see you," Janie said.

Helen had dropped the phone and turned away before she realized what Janie's call might mean. So it was that bad; somebody—Douglas, probably—had called Janie Marshall and told her to come over and stand by. Or had they? Janie had sounded perfectly natural. Still, she was a level-headed girl and she would. Helen seized the phone again and rang the Marshalls'. The indifferent buzzing clattered in her ear. No answer. Janie must have left immediately. She must have been in a terrific rush—as she would have been if Douglas had heard, and knew, and told her to get to Helen's house quickly, before bad news beat her to it.

She ran over to the radio and switched it on. She turned the volume knob as far as it would go, and when the set warmed, it came on in an insane giant's shout. "*Is Your Hair Frowsy, Brittle, Faded? If So . . .*" She spun the dial through every station in the area, but there was no news on. She shut it off.

"Waiting," Mac had told her one time during the war, "is a very hard thing to do, and also very simple. The secret of being a big-league, long-distance waiter is just this: You don't wait at all. You do something else, dig a well, build an apple pie, or whatever, and first thing you know, you've stopped worrying. Then, all of a sudden you'll notice that you're pretty sure everything's going to turn out all right. You get to feeling real good. You begin to be *positive* that everything will turn out all right. And sure enough, it usually does."

"Your own personal system?" Helen had asked him.

"No, my grandmother's," Mac told her. "An expert in heavy waiting. When Grandpop took off for Alaska and all that gold, in '98, she didn't hear a peep out of him for two years. But she was perfectly sure he was not only okay, but rich. She never worried a bit, that last year and a half, after she discovered the system."

"And?"

"He never did write to her. She was sitting in the parlor one day and she heard his step on the porch. She called to him, 'If your boots are muddy, William, go around to the back.' He came in and she kissed him and told him he looked wonderfully healthy. Then she said, 'Where is all the gold?' So he took the $17,000 in dust out of his valise and dumped it on the kitchen table. The old girl had been right all along. See?"

Helen looked at Mac's picture, the one she kept on the mantel over his ferocious protests. "Okay, Skipper," she said. "I see." She picked up a pile of socks and had ruined two of them by the time Janie Marshall showed up. Janie came charging into the house like a small, red-headed fullback. "Hi, sugar," she said. "What's new with all the Wintons?"

Helen stared at her. "Don't you know?" she said. "Didn't they tell you to come over?"

Janie blinked. "They? They? Who's they?" she asked. "Have you been out in the sun too long or something? *You* told me to come over, on the telephone, ten minutes ago. Didn't you?"

"Yes, of course, I did," Helen said. "But I didn't think it was your own idea. I thought Johnny Douglas told you to come over on account of Mac . . . They phoned just a little while ago and told me his engine quit over Bonetown, and I was afraid . . . I wondered . . ."

"Oh, baby, I'm sorry," Janie said. "Nobody told me a thing. Did he get down all right?"

"I don't know yet," Helen said. "They couldn't tell me. I'm just waiting to find out."

"I see," Janie said. She sat down beside Helen on the couch. "We'll both wait," she said. She pulled out a cigarette. "Sometimes I wish the Wright brothers had been drowned at birth," she said.

"Sometimes I wish I'd married an adding-machine operator," Helen said miserably. "No, I don't either. I take that back. I'm glad I married Mac. I wouldn't marry anybody else who ever lived. But still, I do wish he wouldn't fly . . . Or do I? I don't really know." She pushed a sock away and folded her hands miserably.

Janie patted her shoulder. "That's no good, sugar," she said. "You have to take a man the way he is, and you have to let him do what he thinks he must. Nothing else ever worked, nothing else ever will."

They sat there a long time after that in silence, until finally the telephone jangled again.

"I'll get it," Janie said. She spoke briefly and hung up. "Your small son," she told Helen. "He and the Barrett kid made a model plane and he wanted to stay a little longer so they could fly it. I said yes. Okay?"

Helen looked at her for a minute. "I guess so," she said. "Yes, that's all right. If we're going to have another fly-boy in the family, he might as well get an early start at it." Helen stopped speaking suddenly. She saw her own words hanging in the air and she was almost appalled by them. "If we're going to have another fly-boy in the family . . ." She had never let herself think of that before—Mac Junior a flier, like his father? Why not? Indeed, he might as well get an early start at it, and she had better get an early start at accepting it—or whatever else he wanted to do.

And certainly to accept her son's life she must first accept her husband's. Who was she, anyway, to be stamping her little feet and bemoaning her fate? Mac was doing what he had to do, making the contribution he could best make to his world, and if Mac Junior took the same course—well, pies must be built, gold must be dug, waiting must be endured.

She smiled at her friend. "I think I'll make some tea," she said. "We have to wait, but there's no point in starving. I'll make some cinnamon toast, and some tea, and we'll put a ladylike drop of rum in it and sit here in the parlor like gentlefolk."

"Parlor?" Janie asked.

"Parlor," Helen answered firmly.

They had finished the tea when the phone rang.

"I'll answer it, Janie," Helen said. "I'm a new girl now. I think I just finished growing up, about half an hour ago." She walked carefully across the room, took a deep breath and picked up the phone.

"Hi, Mac," she said. "Did you get your boots muddy?"

29

HELEN McCLOY

Murder Stops the Music

FOR THE PROTAGONIST of a number of her mystery novels, Miss McCloy has developed an effective character in the person of Dr. Basil Willing, a psychiatrist who works with the New York Police Department. But you will rarely observe Dr. Willing as he sits taking notes of the ramblings of a patient stretched on a couch. Usually, as here, he finds himself very much involved in the action. Miss McCloy is married to Brett Halliday, a mystery writer too, who created the red-headed Michael Shayne. Recently, in addition to their writing, they have established a literary agency in New York.

SHE WAS LOVELY the first time Basil Willing saw her in the village street. Her dress was white dimity, sprigged with rose-buds.

He asked his neighbor, Paul Amory, who she was.

'Sybilla Swayne from Boston, just nineteen."

She looked different the afternoon she came up the path to Paul's beach cottage. An ugly, muddy stain spread across the billowing white skirt. Paul cried: "Sybilla! What happened?"

"Everything." She was on the verge of tears.

"Is someone following you?" Basil looked towards the dunes. A tall clump of bayberry was quivering.

"I don't think so, but . . ."

Paul said: "This is Dr. Willing. He has the cottage near mine this year."

She turned to Basil. "Aren't you a criminologist?"

He smiled. "Just a psychiatrist who has worked with the police in New York."

"I didn't know that." Paul was surprised. "What happened, Sybilla? Did you see Mrs. Ehrenthal?"

"I saw her all right." The golden skin flushed. Basil made a ·move to go. The girl detained him. "It's nothing criminal, but it is . . . peculiar . . . Every summer this village has a square dance for local charities.

"This year our committee decided to get a paid organizer from New York and the agency sent us Paul. He gave each of us a list of people to see personally. On my list was Gertrude Ehrenthal. She used to be a famous pianist. She's a widow now and wealthy."

"I ignored her wealth," said Paul. "I just wanted her to play for us."

"But what made you think she would?" protested Sybilla. "She has nothing to do with village life or other summer people. She bought the old Ashley place three years ago, that time the Ashleys were so hard up. Jim Eggers, the real-estate man, has been trying to buy it back for the Ashleys ever since, but she won't sell. She didn't acknowledge the printed notice of the dance you sent her, and I was sure she would turn me down, but you were so insistent . . .

"Just as I rang the front doorbell, a big boxer came loping across the turf. I felt quite relieved when the door was opened by a young man, and the dog ran into the house ahead of me. The young man showed me into a drawing room and said he'd tell his mother I was there. The dog crouched on a white bearskin rug. His paws had left a muddy track all over it.

"The son came back with Mrs. Ehrenthal. She was very New Yorkish and clever-looking—"

"What was the son like?" asked Basil.

Sybilla, who was so ready with words for Mrs. Ehrenthal, had none at all for her son. "When I told her about the square dance, she surprised me by saying: 'I'd love to play for an audience once more.' She even explained about not answering our printed notice. It had been addressed to the wrong post-office box—703—and, as hers is 610, she'd only just got it.

"All the time we talked, the dog was roaming the room, leaving muddy tracks wherever he went. A little maid brought in a big tea tray and Eric—the son—set up an old tip table. The dog put its muddy forepaws on my skirt and snatched a cake out of my hand.

"Mrs. Ehrenthal exclaimed: 'Oh, your pretty dress!' I said: 'It doesn't matter.' The dog bounded toward the cake dish on the table and the whole thing toppled over. Tea streamed over the rug and scalded my knee.

"I lost control. I cried out: 'Really, I should think you'd train your dog!' And then . . . Oh, you can never guess what happened. Mrs. Ehrenthal said: 'My dog? I thought, of course, it was yours!'

"Oh, laugh, if you like! But it wasn't a bit funny. I believed her when she said the dog wasn't hers, but she didn't believe me when I said it wasn't mine. She behaved as if she thought I was trying to get out of paying for the damage. She said: 'My dear Miss Swayne, why else would the dog come into the house with you?'

"You see, the son had answered the doorbell and seen the dog with me. He'd told her: 'There's a girl here about the village dance and she's brought her dog.' They'd been too polite to say anything about the dog when they thought he was mine, as I'd been too polite to say anything when I thought he was theirs.

"By this time, the dog had run out an open French window with Eric chasing him, so I was alone with her when I left. I said: 'I never saw that dog before in my life,' and walked out. But I still don't understand it. Why did the dog walk into the house with me?"

"Do the Ehrenthals own another dog?" said Basil. "Perhaps a female?"

"No. She said they'd never had a dog."

"Perhaps the dog belongs to the son," suggested Paul. "Perhaps he acquired it this afternoon and, now the animal's done so much damage, he doesn't dare admit to his mother that it's his."

Basil spoke more thoughtfully. "You say the dog was a boxer. Was he brindled, with a brass-studded collar?"

"Yes. Do you know him?"

"It's just occurred to me that maybe I do."

"You mean Loki?" Paul was astonished.

"Your dog?" Sybilla asked. "Why haven't I seen him before?"

"You never came up here before," answered Paul. "I don't take him to the village."

"But what would he be doing at the Ehrenthals'?"

"I have no idea." Paul let out a high-pitched whistle. "Where is the fellow? Excuse me a minute . . ." He ran down the steps.

A breath of wind sighed and the shadows lengthened. "I must go," said Sybilla. Basil walked down the sandy path with her. As they came to her car, they saw Paul farther down the drive, facing a clump of bayberry. When he heard their steps, he called out in a tight voice: "Willing! Come here—quick!"

The big boxer lay on his side among the bushes, his eyes half-open, filmed and dull. Above the collar, his throat had been slashed. Arterial blood still flowed with a faint pulsation. There was no sign of a knife.

Paul Amory was not the type to show emotion easily, but now his face was as white as the sand.

"Loki . . ." He knelt beside the dying dog. The eyes opened a little wider—questioning, bewildered.

"It's the same dog." Tears came to Sybilla's eyes . . .

At last, Paul stood up. "You said that Eric Ehrenthal followed the dog out of their house. We all three saw something moving in the bushes just as you reached my house. Loki was killed—while we sat talking."

Sybilla protested. "I can't imagine Mrs. Ehrenthal or her son—"

"Can't you? I can." Paul's gray eyes were murderous. "If they dare to come to the dance tonight . . ."

The Village Hall embodied every decorative commonplace of its era—the picture window without a view, pine panels, and a machine-braided rug in strident green. A smaller rug, behind the bar, muffled the bartender's footsteps and, of course, there was a bar lamp with a driftwood base and a shade cut from an old chart of Nantucket Sound.

A long table was laden with casseroles of clam chowder and a handsome, glazed ham with a bone-handled carving knife sharpened to a surgical edge, to cut paper-thin slices. Paul, officiating behind the bar, offered Basil and Sybilla punch and said to Basil: "You know Jim Eggers, the real-estate agent?"

"Who doesn't?" Basil smiled at a gaunt, colorless man waiting his turn at the bar.

Sybilla was looking toward the entrance at the other end of the room. "Here comes Fanny Ashley."

"The one who's trying to buy back the old Ashley place?"

Eggers turned pale eyes on Basil. "What gave you that idea? I made an offer, but I wasn't acting for the Ashleys, as everyone seems to think. I was acting for a lawyer in New York, and heaven only knows who he was acting for. Funny anyone wanting that place."

"Why?"

"It's so big. There are few people today with enough money to keep it up. And nobody local would want it anyway because of the old story. It was ten years ago, before my time on the Cape, but I heard it all from Miss Ashley herself. When she got hard up, she couldn't sell the place at first, so she rented it to some fellow who turned out to be a crook—a French jewel thief known as Lucien Delorme.

"He worked Miami night spots in winter and spent his summers here. When the police surrounded the house, he knifed one of them and escaped. They never did find the loot he was supposed to have lifted off the suckers in Miami. It gave the house a bad name."

"Maybe your New York lawyer is acting for the jewel thief who left some of his loot hidden in the house," suggested Basil.

Eggers grinned. "Could be, but what I don't know won't hurt me. Besides, Mrs. Ehrenthal will never sell. She's putting an oil burner in this fall, so she can spend most of the winter here. It's her son who misses New York, not she! Why, there are the Ehrenthals now."

Paul's hand shook as he ladled punch.

"Let it ride for this evening," advised Basil. "You've no proof the boy killed your dog."

Basil offered Sybilla a cigarette, but his eyes were on Mrs. Ehrenthal. Her sallow face had the stricken look widowhood leaves on some women. Her hair was dark and she wore a black linen dress, with a white bolero.

"Too much black and white," observed Sybilla, critically. "She needs a touch of red."

In the son, the sallowness was a warm olive. It was easy to see why little Sybilla hadn't been able to find words for him. He must have bowled her over.

Mrs. Ehrenthal sat down at the piano, which stood at the other end of the room close to the entrance. Her muscular fingers attacked the keyboard with a hard, brilliant touch, which was almost masculine.

For a few moments, the crowd listened. Then whispers became murmurs and music was played against a sibilant obbligato. Eric Ehrenthal stood beside the piano with Fanny Ashley and Eggers. Basil's eyes were on the group at the piano, when Paul Amory said: "How about more punch?" Just then the lights went out.

The sudden, blinding darkness stilled every tongue. Chords from the piano faltered and stopped.

"*Music ceases,*" whispered Sybilla. "My favorite Shakespearean stage direction."

There was a rustling in the darkness. A voice cried loudly: "It can't be a hurricane. Must be a blown fuse."

"Where's the fuse box?" Basil addressed darkness.

Paul's voice answered: "Just outside the front door, by the piano. If I can only find the gate to this bar . . ."

Basil groped his way through the crowd. He lit a match and saw the fuse box on the wall, outside the entrance. His flame flickered and went out.

"You should use a lighter." Another flame flared. Eric Ehrenthal's striking face was modeled in high relief by shadows. Basil pulled open the door of the fuse box. The main switch had been disconnected.

Basil snapped the switch back into contact. The sluggish, fluorescent lights stumbled into being.

A woman screamed. Fanny Ashley. She was looking toward Gertrude Ehrenthal, slumped forward on the piano. The bone handle of the ham knife protruded from her left shoulder. A thin stream of fresh blood stained the white bolero. A touch of red . . .

In an hour, the crowded room was almost emptied. Sybilla sat close to Eric, sympathetically. Fanny's reddened eyes made her look years older. Jim Eggers and Paul Amory stood looking curiously at a pair of white cotton work gloves the police had found near the piano.

Lieutenant Copley of the State Police turned to Basil. "You and Miss Swayne and Mr. Amory are obviously in the clear. You were all at the bar at the other end of the room from the fuse box when the lights went out. But Miss Ashley, Mr. Eggers and Mr. Ehrenthal were standing near the piano, which is close to the front door and the fuse box, while everyone else was clustered around the supper table in the center of the room. One of those three—Miss Ashley or Ehrenthal or Eggers—must have pulled the main switch and stabbed this woman under cover of darkness."

Basil turned to Eric. "Mr. Ehrenthal, why didn't your mother believe Miss Swayne when she said the dog at your house this afternoon was not hers?"

Eric answered in a voice still numb with shock. "My mother told me she had seen the dog once before, when she drove past Mr. Amory's cottage. Miss Swayne came to us on an errand from Mr. Amory and the dog came with her. Naturally my mother assumed that the dog was hers and that she had been visiting Mr. Amory's cottage the day my mother saw it there."

"What happened when you followed the dog?"

"I couldn't catch up with him."

Lieutenant Copley knew Basil by reputation. "Is it your theory that whoever killed Amory's dog later killed Mrs. Ehrenthal?"

"Yes," answered Basil. "Mr. Eggers, isn't it time you told us who has been trying to buy the old Ashley place from the Ehrenthals?"

"I have no idea. I was approached by a lawyer from New York, Luke Anders."

"Did you know his practice was chiefly criminal?" Basil turned back to the lieutenant. "Was Lucien Delorme ever caught?"

"No. He's been hiding out for ten years."

"Then it's possible his loot may still be hidden in the Ehrenthal house. It's possible he stabbed Mrs. Ehrenthal because she was going to occupy that house all the year round. She wouldn't sell it. That meant he couldn't gain access to it as long as she lived without assuming all the risks of burglary. Her son liked New York—he would probably sell, if she died. Mrs. Ehrenthal was putting in a new oil burner. That could mean digging in the cellar where the loot might be discovered. With her eliminated, Delorme could make a relatively small down payment on the house, recover his loot and disappear."

"But Lucien Delorme isn't here now!"

"Are you sure? What did he look like?"

"Medium height. Stocky, about a hundred and eighty. Sandy hair. Gray eyes."

"Only the height and the color of the eyes need be the same," mused Basil. "He could lose weight. His hair could turn gray or be dyed."

Jim Eggers and Paul Amory looked at one another, each suddenly aware of the other's gray eyes and medium height.

"We never got his fingerprints," said the lieutenant.

"You don't need them now," answered Basil. "Let's assume Delorme returned to Ashley Point ten years later, when he thought enough time had elapsed so he wouldn't be recognized. He would have cover—an occupation that gave him access to everyone in the village."

Copley gasped. "A real-estate agent? Or a paid organizer for charity drives?"

"Are you nuts?" cried Paul. "I was behind the bar when the lights went out . . . nowhere near the fuse box."

"So you were." Basil opened the gate in the bar and stepped behind it. "And you were right here when the lights came on again."

"Whoever pulled that switch had to be standing by the fuse box at the other end of the room when the lights failed," said Paul. "And that's where Jim Eggers—"

The lights went out. Fanny Ashley screamed: "Oh no! Not again!"

Copley shouted: "Get to that fuse box, Rafferty!"

Flashlights moved in the dark. A voice called: "Fuse blown, Lieutenant, but there are some extras."

The lights came on again. Basil was still behind the bar. He rolled aside the small rug there, revealing the electric cord that ran under it to the bar lamp. The insulation had been scraped away. Two copper wires lay exposed for two inches, side by side.

"Two more questions, Miss Ashley: Was 703 the post-office box number for your house when Delorme lived there? And did he keep a dog?"

"Why, it *was* 703 . . ." stammered Fanny Ashley. "And he had a puppy. A boxer. . . ."

"Amory used his foot on the rug that concealed the two exposed wires to rub them together," Basil explained later. "Of course this caused a short circuit and blew a fuse. He knew Mrs. Ehrenthal would be at the piano near the fuse box. As organizer for the dance, he was familiar with every detail of the Village Hall, and in the dark her music gave him the direction. He snatched the ham knife from the table and stabbed her under cover of darkness.

"The fuse box was right beside the piano. He had plenty of time to replace the blown fuse with one of the extras and disconnect the main switch, so that all the evidence would indicate that the lights had been turned off by someone who had pulled the main switch and therefore by someone who was standing close to the fuse box at the very moment the lights went out.

"He was back behind the bar when I asked where the fuse box was, and he took pains to suggest to me that he had been behind the bar all that time by saying that he couldn't find the bar gate in the dark.

"He killed his own dog because it was giving him away. There's only one plausible reason why any dog would enter a strange house uninvited. It must be a house where the dog has lived before with his own master.

"If Amory's Loki had started returning regularly, someone was sure to suspect, sooner or later, that the dog had lived in that house before. The only previous tenant, besides the Ashleys, was Delorme, the French thief, who kept a boxer puppy there ten years ago.

"Delorme risked bringing the dog back to this neighborhood because the dog's appearance had changed, too. He was no longer a puppy and he was useful as a watchdog and body-guard. No doubt Delorme was a dog-fancier in his own way, but he was also a ruthless criminal who didn't hesitate to use a knife on human being or animal if he thought he had to.

"He realized what the dog was doing to him the moment Sybilla told her story and, while she and I were still talking, he went down the drive and killed the dog. It was the dog's own passage through the bayberry bushes that made them quiver earlier that afternoon."

"Then if it hadn't been for the dog you wouldn't have suspected . . . ?"

"Oh, yes, I should. I had begun to suspect Amory was De-lorme long before I worked out the evidence of the dog. Though he spoke English entirely without a French accent, even under stress, he still used the word 'ignore' as the French use it. He said: 'I ignored Mrs. Ehrenthal's wealth.' What professional charity organizer would 'ignore' wealth in the English sense of the word? He meant: 'I didn't know about Mrs. Ehrenthal's wealth,' and that use of the word 'ignore' is French. Also, I thought:

"Why had he sent Mrs. Ehrenthal's notice of the dance to Box 703 instead of Box 610? Was 703 the old box number for that same house? It was, and that number was indelibly associated with that house in Delorme's subconscious. He must have longed nostalgically for the days when he lived there, secure and unsuspected—an unconscious wish that expressed itself in his typographical error.

"The ten-year-old box number and the French use of the word 'ignore' were a sentence in cipher that read in clear: 'I am a Frenchman and I lived in this house ten years ago.' After that, all I had to ask myself was: How could Amory make those lights go out when he was standing so far from the main switch?"

30

DENIS PLIMMER

The Man in the Black Cloak

THERE IS NO PARTICULAR HARM in revealing
that this story was published while Joseph Stalin was
still very much the head of things in Soviet Russia. If
you will read it with that in mind, the effect is more
chilling, though of course "any resemblance to persons
living or dead is purely coincidental." We have saved
this story till the last because it has a bigness of meaning that we hope will leave you with a sobering reflection
on the weakness of man, the greatness of truth. Mr.
Plimmer is a professional writer whose articles and stories
frequently appear in national magazines.

IT WAS JUST past midnight in the Citadel. All day there had been
a hush in its echoing stone halls as the leaders of the huge nation
arrived, one by one.

Marni, the United Nations representative, had flown back from
New York. Noske, the Ambassador to London, had also returned.
The Foreign Minister, the Minister of the Interior, the dozen or
so lesser Ministers of State, all had passed the triply guarded
gates of the huge fortress to which the nation looked for leader-
ship, and gone swiftly to the Dictator's wing.

Few ever penetrated to this almost legendary tower except
those on the highest business of state.

Now the Citadel was silent. Guards stood at each turn in
the passages like men of stone, their tommy guns cradled in the
crooks of their arms. Outside, snow whitened the roofs of the
capital, and the lamps on the sixteen bridges across the broad
Lastra River shone down on solid ice.

Although the sentries at the Citadel never betrayed by so
much as the flicker of an eyelid that they were more than
robots, behind each broad forehead thoughts whirled furiously
as members of the Dictator's Praetorian Guard drove up to the
gates. What did it all mean, the sentries wondered.

Was it war? Were they to fight again?

In the shadows outside the door to the Dictator's apartment, her scrubbing brush in her gnarled hands and the pail of chilly water on the floor beside her, Anna Maravna wondered, too. She had seen so much in her seventy years in the Citadel.

She had scrubbed those flagstones in the days when the Emperor and his Empress, gorgeous in their robes, had swept from the Royal Apartments to the Chamber of State as the strains of Strauss waltzes lifted through the ancient palace.

She had scrubbed the Empress' blood from those same stones that day in 1919 when the old Dictator unleashed the terror he had prepared, and the Lastra's water ran red for miles through the city.

Anna had scrubbed on, even in 1943 when German troops were drawn up just outside the city and the shells from their artillery lobbed into the heart of Dictator Square itself.

Then there had been the peace. Bands played and torches of resinous pine blazed along the battlements. How well she remembered the morning after that night of revelry. For once, the iron rules governing the Citadel had relaxed. She had even seen the Foreign Minister reeling down a passageway, one arm around the old Dictator's pudgy daughter and, in his free hand, an opened bottle of champagne, creaming frothily onto the floor.

But the years that followed were grim.

Rations were cut far below even wartime levels. No heat in the houses. Shops empty except for window-dressed shelves arranged so that foreign diplomats and correspondents could be impressed by the nation's apparent recovery.

At first, there had been an attempt at peacetime living. A few communal housing projects had been built. But then everything had stopped, everything but the tramp of military boots in the great square, the scream of jet planes through the clouds above the city, the rumble of tanks moving out of the factories westward to the nation's frontiers.

"War."

The word had been in every heart. War with the West. War with the makers of war. How many times had the old Dictator told his people of the encirclement policies of his former allies and warned that a national effort at salvation must come before all else! How many times had the pudgy new dictator echoed the words in the short months of his power!

Anna thought about her life as she scrubbed these stones that had known her brush so many, many decades. And now, tonight, with this strange brooding doom hanging heavy over the Citadel, she did something she rarely allowed herself to do. Anna prayed.

She did not stop her work. She did not fold her hands as she had so often done in the great Orthodox Cathedral in the days when the Emperor still ruled. Her lips did not move. But in her heart she prayed to the God of her childhood in the words she had been taught as a child.

Behind her there was a rustle of footsteps. Anxiously she lowered her head over her bucket as three men swept by. She recognized the back of the Foreign Minister and the small hustling body of the Minister of State Security. But the third figure —wasn't he familiar, too? He was tall and gaunt, wrapped in a long black cloak against the deathly chill of those stone corridors. But his eyes above the beard were sharp and eager. She stared in amazement. What could *he* be doing here?

The three men passed swiftly through the door into the Dictator's private apartment while Anna almost held her breath. The man in the black cloak had suddenly lifted her spirit. He was no emissary from a foreign power. He was the companion of death.

After ten minutes the two Ministers emerged. The Interior Minister arrived. Anna slipped back unobserved into the shadows. The stranger in the dark cloak was still inside, but a doctor joined the men.

"Well?" asked the Foreign Minister.

The doctor shook his head. "He can't last the night. There is nothing we can do. His heart is being strangled—thrombosis."

The Foreign Minister sat on the Dictator's desk, nodded a curt dismissal, and lit a long black cigarette.

"It's ironical, gentlemen," he said, when the doctor had closed the door. "The new Dictator always detested the Church, just as the great Leader did. He called it the opiate of the people. True, he took no fresh steps to outlaw religion, but he kept it in the back streets. Even the great Cathedral became a meeting-place for Party congresses. And yet now, on his deathbed, he cries for a priest like a child in the dark. A *priest!*"

The Minister of State Security said, "The Great One would

never have gone soft," and added, "I hope nobody saw that man. It was a very great risk bringing him here."

The Interior Minister nodded. "But it would have been a greater risk for any of us to deny the Dictator his request. After all, suppose he lives? And remembers? Doctors have given up before, only to have their patients recover. And where would we be then? In the uranium mines, I dare say."

The Foreign Minister thought a moment, then said, "There's just one thing that worries me, gentlemen. Not that the Dictator may live. If necessary he could be—well, helped over the stile, I think. No. It's that rascally priest inside there, with his mumbling and his beard and his black cloak. What about him?"

"Are you thinking of the Dictator's confession?" The Interior Minister grinned unpleasantly. "The confession is inviolate. Father Anastatius will never open his mouth, no matter what the Dictator babbles to him. We're quite safe in that direction."

The Foreign Minister shook his head. "I'm not worried about any confession. I'm worried about the simple, overwhelming fact that the Dictator asked for a priest at all."

The plump little Minister of State Security shrugged his shoulders. "Lots of people do when they're up against it."

"You fool!" The Foreign Minister almost spat his contempt. "If this priest lets it be known that he gave the Dictator the last rites of the Orthodox Church, what becomes of our regime? What becomes of our whole political philosophy? What will the people think when they learn that their revered leader, on his death bed, sent for a priest just as if he were any ignorant peasant? It would bring the whole structure of our state philosophy tumbling down like a house of cards!"

He paced furiously across the room and whirled back on the other two, his eyes suddenly blazing.

"You do not understand these people as I do. We frightened them out of their churches, but we never frightened religion out of their hearts. They may not kneel in the great Cathedral when they pray, but they still pray. We cannot silence that.

"This is the only thing that is stronger than we are. Not the Western nations. Not the British. Not the Americans. It is those canting dogs of priests with their superstition. They are in retreat now. They pretend to be loyal to us, but they still believe. Once let this news leak out, and you'll see. It could be the end of everything—with us probably struggling for power among ourselves and the people in revolt with their religious leaders at their head."

There was a stirring at the door. The two men stiffened. The Foreign Minister spoke to the Minister of State Security softly.

"You are armed, of course."

The other nodded and glanced furtively at the others.

"These walls are thick," the Foreign Minister whispered. "That priest must not leave these apartments alive."

The bedroom door opened, and the stately figure of Father Anastatius stood there. He was settling his robe around his shoulders. Anna shrank back farther into the shadows.

He glanced at the three men, then spoke very quietly. "Our brother is gone," he said. "He is with God."

The silence in the room hung heavy. Slowly the Minister of State Security withdrew an automatic from a shoulder holster. Father Anastatius smiled.

"I understand, gentlemen," he said. "I understand perfectly."

He was still smiling when the bullet tore into his heart . . .

In the building on Twenty-eighth of March Street next day the Archbishop faced his colleagues. "Men disappear in this nation every day, my brothers," he was saying, "and no one knows their fate. This is not the first time it has happened to our Holy Order.

"Anastatius was a great servant of God. Perhaps he served Our Lord too well. He left here last night without telling any of us his destination. He has not returned. We can only wait. And pray."

There was a knock at the door, and a young novice entered respectfully. "There is a woman outside to see you, Your Excellency."

"Show her in."

Slowly, fearfully the aged figure of Anna shuffled into the chamber. "You seek Father Anastatius, Your Excellency," she said hesitantly. "You will never find him. He was killed last night. In the Citadel."

"What was he doing in the Citadel, my sister?" the Archbishop asked gently.

Anna's old eyes shone. "A man died there last night. What is it that any priest does in the house of a dying man?"

"A man—?" A light flickered in the Archbishop's eyes.

Anna nodded eagerly. "Yes, Your Excellency. A man."

They gazed into each other's eyes. They were of an age. Their experience of life had been the same. They needed no words.

A Bishop rose. His voice faltered. "Then that is the end of our poor brother Anastatius."

"The end?" The Archbishop's eyes were still on Anna, but they swung away, to the great Crucifix that hung on the wall.

"No, my brothers. It is not the end. I think this is the beginning!"

STEWART BEACH

How to Write the Mystery and Suspense Story

IT WOULD TAKE a far longer analysis than this brief essay could attempt to explore all the forms and mutations of forms which stories of mystery and suspense have successfully taken. But just for the reason that they require extra quantities of imagination and inventiveness on the part of the short-story writer, there is a special fascination about the technique which produces this sort of entertainment.

The technique can take the form of the conventional short-story pattern in which a single character is dominant throughout and the solution of a problem vital to his peace of mind forms the thread of the action. Or it can branch out in a dozen different and captivating ways, sometimes altering its point of view from character to character. And the mystery story can even seem to tell itself backward.

We shall need some definitions before going further, and I shall make these as broad as possible. Some years ago it was the fashion for purists to insist on certain nice distinctions within the field of the mystery story. But today the disposition is away from this.

A *mystery story,* then, is simply one in which a mysterious circumstance crying for solution is presented to certain characters—and to the reader. A detective, professional or amateur, may be called on to direct the job, though this is not a requirement. But *detection of the reason for the mysterious circumstance* is the basis of the story and provides its thread of action, whether it be an actual *detective story* or not. Mystery stories are most often concerned with crime, though they need not be. What engages the attention of the reader is the unraveling skein of events through which a mystery is uncovered. When the mystery is revealed, with the shortest possible tying up of odds and ends, the story races to a conclusion because the interest of the reader has been satisfied.

Suspense stories, on the other hand, do not necessarily involve

311

any mystery at all. Usually they find the principal character, often against his will, in conflict with inimical forces, personal or natural, which he must overcome in order to save his life. Often the nature of his predicament is clear almost from the outset of the story. The suspense turns on developments and the decisions he makes to work out his own salvation.

Two brief illustrations will serve to show the pattern in action:

1. A tough cavalry captain, scouting with a small detail of troopers in the early days of the American West, is ambushed by a larger party of Indians. How will he outwit the enemy, bring his men through to safety and save a settlement it is his duty to protect?

2. A veteran mountaineer, marooned on a desolate slope by an avalanche which has spared him and his companion but wiped out his expected path of descent, must find an alternate route and bring help to the injured comrade.

In each of these situations, the reader understands at the outset the peril of the individual characters. What engages his attention —and it is always important for the writer to know what it is that holds the reader's interest—is the method chosen by the characters to work out their own destiny. When the characters are safe and the dangers overcome, the reader's interest is finished. Once more a quick tying up of odds and ends, and the story is done.

The suspense story, far more often than the mystery story, follows the *unified point of view* type of narration. That is, all of the action is seen through the eyes of a single character. The logic of this rises naturally from the fact that the reader's attention is focused sharply on the principal character, because it is his decisions, and the action flowing out of them, that will influence the success or failure of his dangerous mission.

Both the mystery and the suspense story present a high type of dramatic involvement to the reader. His emotions are quickly engaged, and fiction surveys show that readership is higher on this type of story than on any other. This is not difficult to explain. Just as a shocking murder draws crowds of readers to follow its story as it is developed in the daily newspapers, so a similar crime in fiction exerts the same type of fascination. You will buy each new edition of your newspaper eagerly to find out whether the mystery of the crime has been solved, the murderer caught. You will go on reading a fiction mystery with the same intentness.

Similar influences are at work in the case of the suspense story. Let a tale develop in the press of a workman isolated by some accident on the top of a newly built television tower or a boy lost in a well, and thousands will buy successive editions of the newspapers to read in horror of their plight. We take these things personally. We want to know in detail what happened. This is the dominant fascination of the suspense story.

Although much of what will be said about these two forms of fiction applies as well to the novelette or novel as to the short story, I am concerned here only with the magazine short story of mystery and suspense. In current practice, this means a story from, roughly, three thousand to six thousand words in length (sometimes it can even be told in the twelve hundred to two thousand words of a short-short), and it is unwise to exceed the maximum since most magazines find the longer story difficult to handle.

This was not always the case. A year or so ago I was lunching with two veteran fiction writers who recalled the expansive days of the twenties and earlier when neither would have thought of turning in a short story less than twelve thousand words in length. One of them, indeed, remembered an occasion when a story of his had regrettably worked itself out in just nine thousand words. He had felt it necessary to send a letter with the manuscript, apologizing to the editor for the story's brevity and promising never to do it again. Things worked out all right, though, he said. The editor liked the story and decided to buy it in spite of its lack of substance.

It is fair to say, in passing, that in those days the short story moved at a somewhat more leisurely pace than it does today, particularly in the field of mystery and suspense. Contemporary readers are inclined to be impatient when episodes are introduced which do not lead rapidly to a solution of the mystery or predicament of the principal character. Even when the style *seems* leisurely today, the action itself is speeding rapidly forward. This illusion is heightened by short scenes and constantly changing settings which put briskness and movement into the story. Even when a plot may require that all the action take place in a single house, for example, the same effect is gained by shifting the characters from room to room so that the action is never static.

Because mystery and suspense stories are, essentially, simply short stories of a special sort, I think it will be useful to review the technique of the short story itself before discussing the particular requirements of these forms and pointing out where they may safely depart from the accepted pattern which has been found most successful as the way to construct a short story.

The basic concept of a short story is that it narrates the events of a crisis in the life of a single individual. The crisis must be an important turning point in the life of the story's chief character. Otherwise, it will not engage the attention of many readers. The chief character must be made attractive—in the literal sense of that word. Otherwise, readers will not care to follow his struggle. He need not be someone the reader likes or would care to know. But the reader needs to be drawn to him, to be attracted by him, to have sympathy for his motives as someone whose story he finds fascinating.

To arrange the story in its most dramatic effectiveness, the action should be divided into a *beginning,* a *middle* and an *ending.* Most simply stated, this is the chronological order in which the events of the story take place, though this flow may be interrupted by the device of a *flashback* in which some action previous to the beginning of the story is inserted, not as exposition but as dramatic action recalled in the mind of the chief character. Other than that, the normal development of a short story is chronological.

The beginning introduces the chief character. He should be introduced in advance of, or simultaneously with, other characters since the reader must know immediately on whom to focus his interest. This section states the original situation which provides the crisis, and it may introduce one or more of the minor characters. The purpose of the beginning is to provide the reader with all the preliminary facts which he requires to understand the story. It contains the exposition or background facts. When this section is completed the story flows into the central part— *the middle*—which shows the chief character attempting to solve the crucial problem with which he is faced in the beginning.

The middle. This should be planned as a series of scenes which are in reality tests of the chief character's determination to deal actively with the crisis in his life. They show him overcoming the obstacles which block his way until he hesitates before the final obstacle. His decision here will either crown his efforts with success or determine finally that he has lost the struggle. His decision to make the attempt, no matter what the cost, marks the climax of the story.

The ending. This displays the action which the chief character takes as a result of his climactic decision. It shows his success— or his failure—but in either case the story that began with the beginning is ended with the ending. When a few of the reader's questions have been answered by tying up the odds and ends, the story is over. The reader's interest is completely satisfied.

With this purely structural outline understood, there are a few other points that should be considered, since they play a vital part in a story's final appeal.

First of these is undoubtedly the *unified point of view*. This is simply a shorthand way of saying that all the events of the story are written as they are seen through the eyes and other senses of the chief character. The actions of minor characters are seen through his eyes. Their reactions are transmitted to the reader only as the chief character sees them. At no time does the story enter the mind of a minor character to tell the reader what *he* thinks. Thus, the reader sees minor characters as the chief character sees them. He hears them talk, so that he can make his own estimate of what sort of fellows these minor characters are. But other than that, the reader's point of view is unified with that of the chief character.

This is no arbitrary rule (and, as we shall see, it can sometimes be violated in the mystery story) but a matter of experience based in the story form itself. A good short story is rarely the sum of an exciting series of episodes. The focus of its interest is on a single individual as he drives himself through the action. The reader identifies himself with this character. He reads on because he has been made to care whether this man (or this woman) can solve the problem with which he has been faced at the story's beginning.

The odd thing, which an inexperienced writer may not realize at first, is that to shift the point of view to another character means that he has begun to tell another story entirely. It is not the one he started out with. Because two individuals, however closely allied, have different motives, different qualities, different rewards to gain, a shift of point of view from one to the other means that you are trying to tell *two* stories within a single framework.

The most obvious violation of the unified point of view is to drop one character while you bring another into focus in a different setting, returning later to the first. But the unified point of view must be maintained just as scrupulously in a single scene between two characters. Otherwise the story line is erased, and the sense of conflict in an individual character is lowered if not entirely lost.

To illustrate the point, here is a scene from a story of mine called "Mary Junior" which was published some years ago in the *Saturday Evening Post*. The characters are a young actress (Mary Junior), from whose point of view the story is told, and Peter, a play doctor, who has rewritten her part during rehearsals in a sincere effort to give it greater depth and meaning. Mary Junior has apprehensively consented to the last-minute changes, apparently against the wishes of her mother, Mary Osborne, who is a famous and established actress. The girl has worked hard to realize the new conception of the part, both for herself and because she is half in love with Peter. Peter comes into Mary Junior's dressing room just before curtain time on opening night. Now read the scene at it was written:

Peter came in. She saw his face in the mirror that was studded with bare lamps, and her fingers froze, tipped with grease paint.

"I'll get out if you want me to," he said.

Fingers came to life against her forehead. "Why did you come?"

"I had to tell you how swell you've been," he said. "However it goes, I've never seen anyone put up a greater fight. If you lose, it's my fault now. It means that I asked too much."

Her fingers stopped again while she thought over his words. It was sweet of Peter to try to lift responsibility from her, but he couldn't do that. She still had to fight this through alone. She could feel a beginning tenderness. It was like a memory, but she mustn't let that interfere now. "Peter," she said. "Do you think mother hates me?"

Peter said a surprising thing. He was beside her now, and

she looked up, seeing the planes of his face in sharp shadow from the lamps.

"I think she believes in you more than you or I had ever guessed," he said slowly.

He leaned down swiftly and kissed her on the forehead, then stormed from the room.

"Darling!" she cried. "You'll be all over grease paint!" But now, as the assistant stage manager knocked at her door and called "Curtain!" her heart had the lift of song.

The important thing to note in this scene is that while both characters are dramatically presented under circumstances which have both tension and conflict, Peter is seen only from the point of view of the young actress. The reader must estimate the full meaning of Peter's visit from his words and his attitude, just as Mary Junior must. The reader is never told what Peter *thinks*.

Now I have rewritten the scene so that it shifts the point of view freely between Mary Junior and Peter. Neither character is dominant. Notice how the conflict has been blurred as the story loses its direct line of action—the tension Mary Junior should feel on the brink of her great test as an actress:

Peter came in, and now, for the first time, he was frightened at what he had done. But he mustn't let her see his dread of what tonight might bring.

"I'll get out if you want me to," he said, and braced himself a little against her reply.

Fingers came to life against her forehead. "Why did you come?"

He let a little of his emotion bubble out then. "I had to tell you how swell you've been," he said, and there was much more he wanted to tell her. "However it goes," he went on when she did not react, "I've never seen anyone put up a greater fight. If you lose, it's my fault now. It means that I asked too much."

Her fingers stopped again, and she was thinking over his words. It was sweet of Peter to try to lift responsibility from her, but he couldn't do that. She still had to fight this through alone. She could feel a beginning tenderness. It was like a memory, but she mustn't let that interfere now. "Peter," she said. "Do you think mother hates me?"

The question made him smile a little, because he was remembering the letter from her mother in his pocket. He mustn't show it to her now, but he moved over beside her.

"I think she believes in you more than you or I had ever guessed," he said slowly.

He could not trust himself to speak again. He leaned down swiftly and kissed her on the forehead, then stormed from the room.

"Darling!" she cried. "You'll be all over grease paint!" and she could hear her heart singing inside her.

Outside on the stairs that led to the stage, Peter paused a moment. The smile vanished from his face, and dread was back in his heart.

In this version, the important point to notice is that there are two story lines running at the same time. One of these is the ordeal of Mary Junior on the eve of her debut as a star. The second is Peter's dread that in rewriting her part he has asked more from the girl than she is capable of giving. The two themes are closely allied, but they must always remain separate because they concern the aspirations of two different people. By trying to dramatize both themes, the sharpness of each is blurred.

You can change points of view in a novel; you can sometimes do it successfully in a novelette, particularly in a mystery novelette. Here the greater length gives the reader time to readjust his own point of view. But within the brief limits of a short story, this dip in interest on the reader's part when he shifts his focus of attention can be fatal. If he is strongly absorbed by one character's struggle, he is impatient if he is asked to consider another's reactions. It can make him toss aside the magazine in disgust.

There is another reason, rising naturally out of the brevity of the short story, which argues for the unified point of view. Characterization must be swift—and simple. Much of your story's effectiveness depends on the kind of person your chief character is. A story whose solution requires acts of physical bravery on the part of a man you show to be brave at the outset would have an entirely different inflection if its chief character had never encountered danger before. At the beginning the author establishes his character quickly by giving him a *governing characteristic*.

This *governing characteristic* is really a distillation of the essential man the chief character is. All of his decisions and actions are foreshadowed and governed by it, and this characteristic is dominant throughout the story. You do not have time in a short story to build a complex character. So you stress a single quality in your man on which his success or failure will be built. In a detective story, for example, it may be the brilliant record of the detective in solving murders by depending on his own hunches. By outguessing the criminal he finds him and brings him to justice. So, you tell your reader as you begin the story, "My detective proposes to solve this murder by the same method."

There is another ingredient of every short story which should be mentioned here. This is *conflict*. It means simply that your chief character throughout the story must be in a state of struggle against the persons and circumstances which interfere with the solution of the problem on which the story is based. Sometimes in the mystery or suspense story, because of the nature of the episodes, it may seem that conflict is present intrinsically. But the author must always consider conflict in the sense of his chief character's *personal struggle,* rather than in terms of the exterior excitement of the episode through which the chief character is passing. That is where conflict lies: in the heart and spirit of the character. And unless the writing keeps it actively there, the episodes will be robbed of their excitement.

This is the most simple pattern of any short story. Now let us see how it applies specifically to the story of mystery and suspense.

THE MYSTERY STORY

The three most important ingredients of a successful mystery story are *freshness of story idea, ingenuity of plot—and style.* The first two qualities are basic in creating a memorable story, but the third is equally basic in making it live and furnish entertainment to the reader.

The first of these—*freshness of story idea*—depends entirely on the imagination and inventiveness of the author. I know of no course of instruction which could provide this quality, but I can tell you that for a mystery writer it requires a certain experience of police methods, if detectives and other police officers are to move through your stories. So many mystery and detective stories have been written in the last twenty-five years that it may seem to the aspiring writer he can acquire the necessary expertise in the field just by reading them. But the trouble is that the authors who are experts have built art on reality, so that their police world has become a manufactured one which an unfamiliar author enters at his peril. He begins to invent detectives and uniformed policemen who are not real but caricatures of the more believable caricatures experienced authors have created. Fiction, it cannot be said too often, does not re-create life. It re-creates the *illusion* of life. But to do that, an author must know something of the life itself.

Most of the successful mystery writers I know have made friends with the police, ridden in squad cars on assignments, listened to questions asked, talked about inferences drawn—seen crime very much as a policeman is introduced to it. Crime is people and their backgrounds, developing into suspects and their possible motives, becoming at last, as the web of evidence is drawn taut, discarded suspects and undoubted criminals. But how does this come about? You won't find out by watching television or reading mystery stories. You will find it out only by the experience of knowing police work at first hand.

It is not, you realize, that in knowing how the police go about their business you will find ready-made plots for your stories. The association simply gives you the documentary tools to imagine mysterious crimes of your own, which might well baffle the police. What the experience gives you is the knowledge of how the process of detection would proceed in getting at the root of the crime you have imagined. You know what would be said, and how the medical examiner, the police photographers, the detectives and the uniformed policemen would be deployed. You have the actual experience on which to base your story of detection. You can proceed surely to develop your *story idea* into a *plot* because you know the machinery of detection. Unless you do know it, even a rather inexperienced sub-editor will catch the lack of conviction in your writing.

A fiction writer in any field should observe caution, but it is particularly necessary in the mystery story, which usually deals with the formal processes of the law. For here a slip can often make the writer appear ridiculous. Anyone who chooses to write mysteries had best ground himself in the criminal law before he finds himself quite out of his depth.

Out of a full experience, then, an author is ready to write mystery stories with the assurance of a background of knowledge. How does he find his story ideas? I don't believe anyone can help him there. I have always felt that dependence on imagination was most important—that the story based on some actual crime was dangerous to use as story material, though I know this has been successful where all the real characters and incidents have been suppressed and fictitious ones substituted. But here, as in all fiction writing, the author must call upon characterization to make his story live. In covering real-life crime, newspapers often assign special writers to produce human-interest stories in an effort to explain the background and motives of a criminal. The fiction writer must imagine these, but in imagining them and making them realistic he is satisfying a desire on the part of the reader to understand *why* the crime was committed. He is rounding out the kind of story which often cannot be rounded out in life.

So the secret of a *fresh story idea* lies within the boundless imagination of the writer himself. It is something which grows from his mind to pages of manuscript to a story which an editor will buy and readers will read with fascination. It is based in the experience of the author in the way crimes are treated by police departments. His own experience is the best insurance that it will be fresh and not seem imitative. But there is no other practical shortcut to a great story idea.

The plot. It is in developing the plot that the greatest technical skill is called for on the part of the writer. And this depends entirely on the type of story idea he has chosen. To explain this, it is necessary to explain some part of the two different types of mystery-story construction that are most often followed today.

First, the story in which the unified point of view is followed. This depends on construction in which the chief character, whether an actual professional detective or an individual to whom solution of the mystery is vital, becomes the chief actor in the story. The point of decision is simply this: Is the solution of the mystery itself most important—something which transcends the fortunes of the principal character? Or is the effect on the chief character paramount?

Second, the story in which the solution of the mystery is of first importance. Then, the focus of attention can be placed on this, and the point of view changed as different characters take up the scent. In this case, the reader's interest must be drawn to the nature of the solution itself rather than to its effect on one of the characters. The fate of the characters is secondary to the reader's learning the facts of the mystery. The effect here is almost that of the daily newspaper reports of a developing crime story. To the newspaper reader, the actual persons involved can never be quite real, though the crime or mystery which involves them engages his attention completely. So it is with this type of mystery story. The reader's interest lies in the solution rather than in what happens to the individuals afterward.

In choosing this second type of construction, an inexperienced writer had better be fully convinced that his story idea will immediately command attention and that his plot is capable of absorbing readers completely. Otherwise, there is danger that the story will fail to build interest because the characters themselves do not have sufficient appeal. Above all else, the writer must make certain that there is a sufficient amount of complication and surprise in his plot so that the solution of the mystery will remain in doubt until the climax of the story begins to unravel it.

In this connection, the very nature of "surprise" is worth explanation. It is not the surprise of any of the characters that is important but the genuine surprise—and delight—of the reader as the plot takes an unlooked-for turn. Too often the beginning writer feels that an unusual twist or device at the end of his story supplies the element of surprise. It does only if the reader has been led to expect something quite different. The fact that in the end of a story a criminal is caught through some unintended slip on his part almost never provides surprise, since the reader expects all along something of this sort will be the case. He doesn't know what the slip will be, but he is only mildly interested when the author lets him in on the secret because the presence of such a "device" has been anticipated.

Surprise should not be reserved for the end of a mystery story. In the best of them, there are constant elements of surprise as the plot takes unexpected turns and new information is given to the reader (as the characters turn it up) which adds to his absorption in the narrative. This is one of the genuine tricks of the mystery story.

Without delving into those many mutations which I mentioned at the beginning of this essay, it has always seemed to me that mystery stories divide themselves into two broad types, in so far as technique is concerned. The first is the straight mystery story, which is not too different in its structure from the conventional short-story pattern, unless the writer chooses to tell it through shifting points of view.

In this type, the writer presents a mysterious circumstance in the opening paragraphs which requires solution by the active efforts of one or more characters. The easiest way to think of it is to imagine what you yourself would do if you were the first to encounter such a mystery.

To use a simple example, imagine that you have rented a small place along some deserted strip of ocean to spend your vacation. The first morning you take an early walk down the lonely beach and, neatly arranged on a ledge of rock, you find a man's clothing. A swimmer, you think, but there is no car nearby and when you scan the sea there is no head bobbing in the water. You climb up the rocks but you can see no one on the dunes behind. The thought of a suicide and of calling the police occurs to you, but you cast it aside. There is bound to be some perfectly natural explanation of the pile of clothes. In a moment someone will come along to claim his belongings. You don't want to appear impulsive and silly. You glance down at the sand, and a curious fact is borne in upon you. The sand is hard-packed and your own footprints are the only ones visible leading to the ledge of rock. Quickly you scan the beach for the high-water mark of last night's tide, but this is halfway down to the water. Clearly the sea would have washed away no footprints last night or for several nights. You have been faced by a mystery!

And now, as a writer, you will quickly substitute a character for "you" walking along the beach and decide just what he is to do. You will add other characters—a policeman, surely, and other men and women to complicate the situation as their identities are revealed and their involvement with the events behind this mysterious circumstance of the pile of clothes is made part of your story. Likewise, your chief character must have some reason for continuing to press the solution. Perhaps the local police, for want of other clues, decide on a verdict of suicide, but your chief character believes murder has been done. In any case, from the purely fortuitous discovery of the pile of clothes, he has become entangled in a first-class mystery.

Obviously the success of this beginning plot depends on the ingenuity and imagination with which the writer develops it. But I have chosen it as an example because it illustrates one of the cardinal requirements of a mystery story: Only a fraction of the evidence (the pile of clothes and lack of footprints) is apparent to the chief character when he begins to solve the mystery. He will come upon other facts and other information to supply the reader as his search continues. But the skilled writer will weave these into the narrative in such a way that they provide constant fresh surprise and that they do not hint at the real solution of the mystery until the climax of the story is reached.

This is the trick of the mystery story—adding bits and pieces of information, some of them unproductive scents in all probability, until the real solution is found. To keep faith with the reader, the writer must never withhold information which the chief character knows. To follow the story intently, the reader must be looking over the shoulder of the chief character and he must also be inside his mind. This caution is also true of the story constructed with multiple points of view. The reader has a right to any pertinent information which any of these characters possesses.

The second broad type of mystery story is, of course, the pure "whodunit." This method is more usual with the mystery novel than with the short story, since it is difficult in the brief space of a short story to cast suspicion successively over several characters so that the reader finds it hard to guess until the very end who the criminal may have been. This type of story, when successfully done, has always enjoyed wide popularity. For many devoted mystery readers it has a particular fascination since it permits them to match wits with the writer and try to guess the solution before it is given to them in the ending.

Once more, in the "whodunit" the writer must watch that he keeps faith with his readers and furnishes them with all the information known to his chief character. In addition, skilled practitioners of this form pride themselves on inserting unobtrusively at an early point in the narrative clues to the motivation of the crime which the reader (if he has not done so already) will instantly remember when the solution is revealed.

The writer must also make certain, if it is his purpose to make each of his characters a suspect, that he does not let any of them react to something in the story's development which would make it impossible for that person to be the criminal. For example, if you wish a character to be suspected of one murder and a second related body is discovered, you must not permit this character to express obviously innocent surprise. It will immediately convince your reader that he could not have been guilty of Murder No. 1.

Never, never in a "whodunit" (or in any other short story, for that matter) permit coincidence to play any part in the development of the narrative. This is another point at which fiction departs from life. Coincidence happens frequently in life, but it must never happen in a short story. There may *seem* to be a coincidence in the reappearance of a character at a certain place in the story. But before you have gone much further, you will have had to show that his presence was directly connected with the events of the story you are telling.

The "whodunit" most often employs a professional detective to solve the mystery, though this is by no means an infallible rule. If you have decided to use such a detective in your own story, then this word of caution is necessary: Be sure you invest him with characteristics and individualities which will give him a memorable personality. This is true whether you are using a unified point of view—it need not necessarily be the detective's —or the shifting point of view. Once more the logic of experience dictates this. If the detective is a routine, faceless sort of fellow, the pitch of your narrative will be lowered to a point where the incidents seem dry, without entertainment beyond their documentary importance to the story. But once you have turned loose an interesting, highly individualized personality on your crime clues, the entire story picks up tone, and a quality of entertainment enters the experience of reading.

Beyond this, remember that solving a crime is simply part of the job of a professional detective. The experience will usually have no permanent effect upon his life, other than chalking up another success. Therefore that sense of a story's having changed the life of the characters is lost so far as he is concerned. You can, by your touches of characterization, give his search for the criminal an urgency which it would lack if a colorless detective, however scrupulous, were employed to direct the search.

This brings us naturally to a consideration of *style*—the tone in which a story is written—since in setting the personality of your detective, as well as other characters, you are determining immediately the *style* which your story must take on. You should choose a simple but direct style which does not interfere with the narrative's flow. Beware of "you" as a writer intruding. Do not overornament a style to the point where it seems artificial. The chief point of a style is to create and sustain a story's mood.

With the possible exception of the recent "rough-and-tough" school of mystery writing, there is a definite quality of entertainment in the successful mystery story. Reading one, though it deals with sudden death, is a pleasurable rather than a shocking experience. It is an arm-chair sort of enjoyment and provides for the reader the same kind of excitement he would receive from listening to a skilled raconteur tell a fascinating tale in his living room. The mystery story leans heavily for its success on the art of storytelling.

You will definitely jeopardize the chances of selling a mystery story to the important markets if it lacks this quality. Let me examine that statement in a negative way to show wherein the lack would lie. It might well be in a tragic, depressing treatment. There is rarely much of any satisfaction in a story of that sort unless it is beautifully written and there is some compensating relief for the reader. The lack might also be that you have created dreary characters who do not awaken sympathy in the reader. This is another way of saying that the reader doesn't much care what happens to them and so he does not care about the solution of your mystery.

The importance of this reaction of the reader is one which the beginning writer cannot learn too early in his career. Magazine readers are no captive audience, and they have only to turn the page of their magazine if a piece of fiction fails to hold their interest.

Now let's look at the mystery story constructively, by way of summation, to see what it should contain: 1. It should flow out of a story idea that is fresh and original and that will immediately capture the attention of the reader. 2. Its plot, always directed toward the solution of the mystery, should unfold gradually, and with constant surprise, the events, characters, motives and circumstances which created the mystery in the first place. 3. It should be written with a storyteller's style, full of relish, that will hold the attention of the reader. 4. Its important characters —or at least one in particular—should catch the sympathy of the reader so that he cares strongly about their future. 5. If one of the important characters is a detective, he should be developed with the flair which will make him memorable. 6. Finally (and this has not been mentioned before) if the tale is a tense and gripping one you will be well advised to try to inject some humor. Momentary relief from tenseness, if it grows naturally out of the plot, will cause the reader to plunge back into the maelstrom of events refreshed and ready for more.

One more point before leaving the mystery story: Unresolved danger and unexplained death are the two most dominant facts in fiction. They can never be sidetracked while the writer pursues some other angle of his theme. Until the danger is over or the death explained, your reader will become impatient and irritated if these circumstances are not uppermost in the minds of all the characters. To illustrate, if a secondary part of your theme concerns the fortunes of a young couple very much in love, there must be no emphasis on their personal relationship until the mystery is solved. You may leave your reader in no doubt that they will eventually be married. But you must let him see that now they both realize they have no time to pursue their own romance. Their meetings will be hurried, furtive ones in which they content themselves with the pressure of a hand while their minds are fixed on the mystery. In the mystery story, danger and death are the dominant facts of life.

THE SUSPENSE STORY

The *suspense story* requires no such detailed consideration as the mystery story, since it normally is told in the conventional short-story pattern with a unified point of view. It is possible, when the situation itself is sufficiently commanding, to use a shifting point of view, but I think a writer would be well advised to exhaust every effort to keep the point of view unified in the chief character.

This is because in the suspense story the focus, of necessity, is fixed on the effort of a single individual to overcome danger. There will often be other characters who share the danger, but there will be one individual whose responsibility it is to see that all of them come through the ordeal safely. The technique which will produce the story most effectively is therefore the pattern which the short story most frequently takes.

There will be a problem facing a chief character. The story will be constructed with beginning, middle and ending. The beginning will acquaint the reader with the perilous situation in which the chief character finds himself. The middle will be

plotted to show the tests of increasing intensity which he under-
goes until, at the climax, he will make the decision on his course
of action to overcome the final obstacle. The ending will show
the final high action resulting from the decision which brings
the chief character through to safety.

There is suspense in every short story, of course. Perhaps it
would be simpler to say that every short story *must* generate suspense, even when its theme is a quiet one, because the quality
of suspense does not identify the *kind* of incidents in a story, but
rather the question the writer raises in the reader's mind about
whether the chief character will be able to overcome the tests he
faces in order to solve the basic problem. This question (repre-
senting the quality of suspense) must be skillfully injected into
the quiet story. But in the active one it is implicit in the exciting
nature of the episodes which make up the narrative. Therefore,
the word "suspense" has been taken over to identify this type of
story, which is without an actual mystery but packed with tense
action.

Foreign or other unusual backgrounds are often used as settings, and in the past decade the conflict between the ideologies
of the Eastern and Western worlds has provided many a writer
with serviceable material. But as in the caution that a mystery
writer should be familiar with police methods, so a suspense
writer who intends to deal with spies should have some kind of
experience of so-called intelligence methods, which enables him
to deal with a theme of this sort. Otherwise, his work becomes
imitative and empty, a rehash of phrases he has read rather than
words he has heard. It is the same warning which should be
posted over the typewriter of every beginning writer: "Do not
write about people, backgrounds and themes unless you have
been able to acquire some personal familiarity with them."

This is particularly important with stories set in backgrounds
where there are words and phrases which persons working in-
timately in the field use. Unless you can use them properly, your
story will never ring true. To be sure, you should never fill a
story with technical phrases which the ordinary reader could
not possibly understand, but there should be the illusion of doing so now and then. Once again, it is necessary for fiction to
seem to reflect life without actually reproducing life.

But suspense stories are where you find them, and you may
find them quite easily around home—if you put your mind to

work. The unusual background is not necessary to a tense short story. And if it is a highly specialized background, you will find difficulty in making it come alive within the space of a short story. You will find yourself explaining so much that the narrative will suffer.

Like the mystery story, the suspense story needs attractive characters, men and women about whose fate readers can care. It is as necessary for the reader to have sympathy for the chief character in a suspense story as in any other kind of short story.

But here the *style* must be tense and crisp, swift moving under the pressure of exciting events. Far less than with the mystery story does the storytelling quality seem to be in the writing. But it must be there, just the same, in a strong, documentary sense if you are to bring to the reader your story's exciting best.

CONCLUSION

Successful writers of mystery stories have always seemed to me to be a rather special breed. They rarely write any other kind of fiction and they seem to be absorbed in the plots they dream up. But the ones I know are not dreamy chaps, and the principal impression I draw from them is of an alert, inquiring mind, genuinely excited about some new idea, however trivial, which neatly solves a problem in the story the mind is at work on.

They are men and women who are serious about their work, given to great gobs of research in subjects where they think a story may lie, and no small number of them are impressively erudite in quite unexpected fields where their roving characters have led them. On the whole, they seem a happier group than most writers, having fun in their work most of the time. This may be illusion on my part, but it is the happy way they seem.

If you're that sort of person—with an inquiring mind, a restless curiosity, an infinite capacity for research and a considerable talent for writing—all you need do is write the story. Well, why don't you? I hope it sells!

GLOSSARY OF WRITERS' TERMS

Pattern. The general plan, or technique, by which short stories are constructed.

Plot. The plan and scene sequence of a specific short story.

Story Idea. The original conception or inspiration from which the writer will work his materials into a finished short story.

Scene. The action which takes place in a single setting with a single set of characters. If different action begins with the entrance or exit of a character then a new scene begins.

Chief Character. The central figure in a short story, through whose eyes and other senses the reader sees the story unfold.

Minor Character. Any of the other characters in a short story, no matter how important to the action.

Governing Characteristic. The particular quality of the chief character which shapes his actions throughout a short story.

Unified Point of View. The method of short-story construction by which all action is viewed through the eyes of a single character.

Problem. Dilemma faced by the chief character. Its solution provides the plot of the short story.

Conflict. The constant struggle of the chief character to solve his problem, which provides the driving force of the action.

Exposition. Explanatory information about characters and situations which the reader must know in order to understand the story.

Climactic Decision. The determination of the chief character to take a certain action which will finally solve his problem.

Suspense. The feeling of doubt generated in the reader that the chief character will succeed in his purpose. More apparent in stories of exciting action, but a part of every successful short story.

Flashback. A scene of past action, relived dramatically and actively in the mind of the chief character.

Dialogue. Conversation between two or more characters.

About the Editor

STEWART BEACH, executive editor of *This Week*, has been an expert in the short story for many years. His real training began when he was an instructor in creative writing at New York University. Whatever profit students may have gained from his courses, he says he found his own teaching so persuasive that he became a successful short-story writer himself, and his fiction has appeared in most of the big magazines.

His most challenging association with short stories, Mr. Beach reports, has been the task of selecting them for *This Week*, the Sunday magazine which appears as part of thirty-seven newspapers with a combined circulation of nearly twelve million—the largest magazine audience in the world.

The roster of outstanding authors in this collection is proof that he has earned a reputation as the kind of creative and sympathetic editor who not only develops new talent but draws established writers to his magazine. With the exception of four years' Army service during World War II, in which he attained the rank of colonel, Mr. Beach has spent his life as an editor and writer. He is the author of *Short Story Technique* and the editor of *This Week's Short-Short Stories*.